KINDRED SOULS

"Howdy, ma'am. I'm Prescott Trefarrow."

The woman seemed surprised. "You're the new earl?"

"Yes, ma'am," he said with a grimace. Hearing a total stranger—and a beautiful stranger at that—refer to his title made him feel awkward as hell.

"Welcome, milord," she said, her smoky gray eyes assessing him.

Prescott winced. "Please, ma'am, don't call me that. I'd feel a whole sight better if you'd just call me Prescott. 'Lord' is just too dang formal for my liking. And I'd be happy to call you something other than ma'am, but the fact is, I don't know your name. You ain't told me yet."

She laughed, and Prescott felt the sound wrap around him like a soft velvet blanket.

"If you must know, it's Lucinda," she said, amusement twinkling in her eyes. "Lucinda Trefarrow."

Also by Carol Jerina

A Golden Dream
The Bridegroom

Available from HarperPaperbacks

Kissing Cousins

CAROL JERINA

HarperPaperbacks
A Division of HarperCollins*Publishers*

This is a work of fiction. The characters, incidents, and dialogues are products of the author's imagination and are not to be construed as real. Any resemblance to actual events or persons, living or dead, is entirely coincidental.

HarperPaperbacks *A Division of* HarperCollins*Publishers*
10 East 53rd Street, New York, N.Y. 10022

Cover illustration by Aleta Jenks

First printing: May 1994

Printed in the United States of America

HarperPaperbacks, HarperMonogram, and colophon are trademarks of HarperCollins*Publishers*

❖ 10 9 8 7 6 5 4 3 2 1

Kissing Cousins

1

May, 1891

Prescott reined his horse at the crest of the hill. He removed his hat and scratched his head, feeling more than a little confused. He'd followed the directions given to him by the gent back at the train station in Truro, but he must have taken a wrong turn somewhere along the way. What a man could do on his own in less than an hour—change the course of history, establish an empire, and, in his case, get himself hopelessly lost. Although he hadn't seen a signpost pointing the way to St. Keverne, or to Truro, or to any place else for that matter, he knew the town had to be around here some place. Hell, for all he knew, he might have ridden halfway back to London.

He heaved a frustrated groan and looked from the rise of the next hill, to the gentle valley down below. The lovely sight he saw there had him shaking his head in wonder. What he'd seen of Cornwall so far had been stark and barren looking, not unlike some parts of West Texas, except for the hills and number of wide creeks. But this place was the loveliest he'd ever seen.

At the base of the next hill sat a beautiful garden. Though the thatched roof of the cottage blended in with the surrounding scenery almost to the point of obscurity, the garden itself was a riot of color. Reds, pinks, yellows, blues, and lavenders grew in a wild, tangled profusion, attesting to the love and care the owner gave it. Why, the place even had flowers climbing up the walls of the small stone structure.

A gentle breeze stirred the air, bringing the heady fragrance of the garden up the hill to waft across Prescott's nostrils. He inhaled a deep breath and found pleasure in the aroma. He felt a twinge of remorse as well, for the clean, earthy scent reminded him all too painfully of Waco, Texas, the home of his childhood, the home he and his father and grandfather had fought for and would have been willing to die for had it been demanded of them. The home he'd left only a month ago.

No, he amended, the home he'd been forced to leave, thanks to some stupid inheritance that now made him an earl in a strange land.

The gentle breeze became stronger, turning into a wind and supplanting Prescott's morose thoughts with curiosity as he witnessed a large, light-colored object in the middle of the garden suddenly take flight. Carried aloft by the forceful wind, it sailed upward like a big wingless bird, revealing a head of hair as black as a crow's wing. The hat's owner leaped to her feet among the blooms and reached out, trying to grab hold of it before the wind carried it too far away from her.

Right off, Prescott knew the poor woman wasn't going to be fast enough to catch it on her own. She moved too slowly, and her arms weren't nearly long enough. Figuring he had as good a chance as any of saving the bonnet for her, he squeezed his knees tight around the horse, leaned low and forward, and sent both himself and his mount lunging down the hillside.

For a while, he felt as if he was back home again, able to be himself, with no concern at all for the constraints put upon him this last month by proper British society. Without a care in the world, he rode freely, chasing the wind and the hat, which sailed first to the left, then to the right, then abruptly changed course and headed back to the left again. Squeezing his knees even tighter, he guided the horse each way the wind took the bonnet.

He had just about decided that bulldogging an ornery calf was easier work and that he'd be better off giving up and letting the infernal wind do whatever it dadblamed pleased with the bonnet, when it changed course once again and sailed straight toward him. He leaned far to the side in his saddle, reached out, and caught it by the wide brim. Feeling victorious, he gave off a loud whoop as he headed down the hill, waving the hat in the air. Lord Almighty, he hadn't had this much fun since he and Payne and Chloe fought their way out of a saloon back in San Antone. Only this time he hadn't ended up with a broken nose and a black eye.

A few moments later he reined his horse at the low stone wall surrounding the garden. With the ease of a well-seasoned horseman, he threw his leg over the saddle horn and hopped down. As he advanced toward the gate, he didn't take much notice of the woman who stood there waiting for him.

"I tell you, ma'am," he said with a wide, friendly grin, "if y'all get stiff breezes like that one down here very often, you'd best give some thought to sewing ribbons on your bonnets."

As the woman lifted a hand to brush her windblown shoulder-length hair away from her face, Prescott got his first good look at her and felt his grin slowly vanish. Wide-spaced gray eyes the color of polished charcoal blinked at him, their initial pleasure quickly replaced with a look of disbelief. Her pink, full-lipped mouth opened to say something, but then it quickly snapped shut again, only to be followed by an audible gulp.

He couldn't believe it. He was staring the woman of his dreams square in the face. He had dreamed of her so often, so frequently in the past. But this woman was no come-hither voluptuous figment of his imagination. She was actually a flesh and blood, living, breathing being, who couldn't possibly be the woman he'd dreamed of so often, even though she looked just like that ethereal vision. His dream mate only lived in his mind, coming to him at night to enliven his spirit, to ease away the day's frustrations. No, no flesh and blood woman could ever be his dream mate.

Could she?

"Thank you." There was a noticeable catch in the woman's husky voice as she took the hat from Prescott's slightly shaking, outstretched hand.

"Aw, wasn't nothing, ma'am. It was my pleasure."

Suddenly remembering his manners, he ripped off his own hat and held it in front of him. "That's a right pretty bonnet you got there. It would've been a shame to see you up and lose it to some pesky little ol' breeze."

Feeling warmth creep into her face, she averted her gaze from Prescott and stared down at her hat. One part of the wide straw brim now possessed a mass of creases where his big hand had grabbed it, forever destroying its smoothness. It had been her favorite gardening hat—her *only* gardening hat, come to that—yet she didn't mind his unintentional abuse at all. After all, he had saved it for her.

"Yes, a shame," she said. "Thank you again for rescuing it."

Uncertain what to say to him or what to do next, she turned to walk away.

"Er, ma'am?" Prescott said, suddenly remembering he was lost.

The woman turned back. "Yes?"

"I hate to be a bother. I mean, I can see you're right busy, tending your garden and all, but, er, I think I might be in need of your help."

"*My* help?"

"Yes, ma'am." He hesitated, nudging the toe of his boot in the pea-size pieces of gravel outside her gate. Owning up to a weakness wasn't easy for a man, but it was either own up and ask her for help or continue wandering around Cornwall indefinitely. "I, er, think I'm lost."

"You *think* you're lost?"

"Aw, ma'am, the fact is, I know dang good and well I'm lost. If I had to turn around and go back to where I just come from, I ain't at all sure I could even find my way there. Y'see, I'm new to these parts."

Her eyes twinkled with amusement and a faint smile touched her lips. "Are you really?"

"Yes, ma'am. Course, I suppose you didn't have to be told that to figure it out for yourself."

"Well, I had noticed that your manner of speech is somewhat different from what I'm accustomed to hearing."

"Lots more'n my speech is different, you ask me," he said. "I'll be honest, ma'am. I feel plumb like a lone mule in a stable full of thoroughbreds. Out of place, you know?"

"That's a very colorful way of putting it, but I think I understand," she said, unable to stop herself from warming to the stranger. Ordinarily she made it a practice to reserve any opinions she might have of someone until after she got to know them, for she had learned the hard way that first impressions were not always reliable. But she knew she could rely on her first impression of this particular stranger—he was quite sweet and endearing, if a bit rough around the edges.

"You see," Prescott continued, "before I met up with Henry and let him drag me across an ocean to this place, I was just some ol' cowpoke from Waco."

"Waco?"

"Yes, ma'am. That's in Texas. In America?"

"Yes, I've heard of Texas."

"Well see, that's the thing of it. I'd heard of England, too. I mean, I knew where to find it on a map and all, 'cause as a boy in school I was right good in geography." He grinned lopsidedly. "Course, knowing I had kinfolk living here sort of helped some. Done met my mama's people, but I won't bother you with that story. It's my granddaddy's kin I come to Cornwall to visit. If there's any of them left, that is. But I 'spect I'll be finding that out when I get to his homeplace."

Despite her attempts to keep a straight face, his good-natured, self-effacing behavior had her smiling. "Where, exactly, does your grandfather's kin live, Mr.—?"

"Trefarrow, ma'am. Prescott Trefarrow."

Suddenly, her eyes grew round in surprise. "You're the new earl?"

"Yes, ma'am," he said with a noticeable grimace. Hearing a total stranger—and a beautiful stranger at that—refer to his title made him feel awkward as hell. But he supposed he'd have to get used to feeling awkward. Most likely everyone in England knew about his new status by now. And knowing his status, they'd probably also know he was unmarried. Or "eligible," as one of his aunts in London had called it. Whatever the case, it didn't look as if he'd be any safer from marriage-minded mamas here in Cornwall than he was back in London. "Am I anywhere near to being close to St. Keverne?"

"Quite near, as a matter of fact." She pointed a slender finger to the south. "Continue down this lane for another mile and you'll be there. Had you ridden on a bit farther, you would have seen the signpost just outside the next village. But surely you'll want to be going to Ravens Lair first, won't you?"

Prescott frowned. "I wouldn't be knowing about that, ma'am. Henry told me I was the Earl of St. Keverne. He didn't say nothing about Ravens Lair. Is that close by, too?"

"Much closer than St. Keverne." She turned slightly and pointed to the north. "It's just on the other side of this hill."

"Do tell? Well, I'm sure it's probably a right nice little town, but I've got to be getting on to the house in St. Keverne first. I understand folks might be expecting me, and I sure wouldn't want to keep 'em waiting. Thanks again for all your help, ma'am. Without it, I'd most likely still be wandering around lost."

As he turned, intending to mount his horse, she knew she had to set him straight about his error. "No, wait!" she called out, opening the gate and hurrying after him. "You've misunderstood me."

"'Bout what, ma'am?"

"You don't have a house in St. Keverne."

"I don't?"

"No. Your house is just beyond this hill."

"But didn't you just say that that Ravens Lair place was back yonder?"

"Yes, I did. And it is. Ravens Lair is the name of your house."

"Ravens Lair ain't a town?"

"Good heavens, no. Ravens Lair is the Trefarrow family seat. Your lordship's castle."

Prescott winced. "Please, ma'am, don't do that."

"Don't do what?"

"Call me that."

"Don't call you 'your lordship'?"

"Yes, ma'am. I know you mean well and all, but it just don't seem fitting."

"Fitting or not, milord, that's who you are."

"Maybe to you folks here, but not to me. I'd feel a whole sight better if you'd just call me Prescott."

She visibly stiffened. "Oh, I couldn't do that."

"Why not? It's my name."

"Perhaps it is, but using it would be far too familiar."

"That's fine with me," he said. "Be as familiar as you want. Being called 'lord' is just too dang formal for my liking." A scowl furrowed his brow. "I don't feel like no lord. Don't feel like no earl, either, to tell you the truth. Don't 'spect I ever will feel like one." Glancing up, he saw her blink her wide gray eyes and he knew he was confusing her with his mutterings. "Aw, don't pay no mind to me, ma'am. I'm just letting off a little steam is all."

He was doing much more than letting off steam, she surmised. He was all but confessing that he found his new title and position an uncomfortable encumbrance. Studying him more closely, she noted the look of loneliness on his face. Who could blame him? Perhaps if she were lost and alone in a foreign country as he was she would be lonely and homesick too.

Before she could stop the words, she heard herself ask, "Would your lor—I mean, would *you* like for me to show you the way to Ravens Lair? Purely as a matter of precaution, you understand. I wouldn't want you to lose your way again. This part of Cornwall can be quite confusing at times."

His lonely look faded with the return of his lopsided grin. "If it wouldn't be too much trouble, ma'am, I'd be much obliged."

"Oh, it's no trouble at all, I assure you." Donning her crumpled hat, she turned and latched the gate behind her. "Though, being so near to Ravens Lair already, I seriously doubt you would stay lost for very long. You see, the staff have been expecting you for some time."

"The staff?"

"Yes."

"What staff is that, ma'am?"

"Why, your lor— Er, your staff, sir."

There it was again, Prescott thought with a stifled groan. Though "sir" wasn't nearly as high-and-mighty sounding as "your lordship," it was just as bad. "Pardon my asking, ma'am, but how old are you?"

"Twenty-five." She turned onto a narrow, well-trodden path beside her house and started ascending the hill. "Why?"

"'Cause I just turned thirty-one, and the way I figure it, that puts only six years between us. Now, I'm new here to England and all, and I know you folks do things a sight different from how we do things back home in Texas, but they can't be that different."

"Just what are you getting at?"

"This, ma'am. Back home, we don't call anyone 'sir' unless they're, oh, a good ten or fifteen years older'n us. And even then, it's just 'cause we want to be respectful."

"But you call me 'ma'am.'"

"Only 'cause I'm trying to mind my manners, like my Aunt Em taught me."

"Your Aunt Em taught you very well."

"Thank you. She'd be glad to hear that some of her lessons finally sunk in. I imagine there were times when she had her doubts."

"Why is that?"

"Well, to hear her tell it, I was kind of rambunctious and thick-headed as a boy."

"I've heard that most boys are that way," she said.

"I can't say about most, but my Aunt Em's quick to say that I sure was."

"Well, luckily most boys grow out of being rambunctious and thick-headed." And, from the looks of it, he had grown out of it nicely, she surmised.

"Anyway, I'd be happy to call you something other than 'ma'am', ma'am, but the fact is, I don't know your name. You ain't told me yet."

She laughed, and Prescott felt the sound wrap around him like a soft velvet blanket, totally enveloping him with its luxurious warmth. Lord, he could listen to her laughter for hours and never grow tired of it.

"It's Lucinda," she said.

If someone had come up behind him and doused him with an icy bucket of water, he couldn't have been more shocked. He stopped in his tracks so abruptly that the horse he'd been leading ran into him and almost knocked him to the ground.

"Lucinda?" Recalling the last woman named Lucinda that he'd had the misfortune to encounter, goose bumps grew in profusion on Prescott's flesh. The last Lucinda had come quite close to costing him his life. He'd never forget her, their morning romp in the hayloft of her barn, or her four brothers. They hadn't caught him and the first Lucinda in the act, but they had chased him clear across Texas to San Antonio, then tried to render him a eunuch. They might have succeeded, too, if they hadn't mistaken his identical twin brother, Payne, for him and decided to beat the living daylights out of Payne instead. But then his sister-in-law, Chloe, had pushed him into the fracas, then leaped in herself, and the three of them had dusted the saloon floor with the brothers.

"Yes, Lucinda," she said.

"Er, you wouldn't by any chance have a passel of

brothers hiding over yonder behind them trees, would you?"

"Brothers, hiding behind those trees?"

"Yeah. Big, mean, ugly cusses with low foreheads and beady little eyes who might be itching to try and take a piece of my hide?"

"No, no brothers. I'm an only child."

Thank God for small miracles, Prescott mused. But just because she didn't have brothers it didn't mean she didn't have someone else lurking around to defend her virtue. "How 'bout cousins?"

"Oh, yes, I have cousins. Lots of them." She looked up at him and smiled. "But, er, save for one in particular, at the moment I'm sort of estranged from all the others."

"How about uncles, or a daddy, maybe? You got any of them?"

"My last uncle died some time ago," she said, adding softly, "and I never knew my father."

Though Prescott heard her last remark, he didn't pay much attention to it. He was so relieved to know that he wouldn't have to fight her relations for his life that he blocked out everything else.

"Why do you want to know?" she asked.

"Why?"

"Yes, why?"

Knowing he had to give her an answer, a rational explanation for his curiosity, but unwilling to tell her the whole sordid story, he decided on an abbreviated version. "Well, I guess it's because I've never had much luck with women named Lucy. I wanted to make sure you weren't like the others."

"I see," she said, taking into account everything he'd said, and even that which he hadn't said. But then, he hadn't needed to do that for her to understand.

"You don't go by Lucy, do you?"

"No, normally I'm addressed as Lucinda."

"Good."

"Your last Lucy . . . she had nasty brothers, I take it?"

Prescott nodded. "Very nasty."

"Low foreheads and beady little eyes."

"And not too bright, either. But what they lacked in smarts they made up for in size. The biggest bunch of dolts I've ever seen."

"And mean, you said."

"Oh, Lord, yes." He rubbed the bridge of his nose, remembering just how it had felt to have a huge, ham-sized fist slam into it, break it, and make him see stars.

"I think you should know," she said, "as lord of the castle I doubt you'll be confronting that sort. If you do, you have the authority to deal with them in any way you choose."

"I ain't planning on *dealing* with nobody. That's why I left London and came down here. I had to get away from having to *deal* with folks." Women especially, he thought. His aunts and girl cousins, and all the other marriage-minded mamas and their horse-faced daughters who had taken an instant liking to him when they found out he was titled and figured he might have money—which he didn't. Not to mention the score or more of Payne's ex-lady friends who had mistakened him for his identical twin brother and tried to renew their close relationships with him. Or the husbands of those high-born women who'd had blood in their eyes when they'd met him and tried to settle old scores even after he'd told them he wasn't

Payne. And, of course, he couldn't forget all his brother's creditors, who felt it was Prescott's duty to reimburse them. "I'm kind of hoping Cornwall will be different, Lucinda."

"Oh, it will be. We Cornish are nothing at all like Londoners. Here in St. Keverne, we're much more provincial. Unsophisticated, I suppose you could say."

"Provincial and unsophisticated are fine with me," he said. "That's the kind of roots I come from. Waco's about as ordinary a place as you'll find. Full of plain, ordinary, honest, hardworking folks you don't mind talking to, instead of highfalutin snobs who always put on airs."

Seeing the top of the hill come into view, and knowing Lucinda would soon be leaving him, Prescott felt an urgent need to prolong the conversation with his lovely guide. Out of all the women he'd met in the last weeks, she was the most comforting of the bunch. She didn't make him feel nervous or bumbling, just accepted. He liked being with her, talking to her, listening to her voice. Looking at her pretty face wasn't hard to do either. But the notion of her just turning around and walking away made him feel strangely empty inside.

"You know something," he said. "I don't think I ever got your last name."

"You didn't?"

"No, I don't think so."

"Then I must not have told you."

"We can't let that happen. Seeing as how you're so concerned with us sounding too familiar and all, if I called you by your first name when other folks were around, I just might end up sullying your reputation. Sure wouldn't want to do a thing like that."

"Oh, no, heaven forbid."

"So, what is it?"

"If you must know," she said, amusement twinkling in her eyes, "it's Trefarrow."

2

"Trefarrow?"

"Mmm-hmm. Lucinda Gwendolyn Marianne Trefarrow."

"Well, I'll be danged!" A wide grin split across Prescott's face. "Don't that just take the rag off'n the bush? Here I've been talking to one of my own kinfolk this whole time, and I didn't even know it. We are kinfolk, aren't we? I mean, the name Trefarrow around these parts ain't the same as Smith and Jones back home, is it?"

"No, not quite. Though there are a number of Trefarrows in Cornwall, we're all related to each other, to one degree or another."

"And how are we related? Cousins or something?"

"Yes, cousins," she said. "Distant cousins."

For reasons he couldn't explain, Prescott quickly asked, "How distant?"

"I'm not certain, actually. Just how were you related to the old earl?"

"The old earl?"

"Yes, your predecessor. The one who died and left you the title."

"Oh, him. Well, let me think. I didn't pay too much attention when Henry—Sir Henry Wilberforce, that is—when he told me about my title and lineage, half of which I've done forgot. But I believe he said the old earl was my granddaddy's older brother. If that's who he was, then I expect that would've made him my great-uncle. Or something like that."

"If that's the case, then you and I shared the same great-grandparents, because my mother was the old earl's great-niece. I, of course, being his great-great-niece."

"But what does that make us?"

"I imagine we're third or fourth cousins."

Third or fourth cousins, Prescott thought. In other words, he and Lucinda might share the same last name and heritage, but no matter how you looked at it, she was no better than kissing kin. He liked that notion. Liked it a lot. And knowing their exact status, he was beginning to like her even more.

She came to a halt at the top of the hill and gestured with a nod of her head. "There it is. Ravens Lair. Your new home and castle."

Prescott took one look at Ravens Lair and felt his heart plummet to the level of his boots. The place was more than just the big old house Sir Henry had told him he had inherited; it was huge, with a hundred rooms or more, by the looks of it. And it was most definitely a castle. At least the middle of it was, with medieval-looking arches, turrets, towers, and crenellated battlements sticking up from the roof. All the blasted thing needed, he thought, was a moat and drawbridge and a few knights in dented armor jousting across the lush green valley that made up the lawn. But even without the knights, it was still the ugliest looking place Prescott had ever seen in his life.

It had come by its name honestly, as well. He could see at least a dozen big black birds perched at various places around the rooftop, and even more flew about overhead.

"So that's Ravens Lair, huh?" Though he tried to mask the shock and disillusionment in his tone, he knew he didn't quite make it. A deaf, mute, and blind man could tell he was disappointed, and Lucinda definitely had none of those handicaps.

"Mmm-hmm," she said. "What do you think of it?"

I think I don't belong here, Prescott mused. *I think I want to catch the first boat sailing west and go back home to Texas. That's what I think.* "Kinda big, ain't it?"

"Very big and very old," Lucinda said.

Old was right, he thought. The middle part of the castle looked ancient, almost prehistoric, while the parts that stuck out on either side of the middle looked newer. "Looks like it could use a little work."

"More than a little. Before the old earl became ill and died, it was a constant struggle for him to stay one step ahead of all the repairs that needed doing on a house this size. Needless to say, you can see that he didn't succeed. That's probably what ended his life so soon. He just grew tired of fighting a losing battle with the dry rot."

"Dry rot. Does that mean the roof leaks?"

She smiled. "Only when it rains."

"How often is that?"

"During the summer months, at least once a week."

"And the rest of the year?"

"Oh, just about everyday."

Prescott eyed the lush green valley disdainfully. "That's what I thought. You don't get pastureland like that down there without a good steady rainfall. But hey, that's okay. Rain's good for the herd, right?"

"The herd?"

"Yeah, all the cows y'all graze down there." Her silence and a sudden thought had him asking, "That is grazing land, ain't it?"

"Well, yes. Sort of."

"I thought so. It's too rich and fertile looking for y'all to let it just set there and go to waste. Must have some pretty nice looking cattle around here. Why haven't I seen any?"

"If by 'cattle' you mean cows, then you haven't seen any because we have none."

"Y'all don't raise cows in this part of the country?"

"A few, yes. Some of the tenant farmers keep one or two for milking, but ordinarily they don't raise enough of them for their numbers to constitute an actual herd."

Prescott couldn't hide the shock from his expression. "You're joshing me. With grass like that? Just what do y'all raise?"

With an eloquent thrust of her index finger, Lucinda pointed to the large white mass moving in the distance. Prescott squinted, trying to make out clearly what it was. It seemed to move in a slow, undulating wave, first going partway up the hillside, and then down it again.

Suddenly, shock and disgust churned in his stomach. "Sheep? Lord Almighty, y'all raise sheep here?"

"Yes, but what you see there isn't the whole of the flock," Lucinda said, wanting to assure her cousin, the new earl, that he wasn't exactly destitute, as his tone seemed to suggest, but a man of means to some degree. "That's just a small portion of it. The rest of the flock are divided throughout your small holdings."

"Small holdings, large holdings—it don't make no difference what size they are. I ain't no sheepman. Dadgummit, Lucinda, I'm a cattleman like my daddy before me and his daddy before him. Cows, steers, seed bulls—that's where the money is. You can starve to death raising a flock of stinking sheep. Hell, I'd have been happier knowing y'all raised nothing but horses."

"Oh, we've horses, too," she said.

"You do?"

"Of course."

"Well, thank God for that," he muttered. "Where are they?"

"In the stables."

Although Prescott had a feeling he wasn't going to like her next answer, he couldn't stop himself from asking the question. "The whole herd?"

"If five constitutes a—"

He groaned. "You've only got five horses?"

"We don't— I mean, *you* don't need more than five," she said somewhat indignantly. "A lovely chestnut for riding, two matching grays to pull your carriages, and two Clydesdales for the dray cart. Actually, if you must know, there are seven in all."

"Seven, huh?"

"Yes, if you include the two ponies."

"Ponies," he repeated.

"Yes."

"Little kids ride ponies, Lucinda. Look at me—I ain't no little kid."

"Children aren't the only ones who use the ponies. Hitched together in a harness, they can pull the governess's cart quite nicely."

But Prescott wasn't a governess. Hell, he wasn't sure he even knew what a governess was. It sounded like a lady governor to him.

He glowered down at the broad meadow and the white shape that was still mobile. "I don't like sheep. Don't like 'em one bit."

"Like them or not, as the new earl, they're yours."

"I know—you don't have to remind me." Taking a deep breath to settle his nerves, he changed the direction of his gaze and saw a man on horseback in the distance heading their way. "We raised some pigs once, when I was a boy back on the Triple T. Took a while to get used to 'em, but I managed. Suppose I'll just have to manage getting used to being around sheep."

Lucinda laughed. "You are the lord of the castle, remember."

"What's that got to do with it? A sheep is a sheep, no matter how you look at it." *No matter how you smelled it, either,* he thought.

"Well, you're not required to actually live with your flock. You've shepherds to do that for you."

"Mmm." Eyeing the man on horseback ride ever closer, he asked. "Who's that heading this way?"

Lucinda glanced over her shoulder and saw the approaching rider. Her spine stiffening visibly, she redirected her gaze back to Prescott. "Garrick Emerson, your superintendent."

"My what?"

"Your superin—" She broke off with a sigh of frustration. "I've no idea what you Americans would call him, but here a superintendent oversees the running of your estate—the castle, the gardens, the grounds . . . but primarily your tenant farms."

"Oh, he's the foreman."

"Yes, I suppose," she said crisply.

"His name's Emerson, you say?"

"Garrick Emerson, yes."

"Looks like he's in kind of a hurry, doesn't it?"

Lucinda remained silent, but returned her gaze to Prescott.

"He always ride hell-bent that a-way?"

"Only when it suits him."

Catching the coldness in Lucinda's voice, Prescott glanced at her and saw her veiled look of disgust. Only a minute ago she had been warm and friendly, now she was icy and withdrawn. Though he wanted to know why the appearance of Emerson had caused the sudden change in her attitude, he decided not to make an issue of it. "How long's he been here?"

"In St. Keverne or at Ravens Lair?"

"Either one."

"He's been in St. Keverne all his life," she said flatly. "He was born here. As for Ravens Lair, he's only been superintendent for about two years. The old earl hired him shortly before he died."

"Tell me if I'm wrong, but I get the feeling you don't like him much."

"Like him?" The chuckle she issued held no trace of mirth. "Does that really matter? He's in your employ, not mine."

Prescott was saved from responding to her rather

cryptic comment as Emerson reined his horse abruptly a few feet from where they stood.

"You're trespassing on private land, so get off," the man said to Prescott with a snarl. Then to Lucinda, "And you, witch, get back to stirring your cauldron. You've been warned about showing your face on castle grounds."

Defiance glimmering in the depths of her eyes, Lucinda tilted her head to a dignified pose as she opened her mouth to inform Emerson that words held weight with no one but himself. But her words never had the chance to leave her tongue.

Without warning, Prescott reached up and grabbed the man by the lapels of his coat, dragging him down from his horse with the ease of one handling a lightweight sack of grain. Not letting Emerson's feet touch the ground, he shoved him forcefully against the broad trunk of a nearby tree and hit Emerson's head on the trunk for good measure, dislodging pieces of bark.

"Where I come from," Prescott said, "we don't talk to strangers that a-way, mister. We're more polite. Unless they're toting loaded hoglegs, of course, but I can see that you ain't. Just to set your mind at ease, though, in case you're wondering, I ain't no trespasser. I live here now. And calling a lady a witch ain't good manners a-tall. 'Specially when she happens to be kinfolk of mine."

By the end of Prescott's short speech, the dazed look in Emerson's eyes had vanished. He blinked and nervously glanced past Prescott's broad shoulders, catching sight of the big Western saddle strapped to the back of the lone horse close by.

"You're his lordship, the new earl?"

"That's right." For the first time since he had acquired the title, Prescott liked the feel of owning it. It gave him added authority at a time when authority and power were needed. "I'm Lord St. Keverne."

"Forgive me, milord. I—I didn't know. I'm Emerson—Garrick Emerson—your superintendent."

"That's what my cousin here's been telling me."

"I—I thought you were trespassing. Or worse, a poacher. The woods 'round Ravens Lair have been plagued with poachers lately."

Not rightly sure what a poacher was, but figuring it didn't have much of a legal sound to it, Prescott decided to accept Emerson's apology. "A man's entitled to make an honest mistake every now and again." Though he loosened his grip on Emerson's coat, he still maintained a hold on it, in case the man's friendly attitude took a sudden, unfriendly turn. "But that still don't excuse your rudeness."

"Beg your pardon, milord?"

"You ain't that dense, Emerson. You insulted the lady, not me."

"Insulted her?"

"Yeah, you called her a witch."

"But, milord, she—"

"Ain't no witch," Prescott interrupted firmly as he turned to bestow a boyish grin on Lucinda. "She's my cousin. A Trefarrow, just like me. And the way I see it, Emerson, she's the one you ought to be apologizing to. Ain't that right?"

Emerson hesitated, all but glaring at Lucinda, and Prescott tightened his hold again. "I said, ain't that right?"

"Y—Yes, of course, milord. I apologize, Lucinda."

"That's Miss Trefarrow to you, Emerson."

"Of course. Whatever you say, milord."

"Whatever I say?"

"Yes, milord."

"Then I say, say it to her, not me."

"I apologize for my rudeness, Miss Trefarrow."

"That's better. Much better." Prescott released the man and stepped back. "Last thing we want to do around here is sound like we're too familiar. Might upset some folks that don't need upsetting."

"Yes, milord."

"Everybody ought to know their place," he said, giving Lucinda a conspiratorial wink. "We lose our place, and the whole country's liable to go to hell. Can't have that now, can we?"

"No, milord."

Emerson's voice had taken on a slightly hard edge, but only Lucinda seemed to notice it, and she chose to remain silent. The fact that Emerson had learned the hard way that he couldn't ride roughshod over the new earl as he had the old one was good enough for her. But one thing she couldn't dismiss was how rapidly her cousin had come to her defense. No man had ever defended her that way before, not even as a child, when she'd been lonely and badly in need of love and affection. Realizing it, she felt a place open up in her heart for him, a warm place that grew larger and warmer as the seconds she spent with him ticked past.

"You got work to do?" Prescott asked.

Emerson nodded briskly. "Yes, milord."

"Then I don't want to keep you from it. Go on about your business. Me and my cousin, Miss Trefarrow, have family matters to discuss."

"Yes, milord."

"You can do one thing for me, though, if you don't mind."

"Anything, milord."

"Keep an eye open for a great big wagon headed this way."

"A wagon, milord?"

"Yeah, it's got all my belongings loaded on it. And my valet," he added with a slight scowl. "It's coming from the train station in Truro. You see it, just tell the driver how to get on over here to the house. He might have as hard a time of finding the place as I did."

"Yes, milord." Tugging a lock of hair on his forehead, Emerson turned and mounted his horse.

"I suppose I should be getting on as well," Lucinda said, watching Emerson ride away.

"What's your hurry?"

"I do have work to do."

"You mean your gardening?"

"I know it may not look like much, but if I don't keep one step ahead of the weeds—"

"What weeds? From what I could see of it, there wasn't a one in sight."

"They're there, believe me."

Prescott shook his head in dismay. "Surely the few you've got won't choke out all them pretty flowers of yours in the next couple of minutes. Come on, spend some time with me."

"Discussing family matters?" she asked with a smile.

"Family matters, the price of cotton, the weather—don't really matter much to me what we talk about just so long as we talk."

"Don't you have people waiting for you down at the castle?"

"The people and the castle can wait. Getting to know you can't."

She turned to leave. "You can find me at the cottage almost any hour."

Reluctant to let her leave, he took hold of her arm as she started to walk past him. "You might find this hard to believe, Lucinda, but you're the first friendly person I've come across since I came to this blasted country."

"Surely you jest."

"No, I ain't. I'm dead serious. I've met a lot of folks, but there ain't a one I'd label as just plain friendly. Most of them seemed to be scheming in one way or another, trying to figure out how I could be of benefit to them. Truth is, I'm not much help to myself right now, let alone a bunch of strangers."

Lucinda opened her mouth to protest, but he went on. "But you're different, Lucinda. Out of the goodness of your heart, you helped me when I needed it. And not because you thought I could do something for you, either. I got a feeling it's your nature to be helpful to folks."

"But you did do something for me," she said, surprised by his unexpected forthrightness. "You rescued my hat, remember?"

"Oh, the hat was nothing."

"And all I did was point you in the right direction to the castle."

"Well, as my Aunt Em always says, 'one good turn deserves another.' So how 'bout doing one more good turn and showing me the house."

"Ravens Lair? It's right down there."

"Not the outside. I can see that for myself."

As she directed her gaze at the huge mansion down

below them, she forced herself to suppress a shudder. She couldn't staunch the flow of vivid childhood memories that ran through her mind. The lonely days and nights she had spent inside those dank castle walls, wanting to be loved and accepted by the ones who had raised her and taken care of her, but who had always treated her as the bastard child she was. "You want me to lead you around inside?"

"Yeah. You do know the layout of the place, don't you?"

"Quite well."

"There you go then."

"But Mrs. Sweet and the rest of your staff can show you around as easily as I."

"But that's the thing of it," he said. "I wouldn't know Mrs. Sweet if I saw her. You would."

"Mrs. Sweet is your housekeeper. She's a large, plump lady with gray hair and rosy cheeks and smells of fresh baked bread. She spends a good deal of her time in the kitchens."

"Kitchens? Mercy sakes, you've got more than one?"

"No, I don't, but you do. Or rather, the castle has."

"And I'd find them and Mrs. Sweet at the . . . front of the house?"

"No, at the back. In the east wing, to be precise."

"The east wing, huh?"

"That wing there. The one that extends out to the left of the large front entrance." She started to say more, but broke off with an amused sigh, suddenly realizing that Prescott wasn't as helpless as he pretended, but that he was trying in his own feeble way to make her seem indispensable to him. "Never mind. Come on, I'll show you myself."

"Sure would appreciate it, but I don't want to be no bother," he said as they started down the hillside.

"Oh, you're no bother at all, mil—"

"Prescott. None of that milord nonsense. We agreed, remember?"

"Yes, I remember," she said. "But I can only call you Prescott when no one else is around. If we should, by chance, find ourselves in the company of others, I must defer to your titled status. Not to do so would surely cause much speculation."

"Speculation, huh?"

"That's right."

"You mean gossip, don't you?"

My, but he is bluntly spoken, she thought. "Yes, gossip."

"We can't have that now, can we?"

"Not if you wish to maintain your reputation."

"What's my reputation got to do with anything?"

"Everything, if you must know. You may not like being an earl, but you are one nonetheless, and you must behave accordingly."

She came to a stop and gestured to the huge wooden door in front of them. "Welcome to Ravens Lair, Prescott. Your home."

Prescott opened the front door and felt the hairs on the back of his neck stand at attention at the ominous squeak of the hinges. Following Lucinda into the dimly-lighted house, he saw dust motes floating around, contributing to the fine layer of grit that seemed to cover every available surface—the chipped stone floor, the carved wood panels covering the lower half of the stone walls, the huge pieces of armor that stood like silent sentinels but failed to fill the enormous entryway.

"This place doesn't have ghosts, does it?" he asked, his softly spoken words echoing about them.

"Haven't you heard?" Lucinda said. "All English castles have ghosts. Ravens Lair is no different."

"Well, if they leave me alone, I guess I can learn to live with them."

"There's no reason for you to be afraid. Our ghosts happen to be the friendly type. They do nothing more than rattle around the corridors at night, making odd noises. Of course, those who don't believe in spirits might attribute that sort of thing to the mice in the wainscoting."

"Mice?"

"Mmm-hmm. And occasionally women's jewelry will go missing, only to turn up again in a new location."

"Only women's jewelry, never men's things?"

She nodded. "It's my opinion that the fourth earl is that particular ghost."

"You know which ghost is which?"

"Only that one. And it's purely speculation on my part. You see, the fourth earl was—how shall I put it? Well, he had a certain fancy for wearing women's things. He even demanded to be buried in his favorite frock from Paris and his mother's pearls."

"You're joshing me."

"No, I couldn't be more serious. It's well documented in the family journals. You should read them sometime; they're very informative."

Caught up in Lucinda's story, Prescott's eerie feelings about the castle faded. "Are you telling me that one of my ancestors—one of my *male* ancestors—was buried in a dress?"

"No, and that's the reason I suspect he's the one going about snatching women's jewelry. Oh, the fourth earl requested it well enough, but his son, the fifth earl, had the presence of mind to bury him in men's clothes."

"Thank God for that," Prescott said. "The poor man must have been ashamed of his father's behavior."

"I doubt shame had any part in the fifth earl making

his decision. He was too much the politician to feel that sort of thing."

"How do you know what he felt?"

"Oh, his personal journals were quite thorough too. He wrote that he was hoping to win an appointment for an important position at court. Knowing that a number of his peers and superiors would be attending his father's funeral, and that they would frown upon the old earl's choice of burial garb, they would no doubt frown upon him as well, and he wouldn't get the appointment. The fourth earl was probably so upset by his son's actions that he began haunting these halls, and still does so to this day. But he never hurts anyone. He just wears ladies' things for a while and neglects to return them to their proper place."

Mice in the walls and ghosts roaming the halls in women's clothes. Prescott wondered what other shocking facts he would learn about his family. Not too many, he hoped.

Hearing a sound at the far end of the hall, he peered into the dimness and saw a young woman with an armload of linens coming toward him. At first he thought she might be one of Lucinda's ghosts, but he quickly dismissed that notion when the hazy apparition grew clearer. Suddenly she froze in her tracks, stared at Lucinda, then turned her gaze on Prescott. After a moment, she blinked her eyes and gasped so loudly the sound echoed off the walls.

"Thee's the new earl!"

Thee? Prescott wondered.

"Yes," Lucinda said, "Lord Prescott has finally arrived, Miranda."

"Aye, Lord Prescott, welcome! Mrs. Sweet's been all a-bluster, waiting for thee to—" She gasped again, nearly dropping her bundle as she dipped into a nervous curtsy and turned sharply, yelling at the top of her voice, "Mrs. Sweet! Oh, Mrs. Sweet! The new earl's here. Quick! Put the kettle on!"

"My staff?"

"One of them, yes," Lucinda said.

They walked a bit further along the foyer, past fly-specked mirrors and many closed doors. Prescott supposed they were heading toward the back of the house, where the housekeeper, Mrs. Sweet, resided.

"Is that the reason you live over at the cottage and not here?" he asked.

"What, you mean Miranda or the ghosts?"

"Either one."

"Miranda may have seemed a bit flighty, and I suppose she is at times, but she's a nice girl nonetheless. Be patient with her, will you?"

If I thought it would please you, Lucinda, I'd be patient with the devil himself. The moment the thought entered his head, Prescott felt a rush of heat flow through his veins. He had no idea where the notion had come from, but having had it, he couldn't very well deny it. Nor did he want to. He more than liked his new cousin—his new, *distant* cousin. For reasons he couldn't explain, he wanted to please her more than he'd ever wanted to please any other woman he'd ever met.

"As for the ghosts," Lucinda went on, "it's like I told you—for the most part they're quite friendly. I grew up with them; they're like old friends."

"Then why don't you live here with the others,

instead of alone? Lord knows the place looks like it has enough room."

Lucinda's good humor faded as she glanced about the dreary-looking foyer. Where Prescott probably saw only the neglect and decay, she imagined a sad little girl, lonely and isolated from others her own age. A sad little girl who had suffered unspeakable cruelties, inflicted on her by those who pretended to have her best interest at heart. Genuine love and affection had been rare commodities for Lucinda as a child. They were no less rare today.

"I choose not to live here, that's all," she said.

Seeing the look in Lucinda's eyes, Prescott felt her unhappiness as strongly as if it were his own. Wanting only to comfort her, reassure her, he reached out and took hold of her hand.

The moment his flesh touched hers, a current ignited between them. She obviously felt it as well, because her eyes opened wide and stared at him in surprise. Prescott tightened his hold on her hand, wanting the sensation to continue, to grow stronger. But Lucinda's face suffused with color, and she wrenched her hand free from his. She took a step backward, increasing the distance between them. She had never felt such a strong feeling before, not with any man, and it frightened her.

"Lucinda, we—"

"Milord, milord!"

At the sudden interruption, Prescott turned to see a squat, round-faced, gray-haired woman coming toward him, followed by four other women of various ages, all clothed as the first one in black dresses and white aprons. Miranda, whom he had already met; another young woman who looked to be Miranda's age, height, and coloring; a tall, gaunt lady with iron-gray hair and wire-rimmed spectacles that made her big brown eyes appear even bigger, and, bringing up the rear, one of the oldest, smallest women Prescott had ever seen. As she drew closer, he realized her size was due in part to her hunched-over frame. She had to be at least eighty years old, he decided. Possibly even ninety.

Surely these five women didn't comprise the entire household staff of Ravens Lair? They couldn't possibly handle the work load required to maintain a house this size. But if they were, Prescott could understand why the place was in such a bad state of neglect. Steps would have to be taken to rectify the situation. He would see to it that these women got some help.

"Lord Prescott," Lucinda said, gesturing to the squat, round woman. "This is Mrs. Sweet, your housekeeper."

He extended his hand, but the woman blushed and quickly dipped into a shallow curtsy with a respectful lowering of her head. Taken aback by the unexpected gesture, Prescott let his hand drop slowly back to his side.

"Nice to meet you, Mrs. Sweet."

"Oh, the pleasure's all mine, milord. We've been expecting thee for weeks."

"And you've already met Miranda," Lucinda said, going down the line of women as she made the introductions.

Now realizing that no one would shake his hand if he offered it, Prescott merely smiled. "How do, Miss Miranda."

Miranda curtsied again, her eyes blinking at him

with the steady regularity of a metronome set at two-four time.

"Miranda is your lordship's upstairs maid," Lucinda said, "while Rowena serves as your downstairs maid." Leaning close to Prescott, she added, "Miranda and Rowena are sisters."

Prescott had already figured that much out for himself. "Miss Rowena, nice to meet you."

As the others had done, Rowena curtsied. "Your lordship."

"This is Ursula, Mrs. Sweet's assistant in the kitchens," Lucinda said, coming to the tall, gaunt woman with glasses.

"Howdy do, Miss Ursula."

Prescott heard Ursula's bones creak as she curtsied. "Your lordship. Welcome to Ravens Lair."

"Thank you. Glad to be here." *At least, I think I'm glad.*

"And this is Esmeralda," Lucinda said, coming to the tiny, hunched-over woman whose gaze seemed unable to focus any higher than Prescott's belt buckle. "She's— Well, she's indispensable to everyone here."

"Indispensable," Mrs. Sweet agreed.

"Oh, yes, milord," Ursula said. "We couldn't get along without her."

"Nice to meet you, Miss Esmeralda."

Though she tried to curtsy as the others had done, the simple act of bending her knees threw her so off balance that Esmeralda almost toppled over.

Prescott quickly came to the old lady's rescue by grabbing hold of her arm. Feeling her thin, fragile bones beneath the fabric of her dress, he gentled his hold as he helped her regain her balance. "You all right, ma'am?"

She mumbled something he didn't understand as her tiny little head slowly lifted to look up at him. But he was so tall and she was so short, it took a moment for their eyes to finally meet. And when they did, her response was one that Prescott did not expect.

"Man!" Esmeralda shrieked, flinching from Prescott's touch. "Rape! Rape!"

"No, no, Esmeralda." Lucinda brushed Prescott aside with a quick, apologetic look, and wound her arm around the old woman's shoulders. "It's all right."

"Rape! Rape!"

"No, he isn't. He's Lord Prescott, the new earl."

Esmeralda cast a fear-filled gaze at Prescott. "New earl?"

"That's right, Esme dear," Mrs. Sweet said. "The new earl."

"Where's the old one?"

"He died."

"Died?"

"Yes, two years ago. You remember, don't you?"

The old woman's wrinkles grew deeper, more pronounced as a confused look passed over her face. "I don't remember no one dying."

"Well, the old earl is dead," Mrs. Sweet assured her.

"Naught told me."

"But thee's the one who found him," Miranda said.

Standing closest to Prescott, Rowena mumbled, "Found him, then tried to make his bed up around him. Dotty as a bat, she is."

Mrs. Sweet heard the young maid's remark and shot her a withering look. "You've the silver to polish, Rowena. Get about it. Ursula, take Esme back to the kitchens, and while thee's there, see to the tea. His lordship must be fairly parched from traveling on the road. Hungry, too, I'll wager."

The thought of having to drink one more cup of watery, lukewarm tea had Prescott fighting back a shudder. He'd drunk enough of the stuff in London to float the U.S.S. *Constitution*. Watery tea with sandwiches so tiny they wouldn't keep a child alive, much less a fully grown, hard-working man. Didn't anybody in this blasted country know about coffee?

"Please, Mrs. Sweet, don't go to all that work on my account. I'm fine just as I am."

"But, milord," the housekeeper said, "the old earl always had his high tea at four. It's near that time now. We must maintain the tradition."

Their tradition would likely kill him, or starve him to death, he thought, realizing he had better nip their old habits in the bud right now, while he had the chance. "If it's all the same to you, ma'am, I'd rather have a hot cup of coffee."

"Coffee?"

"Yes, ma'am. The stronger, the better."

Mrs. Sweet's spine stiffened. "The old earl didn't drink coffee, milord. He wouldn't even have it in the house. Said it wasn't a proper English drink."

"Well, that's the thing of it, ma'am. I ain't exactly a proper Englishman now, am I?"

"That isn't my place to say, milord."

"No, ma'am, I realize that. It's my place, and as the new earl, from here on out I'd like coffee served in the afternoon. Tea if we ever have folks drop in for a visit"—which Prescott seriously doubted—"but mostly coffee. In fact, you might want to start keeping a pot of it on the stove in the kitchen. I like to help myself to a cup every now and then."

"Yes, milord."

"And if you're gonna make some sandwiches to go with that coffee, make 'em big ones, would you? Ham, chicken, beef—whatever kinda meat you got already cooked and handy. None of that watercress stuff, though. It tastes like grass to me. And don't cut the crusts off the bread, either. I like crusts. My Aunt Em says eating crusts keeps a man from going bald early."

A noticeable twitch developed in the outer corner of Mrs. Sweet's right eye. "Yes, milord. Will there be anything else?"

"No, ma'am, not just now. But if I should happen to think of something, I'll be sure to let you know."

Mrs. Sweet nodded her head curtly. "Miranda, show his lordship to his room."

"No, don't bother, Miss Miranda. I'm sure you've got more'n your fair share of work to do. My cousin, Miss Lucinda, can show me around, help me get acquainted with the place."

"Miss Lucinda?" Miranda said. "But she's no longer here, milord."

"No longer here?" Prescott turned sharply and searched the vast hall, but he couldn't see any sign of Lucinda. "Where the devil did she go to?"

"To her cottage, I suppose, milord," Mrs. Sweet said.

She had left without saying good-bye to him? Without giving him a chance to say good-bye to her? Though he'd only known Lucinda for a short time, she had become like a lifeline for him, a connection with something familiar and welcome. Now that she was gone, he only felt an odd, inexplicable emptiness inside.

"It looks like I'm gonna be needing you to show me the way to my room after all, Miss Miranda."

"Of course, milord. Follow me, please."

4

Prescott's room lay a good quarter of a mile away from the front entry—up the main staircase in the east wing, down a wide gallery past a score or more of portraits of former St. Keverne earls, and then left along a maze of corridors. He realized that only a lifelong resident of the castle would know the exact location of his room. And, being new to Ravens Lair, he would have to resort to either drawing himself a map or leaving a trail of bread crumbs to find the place next time. But considering the house had mice and all, chances were he'd end up getting lost anyway if he did the latter.

Miranda opened a pair of tall double doors and he followed her through them. One glance at the luxurious chamber told him that "room" was much too humble a word for a place of this size. With all its furniture, it looked more to him like a grand hall, or the lobby of a fancy hotel: two couches, tables of various shapes and sizes, a half-dozen chairs, and two leather wingbacks flanking either side of a massive marble fireplace. But most of the hotels he'd seen didn't have fat, naked cherubs floating among white clouds on a sky-blue ceiling and, Lord help him, this one did.

"This is my room?"

"Aye, milord."

Well, he couldn't exactly complain about the accommodations; they were certainly plush enough. But what did a man do at bedtime? Curl up on one of the couches and let his feet hang over the arm? He'd slept on enough short couches in the past to know that he would have a crick in his neck come morning.

As if in answer to his unspoken question, Miranda opened a connecting door and showed him the bedroom itself. It couldn't compare to the room he'd just left. In fact it outdid it. Where naked cherubs had floated across the other ceiling, well-endowed nymphs cavorted with muscular satyrs in a leafy, flower-strewn glade on this one. With the paintings so faded from age and accumulation of grime, Prescott couldn't be sure, but it looked to him as though most of the participants were doing unspeakable things to one another.

And the bed . . . Lord have mercy, he'd never seen such a big bed before. It looked like it might weigh a good ton. Four massive carved posters supported each corner of the frame and the headboard that climbed halfway up the fourteen-foot-tall ceiling. If that weren't excessive enough, yards and yards of heavy burgundy velvet were draped to conceal whoever slept in the bed.

"The old earl was partial to sleeping here, was he?"

"Oh, no, milord. This isn't the old earl's room. It was his grandfather's. The old earl's rooms are—I mean, they were in the west wing."

"I see." Prescott found it comforting to know that he wouldn't be sleeping each night in the same bed where his great-uncle had died—and had almost been made up in by poor old Esmeralda.

Unable to keep his gaze from straying back to the ceiling, he thought it even more interesting that his great-great-granddaddy, the old earl's father, had had a taste for lecherous artwork. Perhaps because he'd had lecherous habits as well? And if he had, what about the old man's wife, Prescott's great-great-grandma? Had she approved of her husband's predilections with other women, or had she merely tolerated them as most women did? If only these walls could talk, he thought, the secrets they could reveal about his ancestors . . .

He noticed a closed door to the right and nodded to it. "What's in there?"

"Your lordship's dressing room."

"My what?"

"Dressing room, milord."

Miranda opened the door to show him, and Prescott peeked inside. Chests of drawers and ten-foot-tall wardrobes covered every inch of wall space not occupied by doors or windows. In the middle of the floor sat a cheval glass, a chair, and another bed, much smaller than the one in the bedroom.

"And this is your lordship's bathing room," Miranda said, opening yet another door.

Prescott looked inside, prepared to find a bathroom similar to the one they had back home on the Triple T, which was furnished with a wash bowl and pitcher and a mirror above it, and a tub that never quite seemed big enough for him. But the tub he now gaped at would be commodious enough for him and two other people besides. Big enough for him to go swimming in, if the notion struck him.

"Good Lord Almighty! My great-granddaddy must've been an awfully big man."

Would wonders never cease, he thought as Miranda led him back into the first room they'd entered. He had a room for sitting, one for sleeping, one for changing clothes, and one for bathing. And he had thought Texans went in for things in a big way. Little did they know that these English folks could outdo them by a mile.

"Is that it, Miss Miranda," he asked with a smile, "or do you have any more surprises for me?"

She blushed and lowered her eyes. "No, milord, this is all of it. Unless thee'd be wanting to see her ladyship's?"

"Her ladyship's what?"

"Rooms, milord. They're next to yours."

"Naw, I don't think that'll be necessary. I don't have a ladyship. I mean, there ain't no Lady St. Keverne. Not one still alive, anyway. I ain't married."

"Not yet," Miranda mumbled under her breath as she exited the room with a rustle of petticoats and a little sway in her hips that Prescott knew hadn't been there before.

He could handle half-senile old ladies like Esmeralda by making it a point of staying out of their way. But pretty young housemaids like Miranda and her sister, Rowena, were another matter altogether. They could be mighty tempting to a healthy man like himself, but mighty dangerous as well. Previous experience told him he would have to watch out, keep his urges in check at all times, or he might find himself facing the working end of their daddy's loaded shotgun.

* * *

"We have consulted with Mrs. Sweet, milord, and we are assured that we will be dining promptly at eight."

Hargreaves and his "we" business. Prescott eyed his valet's reflection in the dressing room mirror and thought for the umpteenth time that there was something very familiar about the man. But, try as he did, he couldn't quite put his finger on it.

He had noticed the familiarity the first time Sir Henry had introduced them in London. Introduced? What an understatement. Sir Henry had all but forced him to hire Hargreaves on the spot, extolling the seasoned gentleman's gentleman and his many past positions as valet to earls, marquises, viscounts, and one duke. Of course, Prescott had balked at the notion of putting himself and his belongings at the mercy of some stranger, but his objections had made little difference. Henry had merely clenched his teeth—something he did quite often when Prescott talked to him—and told him that no self-respecting peer of the realm would ever think of trying to function properly without the aid of a valet. Prescott had given in, not because he feared for his self-respect, but because a throbbing vein had appeared in Henry's forehead, and he'd feared it might burst.

"Eight, huh?" Prescott said. "Well, if you can wait that long for supper, I 'spect I can too."

Hargreaves closed his eyes and inhaled a slow, deep breath, as if striving for calm. *Well,* Prescott thought, *better that than sporting a throbbing vein.*

"As your lordship no doubt knows by now, we shan't be dining together, *en famille*, as it were. You shall dine alone in the dining room while we shall eat our dinner with your lordship's staff in the kitchens."

Prescott finished buttoning his coat and turned to face the valet. "You know something, Ed? Up until a few weeks ago, I ate all my suppers with my family in a kitchen, just like you intend to do. Only time we ever ate a meal in the dining room was on Sunday, Thanksgiving, or Christmas. And the only time I ever ate alone was when I was out rounding up strays and found myself away from the house after dark."

"But your lordship is no longer in Texas. We are in England, now."

"*We* know that, Ed."

"And it would be more in keeping with the disparities of our positions if you would address us by our surname, Hargreaves, rather than our given name, Edward. Or Ed, as you put it."

"Look, all I'm saying is, before I got myself saddled with this dadblamed title that don't mean a hill of beans to me and probably never will, I wasn't no better than you. The way I look at it, I still ain't. Now I know this may sound strange to a man like you, who's worked for dukes and princes and the like, but I've been dressing myself for years, too."

"But that is why we are in your lordship's employ, to remove that particular burden from your many responsibilities."

"What responsibilities? Hell, man, all I've done since I got to this cursed country is go from one social gathering to another. I'm a working man, damn it. Lollygagging at tea parties with rich folks ain't my idea of being useful."

"Your lordship is bored?"

Prescott took note of the surprise in the valet's voice.

"Hell, yes, I'm bored. I have been since the day I got here. You would be, too, if you were accustomed to working from sunup to sundown on your own land, watching your cattle grow from newborn calves into prize-winning livestock, fighting rains and droughts and cattle rustlers, not to mention blue northers that come up sudden-like and threaten to freeze an entire herd out on the range. Back home, I was of use to somebody; I kept my family fed. Here, I ain't of use to nobody. What I can do they won't let me 'cause I'm a gentleman, and gentlemen ain't expected to do nothing here but sit on their butts while others do all the work for them."

Hargreaves slowly shook his head, contemplating the gist of Prescott's words. "Might we make a suggestion to your lordship?"

"Sure, fire away."

"Well, your lordship's estate appears to be in bad need of . . . shall we say, restoration?"

"You can say that again. I saw the shape it was in the minute I laid eyes on the place. But it's gonna take more than a little patching and mending to get Ravens Lair back to looking the way it once did. And that, Ed old buddy, means having money."

"With all due respect, milord, one must not discuss personal finances with outsiders."

"Hey, you brought it up. I'm merely telling you why restoring Ravens Lair is gonna be next to impossible for me to do. Now if I had money, it might be a different story, but I don't."

"Your lordship must not be too hasty in assuming the worst."

"I'm broke. You can't get no worse than that."

"But we only arrived this afternoon. We have yet

to peruse and thoroughly study the estate's current financial condition."

"You saying I may have some money I don't know I've got?"

"There is that possibility, yes. Ravens Lair has tenant farmers, does it not?"

"Yeah."

"Tenant farmers pay rent."

Prescott nodded his head thoughtfully. "You know, Ed, you may be on to something. I'll look into it first thing tomorrow morning."

"Yes, milord. And, milord?"

"Yeah?"

"The name is Hargreaves."

"Right. Hargreaves."

Thinking the matter settled, the valet turned to leave. "Shall we be needing anything more, milord? Supper—I mean, dinner—will be served shortly."

"Yeah, just one thing."

"Yes, milord?"

"I know you've been busy unpacking my belongings and all, and haven't had a chance to get around the castle yet, meet everybody working here, so I thought I'd warn you ahead of time. It might be a good idea for you to steer clear of Miss Esmeralda for a while."

"Miss who, milord?"

"Esmeralda. She's one of the women working here—the oldest of the bunch. Must've been around when my great-granddaddy was a boy. I'm sure Mrs. Sweet won't mind pointing her out to you."

"What about her, milord?"

"Well, she don't seem to cotton to menfolk too much. Acts downright afraid of us, in fact. Only God knows why, but she took one look at me and screamed rape."

"Milord?"

"I swear, all I did was say hello to her, and she let out with a scream that would curdle your blood. Had me shaking in my boots."

A faint smile touched the corner of Hargreaves' mouth. "Ah, we understand. And we shall do our best to make a point of avoiding this Miss Esmeralda person whenever possible, milord."

"See that you do, Ed. See that you do."

Morning sunlight poured through the leaded windows in the library and flooded down upon the desk where Prescott sat perusing the financial history of Ravens Lair. Business ledgers that went back a hundred years or more rested in a stack to his left. Record books containing the estate's more current transactions were piled in another haphazardly arranged stack to his right. Having already studied the latter, he didn't think he had the strength to look back any farther.

Giving a disgruntled groan, he shook his head and leaned back in the highbacked leather chair. He didn't have to be a banking wizard to know that he'd been correct all along in assuming the worst; the condition of the castle had clearly proclaimed the estate's financial plight. Plain and simple, Ravens Lair had no money. In fact, from what he had seen in the record books, the place hadn't been solvent for years.

Nothing unusual about that, he told himself. Being a Trefarrow and having no money seemed to go hand in hand, and the English Trefarrows were obviously no different from their Texas cousins. But worse than being broke was the fact that Ravens Lair appeared to be heavily in debt. In hock up to its crumbling, crenellated battlements, to be precise.

Glancing down at the page in the open ledger before him, Prescott groaned again. Sir Henry should have warned him that he would find something like this. Learning that he'd inherited a title and would have to leave Texas had been a bad enough shock, but this . . . Jesus, this topped it all. The estate had paid a small fortune to a dozen or more craftsmen, yet he still owed people money. Carpenters and stonemasons in Penzance, plumbers and silversmiths in London, even the very women who cleaned his house and cooked his meals for him. The latter filled him with a sharp surge of guilt.

"Oh, to hell with it." He shoved himself away from the desk and shot to his feet. "I need to get me some air."

He grabbed his coat off the back of his chair and stalked out of the library. And almost ran into Rowena just outside the door.

"Sorry," he grumbled as he moved to walk past her.

"Will thee be wanting your tea soon, milord?" Eager to please, her big brown eyes widened with expectancy. "Mrs. Sweet's got the kettle on."

"No, no tea. Not now. I'm going out for a while."

"Out, milord?"

"Yeah. I want to see the tenant farms." Farmers paid rent, he thought. Maybe a couple of them would want to pay him a little early. Yeah, sure they would.

"Thee'll be back in time for luncheon?"

At the mention of food Prescott stopped and turned around. After the breakfast of cold meats, some kind of salted fish, and braised kidneys that had been waiting for him on the sideboard in the morning room, he wasn't sure he could handle lunch. "What is Mrs. Sweet cooking?"

Rowena beamed. "Steak and kidney pie, milord."

Kidneys again? God in heaven help him. "Make that a plain steak—*beef* steak—cooked rare, with mashed potatoes and gravy, and I'll be here. But no kidneys. You got that, Miss Rowena? No more kidneys."

"Aye, milord."

"And tell Mrs. Sweet that from now on, I want bacon and eggs, and biscuits and gravy for breakfast. Or ham, or sausage, if there's no bacon handy." Thinking more on the matter, and not wanting to sound too difficult, he added, "Pancakes might be nice, too."

"Your lordship didn't fancy the kippers?"

"I don't even know what the dang things are, so I guess I didn't."

"Kippers are fish, milord."

"Good God, no! Not for breakfast. Bacon and eggs, you got that?"

"Aye, milord."

"And you'll be sure to tell Mrs. Sweet what I said?"

"Aye, milord, I will."

Praying she wouldn't forget to pass along his message to the housekeeper, Prescott stalked down the main corridor of the west wing, turned a corner into the old part of the castle, and turned again, right this time, toward the rear entrance. *So far, so good,* he thought, feeling proud that he hadn't gotten lost again as he had when he came down to breakfast. Hargreaves had told him that breakfast would be served in the morning room, and that the morning room was in the west wing. Prescott had started in that direction, but he'd somehow ended up in the music room in the east wing. If it hadn't been for Ursula seeing him take the wrong turn as she returned from a trip to the kitchen garden, he supposed he'd still be wandering around trying to find his way. Starving to death, too, most likely. Though, after the meager breakfast he'd had, starvation might still be close at hand.

"I gotta make myself a map of this place," he muttered as he stepped out of the castle onto the rear terrace that spanned the entire length of the building. "After I figure out a way of making some money."

Thanks to Ursula, who had commented off-handedly that the kitchen garden lay between the castle and the stables as she showed him into the morning room, Prescott soon found himself wandering down a well-trodden path. Herbs and vegetables sprouted in neatly planted rows to his right, while shoulder-high hedges grew in wild profusion on his left. Above the hedges, in the distance, he saw the gray slate roof of a large building. The stables, he hoped. If not, he would have to turn around, head back to the castle, and start all over again.

Moments later, he rounded the corner of the hedge and saw that luck was with him; he was heading in the right direction after all. The young man sitting in the doorway working a ring through a piece of leather harness was the same one who had taken care of Prescott's horse when he'd first arrived at Ravens Lair the day before.

The boy looked up and saw Prescott approaching. Dropping the harness, he leaped to his feet and tugged at a lock of blond hair on his forehead. "Good morning to 'ee, milord."

"Mornin'."

"Would 'ee be wanting a mount to ride?"

"Yeah, I would. But you go on with what you were doing; don't let me disturb you. I can saddle up my own horse."

The young man looked affronted. "But 'tis me job, milord."

"Well, all right. What's your name, anyway? I don't recall Miss Lucinda mentioning it yesterday."

"Thomas, milord. Thomas Sweet."

"You Mrs. Sweet's boy?" Prescott looked for some hint of family likeness, but found none.

"Grandson, milord."

"Well, nice to meet you, Thomas."

Following the boy into the stables, Prescott felt an immediate comfort in smelling the familiar scent of earth, hay, horse, and leather. It smelled just like the stable back home, and looked a little like it, too. The floor was recently swept, harnesses hung neatly off every hook beside each of the stall doors, and at the rear of the stable gleamed a big black carriage. Any horse, he thought, would be proud to call this place home. Any person, too. If he ever got tired of rattling around by himself in the castle, he'd come down here and sleep.

"Looks like you're doing a real fine job here, Thomas."

Thomas looked stunned by the unexpected compliment. "Thank 'ee, milord."

"Keep up the good work."

"I will, milord, I will. Which horse would 'ee be wanting?"

"Oh, the one I rode in on yesterday will do."

"With your lordship's tack, or one of ours?"

"Mine," Prescott said emphatically. "I tried riding English tack in London. Fell off and damn near broke my neck. First time in years I've fallen off a horse. Been thrown from my fair share, but never fallen."

"Thrown from a horse, milord?"

"That's right. Busting broncs." Seeing the perplexed look that crossed the boy's face, Prescott added, "Broncos. Mustangs. They're horses that run wild on the plains in Texas. They've even got 'em as far west as Nevada and California. 'Course, I wouldn't be knowing that firsthand. Just hearsay, is all."

"Broncs." His expression wistful, Thomas tried to repeat the word using Prescott's western accent.

"Yeah, they're mean cusses, the stallions especially. You let 'em stay wild, don't try to round 'em up and tame 'em, they'll come in the dead of night and steal all your mares. Dead of night, hell. I heard of one stallion that used to steal his fillies in the daytime. He was a brazen bastard," he said, shaking his head. "Black as pitch and a good fifteen hands high. Had a mane on him that damn near dragged the ground."

"Milord?"

"Yeah?"

Thomas led Prescott's horse out of the stall and tossed a blanket and the big Western saddle across its back. He seemed to hesitate a moment, biting his lower lip until he worked up the courage to speak. And when he did speak, excitement laced his tone. “Does ’ee fight red Indians in Texas?”

“Indians?”

“Aye, milord, naked savages. I’ve heard tales. Horrible, they were.”

“Naw, we don’t have that kind of trouble these days. Years ago, maybe, back when my granddaddy was working the Triple T, but none recently.”

“Did they really scalp white men?”

“Some did, sure,” Prescott said. “You ask me, it was mostly ’cause the white men that got scalped deserved it. That’s just my opinion, though. History books and old timers will tell you a different story. But if I was an Indian and somebody tried running me off my land, you can be sure I’d try to take a scalp or two before they made me leave.”

“And gunfights?”

Gunfights? Prescott thought. “What about ’em?”

“Wyatt Earp and Doc Holliday—did they really have a shootout with the Clantons at the OK Corral? Were they real men, or just characters in a book?”

“Oh no, they were real men, all right. ’Course, I hear Doc died. Don’t know how or when, exactly, but I think Wyatt’s still alive.”

“Then it is true. All of it’s true.”

“Sure. Happened about ten years ago in a place called Tombstone, Ari—”

“Arizona Territory.” Thomas’s brown eyes were alight with dreamy fascination as he cinched the saddle tightly around the horse’s belly.

“How do you know so much?”

“I read about it. ’Til now, I hadn’t believed it was true.” He breathed a wistful sigh. “The American West must be a wonderful place.”

"Wonderful?" Prescott chuckled. "You been reading too many dime novels, Tom. Ain't nothing wonderful about the West."

"But thee lived there."

"Yeah, in Waco, not Tombstone. We're civilized where I come from. We got trains that stop at all the big towns, telegraph lines, and everything. Some of us even got running water and indoor plumbing."

"No gunfights at high noon on Main Street?"

"Not lately, no."

"No bank robbers? No cattle rustlers?"

"Well now, we still have them. 'Course, we got the Texas Rangers, too. Fine group of men, the Rangers. They do the best they can to keep the peace, but there's always a bad apple or two showing up, causing trouble."

Thomas looped the reins over the horse's head and handed them to Prescott. "I want to go there someday. I *will* go there."

"Where, Texas?"

"Aye. Or Arizona. Perhaps even California."

"Don't know about them other places, but Texas is kinda special. Grand almost. Ain't no place like it that I've ever seen. Plains so flat and broad they seem to go on forever. Skies so pretty a blue you want to stare at 'em 'til you go blind." Prescott shook his head and led his horse toward the stable door. More than anything, he wished he could be there now to see those plains and skies, wished even more that he could be with his family again. But wishing, he knew, wouldn't make it so. From the looks of things, he might not ever see Texas again. But Tom might. A boy his age, with his whole life ahead of him and no responsibilities to tie him down, could do just about anything he wanted.

"Tell you what, Tom. When you settle on a time, let me know."

"A time, milord?"

"Yeah, to head for Texas. You're gonna need to find work when you get there, and I know just the place. The Triple T's always in need of somebody who knows something about horses, and it appears to me that you know quite a lot."

"Work on your ranch, milord?"

"Well, legally it's mine and my brother's. But Payne's a good man. He'll treat you fairly. You give him an honest day's work, he'll give you an honest day's wage. Won't be much, of course, but it'll keep the wolf from the door. He won't let the other cowpokes fun you too much, neither, you being an outsider and all."

"Milord, I—I don't know what to say."

"Then don't say nothing. Just tell me where the closest tenant farm is. All of a sudden I got me a hankering to learn about sheep."

No matter what continent they were raised on, sheep were still sheep, Prescott decided some time later as he bid his last tenant farmer good-bye. The critters stunk to high heaven and were about as stupid an animal as the Almighty could have ever created. Where one went, the rest followed, all staying huddled together in a fat, woolly mass. The only good thing about sheep that he could see was that you couldn't stampede them, no matter how hard you tried. Cows would scatter in all directions at the least unfamiliar noise. Sheep would just run a little way and then stop and start grazing again, as if nothing had happened.

Prescott thought he was headed back to the castle but soon realized he was lost. "Damn it to hell, not again." From the looks of it, he was going to need one map for the house and one for the surrounding countryside. Either that or a guide to accompany him constantly.

He rode over one hill, followed a narrow lane a bit, then veered off and ascended another slight rise. Seeing Lucinda's cottage resting at the foot, he grinned. He wasn't as lost as he thought he was.

The notion of riding past his cousin's place and not stopping occurred to him, but so did the thought of seeing her again. The second notion proved stronger than the first, and he set off at a steady gallop toward her gate.

"Hello to the house!" he called out, dismounting his horse. "Anybody home?"

The door swung open and Lucinda stepped outside, wiping her hands on the bibbed apron tied around her slender waist. Glinting sunlight picked up shimmers of blue amidst her raven-black tresses, and her gray eyes looked pleased when she recognized her unexpected visitor.

"Good day, milord."

"Please, make it Prescott," he said, her immediate smile sending warmth flowing through him. "I get enough of that 'milord' business up at the house."

She walked down the short path to the gate to unfasten the latch, her skirts swishing against the abundant growth of flowers and herbs as she passed by them. "I'm surprised you're out and about today. Not enough work in the library to keep you occupied?"

"Too much work. That's why I'm playing hooky.

But if you're busy, and you look like you are, maybe I ought to—"

"Nonsense. I've just been baking. Come inside. Do you like scones?"

"Are scones them little pie-shaped biscuit things with raisins inside?"

"They're currants, actually, not raisins, and mine are round, not pie-shaped."

Prescott didn't have to think long on the subject, having tasted scones in London, and having liked them. And, since he had eaten so little at breakfast he felt as if it wouldn't take much for him to start gnawing on his horse. But scones sounded a sight more appetizing. "You twist my arm just right, and I might could find it in me to sample one or two."

"Twist your arm?" Amusement danced across her eyes as she gave him a most flirtatious look. "Well, I've Devonshire clotted cream and jam, if that helps any."

"Cousin Lucinda, if I didn't know better, I'd swear you've twisted a man's arm before."

"Figuratively, perhaps, but not literally."

He swept off his hat and followed her inside the cottage, nearly hitting his head on the low doorway. The instant he entered, he felt right at home. The smell of freshly baked bread filled the air, along with the pleasant pungent scent of dried flowers and herbs that hung upside down from the broad ceiling rafters. Looking around the room, he saw she didn't have much, but what she did have was put to good use. A small settee rested beside a fireplace blackened with age and much use, while a large dresser-like piece of furniture filled with plates and pitchers hugged the wall. A square table and two chairs took up the remainder of the floor space.

"You take in boarders here?"

"Boarders?" Giving him a puzzled look, she motioned him to a chair. "Oh, you must mean lodgers. There's barely enough room here for me. Where would I put a lodger?"

"Just asking. I find your home a sight cozier than the castle is all."

"But I thought you Texans appreciated wide open spaces."

"We do, when our wide open spaces are outdoors. Inside, we tend to lean toward cozy." And he could easily grow to like her brand of cozy. Her warmth, her wit, her honesty, not to mention her beauty, were doing things to him that he hadn't thought possible. But now wasn't the time to be thinking of that, or thinking of her doing that with him. "You can't go nowhere in the castle without hearing the echo of your own voice or footsteps. It gets spooky after a while."

She placed a plate of steaming scones down in front of him, along with a pot of strawberry jam and big bowl of yellow-looking cream so thick that the spoon stood upright in it. Prescott wanted to dive right in and start eating, but he remembered his manners and waited until Lucinda had sat down and poured them each a cup of tea.

"You've only spent one night at Ravens Lair, Prescott. Give it some time. I'm sure you'll become accustomed to the castle's size."

"Don't bet on it."

Following Lucinda's lead, and trying not to act too much like a pig, he broke open a scone and plopped a big spoonful of cream on one half of it and a spoonful of jam on the other. When he sank his teeth into it, tasting the blend of bread, currants, thick cream, and strawberry, he experienced a world of pleasurable sensations.

"Mighty tasty, Lucinda. Mighty tasty indeed."

She lowered her eyes and smiled demurely. "Thank you."

"You cook like this all the time?"

"No. Only when the mood strikes me."

"It ought to strike you more often. Tending them pretty flowers of yours ain't your only gift."

Watching him finish off the scone in two bites, she asked, "Is that your way of asking for a second helping?"

"Ma'am, it'd be downright rude of me to do that. My Aunt Em taught me better. But it sure was good. Best food I've had since coming here."

"Then have another, by all means."

"If you insist."

"I do."

Prescott did help himself, and, before too long, the plate of scones was empty. He even polished off a second cup of tea, heavily sweetened with sugar, of course, to mask the bitter flavor.

"Mrs. Sweet could sure learn a thing or two from you," he said, sitting back, replete. "That's the best meal I've had since coming here."

"That's odd. I always thought Mrs. Sweet to be a very good cook."

"She ain't as good as you." *Ain't as easy on the eyes as you, either,* he thought, feeling a pleasurable throbbing begin in the center of his chest. "Boils just about everything. Except them dang kidneys, of course. I don't know how she cooked them. I didn't touch 'em to find out."

"You don't care for kidneys? Not even steak and kidney pie?" The grimace he made was so endearing, made him look so boyish, that Lucinda couldn't help but smile.

"I don't fancy eating innards. Never did. And the only thing I'll eat boiled is chicken, but only when it's fixed with dumplings. The rest of the time, I eat beef, either cooked over an open fire or fried in a skillet 'til it's black on the outside and blood rare in the middle. That's the way we Texans like it."

"Then you should tell that to Mrs. Sweet. I'm sure she would fix your meals any way you wish."

"Well, seeing as how she's already supposed to be such a good cook and all, wouldn't I hurt her feelings, telling her such a thing as that?"

"Prescott, she's in your employ. It's her job to try and please you. You are, after all, the lord of the castle."

"Maybe so, but I learned early on that you don't go around insulting a lady's cooking. Not if you want to stay on her good side, you don't."

"That's ridiculous. You wouldn't be insulting her. You would be advising her. Advice, I'm sure, she would eagerly accept. She knows you're a busy man, that you have important work to do, and that you must have a meal prepared to your liking."

"I ain't that busy. Haven't been since I set foot on English soil. Take this morning, for instance. All I did was look over Ravens Lair's finances and learn what a sad shape the place is in."

"And you probably did it all on an empty stomach, didn't you?"

"What makes you think that?" he asked.

"Because you ate my scones like a man half starved."

"Sorry. Guess I was hungrier than I thought. Didn't mean to make such a pig of myself."

"Oh, don't apologize. It isn't necessary. If you must know, I consider your appetite quite flattering."

"You do?"

"Yes, very much so." She had never cooked a meal for a man before. And it had been years since she'd had the opportunity to share a meal with one.

Suddenly, something Prescott had said registered in her mind. "You said that Ravens Lair is having some financial difficulties."

"That's what I said, all right."

"What sort?"

Prescott hesitated a moment, remembering that Hargreaves had told him never to discuss financial problems with outsiders. But as his cousin and a long-time resident of St. Keverne, Lucinda hardly fit the role of outsider. She more than anyone should know where the situation stood. "The worst kind. We're flat busted."

"What?"

"We're broke. We haven't got a nickel to our name." Heaven help him, he thought. He was beginning to sound like Hargreaves, saying "we" instead of "I." "I owe so many people so much money, I'm surprised bill collectors from all over England ain't at my door right now, trying to beat it down."

"Bill collectors?"

"Yeah, for all the work that's been done and the supplies they used. Carpenters, stonemasons—you name it, I owe 'em. But that ain't as bad as owing the ladies up at the house. Poor things ain't been paid in months. So, you see? I can't very well complain to Mrs. Sweet about not liking her cooking when all this time she's been working for free."

When he stopped talking, he noticed the strange expression on Lucinda's face, and how her slightly narrowed eyes focused on some unseen object in the distance. "What's the matter?"

"Prescott, something is gravely amiss. I'm surprised you haven't realized it yourself."

"Realized what?"

"The condition of the castle, of course."

"The dadblamed thing's about to fall down; I've noticed that."

"Yet you say that you owe craftsmen for, I assume, repairs that have not been made."

Prescott felt as if someone had hit him hard in the center of his chest, or slapped him upside the head and finally woke him up. "That son of a— Emerson's in charge of the books, ain't he? It's his job to pay the ladies' wages and creditors, stuff like that?"

"Yes. He's the estate's superintendent, and handling the books is one of his responsibilities. It has been for the last few years."

"That's about how long he's been stealing from Ravens Lair, too. Bastard's been stealing us blind."

"It certainly appears that— Where are you going?"

Prescott had gotten up from his chair so quickly that it almost toppled over. "To find Emerson, of course. Where is he?"

"I couldn't begin to guess."

"I didn't see him around any of the farms this morning when I was out riding."

"He might be at home."

Prescott headed for the door, grabbing his hat off the wall hook where Lucinda had placed it earlier. "Where would that be?"

"His house is down the lane, toward the village. When you come to a sort of fork, you'll want to—" She broke off with a sigh, remembering that Prescott was still new to the neighborhood and quite likely to get himself lost. "Never mind. I'll show you myself."

6

Prescott gave no thought to propriety or what the villagers might think as he mounted his steed and pulled Lucinda up into the saddle in front of him. He was in a hurry to find Emerson, and they had only one horse between them.

"I had my suspicions, of course," she said. "Emerson always has been something of a scoundrel, even as a boy. But I can't believe he would have the audacity to actually steal from the estate, from dear old Uncle Herbert. His actions are deplorable. Utterly deplorable." She looked over her shoulder at Prescott and saw the angry, determined expression in his eyes. "Uncle Herbert, you see, was the only one who would hire him."

"Looks like Uncle Herbert made a big mistake."

"Well, he really didn't have much choice in the matter. No one else wanted the position."

"No one?"

"No one. There are far too many responsibilities

that go with the job of superintendent. The only others who were even remotely qualified were the tenant farmers, and they—"

"Have enough to do just taking care of their own places."

"Exactly," she said. "Life in this part of Cornwall isn't easy, by any means. The castle may be equipped with all of the latest, necessary conveniences, but the rest of us have very few luxuries."

Wanting to get an idea of how long Emerson had been in a position of authority at Ravens Lair, and how far back his thievery went, Prescott asked, "When did Uncle Herbert hire him?"

"Shortly after he had his first stroke. That was—let me think. Good heavens, it's been three years. He was paying a call on one of the tenant farmers and just collapsed. He was never able to walk again. Sat in a wheel chair when the doctor finally allowed him out of bed, because by then, you see, both of his limbs and one arm were of no use to him at all. He was still quite lucid, though. Still quite concerned about the daily happenings on the estate. So he hired a superintendent to be his eyes and ears and legs."

"Emerson."

"Yes, Emerson. Uncle Herbert took such great pride in Ravens Lair, Prescott. It was his home; he loved it more than anything else in life. And even though I know it must have saddened him not to be able to ride round the estate himself, he made a point of trusting Emerson, of advising him, so that it would be properly run. Unfortunately, his second stroke occurred within a few months of the first, and it left his mental faculties sadly depleted. His speech was slurred, he drooled quite a lot . . ." She shuddered at the memory. "At the end, the staff were caring for him as if he were little better than a baby."

"And that was how long ago?"

"Two years."

"That's a long time for Emerson to have total control of the place. Even longer when you think of all the money he could have been stealing before then. Must've been like turning a kid with a sweet tooth loose in a candy store. Emerson knew Uncle Herbert wouldn't question how he ran the estate or spent estate money, because he knew the old man wasn't in any condition to challenge him. Looks like no one else questioned him, either. The bastard."

"As I said before, I suspected something was amiss. Work that needed doing on the castle was left undone. The grounds became overgrown. But I couldn't tell anyone."

"Why not?"

"Who would I have told?"

"The law, for starters," Prescott said.

"The law?"

"Yeah. Don't y'all have a sheriff around these parts? Somebody hired or elected to keep the peace?"

Lucinda issued a dry, mirthless chuckle. "You'll soon learn that our sheriff is little better than a figurehead. He and the mayor of St. Keverne spend most of their time at the village pub. And as for 'keeping the peace,' as you put it, nothing unpeaceful ever happens in St. Keverne."

"Nothing? No murders, robberies, or drunken rowdies fighting each other on Saturday night?"

"No, nothing. Well, there is the odd squabble or two between neighbors, but nothing of major importance.

We're a very small community. As the new earl, you're the law in this little corner of Cornwall."

"All right, forget St. Keverne. Couldn't you have told somebody in London?"

"Uncle Herbert's solicitors, you mean?"

"They'd do for a start."

"They're the ones who advised Uncle Herbert to hire a superintendent in the first place, right after he had his first stroke. They're also the ones who drew up Emerson's letter of employment, giving him the right to manage the estate as he saw fit. Which he obviously did. No, it would have been useless to go to them. They wouldn't have believed me anyway."

"I don't see why not. You're a member of the family; you live here; you saw what was going on."

"You don't understand," she said. "I'm as much of an outsider as you are. Yes, I have the Trefarrow name, but it doesn't give *me* any special privileges, Prescott. It never has done. And to be seen, or even overheard, consorting with a person like me is not the thing to do in polite society."

"A person like you?"

"Yes."

"You're my cousin, Lucinda. A member of my family. You're not exactly a total stranger."

She hesitated for a moment, wishing she didn't have to elaborate, but she had no choice. He had to know.

"I'm more than just your cousin. I'm your bastard cousin."

There, she thought. She had told him. Now she would see, as she had with so many others, the look of shock, disappointment, and disapproval in his eyes.

Then would come the accusatory tone in his voice as he tried to distance himself from her.

But instead of hurling recriminations at her or stumbling over his words and his feet in an attempt to get away from her, Prescott merely shrugged.

"That don't matter to me none," he said. "Family's family. That's all that counts."

He didn't care? Although shocking, the knowledge pleased her more than she dared admit, causing her to warm toward him even more. Heaven help her, she had finally found a man who seemed not the least bit affected by the matter of her illegitimacy. But perhaps he didn't fully comprehend what she had told him.

"I don't know about Texas, but here in England, one's good name means everything. Because I was born on the wrong side of the blanket, I haven't a good name."

"The hell you don't," he said angrily. "You're a Trefarrow the same as me, and don't ever let anybody tell you different. Dadblast it, Lucinda, we're family."

"But you're a legitimate Trefarrow. I'm not. That's one burden you will never know, one you will never understand for as long as you live."

"You're right about that. Not being in your place, living the life you've led here, I can't understand. But I do understand one thing—it's plumb loco for you to go on shouldering the blame for something your mama and daddy did or didn't do. It's even worse if others blame you for it. How you were born, or when, ain't your fault, and it ain't nobody else's business, either. Besides, none of that matters to me, anyhow. I'm a Texan, remember?"

"Oh, I see. You Texans don't frown upon illegitimacy."

"Not the way you English seem to, that's for dang sure. I can't speak for all Texans, of course, just the ones I know, and they tend to judge a person for what he is, for what he makes of himself, not for what his folks did or who they were. Tarnation, Lucinda, I've known plenty of folks who didn't know their daddies. Known plenty of 'em who did, too. Believe me, you find as many bastards in the second bunch as you do in the first.

"Take that Emerson fella. I'll bet he knows his daddy, but being legitimate didn't do him no good. You're much better than him. You weren't surly to me when we first met. You were kind, helpful, real friendly, and without a doubt the—" He broke off, realizing he couldn't tell her that she was the most beautiful woman he'd ever met. Not yet, anyway. "And the best dang gardener I've ever seen. Why, I know a dozen or more women back home who'd give their eyeteeth to have thumbs as green as yours."

"Green thumbs?" she asked.

"Yeah, you've got a knack for growing pretty flowers."

"Unfortunately, it takes much more than that to garner respect from a lot of my fellow Englishmen. But you'll soon learn that."

Prescott wanted to tell her that he already knew about it, that'd he'd learned it firsthand the minute he'd met the Calderwoods, his mama's people. If he'd only listened to his brother, Payne, maybe he would have been prepared. But he hadn't listened because he hadn't wanted to believe him. He'd been raised to believe that family was family, part of your own flesh and blood, people you treated with respect and affection, who treated you the same way. And if you couldn't be respectful and affectionate, the least you could be was tolerant. But the Calderwoods hadn't been any of those things. From the first moment he'd met them they'd been cold, uncaring, and downright rude. They were so distant that Prescott had likened them to a blue norther, blowing in quickly when he least expected it, and leaving him chilled to the bone with their icy reserve. Why, if Sir Henry hadn't foisted the damn title on him and made him Earl of St. Keverne, he doubted the Calderwoods would have even given him the time of day. His uncles and male cousins had all but turned up their noses when he'd tried to discuss ranching and cattle breeding with them. But being merchants, city folk and all, he supposed they probably didn't know any better.

As bad as the men were, though, his aunts and female cousins had been even worse. Lord Almighty, if they had more than one thing on their minds—getting him married to one of their horse-faced daughters—he'd eat his hat. He had thought that fighting off the Campbell sisters back home had been a chore, but sidestepping the Calderwood girls was ten times worse. They'd been ten times homelier, too. And ten times more determined to make nuisances of themselves. Why, he hadn't been able to walk down a street in London, or even go out for a bite to eat in the evening, without one of them popping up from out of nowhere, grinning like some half-wit, giggling and fluttering her lashes at him. Hoping, he supposed, to capture his attention and affections so that he would propose to one of them. Hell's bells, he hadn't come to England to find a wife.

But he couldn't share his knowledge with Lucinda. Couldn't share the problems he had with the other side of his family, either. She had too many of her own to deal with. One in particular, he thought.

"The way Emerson treated you a while back," he said, "is that the kind of respect you get from folks around these parts?"

"No, I'm happy to say that he's the exception. Everyone else accepts me for who I am." As long as she remembered to stay in her place, she mused, and never tried to defy any of the unspoken restrictions placed on her by her illegitimacy. Like finding the love of a good, decent man, marrying, and making a home for him. And, perhaps the most heartbreaking of all, having his children. "But you'll find out soon enough. Accept it, Prescott, I'm the family bastard."

"You ought not be talking about yourself that way."

"Even if it's the truth?"

Prescott fell silent, unsure of how to answer her. He had lived long enough to know that sometimes even the truth didn't tell the whole story, and that appeared to be the case where Miss Lucinda Trefarrow was concerned. He could understand the position she was in, being a member of the family, yet not being treated as one. Even if she'd had all the ample proof in the world of Emerson's thievery to show the authorities, chances were they wouldn't have believed her or taken her seriously because she was illegitimate, someone not to be trusted.

The unfairness of Lucinda's situation clawed at his conscience. He'd met all kinds of so-called ladies, from the ones back home in Texas to the ones he'd met more recently in London, but Lucinda had far more class, grace, and dignity than any of the others who bore lengthy and legitimate pedigrees.

"I wonder if you'll be able to get the truth from Emerson," she said.

"Don't worry, I'll handle it," Prescott said. He was certain he could, even if he had to resort to beating the truth out of the man. He didn't hold with thievery. Never had, and never would. "If he's only taken a little bit, I might can persuade him to pay it back. Lord knows, we sure could use it."

"And if he's stolen a lot? After all, he's been in authority for almost three years."

"Like I said, one way or another, I'll see to it that he pays it back. Every nickel of it."

"Shilling."

"What?"

"We don't have nickels here," she said. "We have shillings. Pounds, shillings, and pence."

"Yeah, whatever. Money's money, no matter what you call it."

"Go left here."

As Prescott pulled the reins, guiding the horse off the main road onto a narrower path, his forearm casually brushed Lucinda's breast. He felt its firm fullness through the fabric of his shirt and experienced a sharp jolt of awareness in his groin. In another frame of mind, the innocent contact might have affected him more deeply and led him to take actions that might have ultimately eased his recent lengthy bout of celibacy. But Lucinda was the kind of lady who deserved much more than a quick seduction.

Emerson's house, Prescott soon discovered, was little better than a hovel, its thatched roof in bad need of mending, its tiny front garden overgrown with weeds. Even the chickens that clucked and scratched in the dirt out front looked sorely underfed.

"It's a sure thing he didn't spend all his ill-gotten gains keeping up this place." Prescott dismounted first, then helped Lucinda down from the saddle. "It don't even look like it's lived in."

"It is, though. His wife and children are probably inside right now, watching us."

"He's got a wife and kids?"

"Three little girls."

"God help 'em." Prescott had only met Emerson once, but their brief meeting was all it had taken for him to find the notion of Emerson as a husband and family man quite unbelievable. What woman in her right mind would want to marry a rude, surly, disagreeable man like him? Obviously one who didn't have very good judgment where men were concerned.

He knocked on the door, and a moment passed before the weathered panel squeaked open. The tiny, blond head that appeared came no higher than Prescott's knee. He took one look at the pair of huge blue eyes peering up at him, at the little girl's angelic baby face, and he felt the anger in his heart melt into a puddle.

Smiling, he knelt down so that his head was almost level with the child's. "Hi. Is your daddy home?"

The little girl shook her head and stared past Prescott to blink up at Lucinda.

"How 'bout your mama?" he asked. "Is she here?"

Looking back at Prescott, the little girl's cheeks turned a pretty shade of pink, and she stepped back.

"Guess this means we're invited in."

Inside, he found the interior to be quite a contrast from the exterior. Instead of decaying from neglect, the Emersons' home was clean and neat as a pin. He could see no trace of dirt on the bare wood floor or the few pieces of furniture in the small main room. In fact, everything bore the dull gleam of a recent polishing.

His heart leaped in his chest as he looked off and noticed an older child, around three or four years old, standing on a stool at a table, cutting a slice of bread from a loaf with a very sharp-looking knife.

"Lord Almighty, Lucinda, she's gonna cut her little hand off." He crossed the room in three long strides, grasped hold of the knife with one hand and scooped the little girl off her stool with the other. "You ought not be playing with knives, sugar. Where's your mama?"

"In bed, sick," she said.

Her little sister placed a pudgy finger to her lips. "Shhh. Mama seepin'."

"She's sleeping?" Lucinda asked.

"And she left the two of you to fend for yourselves?" It appeared as though Mrs. Emerson was no better than her husband—thoughtless and unconcerned about the welfare of her children.

"Alexandra, Victoria, what are you—? Oh! I didn't know visitors were calling."

Prescott turned at the sound of the female voice. A young woman with a toddler perched on her hip stood in the bedroom doorway. Though her hair was disheveled and her dress wrinkled, she bore an undeniable grace about her that bespoke good breeding. She also looked to him about eight months pregnant.

"I'm sorry, Mrs. Emerson." Prescott deposited the little girl onto the floor and stepped toward the young woman. "We don't mean to be disturbing you when you're resting and all."

"No, no, you're not disturbing me," she said. "We so very seldom have callers here, it's a pleasure when someone deigns to visit us. Please, won't you sit down? It won't take me but a moment to make tea."

"Thanks, ma'am, but we don't want to be a bother."

"Mrs. Emerson," Lucinda said. "Your daughter tells us you're ill."

"Alexandra, I suppose." As her oldest daughter nodded, Mrs. Emerson smiled lovingly. "She's such a dear child. A natural born mother. Always so full of concern for her little sisters, and for me. Always so caring."

"I was making your tea, Mummy."

"Were you, darling? How thoughtful."

Alexandra cast an accusing glare at Prescott. "But he wouldn't let me make sandwiches. He said I was going to cut off my hand. I've never cut my hand before, Mummy."

"Perhaps this gentleman doesn't know that I've taught you all about the dangers of knives and it frightened him to see a little girl your age handling one."

"Well then, he should have asked, shouldn't he, Mummy?"

"Yes, I should have," Prescott said, feeling thoroughly chastised by the little girl.

"Mrs. Emerson," Lucinda said, "do you need us to send for Doctor Goodacre?"

The woman fell silent, her blond head lowering for

a moment as she gazed at all three of her daughters. Then, with a sigh, she placed the youngest on the floor, straightened her spine, and brushed a hand over the generous swell of her belly. "There's nothing the good doctor can do for me that he hasn't already done. Nor for this one, either, I suspect. But you didn't call to hear of my complaints. You're the new earl, aren't you?"

Prescott wished he could contradict her, but he couldn't. "Yes, ma'am, I am."

"Milord."

Mrs. Emerson began to dip into a curtsy, wanting to show the new lord of the manor that she respected him and his authority. But Prescott quickly reached out and grabbed hold of both her arms, pulling her upright again. In doing so, his hands slipped the loose sleeves of her morning gown higher up her arms, and he saw the evidence of old bruises in her pale, too-slender flesh. Emerson, he thought, feeling a powerful surge of anger shoot through him and threaten to overtake his reserve.

"That ain't necessary, ma'am. Not for a lady in your condition."

"You're too kind, milord."

The knowledge that he had made a grave error in assuming that Mrs. Emerson was no better than her husband caused the heat of guilt and embarrassment to steal into Prescott's cheeks. "Kindness ain't got nothing to do with the reason why we're here, ma'am."

"Ah, you must be looking for Mr. Emerson, my husband."

Smart lady, he thought. And obviously too damn good for the likes of the man she was married to.

"Yes, ma'am. Will he be coming home for supper any time soon?"

Mrs. Emerson held her head erect. "I am the last person to be consulted on my husband's activities, milord. He is a man governed by his own whims. And excesses."

"I see." Prescott had a good idea what the lady was really trying to tell him. Emerson wouldn't be home in time for supper, because the man was either out tomcatting, gambling, or getting himself liquored up. For all Prescott knew, he could be doing all three.

"Lord Prescott," Lucinda said, stepping forward, "do you know how to make sandwiches?"

Surprised by the unexpected question, Prescott stared at her. "Sandwiches?"

"Sandwiches." Lucinda gave Prescott a direct look. "Mrs. Emerson and her daughters appear to be in need of sustenance at the moment. She also needs to sit down. Why don't I have a chat with her while you prepare something to eat for them?"

"Good idea," he said, understanding her unspoken message. She wanted to talk with the lady of the house in private, and he was more than willing to let her. She just might find out where Emerson was hiding out. "Sandwiches happen to be a specialty of mine."

"Oh no, it isn't necessary for you to trouble yourself, milord. I can prepare our supper." Mrs. Emerson began moving toward the work table in a slow, waddling gait.

Prescott stopped her. "Maybe it ain't necessary, but it'd sure be my pleasure, if you don't mind, ma'am. You just go sit yourself down over yonder and put your feet up. I ain't made a sandwich since I left Texas, and I'm just itching to make one now. Alexandra, Victoria—you ladies want to help me, show me where your mama keeps all her stuff? I bet we can whip her up one of the best sandwiches this side of the Mississippi."

"Who's Miss Ippi?" Alexandra asked, taking hold of Prescott's proffered hand. Not to be left out, Victoria took hold of his other hand, and they moved to the far side of the room.

"The Mississippi's a river, darlin'. The biggest river in the whole dang world. 'Bout near as big as the Atlantic Ocean in some parts."

As Prescott distracted the two older girls with his tall Texas tales, not to mention his practiced dexterity at slicing bread and meat, Lucinda sat with Mrs. Emerson and the baby, Elizabeth, on the threadbare settee near the fireplace. The two women spoke in hushed tones, Lucinda darting occasional glances in Prescott's direction to make sure he kept Alexandra and Victoria well occupied. Little children, she knew, had remarkable hearing when they least needed it. And they certainly had no need to overhear what their mother was telling her now.

"It's tragic," Lucinda said some time later, as she and Prescott rode away from the house, assured that Mrs. Emerson and her three daughters were taken care of for the time being.

"You're telling *me.* Emerson's an even bigger bastard than I thought he was. Stealing from his boss is one thing, but treating his family the way he does is a sin against man. Barely could find any food in the house. Their clothes were so old and frayed-looking they probably won't make it through too many more washings. Gotta do something about that."

"We can help the children," she said.

"I will; you can count on it. And those bruises on Miz Emerson's arms. Did you see 'em? Lord Almighty, I'd like to give her husband a few bruises, let him know just how I feel about men who beat their womenfolk." Then something Lucinda had said brought him up short. "What do you mean, 'We can help the children?' She needs as much help as they do. Maybe more, a woman in her condition."

"That's just it, Prescott. Her condition is much worse than it appears."

"Worse?"

"Yes. She's dying."

Prescott yanked on the reins, bringing the horse to a dead stop. "She tell you that?"

"Not in those precise words, no. But according to what she said Dr. Goodacre told her, her condition will never improve. Neither will that of her unborn child."

"What's wrong with her?"

Lucinda hesitated a moment, unsure how to phrase her response. In the end, she decided to take the direct approach. Prescott was a man; surely he would understand her bluntness. "She has syphilis."

"What!"

"Emerson, her husband, has given her syphilis."

"God Almighty!"

"The baby has it as well, of course."

Feeling sick inside, Prescott nudged the horse with his knee and set it into motion again. "Couldn't the doc do anything for her, give her something to cure it?"

"I don't know, Prescott; I'm not a doctor. I rather

doubt it, though. From what I understand, tinctures of arsenic and lead are often used to treat conditions such as hers. But arsenic and lead are quite dangerous elements even in minute doses."

"So is the damn disease! Pardon my language."

"It's quite all right. Your anger is well justified. Were I a man like you, I might react the same way."

Thank the good Lord she wasn't, Prescott thought, tightening his hold around Lucinda's waist.

"However, my anger was just as intense as yours when she told me."

"And there ain't no cure at all for her, er, for what she's got?"

"I don't know. I'm confident that if there were a cure, Dr. Goodacre would have tried it long ago. He's a very reliable physician. He's been here since I was a child; everyone in the village trusts him. The sad part about this whole affair is that Mrs. Emerson has no one to turn to at a time like this for help. Her family disowned her when she married Garrick five years ago."

No cure, no family to come to her aid in her time of need, and, from the looks of it, no place to go. Prescott had thought he had troubles, but poor Mrs. Emerson had him beat by a wide country mile. He couldn't just leave her in the lurch like this, though. He had to do something.

"Then I'll just have to write her people and tell them what's going on, won't I? If they've got any shred of decency in them at all they'll come get her and the girls out of that shack they're living in."

"Writing letters won't help."

"Why not? Her people can read, can't they?"

"Her family are all dead."

"All of them?"

"Yes. Except for her three little girls and that pitiful excuse of a husband, she's all alone."

"Not for much longer, she ain't. As soon as I find Emerson and take care of him, I'll move her and the girls up to the castle. Lord knows, it ain't like we're hurting for space. We got room enough to spare."

"Prescott, I know you mean well, but you can't do that."

"Just watch me. Everybody around here keeps reminding me I'm the new earl. Well, it's about high time I started acting like it. Throw my weight around a little, do what suits me. Helping out Miz Emerson would suit me just fine."

"All right, help her. But don't steal her pride. She hasn't much of it now; you can't be so heartless as to want to take even that small amount from her."

Pride, Prescott thought. The one thing standing between a young woman dying in a dingy little hovel and living out the rest of her life in comfort and ease. Folks sure could be ornery when something as paltry as their pride was at stake. But that shouldn't be any great surprise to him. Pride had taken its toll on his family, his mother and father especially. They had fallen victim to it and ended up with nothing but heartache and loneliness and two grown sons who were still little better than look-alike strangers.

"Okay," he said, "if she don't want to move up to the castle, I won't make her. But I'm not fixing to turn my back on them; it wouldn't be right. That family needs help, and I'm going to give it to them. I'll do whatever it takes."

"Just promise me you won't go to extremes."

"Food and clothes and medicine ain't extreme in

my book, Lucinda. They're absolute necessities. Now how the Sam Hill do I get from here to St. Keverne? I gotta find Emerson before nightfall gets here."

"Why the rush?"

"I might find my way back home in the light, but in the dark, I'll probably end up getting lost again." He grinned. "Unless, of course, you'd like to accompany me."

Just as the last rays of daylight began fading in the west, Prescott and Lucinda hit the outskirts of town. Not much larger than the village that sat halfway between St. Keverne and Ravens Lair, the seat of the Trefarrow earldom boasted such luxuries as gas lights and cobblestone streets. Aside from those amenities, and the fact that a few more people lived there, Prescott couldn't tell much difference between this town and the last one they had passed through ten minutes earlier. But then it was getting dark, and he wouldn't have known what comparisons to look for anyway.

"You sure you know where you're heading?" he asked Lucinda.

"Trust me, Prescott. There's only one place Garrick Emerson would be at this time of the evening."

"At the saloon, I'll bet."

"No, and it's a pub, not a saloon. You're in England now, remember?"

"What difference does it make? A watering hole's a watering hole, no matter what you call it."

"Well, it's far too early for him to have gone to a pub. Later perhaps, but not now. At this hour, he's probably having his supper."

"Where at, a hotel?"

"No, at his house. That one, as a matter of fact." She pointed to a graceful, three-story Georgian brick structure just ahead of them.

"That's his house? I thought we just left his house back in the village."

"Garrick has two residences. One where he keeps his wife and children, and another where he keeps—"

"Don't tell me. His, er, lady friend."

"Here we call them mistresses, Prescott."

"Back home we call them that, too, but not in mixed company. How long have you known about him having this other place, and this other woman?"

"I'm not certain how long he's had his mistress, but he acquired the house two years ago."

Prescott had never considered himself a genius, but even a half-wit could figure out the significance of what Lucinda had just told him. "Right after dear old Uncle Herbert hired him."

"You're very astute."

"He sure didn't waste much time putting Ravens Lair's money to use, did he?"

Prescott reined his horse in front of the house, dismounted, then lifted Lucinda down from the saddle.

"You stay here," he said.

"Shouldn't I come with you?"

"No, I don't think that would be a good idea."

"Are you sure?"

"I'm positive."

"Because I wouldn't mind in the least going—"

"Lucinda, sugar, I know you mean well, but keep your pretty little bu—er, neck out of the way. I've handled men much worse than the likes of Emerson. And, in case you haven't noticed, I'm working myself up to a good temper. I get mad like this, my language is apt to get a bit salty. 'Sides, I'm a big boy now. I don't need no lady to hold my hand. Just one to hold my horse so he won't run off and I have to walk back to the castle."

"Prescott, I've heard salty language before."

"Yeah well, you haven't heard it from me. And I'd rather you not think badly of me just yet. That's bound to happen soon enough, after you've known me a while. Now stay here with this horse, and don't move. You savvy?"

Lucinda wasn't sure what "savvy" meant, but she clearly understood Prescott's order and nodded mutely.

"Good girl. I'll be back in a minute."

Think badly of him? She smiled as he ambled toward the front door. She could never think badly of Prescott Trefarrow, no matter what he did. He had ridden into her dull, dreary life on the back of a snorting, prancing charger and changed it forever. He was like no man she had ever met before. Tall, broad-shouldered, handsome as sin; strong-willed yet gentle and kind to every woman he met, regardless of their age or station in life. Think badly of him? No, quite the contrary. If she wasn't careful and didn't guard her heart well, she could easily lose it to him.

Prescott rapped the brass knocker with such force that he felt the whole door shudder. *Good, that ought to get somebody's attention,* he thought. And if it didn't, he'd just keep on knocking until it did.

Within a minute, a young woman in a gray-and-white striped maid's uniform opened the door.

"I need to see Garrick Emerson."

"Mr. Emerson, sir?"

"He is here, ain't he? I was told he would be."

"Oh, aye! That he is, sir. Who may I say is calling?"

"Just tell him the new earl's waiting outside for him, and for him to be quick about it. I ain't got all night."

With a sharp gasp, the young maid bobbed a quick curtsy and vanished into the recesses of the house. Peering through the partially open door, Prescott saw the numerous fineries that furnished the marble-floored entry; crystal wall sconces that reflected gas lighting, gold-framed mirrors and paintings, highly polished tables, fancy-looking vases filled with fresh flowers. The bastard really lived high off the hog here, Prescott thought. Too bad he couldn't say the same about Emerson's wife and children.

"Milord?" Emerson came rushing out of the dining room, wiping his mouth with a linen napkin. A voluptuous blond close on his heels followed, her bosom scarcely covered by a bright blue satin dress and heavy pearl choker. "Is—is there a problem?"

"Yep, there dang sure is. It's a pretty big one, too. You might want to step outside here so we can discuss it man to man."

"Of course. Anything you say, milord."

"Garrick, darling?"

Looking a bit flustered, Emerson turned to the woman. "Isabel, please. Go finish your dinner. This shouldn't take too long."

"He's right, ma'am," Prescott said, sticking his head inside the doorway as Emerson stepped outside. "This ain't gonna take long at all. I'll send him right back in to you as soon as I'm finished with him."

Isabel fluttered her lashes and dipped into a curtsy, showing as much of her generous bosom to Prescott as decency would allow. "Of course, milord."

As Emerson closed the door behind him, he glanced out at the street and noticed Lucinda, who was chatting with a passerby. Later, he would wonder why Lord St. Keverne had brought the village witch with him on seemingly urgent business. Right now he had his lordship's urgent matter to tend to. "I can't imagine what the problem might be, milord."

"Can't you now?"

"No, milord."

"Maybe I can help you out, refresh your memory a little."

"By all means do, milord."

"Well, y'see, I had me a good look at the books this morning."

"What books would that be, milord?"

"The ones in the library that tell me how much Ravens Lair is worth. How much *I'm* worth. Ledgers, I think you call 'em."

"Oh, those books, of course."

"You know which ones I'm talking about now?"

"Of course."

"Not the biographies or the novels, but the ledgers. 'Course, after reading 'em all morning the way I did, I gotta tell you, they tell a right strange story themselves. Part fact, part fiction."

"I don't know what you're getting at, milord."

"You don't?"

"No, milord."

"Well, let me put it this way, Emerson. I didn't much like what I saw."

"I shouldn't imagine you did, milord. The estate is not in a very healthy condition. We're in bad need of capital. We have been for quite some time. Since the old earl passed on, as a matter of fact."

"No, Ravens Lair was in trouble long before that. Near as I can figure it, the castle and the tenant farms started going down hill 'bout the same time you took over as foreman. Er, superintendent."

"Milord! Are you suggesting that I might have had—"

"I ain't suggesting a damn thing, Emerson."

"Then I apologize, milord. I thought—"

"I'm flat-out accusing you."

"Me!"

"Yeah, you. You've been dipping your fingers into my till for two years now, and you're gonna stop it tonight. Right now, in fact."

"Milord, I'll not stand here and be accused of stealing."

"That's fine with me." Before Emerson could react, Prescott drew back his fist and landed a hard right-cross on Emerson's chin, knocking him into a neat row of pruned hedges.

Prescott glanced toward Lucinda and noticed that a crowd had begun to gather in the street behind her. *Gawkers,* he thought with a shake of his head. Well, they would certainly get a bellyfull tonight.

"You're a thief, Emerson," he said in his loudest voice. "A no-good, whoremongering thief. This house of yours? Get rid of it. Come first light tomorrow, you start selling off every stick of furniture you bought for this place with my money. When that's gone, you can sell all them fancy mirrors and paintings and doodads you got inside. And I expect every nickel—er, every shilling of it to be returned to me. You got that?"

"Lord St. Keverne, I swear I—"

"Don't swear at me, Emerson. I hate men who swear in front of ladies. But you know what I hate even more? Men who beat their wives. It tells me they're nothing but cowards. But then that's what you are. A no-good, thieving, whoremongering coward."

"Milord!"

"Oh, one more thing, Emerson. You're fired. Don't you ever set foot on my land again." Not wishing for Lucinda or the crowd to overhear his next remark, Prescott leaned down to the still-prone Emerson and spoke in a low growl. "You do, and so help me God, I'll make you regret it for the rest of your life."

He gave Emerson one last look, then turned and stalked away. Lucinda didn't say a word as he took the horse's reins from her. However, the crowd of men that had gathered weren't so silent.

"Thee'd be the new earl?" one man asked.

"Yep, like it or not, that's who I'd be. Prescott Trefarrow's the name."

"Aye," the man said, nodding at his friends. "We thought that's who thee was. Er, milord?"

"Yeah?"

"Thee needs to have a talk like that with our good mayor. Set him right on his ear, it would."

A few of the other gentlemen chuckled and nodded in agreement. Feeling his anger begin to ebb, Prescott grinned. "He gives you any trouble, you just tell him to come see me."

"That we'll do, your lordship. That we'll surely do."

"I think you've made a lasting impression on your new subjects, milord," Lucinda said moments later, as they headed out of the village.

"I hear you call me 'milord' one more time, I'll put you off this horse and make you walk the rest of the way home. Having to hear it from the likes of Emerson was bad enough; I don't need to hear it from you, too."

"I'm not the enemy, Prescott. I'm on your side."

"You'd better be." He tightened his arm around her waist and gave her a little squeeze that was designed more to reassure himself than to steady her.

"The villagers are apparently on your side as well. They've never said anything, you understand, but it's common knowledge that they have never approved of Emerson or his mistress."

"Yet they kept their mouths shut when he moved her in right under their noses."

"He had authority and power. What were they to do?"

"Tar and feather him? Run him out of town on a rail? That's what I was tempted to do when I saw the bruises he put on his wife."

"The villagers aren't as . . . as straightforward as you are. They're accustomed to seeing their betters live by a different set of standards."

"Decency and honesty is the same to all people in all walks of life, Lucinda. It's what makes all men equal. Just because I've got some fancy title don't mean I'm better than any of them men back in town. And it sure don't give me the right to act the way Emerson did. Not that I ever would, you understand."

"I think the villagers know that now."

"Now? You mean, they didn't know it before?"

"How could they? They hadn't met you until tonight. They'd only heard about you. I suppose they assumed you would be like your predecessor, the old earl, and the earl before him."

"And how was that?"

"Somewhat autocratic, uncaring about them, and totally unconcerned about their hardships. Don't misunderstand me, Uncle Herbert was a decent enough man, but he would have never thought to offer to defend them the way you did tonight. Probably because doing so was just not part of his nature."

"It's just like my Aunt Em always says," Prescott said under his breath. "It all boils down to how you were raised."

"Heavens, except for the odd occasion or two, Uncle Herbert rarely visited the village or St. Keverne. It's only natural the villagers would assume that you would be no different from your predecessors. Your life is nothing like theirs."

"It ain't that different."

"Different enough. You live in a castle; they don't. You have centuries of breeding behind you; some of the villagers couldn't trace their ancestors back any farther than one or two generations. Added to that, you're new here. And you're certainly not English."

"Well, times have changed then, haven't they? The new broom sweeps clean, and all that bunk."

"Yes, well it appears as though the new Texas broom has a very wide brush on it indeed."

"You don't know just how wide, darlin'."

The way he said the endearment in his deep velvety voice made Lucinda's flesh tingle with excitement. Longing began to grow in the pit of her stomach, and she felt strongly tempted to lean her head on the curve of his shoulder, feel his muscled chest against her back, and breathe in the scent of his clean, manly smell. Perhaps even turn her head ever so slightly, look up at him, and gently brush her lips against his. To kiss him, she knew, would bring her such pleasure, such joy.

But, as always, sanity prevailed, and Lucinda resisted the urge. To think of herself and Prescott in such a manner was absurd. Dangerous, too. It could only end in disaster and heartache. Prescott could never be anything more than her friend.

Night had descended in full as they passed through the tiny village outside of St. Keverne and began the final leg of their journey to Lucinda's cottage.

"Will you be able to find your way to the castle?" she asked.

"Well, if I do get lost, I'll just set up camp somewhere and go home when it comes daylight."

"You'd sleep out of doors?"

"Sure. Why not? It wouldn't be the first time."

"But it's likely to rain before morning. I saw clouds gathering earlier."

"Rain, fog—it don't really matter none to me. Once, I had to set up camp in a blizzard. I gotta tell you, we don't get a whole lot of blizzards in my part of Texas, but we did that one year. I was out herding up strays in the far west pasture, 'bout twenty miles or more from the Triple T homestead, when a blue norther struck. It got so cold so quick, and the snow started flying so fast that—" He broke off abruptly and sniffed the air. "Do you smell smoke?"

Lucinda sniffed as well. "Yes, I do. I wonder where it could be coming from?"

"Most likely from one of your neighbors. On a

chilly night like this, a big roaring fire sure does sound cozy, don't it?" He sensed something was wrong when he felt her body grow tense. "What's the matter?"

"I don't have any neighbors, Prescott. At least, none living so close to me that I can smell their fires."

"Maybe it's coming from your place."

"I don't know how it could. I didn't leave a fire burning."

"You sure? You had to have had a fire to make them scones we ate."

"I made certain the flames were doused before we left to find Emerson."

Fearing the worst, Prescott dug his heels into the horse's ribs, and the animal leaped from a canter into a full gallop. Despite the darkness, he managed to cover a good bit of distance on the unfamiliar stretch of road without any mishaps. As they rounded the last curve, they saw a bright glow of light just ahead.

"Lord Almighty, it looks like it's coming from your place," he said, pulling sharply on the reins.

"No, it can't be!"

Before Prescott could voice a word of protest, Lucinda jumped off the horse, stumbled, regained her footing, and began racing toward the burning cottage.

"Damn it, Lucinda, get back here!" He spurred the horse into motion again and caught up with her just as she reached the garden gate. Leaping down from the horse, he wrapped an arm around her waist and stopped her from certain disaster. "You can't go in there."

"I must. It's my home. Everything I have—"

"Ain't nothing in this world worth losing your life over, Lucinda. Nothing, you hear me? Look at that place; it's a tinderbox. You'd be burnt to a crisp the minute you stepped through the door."

"Oh, God!" With a painful sob, she turned and buried her face in his chest. She had lost everything. The few mementos that she had cherished so dearly—the only photographs she possessed of her mother and father, her belongings, even her precious flower garden—everything would be gone.

While in reality it took but a few minutes, it seemed to Prescott as though a lifetime passed as he stood there watching the fire engulf Lucinda's once lovely little cottage. Red flames shot up majestically through the thatched roof, illuminating the moonless night sky. He flinched and ducked down as her windows exploded, sending millions of tiny glass shards in every direction. Not even her garden was spared, the blooms nearest the house scorching and dying from the intense heat.

More than once, Prescott felt tempted to do something, anything, to ease her pain and heartache. But knowing he couldn't, he only held her more tightly to him, muttering soothing words of comfort in her ear until the strong temptation had passed him.

And never once did Lucinda try to leave his embrace, even as she heard the fire roaring behind her, the windows shattering. She welcomed the safe security of Prescott's arms about her and sobbed loudly against his chest.

In the end, when the roar of the flames finally subsided to an occasional hiss and crackle, she did turn her head. But the sight of her burnt-down home brought fresh tears to her eyes.

"Oh, God, Prescott."

"Shhh," he said, stroking her head. "It's all right,

darlin'. Everything's gonna be all right. You're safe and still in one piece. That's all that matters."

"But what will I do? This was my home—my only home. I have nowhere else to go."

"You dang sure do."

"Where?"

"Ravens Lair, of course. You can come live with me."

"Live with you?" The painful loss of her home seemed unimportant compared to the gravity of his suggestion. "I can't live with you."

"Darlin', a family ought to pull together at a time like this, and seeing as how I'm just about the only family you've got, it's only fitting that I take you home with me."

"But I can't—"

"Yes, you can, damn it. You will!"

"Prescott, you don't understand. People in the village are bound to—"

"Talk? Let 'em. Hell, let 'em talk their fool heads off; I don't care. They'd probably talk a whole sight more if I left you out here to fend for yourself. 'Sides, there's gonna be enough speculation as it is."

"Speculation? About you and me?"

"No, about how this fire got started. I got a feeling it wasn't an accident."

"But who would intentionally destroy my home? I've no enemies."

"No, but after tonight, *I* do."

"Emerson?"

"Who else?"

"Oh, no, Prescott. As much as I detest and distrust the man, I can't believe he would do such a thing. How could he? He was nowhere near my cottage when it caught fire. He was in St. Keverne with his mistress."

"Then somebody else must've done it. But I just know down deep in my bones that it wasn't an accident."

Lucinda knew it as well, because she was certain she hadn't left a fire burning in the stove. And even if she had, it would have merely burned itself out as it had on other occasions.

"Come on, let's go home," Prescott said, tugging gently at her waist. "We can come back in the morning and see if there's anything left."

"There won't be," she said softly, taking one last look at the pile of rubble. "Everything's gone. Everything."

8

"Shall we be in need of our riding gear after luncheon today, milord?"

Prescott eyed Hargreaves' reflection in the dressing room mirror as the man helped him with his coat. Back home, he'd gone to breakfast in his work clothes. Here, custom demanded he wear something different for every occasion.

"I don't know," he said. "I haven't decided what I'm going to be doing just yet." That, he knew, would depend on what Lucinda had planned. But considering the events of the night before and the state she'd been in when they arrived at the castle, he rather doubted she planned to do much at all, except maybe mope around a lot.

As the valet attacked the back of Prescott's coat with a lint brush, he noticed a small bandage on the man's hand. "You hurt yourself?"

"It's nothing more than a small scratch, milord.

We had a minor mishap with some broken glass."

"You might want to have Mrs. Sweet take a look at it just the same."

Hargreaves gave him a curious look. "She already has done, milord."

"Then that bandage is her fancy work, is it?"

"Yes, milord."

"Looks like she did a good job. Cotton strip's wrapped around there nice and tight, just the way my Aunt Em wraps them. No dirt'll get in it."

"None at all, milord. Er, milord?"

"Yeah?"

"Your concern for our injury, however minor, is quite generous. Thank you."

"No thanks needed, Ed." He slapped the valet on the back and turned to leave. "I just don't like to see people get hurt, is all. Oh, if I decide to go riding, I'll let you know."

"Thank you, milord."

"And if I do, I think maybe I'll wear my Levis, not them britches with the puffed-out hips."

"Jodhpurs, milord."

"Whatever. In fact, why don't you just shove 'em way back in the back of some drawer?"

"Milord, as a peer of the realm, you—"

"Look like a pantywaist in them damn things. Feel like one, too. I'll just stick with the Levis, all right?"

"Of course, milord."

Leaving his bedroom, Prescott went down the hall to the suite of rooms where he had installed Lucinda the night before. He paused a moment outside the door, wondering if he should knock. But thinking better of it, he decided to leave well enough alone. She might still be sleeping, and after the night she'd had, the poor girl probably needed all the rest she could get.

A damn shame, her losing everything she owned in the fire, he thought as he headed toward the old part of the castle and the main staircase. A fire caused by God only knew what, or better still, who. Prescott had a strange feeling that someone had caused it, because it sure hadn't appeared to be a case of spontaneous combustion. Though Emerson seemed to him the most likely culprit, common sense told him that it wasn't possible, because he and Lucinda hadn't spotted anything or anyone on the road leaving St. Keverne. But if Emerson hadn't done it, who had?

Prescott shook his head. The answer to that question would probably remain a mystery for a long time to come.

Mrs. Sweet was putting the last of the chafing dishes on the sideboard as Prescott entered the morning room.

"Will Miss Trefarrow be joining your lordship for breakfast?"

"I wouldn't know, Mrs. Sweet. She wasn't in too great a shape when I brought her home last night. I heard her crying all the way down the hall in my room. She might not feel like eating a thing this morning." He, on the other hand, felt hungry enough to eat a whole steer and chase it down with a side of pork.

Though he knew the housekeeper was watching him, probably waiting for him to help himself to the abundant meal she had prepared, he refrained from doing so. What a thing for a grown man to have to own up to, he thought, cautiously eyeing the array of covered dishes Mrs. Sweet had arranged on the sideboard. He was afraid to lift the lids and see what she had fixed him for breakfast. Afraid because, deep down, he had a feeling that she had probably fixed him kidneys and kippers again, and he figured she would keep on fixing them until either he learned to like them or he starved to death.

"Miss Trefarrow's a strong lady, milord. Thee shouldn't worry too much about her. She'll come 'round in time."

"Yeah, that's what I figure. We just gotta let her do it in her own good time is all."

"I'll have one of the girls take a tray up to her rooms then, shall I?" Mrs. Sweet tried not to smile at the way his lordship kept looking at the sideboard.

"That's very kind of you, Mrs. Sweet, but it won't be necessary."

Prescott turned at the sound of Lucinda's voice and watched her come into the morning room.

"No trouble at all, Miss Lucinda." The housekeeper gave Prescott a mischievous glance. "Enjoy your breakfast, milord."

Ignoring Mrs. Sweet's sardonic rejoinder as she left the room, Prescott smiled at Lucinda, thinking how fresh and well rested she looked despite last night's ordeal. She was certainly easy on the eyes this morning, with her black hair piled high atop her head, her dark gray eyes sparkling like enormous jet crystals, and her pale skin blooming with a healthy pink blush.

"I kinda figured you might want to sleep in this morning," he said.

"I thought about it, but I couldn't. I have far too much to do."

"That's right. You and me were gonna go back to the cottage, see if anything was spared, weren't we?"

"I think that would be a waste of time, Prescott." She joined him in front of the sideboard. "I've never been one who believed in ever wasting time. It's far too precious. I've lost my past and everything from it, so I'll put it behind me where it belongs and go forward."

Damn, but she was some lady, he thought. She was optimistic, good natured, and pretty as well. A downright lethal combination. "Good. That's what I like to hear. So what do you plan to do today?"

"I thought I might help you. If you wish me to help, that is."

"Darlin', I'll be grateful for all the help I can get. The question is, though, what can you help me with?"

"Well, we could begin with the estate ledgers."

Prescott's good humor visibly faded. "Do we have to? I spent all yesterday morning going over those books, and I can tell you right now, the story they tell ain't a pretty one."

"Perhaps you read them wrong."

"Could be, anything's possible. But I doubt it."

"Then after breakfast we'll have another look at them, shall we? Just to make certain."

"Yeah, breakfast." Looking back at the sideboard, Prescott felt his spirits sag even more. Before he could accomplish anything, he had to get through Mrs. Sweet's breakfast. He didn't know if he had the stamina.

"What have we here?"

"I wouldn't know," he said. "I haven't worked up enough courage to find out."

"Shall I look for you?"

"Be my guest. Just let me know if you come across anything that looks like kidneys or fish in them bowls."

Lucinda went down the line, lifting off the covers on the chafing dishes. "Eggs . . . sausages . . . chops . . . and what's this?" She leaned down and sniffed into the steaming dish. "Mmm, spiced apple-and-nut compote. Mrs. Sweet's recipe, too; I can smell the cinnamon and cloves. She's trying to impress you, Prescott. She rarely makes spiced apple-and-nut compote."

So far the breakfast sounded very good, he thought. "You find any biscuits and gravy over there?"

"Biscuits and gravy?" The mere thought of a sweet biscuit topped with thick, gooey gravy made Lucinda wince.

"Not your kind of biscuits, darlin'. My kind. The thick, fluffy ones."

"Let me see." She lifted another lid, then smiled at him. "Will scones do?"

"Are you kidding? Move over. I'm starved."

Lucinda delighted in the way Prescott ate. He piled his plate high not only once, but twice, then went back for a third helping of scones and apple-and-nut compote, washing it all down with cup after cup of hot black coffee. How one man could consume so much food in such a short amount of time and not possess any extra weight was a mystery to her. Even more surprising was the fact that Mrs. Sweet had prepared a large urn of coffee. Until Prescott's arrival, coffee was unheard of at Ravens Lair. But then, Mrs. Sweet had prepared her famous compote for him; what else should she have expected? The man definitely had a way with women.

Later, in the library, Lucinda saw what Prescott had meant by the ledgers not telling a pretty story, but the story they did tell was quite significant.

"It's as bad as I said it was, isn't it?" he asked.

"Not entirely. In this case, looks are quite deceiving. Emerson has falsified many of the entries."

"How can you tell?"

"Well, this entry here is a prime example." She turned the ledger so that Prescott could read it over her shoulder. "Over five hundred pounds for imported French wines and Napoleon brandy? That's ridiculous. Anyone who ever knew Uncle Herbert would know that he would never have approved of a purchase of French brandy. He would have thought it disloyal to the crown. I could understand if this were a receipt for a crate of blended Scotch whiskey, but not French brandy. Besides, if you'll bother to check the cellar, you'll find that it's full of wine and spirits that haven't been touched in years. And I'd be willing to wager that this purchase here is not among the inventory."

"You're joshing me," Prescott said with admiration in his eyes.

"Emerson has been as inept in his thievery as in his record keeping," she said. "No wonder you couldn't make any sense of this mess."

"How come you can?"

"I knew Uncle Herbert, that's how. I knew what he liked and disliked, and what he would and wouldn't have condoned. His age and failing mental faculties wouldn't have changed his basic beliefs. At least not to this degree. Oh look, here's another. *Pâte de foie gras Strasbourg.*"

"That don't sound English to me."

"It isn't. Oh, Garrick, you're not the clever Dick you think you are. We've got you dead to rights with this one."

"What do you see that I don't?"

"The date this foie gras was purchased," she said, pointing a finger to the entry in question. "It's a full five months after Uncle Herbert died."

"What did you just call him?"

"You mean, 'clever Dick?'"

"Yeah. Is that supposed to be like smart Alec or something?"

"I suppose. But Garrick isn't either, I assure you. He never was. Even when we were children, he thought himself the cleverest boy around, far superior to the rest of us. And the liberties he took with—" She broke off and shook her head briskly. "Needless to say, if Uncle Herbert had known, he never would have hired Emerson as estate superintendent."

Curiosity had Prescott asking, "What kind of liberties?"

Lucinda hesitated a moment. "Let's just say they were the kind totally unacceptable to polite English society."

Polite English society? Prescott could think of only one thing that that could mean. "You're saying he messed around with girls out of his class?"

"He tried."

Her quiet remark caused the hair to stand on the back of Prescott's neck. "With you? He tried to mess around with you?"

Surprised by his quick astuteness, Lucinda turned so rapidly to stare at him that her nose almost bumped his. Each pulled back a scant space. He noted the blush rising in her cheeks and knew his assumption had been right on the mark.

"He did, didn't he? That bastard!"

"He only tried, Prescott. He never succeeded. I made certain of that."

"With a well-aimed kick, I hope."

A faint smile touched her lips. "I'm a lady. I would never resort to such a physical act. I merely used my wits."

"How?"

"I cursed him," she said simply.

"Cursed him? You called him a couple of foul names, and it stopped him?"

"Prescott, profanities have never crossed my lips."

"But you just said—"

"That I cursed him. And I did. I told him that if he touched me, or if he ever came near me with lust in his thoughts, I would call upon the ancient Druid forces and shrivel up that which makes him a man."

Curses . . . ancient Druid forces . . . Prescott couldn't make any sense of what she was talking about. Then suddenly it hit him. The first day he had met the two of them, Emerson had called Lucinda a witch and told her to go back to stirring her caldron.

"I suppose," she went on, "the thought of being rendered a—a eunuch for the rest of his life frightened him. One might even assume that I helped to put the fear of God into him. For a time, at least."

Feeling his anger at Emerson slowly evaporate, and his admiration for Lucinda increase, Prescott said, "He actually believed you could do such a thing? Shrivel up his manhood, I mean?"

"Obviously. He hasn't come near me since the day I put my curse on him."

Prescott placed a hand on Lucinda's shoulder, his thumb grazing the ridge of her collarbone as his fingers rested on the back of her neck. "You're some lady, darlin'."

His innocently spoken endearment, coupled with the

warm touch of his hand, made her glow deeply within, a slow, smoldering glow that would have grown warmer had she allowed it to do so. But such thoughts, such feelings for him were far from acceptable. She had to keep their relationship, such as it was, on a purely platonic level. To do so would be extremely hard, but not to do so would be courting certain disaster. For him as well as for her.

Banking down her burgeoning emotions, she turned her full attention back to the ledger. In a matter of moments she made a startling discovery that was sure to please Prescott. "I think I've just found something."

"What?"

"The estate isn't totally ruined, as you suspected. It has some working capital. Not a lot, you understand, but some."

"Is there enough to pay all the hands on the estate their wages for the month?"

"Oh, yes."

"Well, that sure is a load off my mind. I figured I was gonna have to let most of them go."

"They wouldn't do that, you know."

"Do what?"

"Go."

"You mean, they'd work here without pay?"

"They have done in the past; why wouldn't they now? This is their home, Prescott. Most have lived here all their lives. Like our ancestors, they've seen both good times and bad and, throughout it all, they've stayed on. Ravens Lair is as much theirs as it is yours. And by this time next month, there'll be even more money coming in."

"How do you figure that?"

"The shearing season is due to begin almost any

day now. As soon as the shearers arrive, in fact."

"How is shearing a flock of mangy sheep gonna make money for Ravens Lair?"

Lucinda gave him a half-surprised, half-impatient look. "You are new here, aren't you?"

"I'm as green as they come, darlin', where sheep are concerned. I'm a cattleman, remember?"

"Well, Mr. Cattleman, you're about to learn that raising sheep is quite a bit more lucrative than your endeavors at bovine husbandry."

"How? A sheep's a sheep. Ain't no way you can compare them to cows."

"I wasn't trying to, believe me."

"Good, 'cause they're nothing alike. Cows give you milk, butter, and cheese when they're alive, and beef and leather when they're dead. And all sheep do is eat up your grazing land and stink up the place."

"Not quite. You've forgotten that they also produce tons of wool every year, for a good many years. Not to mention mutton and lamb when they're dressed."

"Wool?"

"Yes, Prescott, wool."

"I don't like wool. Can't wear the stuff. Never could. Last time my Aunt Em made me wear it, it made me itch so bad I scratched half the hair and skin off my legs."

"You obviously weren't wearing merino wool then."

"Wool is wool, darlin'."

"No, merino wool is different. It's the finest wool you can find, and the only kind of lamb we raise at Ravens Lair. Not only that, Lord Prescott Trefarrow, Tenth Earl of St. Keverne, by the first of May, when the shearing season ends, that itchy, scratchy wool you seem to detest so much is likely to be the only thing that will put this foundering estate of yours back on its feet again. So if I may give you a word of advice—don't be so quick to condemn the product or the stinky animals that produce it."

Prescott knew when to argue and when to keep his mouth shut. Obviously Lucinda knew what she was talking about, and he took no offense at her bluntly-spoken words. And he did take them to heart. "Well, in that case, I might just take a liking to the little critters, seeing as how they're so useful and all."

"A wise decision."

"But I won't eat them."

"You won't?"

"Nope, I sure won't. I had me some mutton once, and hated every bite of it."

"Not every bite, Prescott."

"Yes, every bite."

"Oh, really? Then why did you go back for a second helping at breakfast? A very generous second helping at that."

"I didn't eat no mutton at breakfast."

"Yes, you did. I saw you eat it."

"Dadblast it, Lucinda, I had sausages and some itty-bitty chops this morning. I did not have mutton."

Unable to stop herself, she laughed. "Prescott, the sausages and 'itty-bitty chops' were mutton. Well, spring lamb, actually, but it's almost the same as mutton."

"You're joshing me."

"No, I'm quite serious."

"I ate lamb?"

She laughed again at the horrified look on his face. "Yes, and furthermore, you enjoyed it."

As he considered the notion for a moment, his expression of horror changed to one of acceptance. "You're right, I did. I'll be damned, I actually ate lamb and liked it."

"Before you know it, you'll be eating kidneys and kippers like a proper Englishman."

"Kidneys and kippers?" Prescott straightened sharply, then moved away from the desk. "Don't bet on it, darlin'. I draw the line at eating kidneys and kippers. I got too much Texan in me to sink that low."

"We'll see," she said with a quiet smile as she closed the ledger.

9

As Lucinda had told him, shearing season began the moment the shearers arrived at Ravens Lair two days later. The shearing shed, Prescott learned, was over a half mile away from the castle, nestled in a quiet little valley. Well, he thought, it would have been quiet if there weren't so many noisy sheep around.

Standing in the doorway of the shed with the estate hands, with the first of the flock to be sheared waiting in the holding pens nearby, Prescott watched the dozen or so men ride up in their wagons. Dawn had just broken, and the men piled out quietly, somberly, one or two looking the worse for wear with their bloodshot eyes and gray-tinged faces. Drunks suffering hangovers, he told himself, feeling sympathy for the men. But his sympathy faded when the first few sheep were led into the big, open-air shed and the shearers knuckled down to work.

Though short of stature, the men possessed

powerful arms. A necessary quality, Prescott decided, considering each one had to hold down an unruly sheep with one hand and shear the wool off its back with the other. One sheep to one man—that was how it went with all the shearers. They would wrestle the bleating animal to the floor, cut off its wool with hardly a scratch, then as the near-naked critter staggered out of the shed, many pounds lighter, another, fatter-looking sheep would take its place.

Hours passed, and the first flock of sheep in the holding pens gave way to the second. Prescott watched in wonder as a mountain of wool began to pile up in the far corner of the shed. If the shearers continued at their present rate, Prescott knew the pile would reach the open-raftered ceiling by the end of the day. Yet they had only begun the shearing process, and there were thousands more sheep left to clip.

"We're gonna run out of room in here before the day's over," he told Lucinda when the shearers stopped for lunch.

"No, we won't. They'll start bundling it soon." She had spent most of the morning helping Mrs. Sweet and the others prepare a substantial meal for the men. Now she handed out the last of the thick sandwiches and mugs of hot tea to the shearers, then turned and walked away from the crowd with Prescott.

"Where does it all go from here?"

"A good deal of it will go to Scotland."

"What's up there?"

"Only some of the finest woolen mills in the world. We've a long-standing contract with two of the oldest."

"Oh, I didn't know."

"Well, how could you? You don't wear wool."

"Look, I'm sorry about that."

"What, that you don't wear wool? There's no need to apologize for that. A lot of people don't wear it."

Reaching a far enough distance from the shearing crowd, Prescott stopped. He stopped Lucinda as well, taking hold of both her arms and turning her to face him. "That's not what I mean. I'm sorry for the way I behaved the other day."

"The way you behaved?"

"Yeah, like an idiot. Which I suppose I am, when you come right down to it. Hell, Lucinda, I'm a cattleman, not a sheepman."

"So you've said. Many times."

"Well, I am, dang it."

"But you're learning about sheep now, aren't you?"

"More by the minute," he muttered.

"And they're not as destructive to the land as you thought they were, are they?"

"I'll answer that when I see how fast the grazing pasture grows back."

"In fact, they're quite charming."

Charming? He gave her a speculative look, wondering if she could smell the same stench he could. But he decided not to broach that issue. Instead, he started walking again, toward a grove of trees atop a hill.

"So tell me, once all that wool gets to the mills in Scotland, what happens to it then?"

"Well, they'll clean it, of course. Then they'll dye it, spin it into yarns, and weave it into woolen fabrics. The wool we don't transport will stay here."

"You mean, you'll keep it back there in the shed?"

"No, of course not. It's badly needed; it can't just go to waste. It will be equally divided among the tenant farmers. They're responsible for our having it; they should reap the benefits from it as well."

"What will they do with it?"

"The same as the mills do in Scotland—clean it and spin it into yarns and make sweaters for themselves and their children. Our winters here in Cornwall might not be as harsh as in other parts of England, but I assure you, a thick woolen sweater on a nippy day is quite a comfort."

They reached the top of the hill, and Prescott looked down at the beach below them, awed by its rugged splendor. White-capped waves rolled in from the sea and exploded loudly on the jagged rocks that jutted up from the white sand like small, gray-black monoliths. Closer to the base of the hill on which he stood, he saw niches in the rocky soil, some so deep they seemed to disappear completely from sight.

"Lord, it is pretty here."

"Isn't it."

"Nothing at all like Texas. At least, nothing like my part of Texas."

"Cornwall isn't like any other part of England, either. It has its own particular beauty. It's stark and harsh and oftentimes very cruel, but it is beautiful."

Cornwall wasn't the only beautiful thing, in Prescott's opinion. He gazed at Lucinda's profile as she stared down at the crashing surf. The slight upward tilt of her nose was exquisite as were the gentle fullness of her pink-tinted lips. And the way the wind tore at her raven black hair, threatening to tear it loose any minute from the tight coil around her head, suddenly gave him an impossible urge. He wanted to rip the pins right out of her neat little braid, shake her long tresses loose, run his fingers through them as he turned her face up to his, and kiss the very daylights out of her.

Cut it out, you old horny toad, he told himself. Lucinda was a lady—a refined young lady with more class in her little finger than most titled women could ever dream of possessing. And he was supposed to be a gentleman. But at the moment he felt more like a randy old billy-goat.

No, he wasn't a gentleman. Probably never would be, either, the way he felt. He had as many faults and weaknesses as the next man. Maybe more, considering his main weakness these days seemed to be a black-haired, gray-eyed woman who thought of him only as a friend. Or, worse a distant cousin.

"Now that you've seen how the shearing process works," Lucinda said, turning to face him, "aren't you the least bit curious as to how the sheep are—I believe you call it 'rounded up?'"

A slow grin spread across Prescott's face. "I already know how that's done, darlin'. I've seen the dogs that run their little legs off chasing the silly critters."

"You have?"

"Yeah. Went out riding yesterday morning and watched them for a while."

"I suppose you're going to tell me now that you don't like dogs, either."

"Naw, I like dogs. Fact is, I got me a couple of old hounds back home. They never chased my cows, though. I'd have shot them if they had."

"They're lap dogs then, are they?"

"Reb and Old Blue, lap dogs?" He chuckled. "They've tried a couple of times, but Aunt Em's cat won't let them in the house. No, Reb and Old Blue earn their keep in their own way. They're the finest pair of hunting dogs in Waco. They can sniff out a covey of quail before the birds even know they're on to them. Many's the time I've watched them sneak up on a nest, real quiet like, then just stand there and wait 'til I find them."

The tone of his voice, coupled with the far-away look in his eyes, spoke volumes to Lucinda. "You miss it, don't you?" she said.

"Hunting quail with Reb and Old Blue?"

"No, Texas. Your home."

He rubbed the bridge of his nose, pushing his wide-brimmed Stetson back from his forehead. "I'd be a damned liar if I said I didn't. Yeah, I miss it. 'Til I met up with Henry, the only other place I'd ever been outside of Texas was Louisiana. And that was just to visit kinfolk. My Aunt Em's oldest girl and her family live outside Baton Rouge."

"Tell me about them."

"Aw, you don't want to hear about them."

"Why wouldn't I? They're my . . . kinfolk too, aren't they?"

"Now that you mention it, I guess they are."

"Then tell me about them. What's her name?"

"Aunt Em's oldest daughter?"

Lucinda nodded.

"Frances."

"And she's married, with a family, you said?"

"Yep. Got herself a husband and four kids. She ought to be a grandma just any day now."

"Then she's older than you."

"Much older," he said, and went on to explain how Frances and her two younger sisters had been more like his older sisters than his cousins as they grew up together on the Triple T. "It wasn't easy for Aunt Em, raising three little girls alone without a husband. He died, you see, right after their youngest was born. That's when Aunt Em moved back home. She's spent most of her life taking care of my daddy and granddaddy and raising kids. First her own, then me, then Chloe when her folks died."

"Chloe is—?"

"My brother Payne's wife." He wanted to explain to Lucinda that he had once been engaged to Chloe, but that his brother, Payne, who had come to Texas from England, where he'd been raised and educated, had kidnaped her on the day of their wedding and later married her himself, after he'd gotten her with child. But it was all too complicated, and besides, he didn't think Lucinda would understand. In fact, she might get it into her head that he still carried a warm spot in his heart for Chloe. Which he did, of course, but not in a lover-like way.

"Your Aunt Em sounds like a very remarkable woman."

"Oh, she is. Woman's got a heart as big as Texas. Strong as an ox one minute, and dainty as a China doll the next. But that's the kind of women you find back home. Good women, that is. We got our bad ones, just like everybody else, but it's the good ones you remember the longest."

"So, you grew up surrounded by women."

"Outnumbered was more like it."

"I have a feeling you loved every minute of it, being the youngest and the only boy."

"Loved it? Darlin', there were times when living with all those women was nothing but pure, unadulterated hell. Pardon my language. When I was little, my cousins used to dress me up in girl's clothes, like I was a doll or something. If that wasn't bad enough, they'd make me sit through their dang tea parties with them and play with their dolls. I thought I was spared forever when they all married and left home. But then Chloe came along and dashed that notion to smithereens. The girl all but latched herself onto my shadow. I couldn't go anywhere without her traipsing along behind me, getting in the way, saying all kinds of crazy things that usually embarrassed the daylights out of me."

"Just as I thought," Lucinda said. "You loved every minute of it."

A twinkle appeared in his eye as his mouth formed a slow grin. "Maybe I did just a little bit."

If nothing else, he thought, living with his aunt, his cousins, and Chloe had given him a fine appreciation for women. In fact, he more than appreciated them. He admired them, respected them, and if he didn't watch himself, he could easily fall head over heels in love with one in particular.

"We'd best be getting back," he said.

"Yes, we should. The shearers probably finished their noon meal some time ago."

As they turned to descend the hill, Prescott stopped her. "Thanks for bringing me here, and telling me about the wool and all."

"It was my pleasure."

"Maybe we can do it again sometime."

"What, discuss wool?"

"No, come up here and talk." *Steal away from the castle, just the two of us, and sit for hours, looking at each other and sharing our lives.* "Maybe even bring a picnic basket."

"A picnic. Now that would be lovely. Perhaps after all the shearing is over."

"That'll be in—what, a week?"

"Oh, less than that. The shearers are very quick at their work."

"It's a date, then."

But as Prescott descended the hill behind Lucinda, he wondered if he could wait that long to be alone with her again. Hell, he'd have to. He would wait a lifetime, if necessary.

10

Lucinda hummed a chipper little tune as she descended the stairs on her way to breakfast. She had heard Prescott singing it one morning as she passed his room—something about a yellow rose in Texas, she believed. Though the words made very little sense to her, the melody was catchy and spirited, and it more than matched her good mood this morning.

How strange that she could feel so wonderful when less than three weeks ago she had lost her home and all of her possessions. Yet she felt utterly fantastic and was beginning to love the life that the unkind fates had dealt her. Why shouldn't she? The shearing had ended a few days ago, the amount of wool they had collected far surpassed that of last year's, and, with nothing important left to occupy his time for the next few days, Prescott was going to take her on a picnic as he had promised.

She reached the foot of the staircase just as

Prescott's valet began to ascend it. "Good morning, Mr. Hargreaves," she said with a bright smile.

"Miss Lucinda." His face devoid of expression, the valet merely bobbed his head and hurried by her.

What a thoroughly somber person, she thought as she made her way down the hall to the kitchens. Quite strange, too. He'd always been polite to her the few times she had encountered him in the castle passageways, yet he could never seem to spare the time to say more than two words of greeting to her. Simple good mornings and good evenings; that was the full extent of their conversations to date.

Granted, he was valet to an earl, a slightly higher status than that which she or any of the others held at the castle. But he was still a member of Prescott's staff, and staff usually stuck together. Not Hargreaves, though. He seemed to deliberately hold himself apart from everyone else even though his duties certainly weren't more taxing than anyone else's. On more than one occasion, Prescott had told her how little he relied on Hargreaves' services, preferring instead to do almost everything himself. She had to wonder why the man always seemed so preoccupied when he had so little to do.

Yes, very strange indeed, she thought as she entered the kitchen and found the housekeeper and the maids busy about their work.

"Good morning, Mrs. Sweet."

"Morning, Miss Lucinda. Shall thee be having breakfast in the morning room as usual?"

"Yes. I just thought I'd pop in first and ask if you wouldn't mind preparing a small picnic hamper for us."

"For thee and his lordship?"

Lucinda started to answer, but she hesitated when she noticed the curious stares that Miranda, Rowena, and Ursula were giving her. In an instant, she knew she had almost forgotten her place and crossed that invisible barrier that separated her from the others. But she was no different. In fact, if the truth were known, her position at the castle was the most tenuous of all, considering she was nothing more than a poor, homeless relation of the earl's.

"For his lordship, yes," she said. "Now that the shearing has ended, and before we begin the haying season, he mentioned something about wishing to see more of the estate."

"He's doing that now," Rowena said snidely.

"His lordship has already left the castle?"

"Aye, he's been gone for quite some time," Miranda said. "Left early this morning, he did. Had Tom saddle his horse afore first light."

"Oh. Well then, I suppose he'll be occupied for the rest of the day. I'm sorry I disturbed you, Mrs. Sweet."

"Thee didn't disturb me, child. Now run along and have your breakfast."

Disheartened that her picnic with Prescott would have to be postponed, Lucinda turned to leave. But her footsteps faltered slightly when she reached the baize-covered door that led to the hallway.

"That put her in her place, didn't it?" she heard Miranda whisper.

"Uppity chit needed it," Rowena replied. "Always acting like she's better'n us."

"Always chasing after his lordship, too," Ursula said. "Don't think I haven't noticed."

Despite the stinging words, Lucinda held her head high and pushed open the door. At the same moment,

Prescott almost barreled into her, shirtless and carrying a large bundle in his arms.

"Lord Almighty, Lucinda, get me some warm milk quick."

"Warm milk? Of course. Mrs. Sweet, his lordship needs some warm milk."

The housekeeper whirled around and stared at the two of them. "Warm milk?"

"Yeah," Prescott said. "And put it in a bottle."

"A bottle, milord?"

"One with a nipple on it, if you have one handy. And if you don't, he'll just have to make do with a sugar teat."

Miranda and Rowena stood as still as marble statues as Prescott deposited his bundle onto the table at which they had been working. Their mouths dropped open, and their eyes fixed in fascinated wonder at the corded muscles on his arms and shoulders and at the broadness of his bare chest, covered ever so lightly with dark swirls of hair.

Though not in the least bit displeasured by the sight of Prescott's naked upper torso, Lucinda could only think what a perfect pair of hoydens the sisters were. For reasons she couldn't explain, their behavior angered her immensely. "Ladies! Do as his lordship wishes. Find him a bottle."

"But there ain't none, Miss," Rowena said.

"Aye, we've not had need of baby bottles in the castle for years," said the pinch-faced Ursula.

"Then get me a towel," Prescott said as he slowly began to unwrap his bundle.

"Ow!" Miranda squealed when the squirming, wet creature inside the bundle became visible. "Mrs. Sweet, his lordship has brought a lamb into your kitchens."

"A lamb?" The housekeeper bustled toward them with a clean linen towel. "Milord, I must protest. I don't allow animals of any sort in my kitchens. Not live ones, at any rate."

"Well, this one's not gonna be alive much longer if I don't get some warm milk into him," Prescott said. "Poor little thing's an orphan."

"An orphan?" Lucinda saw the look of concern on Prescott's face and wondered if he truly disliked sheep as much as he had said, or if he had spoken out of ignorance, as a man who had been exposed to nothing but cows. She suspected the latter was the case, because he certainly appeared to care a great deal for the welfare of this particular little foundling.

"Yeah, I came across him out in the pasture," he said, "laying right next to his dead mama. She must've died just as he was born. See? He's still wet from the afterbirth. He couldn't have been out there long. Maybe I got to him in time. Thanks," he said as Mrs. Sweet handed him the towel and a glass of warm milk.

He rolled up the towel, then dipped a good two inches of it into the glass. Carefully, he inserted the dripping end into the lamb's mouth, holding his middle finger inside it so the lamb would have something to latch his tongue onto. In an instant, the baby animal began to suck loudly.

"This ain't gonna last him long," Prescott said, removing the towel and dipping it into the glass again.

"No, it's not," Lucinda said as an image suddenly flashed through her thoughts. "Just a moment. We do have bottles and nipples here in the castle."

"Not likely," Ursula said. "Got rid of the last of

them years ago, when the last Trefarrow babe was weaned."

"That last Trefarrow babe was me," Lucinda said. "And I believe there were some kept in the nursery. It wouldn't hurt to check to see if I'm right."

"Waste of time, I say."

Lucinda ignored Rowena's muttered comment, intent on helping Prescott save the little lamb. "Miranda, would you dash upstairs and check the pantry there?"

"Miss?"

"They should be in a rather large box. A pink or blue one. It's been so long since I last saw them, I'm really not sure which color." She glanced at the maid, expecting to see her dashing toward the door. Instead, Miranda continued to stand rooted to her spot next to Prescott, a look of righteous indignation glaring in her deep brown eyes. Lucinda felt her patience diminish. Heaven save her from class-conscious servants. "Please, Miranda. As you can see, his lordship is quite worried about his lamb."

"Now hold on a minute," Prescott said. "This ain't *my* lamb."

"That's what you think," Rowena muttered.

"He's just *a* lamb. All I did was find him and bring him here. But if there's any bottles handy, I'd sure appreciate you fetching them for me, Miss Miranda. This little boy here's about to suck the skin right off my finger."

"Yes, milord." Blushing from Prescott's attention, Miranda bobbed a curtsy and sprinted for the door.

Mrs. Sweet edged closer to the table to examine Prescott's orphan more closely. "I think your lordship is mistaken."

"'Bout what?"

"About this. See? This isn't a little ram. It's a little ewe. A female."

Prescott eyed the area which Mrs. Sweet was indicating with her wooden spoon. Even a lifelong cattleman such as he could see that a certain vital male appendage was missing. "Well, that figures," he said.

"What does?" Lucinda asked.

"I'm always coming to the aid of females in distress. Looks like this time's no different."

"I'm sorry about us missing out on our picnic," Prescott said some time later, as he and Lucinda sat in the library. "I was really looking forward to it. But after I found that lamb, Tom needed me down in the stables, and we got to talking about Texas and, well, I guess the time just got away from me."

Lucinda had been looking forward to it as well, but she didn't dare admit as much to him. It would be too forward and unseemly of her. "We'll have other days for picnics. Summer shall be starting soon, and the weather will be warmer, the winds calmer."

"But haying season will be on us by then, won't it?"

"Yes. Perhaps after haying season."

"We'll see." But Prescott wasn't going to hold his breath. He had a feeling that any time he made plans to spend a day alone with Lucinda, something would happen. Rains, floods, a freak ice storm in the middle of July—anything out of the ordinary, just to interfere with their plans. Dadgummit! Being an earl was cutting too dang deep into his courting time.

Lucinda glanced down at the pile of journals on the desk in front of Prescott. "Studying the family history as I suggested, are you?"

"I don't know how much studying I'm doing. I'm having a hard enough time just trying to read it. Our ancestors don't appear to have been very good spellers, and their penmanship is more like chicken scratchings. Near as I can figure, though, we Trefarrows weren't always sheepherders."

"We weren't," she said.

"What did we do?"

"Oh, lots of things. At one time, we owned and operated a number of tin mines in the north of Cornwall."

"Did we make any money at it?"

"Quite a lot. As it happens, if it hadn't been for our tin mines, the castle wouldn't have the east and west wings and all its conveniences."

"If it was so profitable, how come we stopped mining the stuff?"

"To put it simply, the veins of tin grew so scarce that it became an unprofitable venture to mine it. That's when we turned to raising sheep."

That sounded like a reasonable enough solution to Prescott. Any sensible businessman would move on to another moneymaker when the old one played out. "What did the old Trefarrows do for income before they mined tin?"

"Oh, farming mostly, I suppose."

"They were sodbusters?"

Lucinda hid a smile, unsure if she would ever get used to hearing Prescott's colorful Texas colloquialisms. "They didn't remain farmers, of course. Probably because it wasn't a very lucrative endeavor in this part of England. Not being a farmer, I can't be certain, you understand, but I believe the soil here is much too thin and rocky for agricultural purposes. However, our rocky shores did lend themselves to the success of another of their enterprises."

"What would that have been?"

"Smuggling," she replied with a glint in her eye. "The early Trefarrows were rather good at smuggling."

Prescott stared at her in disbelief. "You mean to tell me that our ancestors were a bunch of thieving crooks?"

"Not all of them. Just the ones who didn't agree with the king's ban on French imports during Napoleon's reign. But don't think too badly of them. They weren't the only ones smuggling goods from France. At that time, half of England dabbled in illegal trade of one sort or another."

"Why would I think badly of them?" Prescott said. "I admire a man who does whatever it takes to keep a roof over his head and food in his family's belly. I'm just surprised is all, considering that dear old Uncle Herbert was such a dang patriot."

"You have to understand that all this took place before Uncle Herbert became earl. His father truly fancied his French wines and brandies, and he went to any length to get them. And his wife loved wearing French silks, satins, and muslins from the most fashionable Parisian designers of that time. You should see her gowns and some of the men's garments that are stored in trunks up in the attics. Some look as if they've never been worn."

"I'll have to take a look at them some time." Prescott hoped he hadn't sounded uninterested. Looking at clothes from a bygone era wasn't high on his list of things to do. Likely as not, that kind of activity deserved a place closer to the bottom.

"What was it you said the other day?" he asked.

"About what?"

"About calling up ancient Druid spirits when you cursed Emerson. What did you mean by that?"

A flush of alarm crept into Lucinda's cheeks. "I meant nothing by it. I wasn't serious, Prescott. I only said that to Garrick to frighten him into leaving me alone. Heavens, I wouldn't know how to begin to call up an ancient Druid, much less how to curse someone. I'm not a witch."

"Oh, I know you're not."

"Then why did you ask?"

"Because I think I saw some mention of Druids in one of these journals. I just thought there might be a connection is all."

"Well, there is, I suppose," she said. "You see, Druids once ruled here many centuries ago. Long before King Charles II ever thought of bestowing the title of Earl of St. Keverne on the first Trefarrow."

"Were they practitioners of witchcraft?"

"Frankly, I know so very little about them I couldn't say for certain. However, some scholars believe they were witches of a sort. I do know from my history lessons at school, and from what I've read in these journals, that, witches or not, they were a peaceful, intelligent race. But then Julius Caesar came along with his Roman soldiers and put an end to all of that. Unfortunately, he managed to put an end to the Druids as well."

"Every last one of them?"

"Well, they don't gather together at the village chapel every Sunday, if that's what you mean," she said, a thought suddenly coming to her. "But one does hear rumors."

"Rumors?"

"Yes. Each year on All Hallows' Eve it's said that men and women in long black cloaks gather in the dead of night at certain places about the neighborhood where there used to be huge groves of oak trees. Oak groves, you see, were where the ancient Druids once worshiped. At any rate, these black-cloaked figures have been seen dancing slowly around in a circle as they call to the spirits of the ancient ones in foreign-tongued incantations. Within days after they've been sighted, strange things begin to happen. Certain people develop ugly facial warts, while blemishes vanish completely from others' faces. Men are attracted to women they'd hardly noticed, and milking cows suddenly go dry."

Though sunlight streamed into the library through the windows, warming the room, Prescott felt goose bumps come to life on his flesh. "That yarn's about as spooky as the one of the ghost we've got on the loose here in the castle. The one that wears women's clothes and jewelry. If I didn't know better, Lucinda, I'd swear you were trying to scare me."

"Why would I do a thing like that?" she asked, turning her head slightly so he wouldn't notice the almost imperceptible twinkle in her eye.

"I don't know. You tell me."

"Well, you asked me about the Druids, and I merely told you what I knew about them."

"Uh-huh, sure."

"Oh, there is one more thing you might find interesting."

"I'm afraid to ask, but what is it?"

"You know all the ravens that fly about the estate?"

"Yeah."

She leaned close to him and lowered her voice to a whisper. "They weren't here before the Romans arrived."

Prescott couldn't be sure if it was the huskiness of Lucinda's voice, the faint scent of her cologne, or what she was going to tell him next. He only knew that his goose bumps were growing and multiplying, and that his heart was threatening to leap right out of his chest. "They weren't?"

"No, they weren't. The last Druid priest who ruled this region called them out of the heavens as the Romans burnt down the oak forest. There was a forest here at one time, you know. Huge oaks that towered halfway to the sky. But as the soldiers tortured the old priest to death, he cursed both them and this land. We've never had an oak tree grow here since that time, but we've still got the ravens. That's how Ravens Lair got its name." With a coy blink of her captivating gray eyes, she moved slowly away from Prescott to stand on the far side of the desk.

For a long moment he could only stare at her, one part of him knowing he was an idiot for considering the story even remotely plausible, while the other part of him wanted her so badly he ached inside. "You expect me to believe that hogwash?"

"No," she said simply. "I don't expect you to believe anything."

"Well, good, 'cause I don't. Not a word of it."

"That's entirely up to you, of course."

"And while we're at it, I don't believe we've got some panty-waist ghost roaming the halls of this castle, either."

"I understand your doubts."

"If we did have a ghost, I would've heard or seen him by now."

"All right."

"Dang it, Lucinda, stop being so blasted agreeable."

"Would you rather I disagree with you, perhaps start an argument?"

"Why not? It's been a while since I had a good fight. One might feel real good about now."

"That's ridiculous. There's no need for us to fight or argue. That is, of course, unless an argument is the only way you know of to calm your nerves."

"Nerves?"

"Yes. Why don't you just admit it, Prescott—hearing tales of ghosts has scared you."

At her smile and her teasing look, he pushed back his chair and circled the desk to stand beside her. "Right now, darlin', scared is the last thing I am."

She saw the heat in his eyes and knew what it meant. Trying to tease him with her tale of ancient Druids and curses, she realized, had been a big mistake. Instead of frightening him a bit, as she had hoped, it had enticed him, and now she didn't know what to do to stop his obviously rising passions. But if the truth were told, she wasn't sure she really wanted to stop them. Perhaps that was why she had goaded him in the first place—to wake him up, to make him take notice of her.

She didn't budge as his hand came up to her cheek. But the instant he touched her, his finger gently caressing her skin, she felt a jolt of heat rush through her frame. Her eyes widened, the irises growing dark with emotions and longings she had kept buried deep within her soul. Feeling her mouth suddenly become dry, she parted her lips and licked them lightly with her tongue.

Prescott couldn't take his eyes off her mouth. He wanted to kiss it so badly it hurt. It would be so easy for him to wrap her in his arms and hold her tight against him as he captured her lips and plunged his tongue deep into her dark honeyed recesses. Easy, yes, but what about afterward, when the kiss ended? He couldn't just go on about his business as though nothing had happened. Kissing Lucinda once, he knew, wouldn't be enough. He'd want to go on kissing her until she begged him for more—for everything. And, by God, he'd eagerly give in to those pleas.

"Oh, what the hell."

He started to reach for her, but the library door suddenly burst open and Mrs. Sweet rushed in, not only putting an end to Prescott's plan, but dampening his rising ardor as well.

"Beg your pardon, milord, but there's an urgent matter that needs looking after."

Prescott faltered for a moment, silently cursing the fates and everyone else he could think of. But as he moved past Lucinda to stand near the window he prayed that the worried-looking housekeeper hadn't noticed what had been about to transpire. "What is it, Mrs. Sweet?"

"It's Mrs. Emerson, milord. The poor thing's gone into labor."

"She can't have done," Lucinda said. "It's too soon."

Prescott wondered why the housekeeper had come to him with such a problem; he knew next to nothing about delivering babies. "If the woman's having her baby, Mrs. Sweet, run fetch a doctor for her."

"She can't," Lucinda said.

"Why not? Oh, never mind. Mrs. Sweet, send Tom to fetch him."

"You don't understand, Prescott. Dr. Goodacre isn't in the village today."

"Not in the— Where the devil is he?"

"Truro, milord," Mrs. Sweet said. "Gone to meet his widowed sister at the train."

"I had to ask," he muttered. "Well, what do you expect me to do about it, Mrs. Sweet? I'm no doctor. I can't help Mrs. Emerson."

"No, but I can," Lucinda said as she started for the door.

"You?"

"Yes, me. I've helped Dr. Goodacre deliver babies before. Mrs. Sweet, I'll need a lot of clean linens—as many as you can spare—and some strong soap. The stronger the better. And you'd better send word to Tom that I'll be needing the governess's cart brought round to the front."

"Yes, Miss." The housekeeper bobbed a quick curtsy and trundled out of the library.

"You're a midwife?"

Lucinda stopped in the doorway and looked back at him. "When the occasion calls for it, yes. And it seems as if this is one of them. Now, if you'll excuse me, I really must hurry."

"Hang on. I'll go with you."

"Oh, really, Prescott, you'll only get in the way. Stay here." Suddenly she hesitated. "However, on second thought, perhaps you might be of some help after all."

"You want me to help?"

"Yes."

"Well, all right. But I think I'd better tell you, I've never delivered a baby before. Calves and foals, sure, plenty of times, but never a human baby."

"Don't worry about the baby; I'll deliver it. You just take care of the children."

"Hey, you're looking at a man who likes kids."

"I wonder where the Sam Hill Emerson is?" Prescott said as he guided his horse around a curve in the road.

"I wouldn't want to hazard a guess." Sitting in the little governess's cart, Lucinda flicked the reins over the ponies' backs, spurring them to move faster. "However, one thought does come to mind."

"Yeah, that thought came to me, too." Emerson, he suspected, was in St. Keverne with his mistress instead of at home with his wife where he belonged. "If he is, the man ought to be horsewhipped."

"Whipping Garrick Emerson wouldn't be a suitable enough punishment."

"I know, darlin', but it sure would do for starters."

When they arrived at the Emerson house, they saw no one. Lucinda climbed out of the cart and handed her supplies to Prescott.

"Until I get inside and have a look," she said, "I have no way of knowing how far along Mrs. Emerson is into her labor. If this one is anything like her others, I suspect it's going to take quite a while."

"How long is a while?"

"Hours, perhaps even days—I'm not really sure."

"Days? Good Lord!"

"She's a very small-boned woman, Prescott. Need I explain further?"

"No, that's all right, I understand." Women and their problems had always been a mystery to him and, as far as he was concerned, they could remain a mystery. He had enough to handle just being a man.

As she had the first time, little Victoria answered Prescott's knock at the door. The worried and frightened expression on her face tore at his heart.

"You're Victoria, aren't you?" Lucinda asked as they entered the house. At the little girl's nod, she added, "Well, Lord Prescott and I have come to see your mummy. We hear she's not feeling well, and we're going to try and make her all better. Is she in her bedroom?"

Again the child nodded and pointed to the nearby closed door. "Exie and Izzabeff."

"Your sisters are in there with her?"

"Uh-huh."

A loud, painful wail emanated from the other room, causing Prescott's stomach to twist into knots. God, he had never felt so useless. If it had been a cow or a mare about to give birth, he'd know what to do. But not this time. Not with a woman in the throes of hard labor.

Feeling the need to do something, he started for the door, but Lucinda stopped him with an outstretched hand. "No, you stay out here."

"I just thought—"

"Yes, I know. I want to help her as well. But you can be more help to her by staying here with the children. I'll send the other two out to join you in a moment, as soon as I get things ready."

"All right," he said, liking the sound of her idea. "You want me to boil some water or something?"

"Yes, that would be nice." She placed her hamper down on the kitchen table and began to unpack it. "Boil some water and make tea for yourself and the girls."

"Tea?"

"Mmm, and sandwiches, if they've enough on hand. If Victoria is any indication, I would have to say that no one has had anything to eat since this whole ordeal started."

"I can handle feeding them. You just take care of their mama."

Her arms loaded with clean linens and the large bar of strong soap, Lucinda headed for the bedroom. The door swung open wide to her touch, and Prescott looked inside, catching a glimpse of the woman who lay in a twisted mass of sheets on the bed. Rage surged through him at the sight of her face, all swollen and covered in darkening bruises, given to her, he suspected, by her husband.

"Bastard," he muttered.

"Let's go out here and see what Lord Prescott is doing, shall we?" Ashen faced at what she had discovered, Lucinda came out of the bedroom, leading Alexandra by the hand and carrying Elizabeth on her hip. "Oh, look! I think he's going to make you something to eat, like he did the last time he was here. Is that what you're doing, Lord Prescott?"

"Er . . ." Sickened, enraged, and trying desperately to remain calm, words eluded Prescott.

Lucinda didn't have to be a mind reader to know what he was thinking. She had come to the same conclusion herself the instant she had seen Mrs. Emerson's condition. Garrick had beaten his wife unmercifully and walked out on her, totally unconcerned that his abuse had sent her into labor. But enough violence had transpired already; the girls certainly didn't need to see more of the same.

"Lord Prescott! You are making the children's tea, aren't you?"

He banked down his anger long enough to stare at Lucinda. "What?"

"I said, aren't you making their tea?"

"Er, yeah, tea—I'm just fixing to get on it."

In his present state he couldn't boil a kettle of water, let alone make a proper tea for the children. "On second thought," she said, "I've a much better idea. Why don't you take the girls out for a while?"

"Out? Out where?"

She sat Elizabeth down on the floor and sidled close to him. "Get a hold of yourself, Prescott," she whispered in his ear. "You must remain calm. You must."

"Don't you think I'm trying?" he said through clenched teeth. "But it ain't all that easy. Damn it, I saw what that bastard did to her."

"I know. It's horrible, and she's suffering because of it, but don't compound her agony with your unnecessary display of outrage. Think of her and the children. At this moment, you must think only of them. Do you understand? Heaven only knows what they've seen."

Knowing she was right, Prescott banked down his

rage even more. There would come a time when he would personally avenge the pain Mrs. Emerson now suffered. Sooner or later, Emerson would pay for what he had done to his wife.

Gazing down into the three upturned, anxious faces that watched him, he forced a grin. "What do you ladies feel like doing, huh?"

"We mustn't leave Mummy," Alexandra said.

"Miss Lucinda will take good care of her," he said. "Won't you, Miss Lucinda?"

"Of course I will."

"Now, what do you say we all—"

"No!" Alexandra said, backing away from him. "She needs us."

In desperation, Prescott looked at Lucinda for guidance. "What do I do now?"

"Oh, for God's sake, Prescott, use your imagination. Take them for a long walk—down to the beach, perhaps—or read a story to them. Anything to keep them distracted. They mustn't think of their mother laboring away in agony like this. Look at them. They're frightened to death as it is, the poor little things."

Another wail erupted from the bedroom, more pitiful sounding than the one before it. Prescott racked his brain, trying to think of something to do. He liked kids well enough, but he'd been around them so seldom, he wasn't sure how to handle them. *What in God's name,* he wondered, *could a grown man do to entertain three little girls?*

Then he remembered the pony cart waiting outside and the solution came to him. "Don't worry, Miss Lucinda. I know just the thing to do. The four of us will go up to the castle and have ourselves a tea party."

"Oh, that's a splendid idea, Lord Prescott!" Knowing that he had finally regained his composure, Lucinda had never felt more relieved. "Doesn't that sound delightful, ladies? A tea party."

"At the castle?" Alexandra asked, excitement slowly replacing the fear in her eyes.

"You bet," Prescott said. "Nothing's too good for little ladies like you three. We'll go first class all the way. Do it up right with—with—" He looked at Lucinda for help.

"Scones with jam and ham finger sandwiches," she said. "I think I even saw Mrs. Sweet making some of her tiny iced cakes this morning. There are probably still a lot begging to be eaten."

"That's settled, then," Prescott said. "You girls run get your things together. Grab your dollies and whatever else you want to take to the tea party."

"But we haven't got dollies," Alexandra said. "Papa never gave—"

"Well, no matter," Lucinda interrupted, patting Alexandra's pale blond head. "We've hundreds of dollies in the castle nursery."

"Hundreds?" Alexandra's eyes glittered with excitement.

"Yes, and you can play with all of them if you want."

"Did you hear that, Victoria? They've got dollies at the castle."

A sharp pain tugged at Lucinda's heart as she watched Alexandra help her little sisters gather up the few toys that they thought vital. Though many years separated her from the girls, they had a lot in common. They had a father who cared so much for his own lascivious comforts that he neglected to provide them with the most basic of necessities. She'd had a father who hadn't even known of her existence; he'd merely taken his pleasures with a nobleman's niece one night, then left her to die in heartbroken disgrace. But at least the little girls had a mother who loved them. Lucinda couldn't even make that claim.

"Are we ready to go?" Prescott asked.

Eager to get underway, Alexandra and Victoria beamed, chattering softly of tea parties and iced cakes and dollies. Baby Elizabeth, resting on Lucinda's hip, could only look confused and unsure of the whole situation.

"I guess we'll be taking the governess's cart, won't we?" Prescott asked.

"Under the circumstances, I think that would be much better than trying to sit all four of you on the back of one horse," Lucinda replied.

"Right. Well, let's get going. Come here to me, Peanut. You can sit in my lap and help me drive." He reached out to take the baby, but she wrapped her little arms tightly about Lucinda's neck and hid her face.

"Her name is Elizabeth, Lord Prescott, not Peanut," Alexandra said, not really sure what a peanut was.

"Well, she looks a lot like a peanut to me. Looks like she's kind of scared, too."

"She can be quite impossible at times," Alexandra said with all the impatience of an adult. "Do come on, Elizabeth. We must hurry."

A wail much louder and stronger than any Lucinda had ever heard came from the bedroom. Knowing she could waste no more time, she thrust Elizabeth into Prescott's waiting arms and pushed him toward the door. "Take care of them."

"You take care of their mama," he said, and then, as an afterthought, he bent down and kissed her cheek. "Let me know how it turns out."

"I will."

Once outside, Prescott settled the little girls on one side of the tiny cart, with Alexandra holding Elizabeth in her lap, then he climbed onto the seat facing them. Hell of a thing, he thought as he flicked the reins, sending the ponies lurching into motion, a grown man having to ride side-saddle in an itty-bitty cart with a trio of children. He just hoped the ponies had no trouble in conveying them all the way to the castle. If not, he supposed he'd just have to climb out and walk. But above all, he prayed that nobody saw him in such a predicament.

They made it to the castle in a slow, steady progression, the ponies faltering only once, when the narrow lane grew steeper toward the top of the hill.

"Sturdy little fellas, ain't they?" he said.

"They're beautiful," Alexandra said.

Prescott heard the wistful tone in her voice and smiled. He had a feeling he had just discovered something that he had in common with the child. "You like horses?"

She nodded. "Mummy has promised to teach me how to ride when I'm old enough."

"Back home in Texas, you'd be old enough now. But I guess they do things kind of different here in England. How old do you have to be?"

"Mummy said when I'm five," she said.

"That's a good age to learn to ride. Four's better, though, don't you think?"

Alexandra dipped her head. "It would be lovely, Lord Prescott, but I'm not old enough yet. And Papa hasn't enough money to buy us a pony."

Hearing the little girl defend her father only served to renew his anger toward the man. Emerson had stolen more than enough money to buy his daughters one small pony, yet he had chosen to lavish all of his ill-gotten gains on his floozie and his other home.

"How old are you now?" he asked.

"Four. But I shall be five in July."

"That's just a few months away. Do you think your mama would get mad if you learned to ride now?"

Her blue eyes widened with anticipation. "Now, Lord Prescott?"

"Sure, why not? I've got the ponies right here. I know they're kind of fat and all, but you riding them everyday will soon give them the exercise they need."

"Oh, may I?"

"Anything you want, darlin'. In fact, if you or your sisters want anything at all, you just come ask your old Uncle Prescott."

"*Uncle Prescott?*" Alexandra asked.

"Yeah, I kind of like the sound of 'uncle Prescott' better than I do 'lord Prescott.' It's friendlier."

Hours later, Prescott found himself regretting having made such a rash promise to the children. From the moment they arrived at the castle and he tried to hand them over to Miranda for safekeeping, Alexandra clung to him like a little shadow. Victoria followed closely in her older sister's wake, and both vented their curiosities about Ravens Lair and the nurseries and all the toys with an indefatigable eagerness. And baby Elizabeth, who had been so shy of him at first, refused to let anyone but Prescott hold her, or feed her, or change her diapers when that unfortunate time rolled around.

Which seemed to be a little too often by Prescott's way of thinking.

The only thing that seemed to quiet them down was the newborn baby lamb they discovered in a large basket in the corner of his bedroom. How the animal had found its way there, Prescott wasn't sure, but he had a good idea that Mrs. Sweet was responsible for moving it up from the kitchen.

"Shouldn't he be out playing with all of the other little lambs, Uncle Prescott?" Alexandra asked.

Holding a baby bottle full of milk, Prescott knelt down on the floor beside the little girls, who hovered around the basket petting the lamb. "It's a she, darlin', not a he."

"How do you know?"

"Oh, that's easy. You just look—" He broke off, realizing he couldn't tell an impressionable four-year-old how one determined the sex of an animal by sight. "Er, it's just something that we sheepmen know. And I know that this is a girl."

"Well, shouldn't she be outside?" Alexandra persisted.

"Sure she should. And when she gets bigger, we'll put her out to play in the pasture with all her little friends. But for right now, she's better off staying here. You want to feed her?"

"Yes, please." Alexandra took the bottle from him and poked the nipple into the lamb's waiting mouth. "What's her name?"

"Name?" English people didn't go around naming their sheep, did they? No, of course they didn't, he decided. They couldn't; there were too dang many of them. "Er, I haven't given her one. Haven't had the time, really. I just found her this morning."

"But she must have a name, Uncle Prescott," Alexandra said. "Mummy says that all God's creatures must have names."

"Your mama's right about that. You want to give her a name?"

"May I?"

"Sure, go right ahead."

Alexandra thought about it for a moment and then smiled. "Princess. We shall call her Princess."

"Sounds like a good name to me." Feeling someone watching him from behind, Prescott turned and saw Hargreaves standing in the doorway. "Hey there, Ed."

Hargreaves stiffened slightly at the earl's persistent use of his given name. "Milord."

"Girls, this is Mr. Hargreaves. He works here in the castle. Ed, this is Alexandra, Victoria, and the little one there making a puddle on my rug is Elizabeth."

The very proper valet eyed the children with a mixture of disdain and amusement. "Ladies."

"We've just named Uncle Prescott's new lamb, Mr. Hargreaves," Alexandra announced.

"A worthy endeavor indeed, Miss. Beg your pardon, milord, but might we have a moment of your time?"

"Sure. Girls, why don't you finish feeding Princess and then head on up to the nursery. But don't go climbing the stairs until Miss Miranda or Miss Rowena come to fetch you. Wouldn't want y'all falling down and getting hurt or nothing."

"Oh, we shan't, Uncle Prescott."

"Good. In the meantime, I'll see what I can do about finding some more diapers for Elizabeth."

Leaving the children in his room, he walked with

Hargreaves out into the hall. "I think we're gonna need us a nanny, Ed. The sooner we can find one, the better. Changing diapers ain't exactly my line of work."

"Is this to be a permanent arrangement, milord?"

"Well, they're gonna be here a while, if that's what you're asking."

"How long is a while, milord?"

"That all depends. See, their mama's having another baby, and from what I've been told, it ain't gonna happen real quick like."

"We understand, milord."

"What was it you wanted to see me about?"

"Ah, yes. Mrs. Sweet wishes me to ask you if the children shall be having their tea early in the nursery, as is the usual custom, or if they shall be dining *en famille* with your lordship at a later hour this evening?"

"Oh, hell, Ed, I can't let those three little girls eat all alone. Why, Elizabeth ain't even old enough to feed herself. I 'spect they'll be better off eating with me."

"Whatever your lordship wishes, of course. But might I make an observation?"

"Sure, fire away."

"With children of that age, dining at a later hour might not be a wise decision."

"Yeah, you're right. I forgot that kids need to go to bed early."

"Precisely, milord. And dining formally *en famille* in the dining room might be courting disaster, especially where baby Elizabeth is concerned. The velvet cushions on the chairs are quite old, and I doubt they could withstand the, mmm, shall we say added dampness that she would most certainly bring to them."

"Not to mention the food they're all liable to spill." Prescott scratched his head, wondering how he was going to figure his way out of this situation. "Sounds to me like you know a little bit about kids, Ed."

Hargreaves held himself erect, his expression blank as he cleared his throat. "We have held previous posts in households where there have been children present, milord."

"Little ones their age?" he asked, cocking his head toward his bedroom door.

"Children of all ages, milord."

"Then seeing as how you've got more experience with them than I do, what do you think I ought to do?"

"Quite simply, milord, you should dine with them in their environs."

"Yeah, now that you mention it, that's a dang good idea. Eat with them in the nursery, and if they spill anything, it won't matter." Prescott slapped a hand heartily across the man's back. "You're okay, Ed. At first you came across as kind of pompous, but now I see you've got a level head on your shoulders."

"Thank you, milord."

"Don't mention it. Pass the word along to Mrs. Sweet, would you?"

"Of course, milord."

As Prescott turned and reentered the bedroom, closing the door behind him, the valet muttered, "And the name is Hargreaves, milord. Not Ed. Hargreaves."

12

A faint noise roused Prescott from sleep at the same moment that he felt a warm dampness growing in the bed beside him. Elizabeth, he realized, had wet her diaper again.

He very carefully unwound himself from the tangle of little arms and legs and climbed out of bed, not wishing to disturb the three children who continued to sleep so peacefully. He tiptoed across the carpeted floor, grabbed his heavy robe off a nearby chair, and pulled it on as he opened the door. The faint noise he'd heard had been Lucinda entering his sitting room.

"Oh, I'm sorry," she said, holding the lamp she carried high in front of her. "I didn't mean to awaken you."

"You didn't. I wasn't getting much sleep anyway." Despite the dimness of the lamplight, he could see the weariness etched on her pretty features. Something told him that she hadn't come to him at this late hour with good news.

"Are the girls all right?"

"They're fine," he said. "We played with the dolls and the baby lamb most of the afternoon, then they ate like they hadn't had a good meal in weeks, and they fell asleep. In my bed."

"Your bed?"

"Yeah, my bed."

"But shouldn't they be upstairs in the nursery?"

"I tried putting them to bed up there, but it didn't quite work out the way it was supposed to. They wanted me to tell them a story, and I did. Fact is, I told them every bedtime story I could think of, and they still wanted more. So I brought them down here and read to them 'til they dropped off." Feeling a growing chilliness beneath his robe, he pulled the heavy fabric away from the damp spot on his leg. "Elizabeth just wet the sheets."

Lucinda glanced at the partially closed door behind him, a look of arrant sadness contorting her features. "Poor little things."

"How's their mama?"

"Anne is—" Lucinda broke off and began to tremble, her small amount of strength vanishing altogether.

"Oh, God, darlin'." Prescott crossed to her, took the lamp from her fingers, and wrapped her in his arms, holding her close as she sobbed uncontrollably. *Heaven help and protect the innocents in this world,* he thought. Especially the three little motherless angels now asleep in his bed.

Some time later as her weeping began to subside, Lucinda regained the strength to speak. "Anne was such a lady. So delicate, so refined, and such a wonderful mother. She didn't stand a chance, Prescott. Not the smallest shred of a chance."

"Now, don't go blaming yourself. You did everything you could to help her."

"I know, I know. Dr. Goodacre said the same thing, but it doesn't lessen the emptiness that I feel."

"The doc was there?"

"He arrived at the cottage moments before Anne finally gave birth. He did everything he could, but even he couldn't save her. Garrick had kicked and beat her so badly this time, she just didn't have the strength to survive. Dying was probably the greatest relief she could find."

"Is that what the doc said?"

"Oh, he didn't have to say anything. The moment I saw the bruises on Anne's abdomen, her condition was obvious to me."

"And the baby?"

Lucinda shook her head. "According to Dr. Goodacre, he must have expired during the beating."

A sickening, red-hot rage begin to build up inside of Prescott. He couldn't understand how a man could kick his pregnant wife and unborn child so severely that it would kill them both. But then, Emerson wasn't a man, not in the truest sense of the word. He was an animal, and animals of his kind had to pay for their crimes in one way or another.

"Are you gonna be okay?" he asked.

"I'll be fine." But Lucinda knew that it would take days, weeks, perhaps even months for the vivid images of Anne Emerson and her tortured screams to fade from her thoughts. Those would linger with her for a long time to come.

Unable to stand still, and feeling a need to do

something immediately, Prescott stepped out of their embrace and turned toward the bedroom. "Would you mind staying with the girls for a while?"

"Of course not, but where are you going?"

"I need to go out."

"Go out, at this hour?"

"Yeah. I got a bad taste in my mouth. Maybe some fresh air will get rid of it."

"But it's pitch black out there. And it's beginning to rain. You'll get lost and catch a chill."

"Don't worry, I'll be all right. I won't go anywhere I haven't been before."

In that instant, watching the way he held himself so rigidly, so determinedly, Lucinda had little doubt as to what his intentions and his destination were. "Oh, for God's sake, Prescott, you can't be thinking of doing something rash."

"No, not rash. It's something I should have done months ago."

"You mean to take the law into your own hands, don't you?"

"Since the first day I got here, Lucinda, you and everybody else have been telling me that I'm the earl, the law of the land around these parts. It's about time I started acting like the law, don't you think?"

He slipped quietly into his darkened bedroom, the dim light shining from Lucinda's small lamp in the sitting room barely illuminating the three tiny forms in the middle of his bed. But the sight was enough to pull at his heart, remind him of his own childhood. He knew what it was like to grow up without a mother, to wonder what she looked like, to wish he could hear her talk and laugh just once. His Aunt Em had been a wonderful substitute—loving, giving, and stern when necessary. But the fact remained, she had been only his aunt, not his real mother.

He paused to cover the children with the blankets they had kicked off, and then he went into his dressing room. But when he tried to close the door he found Lucinda was right behind him.

"This is insane, Prescott. What you're thinking of doing is absolutely insane."

"Emerson kicked his wife and baby to death. He deserves a dose of his own medicine, Lucinda. You know it, and I know it."

"An eye for an eye—that's what you're saying, isn't it?"

"Yeah, I guess it is." He pulled off his robe and would have undone the buttons on his trousers if Lucinda hadn't been watching him. "Would you mind turning around? I've gotta get out of these wet pants."

"Yes, I do mind. Keeping you in those clothes just might stop you from doing something idiotic."

"Fine. We'll do this your way." He opened the top two buttons and was about to go for the third when Lucinda gasped and whirled around.

"You can't be serious about confronting Garrick tonight," she said.

"I can, and I am. Beating the living hell out of a bastard like him is a fitting punishment in my book, 'cause this time he's gonna be up against a man his own size, not a frail, sickly woman."

"Prescott, two wrongs never make a right. Your beating Garrick won't bring Anne and the baby back. They'll still be dead."

"I can't just let it go and forget about it," he said, pulling clean trousers out of his wardrobe.

"That's not what I'm asking you to do. I just think you should stop and consider your actions before you take the law into your own hands."

"Somebody's gotta do something, and it might as well be me. From what I've heard, the sheriff in these parts is little better than useless."

"He's not useless. He's a good man. Not as well trained as the bobbies in London, perhaps, but he does his job well enough."

"All right, maybe he does do his job as well as he can, but does he know anything about handling a murder?"

"Murder?"

"Yeah, murder. When a man kills his wife and unborn son the way Emerson did, he's a murderer, no matter how you look at it. Now, I don't know how you people here in England handle your murderers, but back home, we hang 'em."

"We hang ours as well," she said. "But we let the law do it for us."

"Yeah well, both you and I know how those laws work. Not nearly fast enough."

"Nevertheless, the sheriff should be the one to arrest Garrick and incarcerate him until it's time for him to stand trial for his crimes. It's the civilized thing to do."

"Civilized, hell. By the time Emerson gets his mangy carcass tried, he can be long gone from here. No, it's not going to work that way this time."

"You may be Earl of Ravens Lair, but even you have your limitations."

"Maybe," he said, pulling on a warm, clean shirt. "Maybe not."

"Oh, for God's sake, Prescott, need I remind you

that you're no longer in Texas? You're in England now. Your form of Wild West justice simply will not work here."

"We'll just see about that."

"Listen to yourself. You're talking like some barbarian from the Dark Ages. You cannot appoint yourself Garrick Emerson's judge and jury, and you certainly can't form a one-man lynch mob and hang him." When Prescott didn't immediately come back with a biting response, Lucinda knew it was time to take a different approach, to appeal to the kinder, gentler side of his nature. "For God's sake, think of the children for a moment. They've just lost their mother, and their father is—is— Well, it's obvious that he doesn't care for them. He probably never did. Anne's family is all dead, as is Garrick's. Those three little girls asleep in your bed in there have no aunts, no uncles, no cousins. No one, Prescott. No one at all."

"Wrong," he said. "They've got me."

Lucinda whirled around and stared up at him in astonishment, a small part of her relieved to see that he was now pulling on a heavy, sheepskin-lined coat. "You're willing to take on the responsibility of raising them?"

"Why not? My Aunt Em always said I was one of the best at dragging home every stray pup I could find."

"But Alexandra, Victoria, and Elizabeth aren't puppies. They're little girls."

"I know that. But they're not much different from little strays when you stop and think about it. They need a home and somebody to love and take care of them. Lord knows, I got a home for them. This place is big enough to house an army of little girls. And in my own way, I suppose I can give them love. Hell, I even got enough money now to hire somebody to take care of them."

"You're talking as though you're thinking of adopting them."

"If it comes to that, yeah, why not?"

"For one thing, you're not married. Bachelors can't adopt children. Little girl children especially."

"Okay then, I won't adopt them. I'll just get the judge to make them my wards. Alexandra already calls me Uncle Prescott. Whatever the outcome, they'll be my responsibility, not Emerson's. The less they have to do with that piece of white trash, the better. Now you keep an eye on them for me while I'm gone, y'hear? I won't be gone too long."

Lucinda could only stare in silent wonder as Prescott slipped through the door that connected his dressing room to the outside hall. Would the man never stop surprising her? From the first moment she'd met him he'd been a constant source of amazement to her, so unlike any other man she'd ever known. He opened his arms and his heart to orphaned sheep, motherless children, and homeless spinsters like herself. Yet in the same breath he could speak of beating a man senseless as an act of retribution for a dead woman he'd seen only twice. He had so many different sides to his character, she didn't think she would ever see them all. But of all the sides she had seen, she supposed that his gentleness and caring far outweighed his frightening vengefulness, and, in her mind, that made him a man among millions.

* * *

Despite the wind and chilly rain that pelted him, Prescott felt a trickle of perspiration run down his back as he arrived in the village a half hour later. The notion of having it out with Emerson again didn't set well with him, but he knew it had to be done. Emerson and others like him in these parts had to know that the new earl wasn't going to put up with men who beat their wives. Or their kids, either, for that matter. If they wanted to fight somebody, they could take him on, but not their children and womenfolk. That sort of thing just wasn't fitting.

Emerson's house looked peaceful enough to Prescott as he reined his horse at the front gate. He looked around, hoping to see some of the villagers still out and about in case he needed their help. But at ten o'clock on this rainy night the street was empty. Not for long, though, he told himself, climbing down from the saddle. He intended to raise a loud enough ruckus with Emerson to disturb the sleep of even the hardest of hearing.

He went up to the front door and knocked, praying that nobody would answer it so he'd have an excuse to kick the dang thing down. But somebody did answer it; the same little maid who'd opened it for him the first time.

"Milord!"

"I've come to see Emerson," he said.

"But milord, Mr. Emerson be abed at this hour."

"Then you'd best go wake him up, girl, 'cause if you don't, I will."

"Yes, milord." She bobbed a quick curtsy and dashed off into the house.

Having time to think as he stood in the rain, Prescott wished he'd told the maid to go find herself a good hiding place, and that he'd go wake up Mr. Emerson. He'd bet that seeing him burst into the bedroom would sure put the fear of God into that bastard. Probably the last person Emerson expected to call on him on a night like this was the new earl.

A moment later, the maid appeared again, slightly flushed and breathless from having run up the stairs. "Mr. Emerson said to tell your lordship he'd be right down. Miss Isabel says thee's welcome to wait in the parlor."

"The parlor? Fine, I'll do just that. Now why don't you run on down to the sheriff's house for me."

"The sheriff, milord?"

"That's right. Tell him the earl needs him."

"Yes, milord. I'll just run fetch me cloak."

"No, no need for that. Here, take my coat. I don't 'spect I'll be needing it 'til you get back."

He slipped the garment over the maid's slim shoulders and watched her knees sag under the considerable weight. "Now, you run along. And, er, take your time."

"Yes, milord."

Prescott waited until she was out of sight down the street before he entered the house. He started to close the door, but decided at the last moment to leave it open. No telling who might need to make a quick exit before the night was over.

Like his vestibule, Emerson's sitting room was furnished with just about the best that stealing from Ravens Lair for years had gotten him: plush sofas and chairs, dainty little tables with marquetry-inlaid tops, and fancy-looking paintings on the walls. It didn't look to Prescott as though Emerson had put much effort into trying to sell off his ill-gotten gains, which no doubt explained why he hadn't gotten back any of his money yet.

"No-good bastard," he muttered.

"Beg your pardon, milord?"

Prescott turned and saw Emerson standing in the doorway, tying the sash of his heavy silk brocade robe. His wife and kids had been forced to wear rags, yet Emerson and his floozie dressed in the finest that money could buy. Ravens Lair's money at that.

"I said, you're a no-good bastard, Emerson. I've met some sons of bitches in my time, but I gotta tell you, you take the cake."

"You've come at a rather late hour to hurl verbal abuses at me. Couldn't it have waited until morning?"

"'Fraid not. This has to be done now. And before the night's over, I'm gonna be hurling more than verbal abuses, Emerson."

"What do you mean?"

"I mean, I'm gonna beat the hell out of you the same way you beat the life out of your wife and son." The startled look on Emerson's face told Prescott that his announcement had hit home.

"Son? I have a son?"

"No," Prescott said, stalking toward him, "you *had* a son. But you killed him along with your wife when you kicked her to death."

"No, I—" Emerson broke off, stunned by the news. "Anne's dead?"

"Ain't that what I just said? You deaf as well as ornery and stupid?"

"She fell. Anne fell, do you understand? She's always falling. I didn't kick her."

"That ain't the way I hear it."

"I swear I didn't kick her. She fell!"

"But you did beat her, didn't you?"

"I—I may have done. We had an argument, you see. We always argue when we're together. That's why I live here with Isabel—er, Miss Martins. I can't abide a woman who talks back to her husband, as Anne constantly talked back to me. This afternoon, when she raised her voice, I—"

"Slapped her."

"Yes."

"Then when she tried to defend herself, you hit her in the face with your fist. You hit her so damn hard, Emerson, you broke her jaw."

"No!"

"Yes! Don't lie to me, you son of a bitch, I saw her face. I've cracked enough jaws in my day to know one when I see it, and hers was more than broke—it was shattered all to hell."

"Sh—she was hysterical."

"No wonder, you hitting her the way you did."

"She wouldn't stop badgering me, begging me to come home to her and the children. I can't live there in that hovel with them. I have a position to maintain. And I have my needs; I'm a man, and Anne was never able to fulfill them."

"So you let your wife and children wear rags and starve while you shack up here with your whore."

"Isabel is no—"

"She damn sure is. She lives here in this house with you, she sleeps in your bed, she wears the clothes you buy her, and she ain't your wife. If that don't make her a whore, I don't know what does."

"She's my mistress. All English gentlemen of breeding have mistresses."

"I know a couple that might disagree with you on

that score, Emerson. But then you ain't no gentleman, and you sure as hell ain't got no breeding."

"I must object, milord."

"Well, a man's gotta do what a man's gotta do."

"I—I have the right to defend myself against such unjust allegations."

"Defend yourself? You're right about that." Prescott swung his right fist upward so quickly that Emerson didn't have time to duck. The punch landed soundly on Emerson's jaw, not only cracking it, but knocking him backward against the wall.

Though pain registered in Prescott's knuckles, he ignored it. "How does it feel, Emerson, knowing you're up against somebody who's bigger'n you, who's not gonna listen to any of your shit? Don't feel too good, does it? Must not have felt too good for your wife, either, having you use her as a punching bag."

A trickle of blood seeped out of the corner of Emerson's mouth as a look of burning rage passed across his eyes. "You—you upper-class scum are all alike, always taking advantage of us poor working-class sods."

"Don't insult me that way, Emerson. I ain't upper class."

Emerson pushed himself away from the wall and lunged for Prescott. Prescott took a quick step to the side and stuck out his foot, tripping Emerson, but grabbing him by the collar of his robe before he fell to the floor.

"Good move, but not good enough," Prescott said, hauling the struggling man around the room like a heavy sack of grain. "See, I've done this before. Best saloon brawl I was ever in, a fella tried coming at me headfirst that way." He rammed the man's head into the doorjamb. "Oops, where did that come from?" Then he rammed Emerson's head into the wall, cracking the plaster and the strips of lathing behind it. "Looks like you ain't having any luck at all."

Catching sight of the front window, Prescott took aim and flung Emerson with all the strength he could muster. Glass shattered as Emerson's body sailed out into the night.

Hmm, Prescott thought as he followed his opponent through the newly made opening. He hadn't needed to leave the front door open after all.

Sheriff Penhalligan lumbered up the street, still half asleep despite the cold air that blew up his long nightshirt. He'd been looking forward to meeting the new earl, but he hadn't quite envisioned their first meeting taking place in the dead of night this way.

"Thee's certain his lordship wanted to see me?" he asked the young woman who trotted alongside him, her short limbs having some difficulty keeping up with his much longer strides.

"Aye, sir. That's what he—" She broke off, spotting two men in front of her place of employment instead of inside it, where she had left them. "Oh, my! What are they doing?"

The sheriff took one look at the tangling pair and knew his first meeting with the new earl was going to be a memorable one. "Nothing a young lady your age should concern herself with. Better run back to my house and stay there."

"But, sir—"

"Don't argue with me, miss. Do as I say. Now go!"

His nightshirt flapping against his bony ankles, the sheriff hurried on ahead, believing that his order had been obeyed. Emerson's young maid, however, stood rooted for a moment, then followed more slowly in the sheriff's wake. What she saw when she drew closer to her employer and his late-night caller, the new earl, made her gasp. Lord Prescott was giving Mr. Emerson a sound thrashing.

"'Bout time," she muttered to herself.

"What's all this, then?" the sheriff asked as he approached the scuffling pair. But, on closer inspection, he realized it really wasn't much of a scuffle at all, considering one had a definite advantage over the other.

"You the sheriff?" Prescott asked.

"Aye, that's who I'd be. Sheriff George Penhalligan. And you, sir, are—?"

"Pres—er, Lord St. Keverne, the new earl 'round these parts."

"Ah, yes. I was told your lordship wished to see me."

"That's right, I did."

Penhalligan paused, waiting for the new earl to explain further but, when Prescott didn't, he asked, "What do you wish to see me about, milord?"

"About this slimy polecat here." Prescott hauled Emerson to his feet and turned him so Penhalligan could see the man's face. Taking a look at it himself, he felt right proud of the way he'd kept his temper in check. Only one of Emerson's eyes was swollen shut, and he'd only lost two teeth instead of a whole mouthful, as had often happened when Prescott got in a fight.

"Slimy what, milord?"

"Polecat. You might call them by a different name here. Skunk?"

"Your lordship is comparing Mr. Emerson to vermin?"

"Yep, that's exactly what I'm doing."

"But milord, Mr. Emerson is an upstanding member of the community."

Prescott turned Emerson's collar loose, and the man slid into a nerveless mess in the middle of the cobblestone street. "He ain't upstanding no more. 'Course, it only seems a fitting ending for a thief and a wife beater, don't you think?"

"A thief and a wife-beater? Mr. Emerson?"

"Oh, more'n that, sheriff. Lots more."

"What could be worse?"

"How 'bout a murderer? See, he killed Mrs. Emerson and their baby son."

"You have proof of this?"

"Yeah, their bodies are back at his house right now. Not this house here. His other one, where his wife and kids lived. For all I know, Dr. Goodacre might still be tending to the newly departed."

"No, that's not the sort of proof I meant."

"Two dead bodies ain't good enough? What the hell kind of proof do you want?"

"An eyewitness to his alleged assault of Mrs. Emerson would be most helpful, milord."

Immediately, images of Alexandra, Victoria, and Elizabeth flashed through Prescott's mind. He was almost certain that they had seen Emerson hit and kick their mother, but he couldn't tell Penhalligan that. They were still little better than babies and had been put through enough torment for one day, for a lifetime even. He couldn't very well ask them to testify against their father now. Perhaps when they were older and could more easily understand the gravity of the situation, but not now.

"Two dead bodies, and my word and the doc's against his ain't good enough, is that what you're saying?"

"Oh, for me, aye. It would be good enough for me, milord, but I'm not a judge. Come to that, I'm not a solicitor, either. But I do know that our English courts are quite particular about having substantial proof."

"Oh, never mind. Damn judicial systems." Prescott knew there had to be a way of not only punishing Emerson, but getting him put quickly behind bars so he couldn't do any more harm. Then it came to him. "You may doubt his being a murderer, but there ain't no doubt at all that he's a thief. And before you ask if I've got proof, the answer is, Yes, I do. Very substantial proof, as a matter of fact. I've got ledgers and journals with his handwriting back at the castle that prove he's been stealing from Ravens Lair for years." He waved a hand at the house behind him. "This place and everything in it rightfully belongs to me."

Penhalligan glanced up at the house and saw the scantily-dressed, lush-figured silhouette of a woman standing in the doorway. "Everything, milord?"

Seeing Emerson's mistress eyeing him with uncertainty, Prescott shook his head firmly. "Oh, hell no! She's his, not mine."

"Ah, I see."

"Now, I've tried to be fair about all this, Sheriff. I really have. When I found out what he'd been doing, I gave him a chance to pay me back. Well, not me, exactly, but Ravens Lair. I told him to sell off everything, and even gave him plenty of time to do it. But by the looks of it, he's still living high off the hog and don't intend to pay back one red cent."

"I see," Penhalligan said, nodding his head sagely. "So does your lordship wish to swear out a complaint against Mr. Emerson?"

"A complaint, are you joshing me? I want his sorry ass thrown in jail for the rest of his natural life, that's what I want."

Penhalligan appeared a bit flustered. "I'm afraid that will be impossible, milord."

"Why the hell will it?"

"Simply put, milord, the village doesn't have a jail."

"No jail?"

"No, milord."

"What about St. Keverne? Is there a jail down there?"

"There used to be, milord. But unfortunately, it burnt right down to the ground last year, and they've not yet been able to raise the funds to replace it."

"No jail." Prescott raked a hand through his hair in disbelief. "I'll be damned. I never heard of a place that didn't have a jail."

"Thee has now, milord."

"Just where have you been putting all the criminals who break your laws?"

Feeling embarrassed at his village's lack of detention facilities, Penhalligan cleared his throat and said quietly, "We put them under house arrest, milord."

"House arrest."

"Aye, milord."

Prescott couldn't dismiss the image of a man committing a crime then being forced to live in the comfort of his own home as punishment. What a hell of a place, he thought.

Suddenly the gears in his mind started clicking. House arrest. Home. His home, Ravens Lair, was a castle. A very, very old castle.

"I got it," he said with a self-satisfied grin. "I know the perfect place to put his sorry ass."

"Milord?"

"He can be under house arrest with the other rats in my dungeon."

"Your lordship's dungeon?"

"That's right, Penhalligan, my dungeon. Come on, give me a hand here." As he reached down to hoist the unconscious Emerson to his feet, the sheriff hurried to assist him.

"But, milord, the dungeon at Ravens Lair hasn't been used in centuries. The conditions there are probably most inhumane by now."

"You've seen it?"

"Aye. Once, as a lad, some chums and I sneaked into the dungeon to have ourselves a look. A frightful place it was."

As they tossed Emerson's limp body onto the back of Precott's horse, Prescott asked, "Had a lot of spiders, did it?"

"Aye, as well as shackles and chains on the wall, and other devices I dare not mention."

"Sounds good to me. Emerson here ought to feel right at home."

An hour later Prescott trudged up the cellar stairs, brushing cobwebs off his arms and shoulders. Though it was long past midnight, and he had just exerted a good deal of energy getting his semi-conscious prisoner settled into the darkest, dankest cell he could find in the dungeon, he felt wide awake, not the least bit tired.

Too much excitement, he told himself. Too much worry, too. The sheriff had been right—the dungeons at Ravens Lair hadn't been used in centuries, and they looked it. The condition of Emerson's cell was questionable at best, and it looked as if one good shove would tear the door clean off its hinges. The rusty shackles on the wall hadn't looked much stronger, either, but they would serve their purpose until Emerson went to trial for his crimes.

As he closed the cellar door behind him and started down the hall, he thought of a remedy for his sleepless state, one that had served him well in past years. A good stiff shot of bourbon would help to settle him down.

However, upon reaching the library and lighting a lamp to aid him in his quest, he soon discovered that the castle had no bourbon on hand. Only a bottle of something labeled Single Malt Whiskey from a distillery in Scotland. Prescott frowned. What the hell was single malt whiskey?

Only one way to find out, he decided, removing the stopper. Besides, sampling the stuff himself would be much better than waking up Mrs. Sweet from a sound sleep and having her take a midnight inventory of the castle's liquor supply. He knew she wouldn't appreciate that. But first thing in the morning he would make sure that a bottle or two of Kentucky's finest bourbon was added to her next shopping list.

He took a precautionary sniff, wanting to make certain he would be drinking whiskey and not furniture polish that somebody had poured into an empty whiskey bottle. His Aunt Em had made that kind of substitution before without telling anybody. Unfortunately, to his everlasting regret, he'd been the one to make the discovery.

Satisfied that the bottle contained spirits and that no one was awake at this hour to catch him, he turned the bottle up to his lips. A healthy swig had a pleasant fire burning at the back of his throat, one that burned all the way down to the pit of his stomach. It settled there into a nice, comforting glow that instantly obliterated some of the day's tensions.

"Mmm, not bad," he muttered, and took another swig. Single malt whiskey wasn't bourbon and never would be, but it wasn't bad. In fact, if he had to, he could probably get used to the stuff.

Morning arrived with the normal sort of sleepy lethargy that evolved over the hours into a hectic hustle and bustle. After a cup of tea, the housemaids began scurrying about the kitchen, helping Mrs. Sweet prepare breakfasts for the earl, his guests, and the rest of the household staff. Tom came in from the stables just as his grandmother pulled the first tray of hot scones from the oven.

As was his habit, Hargreaves came down to prepare a tray before he returned with it up to his rooms in the servants' quarters. Although he was technically part of the staff, and therefore no different from any of the others, he preferred to keep himself distant, neither associating with them nor allowing himself to be involved in their petty squabbles. And he also wished to avoid having another unpleasant encounter with Esmeralda, whose mental faculties were somewhat questionable. Only two days ago the old lady had called him "young master" and tried to tie a bib around his neck.

Reaching the foot of the stairs, he turned, intending to go to the kitchen, but an odd noise coming from the direction of the library stopped him. He listened intently for a moment, trying to decipher the strange sounds. In the end, he could only conclude that a wounded animal had somehow made its way into the castle overnight and was now letting its presence be known.

Suddenly, he had another thought, one more frightening, and he all but raced toward the closed library doors. First his lordship had brought home a poor relation, then a baby lamb, and then three little girls. Heaven only knew what he'd dragged in overnight.

"Oh, God, him and his strays," Hargreaves muttered as he flung open the doors.

"There's a yeller rose in Texas that I am gonna seeee . . . Da-da-da dum dee da-da . . . not half as much as meee . . ."

His voice ringing loudly and unpleasantly off-key, Prescott lay on the leather sofa, his booted feet hanging off one arm and his head lolling off the other. In his hand an empty bottle waved back and forth in the air.

"Milord!"

"I cried so when I left her . . . it dang near broke my heart, but da-dum dee dum dee da-da . . . we never more would part."

"*Milord!*"

Prescott turned a pair of bleary, red-rimmed eyes toward the doorway and grinned broadly. "Ed! How you doin'?"

"Better than you, I dare say, milord."

"Come on over here and have a drink."

"It's a bit early in the day for us to begin consuming spirits, milord. We normally wait until early evening." Hargreaves cautiously made his way to the sofa, hoping he could maintain a certain degree of decorum about this most unsavory situation. One of them had to remain dignified, and since his lordship seemed totally incapable of doing anything at the moment, except perhaps passing out, he supposed the dignity was left up to him. What an absolute heathen, he thought.

"It is evening. Fact, it's past midnight."

"Well past, milord."

"Huh?"

"It's morning, milord."

"Morning?" Prescott struggled to turn over, intending to look out the window, but he turned much quicker than he planned to and fell off the couch onto the floor. "Danged if it ain't."

Grumbling beneath his breath, Hargreaves helped Prescott to his feet. "Has your lordship been to bed yet?"

Prescott frowned, trying to recall. "I think so. Once. Oh, yeah, now I remember. The baby peed on the bed last night and got me all wet. Then Lucinda came home and I went out. Hey, did you know we've got a dungeon here?"

"Yes, milord, we knew."

"It's old. And dirty. Somebody ought to clean it

up. Not too clean, though. Bastard like Emerson don't deserve a clean jail cell. Better off sticking him in a pigpen where he belongs. We got any pigs here, Ed?"

"Not to our knowledge, milord."

"We ought to get us some." Prescott waved his empty whiskey bottle in the air, bringing it dangerously close to Hargreaves' head. "Big old fat, dirty pigs that snort and wallow around in mud all day. Bet Emerson would feel right at home in a pig—Hey, what are you doing with my drink?"

Hargreaves wrested the empty bottle out of Prescott's hand. "Putting it aside, milord."

"Oh, is it all gone?"

"Yes, milord. You've drunk every last drop of it."

"Did I? I'll be. I thought I only took a couple of drinks. Well, that goes to show you how much I know."

"Yes, milord."

"You know, that single malt shit is dang good stuff, even if it ain't from Kentucky." Prescott burped loudly. "Scotland."

Hargreaves winced at the smell. "Beg pardon, milord?"

"I said it comes from Scotland. Funny, ain't it? I thought them sissy Scottish boys from up north only wore short skirts. Didn't know they could make whiskey as good as this. Still, it ain't quite as good as Kentucky sour mash. Now there's a drink for you. Put hair on your chest."

"Yes, milord." Bearing most of Prescott's considerable weight, Hargreaves headed slowly for the library door.

"Mescal, though— Whoa, boy! That shit'll make you go crazy. Heard that a couple of good old boys back home even went blind drinking that stuff." Now halfway across the room, Prescott came to a sudden stop, wrapping an arm around Hargreaves' neck and holding tight. "That wasn't mescal I was drinking, was it? Tell me it wasn't mescal."

"No, milord."

"You sure?"

"We could almost swear to it, milord."

"'Cause I think I done swallowed the dang worm."

Hargreaves didn't know what mescal was, nor did he wish to know what a worm would be doing in it, so he let the matter drop. He only prayed his lordship would let the matter drop as well and cease speaking. Unfortunately, his prayer was not to be answered.

"Where we goin'?" Prescott asked as Hargreaves led him down the hall and up the stairs.

"To your lordship's room."

"My room?"

"Yes, milord."

"Hey now, you ain't gonna try to undress me, are you?"

"No, milord."

"'Cause I don't like that, Ed. I don't like that one bit."

"I quite understand, milord."

"Nothing against you. You're a fine man. Kinda stiff, but you're all right."

"Yes, milord."

"See, the thing is, I been undressing myself since I was a little bitty boy."

"Yes, milord."

"Having another grown man take my clothes off of me makes me real uneasy-like. I ain't no sissy-boy, Ed."

"Of course not, milord."

"I like women."

"Yes, milord."

"'Course, it's been quite a while since I last—" Prescott broke off as a wave of nausea washed over him. "Oh, Ed, I don't feel so good."

"We understand, milord. We'll get you into bed and your lordship can—how do you Americans put it? Ah, yes, sleep it off."

"Yeah, sleep. That sounds pretty good. Tried to do that last night, but the baby peed on the bed."

"So you've said, milord."

"Pretty little baby. All three of them girls are pretty little babies. Like a little trio of blond, blue-eyed China dolls. Their mama's dead, you know?" Drunken tears welled up in Prescott's eyes and his voice developed a catch in it. "Sorry son of a bitch killed her."

"Milord?"

"You heard me. That bastard Emerson killed their mama. I know it as well as I know my own name, and them three little precious babies saw it all. I never knew my own mama, now they won't ever get to know theirs. Knew my daddy, though. Fine man. Real fine. Salt of the earth, my daddy was. He'd give you the shirt right off his back, and don't think them damn Calderwoods didn't try and take it, 'cause they did. Took his shirt, his pride, and in the end even took his wife. Would've tried to take me and Payne from him, but . . ."

Unable to make sense of half of his lordship's drunken ramblings, Hargreaves decided to ignore him. He had enough of his own problems with which to contend, the first and foremost being to get the tenth earl of St. Keverne safely settled into bed.

Hearing a noise out in the hall, Lucinda leaped out of bed and grabbed her robe. Thank God, Prescott had finally come home. She had waited up half the night for him, only to end up going to bed just before dawn, still quite concerned about the outcome of his confrontation with Emerson.

As she opened the door, Hargreaves was just passing her room, half-carrying, half-dragging Prescott down the hall to his chambers. "Oh, my! What happened?"

"His lordship isn't feeling well, miss. One too many drams of whiskey."

"Oh, whiskey." Lucinda willed her pounding heart to return to a more natural rhythm. At first she had feared that Prescott's condition was due in part to injuries he might have sustained from Emerson.

"Yes, miss," Hargreaves said. "We've learned through the years that when one is overcome with drink, as his lordship is, the only solution is to put one to bed and let one sleep it off."

"That sounds like a very good— No, no! You can't do that."

"Miss?"

"You can't put him to bed. Well, not his bed at any rate. The children are still in it."

"Ah, yes, the children. We had forgotten."

"They mustn't see him in this condition."

"No, of course not, miss."

"They wouldn't understand, and we mustn't alarm the poor little things any more than they already are. Their mother died yesterday, you know."

"So we were told, miss. But if not his lordship's bed, then whose?"

"Oh, heavens. Well, mine, I suppose."

"Yours, miss?"

"Yes. It's right here, and I know it's fit to be slept in. I have no idea what condition the other bedchambers are in; it's been years since anyone has had need of them. And we can't put his lordship in just any room."

"No, miss." Although Hargreaves did envision a pile of hay in the stables as a suitable enough place for this drunken earl. At least the American would feel right at home there.

"Here, bring him on inside. I'll just have a quick look at the children to make certain they're still asleep, then I'll come back and gather up a few things."

"Yes, miss." As Lucinda hurried down the hallway, Hargreaves dragged his heavy burden inside the room. In his years of service as a gentleman's gentleman, he had taken orders of all kinds, even those he considered questionable. But this had to be one of the most highly questionable orders he had ever received. A young lady, even one of lesser breeding, giving up her own bed to a drunken lord? While it might be considered charitable in some circles, in others it would be looked on as a gross breach of propriety. But then, the entire castle household seemed to fit that mold.

Prescott, still muttering a disconnected monologue of his life story, didn't protest when Hargreaves lowered him to Lucinda's unmade bed and began pulling off his clothes. The boots came off first, of course, handled with great care due to the dried mud and manure caked on the heels.

"I didn't love her," Prescott said, his arms flung

out wide on the mattress as he let Hargreaves do his work. "Thought I did for a while, but I really didn't. Just needed a wife, and she was handy. Chloe was sweet and all, and I'd have done anything for her, but if I'd married her, we'd have both been miserable. She's better off with Payne."

"We're sure she is, milord." Any woman on the face of the earth would be better off with any other man where this lout was concerned, Hargreaves thought to himself. "Let's slip out of these trousers now, shall we?"

Prescott lifted his head and looked down the length of his body as the valet undid the fastenings on his britches. "He's my twin brother, you know."

"This Payne person you're speaking of, milord?"

"Yeah. My identical twin." He continued to stare at Hargreaves, a frown forming on his forehead. "You know something, you look a little bit like him. Damn! Is that you, Payne?"

"No, milord. We are Hargreaves, your lordship's valet. In the future, please be so kind as to remember that. We are not Ed. We are Hargreaves!"

"Yeah, I know, I know." Prescott's head flopped back onto the bed as an all-consuming dizziness washed over him. "I swear, Ed, that worm's done got me. I thought it was laying dead in the bottom of that bottle of mescal, but it wasn't; it was alive. Still is, too. I can feel the dang thing crawling around inside my belly right now."

His face set in stony angles, Hargreaves refused to reply. He knew that this uncouth American would never learn the proper sort of behavior for a noble member of the peerage. He may have been born into a noble family, but he had not one ounce of nobility about him. It would take him a hundred years or more to acquire that sort of breeding. But, with luck, he would leave within the year.

Finished with his most unsavory task to date, Hargreaves flung a sheet over the top of the new earl and exited the room.

Unaware that his valet had departed, Prescott continued to mutter to himself about the dangers he faced from the worm. "If I keep this up, I'll go blind and crazy before I'm forty. God, why is it so hot in here?" He kicked at the sheet, succeeding in uncovering only one long, hairy leg. "Somebody put out the fire or open up a window. I'm 'bout to melt."

He drifted off into a light sleep, vaguely wishing that his dream mate would come to him as she had so often in the past and ease his pain. But his dream mate didn't come, and he knew deep in his soul that she never would. She was no longer a dream to him, but a real person, one who knew pain and heartache and loneliness as deeply as he did. One, furthermore, who was probably going to be mad as hell at him for drinking so much mescal and swallowing that damn worm.

The feeling of something soft and warm fluttering over him pulled Prescott out of his light sleep. Ed, he told himself, was beginning to act like an old mother hen. He opened one eye to a narrow slit, intending to let his valet know just how much he didn't appreciate all the attention. A man in his condition needed to be left alone, not hovered over.

Though at first slightly blurred, his gaze began to sharpen, finally focusing on something that both shocked and pleased him. Mere inches from his nose were the tops of a pair of creamy breasts nestled inside a white lacy gown. Both of Prescott's eyes opened wide and he inhaled slowly, the faint scent of roses drifting up from the generous cleavage making him smile.

"Ed, you lucky bastard. You've got tits."

Embarrassed color suffusing her face as she jerked upright, Lucinda clutched the folds of her dressing gown close to her throat. Heavens above, she had thought he was asleep. Had she known he wasn't, she wouldn't have put her reputation at risk by returning to the room to collect a change of clothes. And she certainly wouldn't have pulled the sheet over him when she'd seen him lying half uncovered in bed. What he must be thinking!

"Prescott?" She called his name softly, wanting to allay immediately any misconceptions he might have made about her. But the heavily lashed lids had already closed over his bloodshot green eyes and soft snores were coming from his lax mouth.

Certain that he was finally asleep, she quietly gathered up her clothes. But as she started to leave the room a moment later, an urgent need made her pause and take one last look at him. He looked so handsome asleep there in her bed, so right at home. She wondered how it would feel to lie next to him, to smell his manly scent, to sleep in the warm security of his embrace throughout the night. Probably quite wonderful, she thought. Too bad she would never get the chance to experience such a wonder.

14

"Why isn't Uncle Prescott coming with us?" Alexandra asked.

Because the fool finished off a half bottle of whiskey and is as drunk as a besom. The moment Lucinda had the thought, she knew full well she couldn't relay that fact to the girls. At their impressionable ages, they wouldn't understand.

"I'm afraid your Uncle Prescott is feeling a bit under the weather today." With baby Elizabeth perched on her hip and Victoria holding on tight to her hand, Lucinda let Alexandra lead the way up the narrow staircase to the attics.

Both she and the children were in desperate need of clothes. What few things she'd had had gone up in flames along with her house. The children, on the other hand, needed things more suitable for their new station in life than the clean rags they were wearing. But with Prescott feeling so "under the weather" until heaven knew when, and with no money to purchase new garments, the only solution to the problem that Lucinda could see was to take them on an excursion through the trunks in the attic.

"What's that mean, 'under the weather,' Aunt Lucinda?"

"Er, it means that he's ill," she said. "But you're not to worry. He'll be right as rain in a few days."

"Is he going to have a baby like our mummy?"

"A baby? Certainly not. Men can't have babies, Alexandra. Only women can have them."

"When are you going to have a baby, Aunt Lucinda?"

Ah, the incessant curiosity of the innocent, Lucinda thought, hiding a smile. "I don't know."

"Don't you want one?"

"Perhaps some day." If only she could find the right man—and one who would have her—before she was too old to conceive. In some respects, Prescott seemed almost to be the right man. He was certainly sweet and kind and extremely gentle with her and the children and the other members of the household staff; qualities she most admired in a man. Of course, he had a man's temper, but he had only exhibited it when the situation warranted, which wasn't often, thank heaven.

Without warning, a wispy image of herself and Prescott in the years to come floated through her mind. She could see them marrying, having children, then grandchildren, all the while growing old together happily.

Realizing the disastrous direction in which her thoughts were headed, she gave her head a brisk shake. "Right now," she said, "we should be thinking of finding all of us something to wear. Not babies—clothes, all right?"

"All right," Alexandra said. "I want a red dress."

"Red? Victoria darling, watch this last step, it's rather a steep one. There's a good girl."

"Yes, I like red, Aunt Lucinda."

A short trek along a narrow corridor led them to a door. Lucinda released the toddler's hand long enough to dig down into the pocket of her skirt for the key she had put there earlier. "Well, if we can find a red dress near your size, Alexandra, you shall certainly have it. Now, Victoria, you're not to go wandering about exploring on your own, do you understand? You're to stay close to me at all times."

The toddler looked up at her with wide blue eyes full of innocent wonder. "Why?"

"Because there are lots of boxes and trunks inside, and I wouldn't want you climbing on them and getting hurt."

"I won't let her climb on anything, Aunt Lucinda," Alexandra said sagely.

"Good girl. I knew I could count on you, Alexandra."

Lucinda opened the door and they entered the vast, dusty world of Ravens Lair's attics, where centuries' worth of Trefarrow family relics, discards, and once-cherished memorabilia lay ignored in piles. In the first and largest of the rooms, old pieces of furniture were stacked nearly to the ceiling. A second and smaller adjoining room had become the final resting place for landscapes, still lifes, and portraits of family members deemed unworthy of hanging in the hallowed second-floor gallery. Here, too, were odd knick-knacks and crates of books and ledgers.

Having gone searching for clothes in the castle's attics the morning after her cottage burnt down, Lucinda couldn't help but notice that a number of the boxes now lay open, their contents spilling out onto the bare wood floor. Strange, she thought, studying one or two pages from a journal. She couldn't recall this clutter being here before. But perhaps it had been here and she had merely failed to notice it. Ignoring something so obvious as a messy storage room was easily understood, considering her state of mind at the time of her first visit. One couldn't lose one's home and everything one held dear in life without suffering some small degree of shock.

"Are we going to tidy it up, Aunt Lucinda?"

"No, we aren't, Alexandra." She looked down into the child's wide, inquisitive blue eyes and smiled. "The person who made this mess can do that."

"Do ghosts tidy up?"

"Ghosts?" Alexandra's unexpected query made Lucinda laugh. "Whatever gave you the idea that a ghost did this?"

"We heard it."

"You heard a ghost here in the attics?" Both Alexandra and Victoria nodded. "When?"

"Last night," Alexandra said.

Lucinda decided that the child's accounting could only be that of an active imagination. They couldn't have heard anything, especially not a ghost. After all, they had only arrived at the castle yesterday, and last night they had slept in Prescott's room.

"The ceiling squeaked like someone was walking on it," Alexandra added. "They went from one side of the room to the other and back again, making all sorts of noises. Didn't they, Victoria?"

As the three-year-old nodded, Lucinda felt a cold chill crawl up her spine. There had been stories of ghosts haunting Ravens Lair for centuries, she had even told Prescott about them, but that's all they had been—stories. Yet these two impressionable little girls actually thought they had heard one of those ethereal apparitions walking across the ceiling.

Ridiculous, she told herself. Such a thing was absolutely ridiculous, because there were no such things as ghosts. Elderly, absentminded maids who took pieces of jewelry and ladies' finery from one room only to leave them in another, yes, but Esmeralda was not a ghost.

"We screamed out ever so loudly," Alexandra said.

"You did?"

"Mmm-hmm. That's when Uncle Prescott came and took us to bed in his room."

"Then Uncle Prescott must have heard the ghost, too," Lucinda said.

"No, he didn't. We told him about it, but he said our screams must have frightened it away."

The more she thought about it, the more Lucinda realized that Alexandra had to be telling the truth, not simply employing an active imagination as she had first assumed. It was quite obvious that these trunks and crates had been tampered with. For someone to go to the trouble of searching them, they would have to move things about, and moving things would most certainly register in the rooms below. As it happened, the rooms lying directly below the attics were the nurseries.

"He said we should always let someone know when we're afraid."

"Uncle Prescott's right, you should," Lucinda said, wanting the children to know that they would be safe and protected while under Prescott's watchful care. "Any time you feel frightened, you're to call out for help, do you understand?"

"Even late at night?" Alexandra asked.

"The hour doesn't matter. Someone will hurry to you to scare away all the bad dreams. And don't worry about hearing any more noises like the ones you heard last night."

"Did we really scare the ghost away?"

"That wasn't a ghost you heard, Alexandra."

"It wasn't?"

"No. It was probably just one of the maids rummaging around up here, looking for something."

"They wanted pretty new frocks, too?"

No, more like papers or documents of some sort, Lucinda thought, eyeing the loose pages scattered over the floor. "Well, if that's what they were looking for, they didn't find it here, did they? The clothing trunks are in the next room, but they probably didn't know that." Or they had known it and hadn't cared. "Come on, let's go see what we can find."

"Remember, I want a red frock," Alexandra said, following Lucinda.

"Yes, darling, I remember."

"With lots of lace and ruffles."

"We'll see, Alexandra. We'll see."

The morning's foray into the attics resulted in each of the girls acquiring a dozen frocks and a few necessary undergarments that, though previously worn by much earlier juvenile inhabitants of the castle, still looked relatively new. Lucinda even found some more things to add to her meager wardrobe. Alterations would have to be made, of course. Most of the little dresses had been made for children living in a much earlier time, but Lucinda felt certain she could handle the chore. She would have to; because the castle hadn't had a full-time seamstress living on the premises since the demise of the late earl's wife nearly thirty years ago.

On their return from the attics, Lucinda stopped by the sewing room near the nurseries on the third floor. The tapestry looms and the cupboards once bursting with fabrics, silk threads, and yarns now lay covered in dust. Though the room had the appearance of not having been entered in years, it brought to mind many memories of Lucinda's childhood. She had spent countless hours alone here, keeping out of everyone's way as she made clothes for her dolls and dreamed of what her life would be like when she became a woman. Well, she was that woman now, but she still had to wonder what the fates held in store for her.

"We'll just leave everything in here," she said, depositing the armload of dresses onto the wide worktable in the center of the room. "I'll get to them as soon as I can."

"Why can't we wear them now?" Alexandra ran her small hands over the deep burgundy velvet skirt of the dress she had chosen as her own.

"Because now it's time for us to have our elevenses. Besides, nothing here fits you properly. This one's a bit too long for you, and the others need to be taken in for your sisters."

"But I wanted Uncle Prescott to see me in my new red frock."

"He will, darling, but not right now. He's still asleep, remember?"

"That's right, I forgot," Alexandra said. "He's under the weather, isn't he?"

"Yes, he is." And when he awakened, he would probably suffer greatly for his indulgences, Lucinda thought with a sympathetic smile. Why she should feel sympathy for a man who had imbibed so much whiskey that it had rendered him unconscious she wasn't sure, but she did. She supposed that Prescott, like everyone else, had his own demons with which to wrestle. He merely chose to wrestle his with the aid of a bottle.

"When will he be better, Aunt Lucinda?"

"That's hard to say, Alexandra."

"Why is it, don't you know?"

"No, I don't. You see, I've never been under the weather as your Uncle Prescott is, so I can only guess. He may be up and about this afternoon in time for tea, his old chipper self again, but then, he may not come around until some time tomorrow."

"I don't think being under the weather is very nice."

Lucinda lovingly ran her hand over Alexandra's head. "No, darling, I dare say it isn't."

His head throbbing unmercifully as he slowly made his way down the main staircase, Prescott realized how grateful he was that the bright light of day had diminished into the subtle glow of early evening. The way he felt, having to look at bright light would probably kill him, for not only did his head throb, his eyes seemed to pulsate on their own, threatening to pop right out of their sockets each time he shifted his weight to take a step. But beyond all the physical agony he presently experienced lay the vague residue of an image that not only concerned him, but frightened him as well. For reasons he couldn't explain, he had a feeling that Hargreaves wasn't the man he'd first thought he was.

"Have we decided to have our tea early with Miss Lucinda and the children, milord?"

Prescott flinched, hearing his valet's voice directly behind him. He came to such a sudden stop that his head throbbed more unbearably, making him realize he couldn't make such abrupt movements in his present condition. Turning slowly, he tried to keep his eyes focused on the valet's face, but he soon realized that his gaze wanted to wander lower, to the man's chest. Giving in to the need, he saw that Ed's chest was as flat as any other man's, that he didn't have so much as a paunch to mar his well-maintained torso. Prescott had to wonder where the devil he had gotten the idea that Hargreaves had breasts.

"Tea?" Though he tried to speak softly, the sound of his voice reverberated loudly in Prescott's head.

"Yes, milord. We know that it's rather late, but your lordship did miss luncheon."

"I know I did, Ed. Thanks all the same, but I don't want any tea. What I *need* is coffee. Strong, hot coffee. The blacker, the better. A whole pot of it."

"Nothing to eat, milord?"

"Good God, no!" The very thought of putting solid food in his mouth caused Prescott's stomach to churn. He could still taste the worm he'd eaten earlier. Or had the worm actually eaten him? At this point, he wasn't sure.

"Very well, milord. We shall inform Mrs. Sweet that your lordship requests only coffee."

"Yeah, you do that, Ed." Taking a deep breath to bank down his rising gorge, Prescott started across the foyer to the library. He had work to do, and though he was in no shape at the moment to tackle it, he had to at least try.

He got no farther than a few feet when Hargreaves called out to him. "Milord?"

Coming to a stop more slowly this time, Prescott looked back at the valet. "Yeah?"

"Miss Lucinda and the children have been most concerned about your lordship's, er, shall we say condition? Does your lordship wish us to inform them that you are up and about and ready to receive visitors?"

Seeing Lucinda would be nice, Prescott thought. Listening to her soft, calming voice might make his head stop throbbing, or at least make it feel a little more tolerable. But he wasn't so sure that he could endure the little girls just yet. Like most children, they had a tendency to get a tad loud, and right now he didn't need loud, he needed all the peace and quiet he could get. "Maybe later, Ed. When I'm feeling more sociable."

"As your lordship wishes."

Prescott watched the valet turn to leave, but a sudden thought made him call out to him. "Er, there is something you could do for me, if you wouldn't mind."

"Of course we wouldn't, milord. After all, it is our job to serve you."

"Well, it's not exactly me who needs serving."

"Milord?"

"You see, Ed, we've got ourselves a . . . a guest, I 'spect you could call him."

"A guest, milord?"

"Yeah. He's staying down in the dungeon."

Hargreaves only reaction was to blink once. "In the dungeon?"

"It's a long story, and I ain't in no shape to go into it now, but I'd appreciate it if you'd see to it that he got something to eat 'fore the night's over. Don't give him anything too fancy. Bread and water'll suit him just fine."

Bread and water for a guest? Hargreaves resisted the urge to shake his head in disapproval. "Of course, milord. Will there be anything else?"

In response, Prescott waved a hand and turned to stagger into the library, shutting the door quietly behind him. If he could make it through the rest of the evening without disgracing himself, or falling down dead outright, he knew he could make it through just about anything. Somehow he was going to outlast this terrible physical affliction that the Almighty had decided to bestow on him and, when he did, he would never take another drink of single malt whiskey from Scotland again. Worms or no worms, the stuff was more deadly than any bottle of mescal he had ever tasted.

Gingerly sitting down at his desk, he eyed the few letters that awaited his inspection. How the devil was he supposed to read? His eyes could barely focus. And who the devil would be writing him anyway?

"Probably more bills," he muttered, and started to

toss the envelopes aside. But, noticing a familiar scrawl on one of the letters, he grabbed them up again. "Chloe?"

Praying that nothing bad had happened to his family back home in Texas, he quickly ripped open the envelope and pulled out the letter. After reading only two lines, he began to relax, his fears gradually dissipating. According to Chloe, all was well with everyone. Though Payne's education had been late in coming, he was doing a fairly good job of learning how to run the ranch. He'd gone on his first spring roundup with the hands, and had come home with stories of how he'd branded over a hundred head of new calves without branding himself once in the process.

Prescott laughed, envisioning Payne clearly. "The question is, little brother, how many times did you fall off your horse lassoing the silly critters?"

Reading on, he learned that Aunt Em had planted her garden, and that they'd be harvesting their biggest crop yet of okra, corn, potatoes, and green beans come summertime.

"God, what I wouldn't give for some of Aunt Em's delicious home cooking."

The Campbell sisters asked about him every time Chloe went to Waco. They were still unmarried, if Prescott was interested. Perhaps he should write to them, let them know what life in England was like.

"I got enough womenfolk in my life now. Too many, in fact. I dang sure don't need to add those three to my worries."

Though Chloe didn't have much to say about herself, she couldn't say enough about the baby. It seemed as though Prescott's little five-month-old niece was growing like a weed, had the smile and laugh of an angel, and was cutting new teeth almost daily.

He put the letter aside, the ache in his head descending and centering itself more closely to his heart. Lord, but he missed his family. What he wouldn't do, what he wouldn't give to see them, be with them again. The castle and estate of Ravens Lair might be his, but it wasn't home, and it never would be. Home to him was the rolling hills, the wide, grassy plains of North Texas, and the meandering Brazos River. Home was the people he loved most in this world, not this damp old castle that creaked and groaned every time the wind picked up.

"Cut it out, Trefarrow," he admonished himself, tossing Chloe's letter aside and grabbing the next. "You'll be bawling like a homesick baby in a minute."

The next letter obliterated any thoughts Prescott may have had of Texas and the ones he loved and had left behind. Cold fingers of dread raced up his spine as he read the neatly written lines on the expensive linen stationery.

"No!" he yelled at the top of his voice. "Damn it to hell, no!"

Lucinda, who had been walking past the library, heard his outburst and rushed in. "Prescott, whatever is the matter?"

"I'm doomed. Hell, darlin', we're all doomed."

"What is it?"

Unable to stand the renewed pain in his head, he lowered it to the desk, using his bent arm for a pillow. "They're coming here to Ravens Lair. God help us all."

"Who's coming to Ravens Lair?"

Without lifting his head, he held up the letter for her inspection. "Them, that's who."

Lucinda took the letter from him and as she read, she began to understand the reason behind his sudden outburst. "The Calderwoods and guests?"

"That's right."

"Aren't the Calderwoods your—"

"Yep, my mama's people." He looked up at her. "There's gonna be twenty of them."

"We can certainly entertain that many."

"Entertain them? Darlin', you're gonna have a hard enough job just trying to survive them. 'Cause when they all get here, we're not gonna stand a snowball's chance in hell."

"Honestly, Prescott, how bad could they be?"

"As bad as a plague of locusts. No, worse than that. They'll descend on us—them and all the friends they're bringing—and there won't be nothing left of us when they leave."

Lucinda knew she had to do something to reassure him—say the right thing. However, that right thing seemed to elude her. "They're not arriving until the end of the month. That gives us over three weeks to prepare for them."

"Three weeks, three months—we wouldn't have enough time if we had three years."

"But they say here in the letter that they'll be gone within a fortnight."

"A fortnight is two weeks, ain't it?"

"Yes."

Prescott shook his head. "No, that's too long. I spent dang near a whole month with those people, and I learned that two hours at a stretch is about all I can take of them. They'll run me crazy in two weeks—I just know they will."

"Oh, don't go on so. It probably won't be that bad, having them here."

"You don't know what bad is, darlin'. But you're fixing to find out."

15

Preparing for the arrival of the Calderwoods was like getting ready for a major battle. At least Prescott looked at it that way. But, never being one to join in a battle when it wasn't in his best interest to do so, he stayed well out of everyone's way, especially that of the housekeeper's.

Putting herself in charge of the cleaning brigade, Mrs. Sweet brought in every available woman she could find in the village to help her meager staff sweep, dust, mop, and polish every inch of floor, wall, ceiling, and furniture they came across. Empty bedrooms in the west wing that hadn't seen the light of day in years were readied for the arrival of his lordship's relatives and their friends. And when the west wing was finished, Mrs. Sweet's army began to tackle the east wing. That was when Prescott put his foot down.

"Enough's enough," he told Lucinda as they examined one of the spare bedrooms in the east wing. "I may have to spend my days with them people just to be sociable, but I'll be danged if I'm gonna spend my nights with them sleeping right down the hall from me."

"Be reasonable, Prescott. All we need is two extra bedrooms, and the only other rooms available are here in the east wing."

"I don't care. Double them up in the west wing if you have to, but keep them away from me."

"Double them up?"

"That's right."

"How do we do that?"

"Easy. You make them sleep two and three to a bed. Or better yet, spread pallets for them on the floor."

"We can't do that. It's—it's inhospitable."

He gave her a glare. "So are the Calderwoods."

"Oh, for heaven's sake, they're your family."

"I know." He groaned. "Don't remind me."

Lucinda took a deep breath and tackled the issue from a different angle. "Need I remind you that they're only going to be here for a few days?"

"That's what you think. I know my kinfolk better than you do. They're all alike—every last one of them. They may say they're only gonna be here for a few days, but I'll bet you a dollar to a dime they figure out a way of staying on for a month or more." He fell silent for a moment, a thoughtful frown forming on his forehead. "I gotta come up with a way of getting rid of them."

Surprised by this mean-spirited streak in him that she had never before seen, Lucinda could only shake her head. "They're not even here yet, and you're already scheming how to rid yourself of them."

"Yeah, it's called self-defense, darlin'."

"Self-defense, indeed. I suppose if they make too many demands on your time you'll toss them down in the dungeon with Garrick."

"Hey, now there's an idea! Naw, that wouldn't work."

"Of course it wouldn't."

"The dungeon ain't nearly big enough for that bunch. The walls and chains ain't sturdy enough, either."

"Oh, you're impossible, Prescott Trefarrow."

"No, darlin', I'm desperate. There's a difference. I don't think I've ever been this desperate in my life. You don't understand. The Calderwoods— well, they ain't like you and me. They ain't like anybody we know, as a matter of fact. What in the Sam Hill am I gonna do?"

The concerned tone of Prescott's voice told Lucinda that he was more than a bit upset with the pending arrival of his relatives; he was truly worried. And she thought she knew why. Though he had told her very little about his life prior to coming to England, she knew enough to know that the Calderwoods had treated his father and mother and, later, his twin brother Payne quite badly. They had been cold, supercilious, judgmental people, believing themselves to be in the right while everyone else was in the wrong and therefore not worthy of their attentions, let alone their affections. Prescott, on the other hand, was one of the most generous, caring men Lucinda had ever known. And, as such, how could he pretend to tolerate even for a short time those who had been so cruel to family members he had loved? He couldn't, of course, and therein lay his dilemma. If he refused to let them come to Ravens Lair, he would be no better than they. Yet, not being a hypocrite, he couldn't welcome them with open arms, either.

"You'll do what you have to do," she said, wishing she could ease his concerns. "I know you're not pleased with all this, but you can't turn your back on them."

"You're telling me. They might try to stab me."

"Oh, rubbish. They'll do no such thing. In a pinch, simply stay out of their way and let them entertain themselves for the length of their visit."

"Yeah, I suppose I could do that."

"After all, you are the Earl of St. Keverne, and as such you have certain responsibilities that must be seen to daily."

"I do? I mean, yeah, of course I do."

"Naturally, I'm not suggesting that you should always absent yourself from their activities. You would have to join them a time or two. After all, this is their holiday, and they are traveling all the way down from London just to visit you."

"Some holiday it's gonna be," Prescott muttered, "calling on kinfolk they don't even know."

Holiday. The word slowly took root in Prescott's mind and began to grow. Holiday, holiday. The Calderwoods were coming the first of July.

"Damnation, darlin', that's it!"

"What is?"

The smile that split across his face seemed to light up the whole room, and it caused Lucinda's heart to trip inside her chest.

"We're gonna give those people the biggest, the best dang holiday they've ever had."

Her wide gray eyes blinked in confusion as he drew close to her. "We are?"

"You bet. This'll be one visit they never forget." Beaming, he grabbed her by the shoulders and would have given her a hug had not another feeling suddenly took hold. Before his conscience had a chance to take hold, he lowered his head and claimed her lips with his.

Prescott meant only to give her a kiss of thanks for coming up with the solution to his problem. But the moment his lips touched hers and he tasted her intoxicating sweetness, his gratitude evolved into something more potent, something that unlocked all the emotions and needs he had kept suppressed for so long. A warmth began to spread through his loins, a warmth that grew slowly, steadily into a blazing inferno.

Unprepared for the onslaught of Prescott's kiss, or for the intense hunger she felt behind it, Lucinda all but reeled in his embrace. Her limbs suddenly weak, she let herself melt against him. All too soon, she realized just how well, just how perfectly they fit, their forms contouring to one another as if they were meant for each other, as if they were made to be together. She had never felt this way with any man before—so wanted, so needed, so, oh, God, so loved. She wanted this moment to last forever. And if it were at all possible, she would willingly crawl inside Prescott's skin and become a part of him, never to be separated.

Sanity returned to Prescott when he realized what he was doing and to whom he was doing it. Breathing hard, he slowly pulled away and stared down at Lucinda's still-closed eyes. Her lips, still flushed and parted, continued to beckon loudly to him, begging him to resume his lustful attentions. But he had just enough presence of mind to ignore their call.

"Whoa!" he said. "What the hell just happened?"

Lucinda opened her eyes and tried to focus on him. "Huh?"

"Come on, darlin', snap out of it. You keep looking at me like that, I'm gonna be tempted to do something that we both might regret."

Lucinda swallowed and blinked, dragging deep breaths of air into her lungs in the hopes that the simple act of breathing would restore her self-control. "I—I don't know what you mean."

"Yeah, just like I thought. You felt it too, didn't you?"

"Felt what?"

"That kiss we just— Oh, but that wasn't just any kiss, was it? Hell, darlin', that was a"—he wracked his brain for just the right word— "a *kiss.*"

"Yes, it was, wasn't it?"

"You kiss men like that often?"

The last shred of her sensual lethargy fled in the face of a surge of indignation. She stiffened her spine and stepped well away from him. "How dare you insinuate such a thing! I'll have you know that I don't kiss men at all. You happen to be the first."

"Good thing. You kiss like that all the time, why, half the men in this country would be killing each other just for you to give them a little peck on the cheek."

"Oh, really, Prescott. It was nothing more than a friendly kiss between cousins."

"Ha! There wasn't a dang thing cousinly about that kiss. You know it, and I know it, 'cause we both felt it."

"I know no such thing, and how do you know what I felt?"

"'Cause I felt you feel it, darlin'."

She made small, flustered sounds for a moment until the ability to speak came back to her. "You're making a mountain out of a molehill."

"I'm not, but kissing me that way, you almost did. If we hadn't stopped— Well, it's just a good thing we did stop. A man in my condition can't take too much of that at one time without wanting a whole lot more."

"What on earth are you talking about?"

"I know you're a sweet young thing, darlin', but you're not quite that inexperienced."

"About some things, I am. Namely, understanding riddles like yours."

"Riddles?"

"Yes, riddles. One moment we're talking about feelings—*my* feelings in particular—and then it's mountains and molehills, and then something about you being a man in some kind of condition. I just don't—" She broke off abruptly as the answer came to her in a flash. Before she could stop herself, she glanced down at the front of Prescott's trousers, which now possessed a bulge that she hadn't noticed before. Heat instantly suffusing her face, her gaze flew back up to his. "Oh, my!"

"So you do know what I'm talking about."

"Oh, my word, yes!"

"Now don't go getting all flustered on me, darlin'."

"I'll be as flustered as I please, thank you. That—that's not my doing."

Prescott laughed. "No, I admit it's partly my doing. But you helped a little."

"I did no such thing."

"Look, don't get scared. It's just a natural part of me being a man. It ain't the least bit harmful. Well, not all the time, least ways."

"But it is unseemly. Make it go away."

"It will. You just gotta give it some time is all."

Not knowing what to do, or how to hurry up the departure of his "condition," she turned around and headed for the bedroom window. "A change of subject is called for right about now, don't you think?"

"Yeah, that might work." Though deep in his heart, Prescott couldn't guarantee it. His "condition" seemed to have developed a mind of its own. Instead of fading away, it kept getting stronger.

"Good."

"So, what do we talk about?"

She eyed the draperies. "These curtains. I think they should be taken down and thoroughly cleaned, don't you?"

Willing to go along with her game because he didn't know what else to do, he walked up behind her and eyed the old, faded fabric. "I don't know. They look to me like they'd fall apart in the first wash."

"Well then, perhaps we should consider replacing them."

Prescott took a deep breath and realized he had done the wrong thing. Not only did he get a faint whiff of the dust that still lingered in the room, but along with it was the heady fragrance of Lucinda's clean, flowery scent. It only served to entice him more, making his condition all the more unbearable.

"Oh, hell," he groaned, grabbing her shoulders and turning her around to face him. "Nice try, darlin', but you'd better face it—I have. We're doomed."

Letting hunger guide his every movement, his head descended and his lips claimed hers. Lucinda issued a tiny whimper of protest in the back of her throat before she gave in to the sensation again and melted against him. The need for him to hold her, to kiss her again was so strong, she couldn't deny it.

Obviously, he was right, she thought dazedly. They were doomed. Her mind kept telling her that she belonged to Prescott in every way that mattered, so she might as well accept her fate willingly. Heaven knew, her heart and soul already belonged to him, and it was just a matter of time before she knew her body would be his as well.

Lips parted and tongues explored. Hands slowly searched into private places hidden by clothes, finding regions that tantalized and excited and elicited soft little cries. Needs grew stronger.

But, once again, reason returned.

His heart beating a ragged tattoo in his chest, Prescott pulled away and held her at arm's length. "That settles it. You and me are getting married."

"What?"

"You heard me. I said we're getting married."

"Married!"

"That's right. We can't go on like this and still be decent. Hell, *I* can't go on like this and *you* still stay decent."

"But I can't marry you."

"Why the hell not?"

Pain suddenly began to replace the joy in Lucinda's heart. The two of them holding each other and kissing each other had all been so beautiful, so right, and then he had gone and destroyed it all with his unorthodox proposal. "We just can't, that's all."

"Oh, no. You've gotta give me a better reason than that."

"I don't know what to say."

"You don't have to. I know. It's because we're cousins, isn't it?"

"That's part of it, yes."

"We're third cousins, darlin'. Or is it fourth; I forget. Oh, hell, it don't make no never mind no how. We're not that close. Ain't nobody gonna say nothing."

"That's where you're wrong. They will say something, don't you see?"

"See what? We're two people who want each other. Just 'cause we're cousins shouldn't keep us from doing what's right. Besides, cousins get married all the time."

"Not cousins like us." Lucinda turned away, not wanting Prescott to see the tears that were welling up in her eyes. "You forget, Prescott. You're an earl."

"So?"

"You're an earl, and I'm a bastard."

Grabbing hold of her shoulders, he whirled her around to face him. "Dammit, now don't you start talking like that. I've told you before, I don't hold with you calling yourself that name."

"Even when it's a fact that neither of us can ignore?"

"I'm not ignoring it. It just don't matter to me, that's all."

"Well, it matters to me. And I assure you, it will matter to everyone else."

"Yeah, but I ain't marrying everyone else, darlin'. I'm marrying you."

"No, you're not. I can't let you destroy yourself. I won't let you."

Tears streaming down her cheeks, Lucinda raced out of the bedroom.

Prescott stood there for a moment longer, stunned that she could be so concerned about what everyone else would think. He didn't care what anybody else thought. He loved her, and he wanted to be with her. He wanted to share his life with her. He wanted to watch her grow old, surrounded by their children and grandchildren, and, if God was willing, their great-grandchildren.

"Dammit to hell!" He turned and raced after her.

16

Lucinda's skirts flew behind her as she raced down the stairs. Prescott caught up with her before she could reach the second floor landing. He had no idea where she was running, nor did he care. He grabbed hold of her arm and directed her toward his room.

"Please, Prescott, let go of me."

"Nope. We need to have ourselves a little talk, darlin'."

"We've talked enough."

"The hell we have."

As they passed by a doorway, Miranda suddenly appeared and Prescott stopped. "The kids are taking a nap," he said.

Confusion flooded the young upstairs maid's face as she bobbed a curtsy. "Yes, milord."

"No, dammit. They're napping now, but when they wake up, you watch them."

"Watch them, milord?"

"Yeah, watch them."

"But I ain't a nanny, milord. Governess, neither."

"All you gotta do, Miss Miranda, is just watch them. Play with them, read them a story, do whatever the hell you think will keep those three little girls happy for a while." *Happy, occupied, and well out of my way,* he added silently.

"Milord?"

"Just do it, Miss Miranda."

"Y—yes, milord."

Reaching his quarters, Prescott ushered Lucinda inside the sitting room. "Now then, all this nonsense you've been blathering about is—"

"We've succeeded in mending that rip in your lordship's trousers," Hargreaves said, appearing sullen-faced in the bedroom doorway.

"Damnation!" Prescott couldn't hide his frustration. Who the devil was going to pop up next? Miss Esmeralda? Lord help him if it was that poor old soul.

"In the future, we would appreciate being notified of any rips and tears in our garments. As your lordship well knows, the sooner we mend them, the better. Your lordship's wardrobe is not that extensive."

Holding on to Lucinda with one hand, Prescott motioned to the door with the other. "What I got suits me, Ed, but I'll be sure to keep that in mind. Now would you leave me and Miss Lucinda alone for a while? We've got some important family business to go over."

"Yes, milord." Hargreaves started for the door, but he stopped and looked back at the pair, noticing the redness about the young woman's eyes. "Will your lordship and Miss Lucinda be having your elevenses here or in the morning room?"

"The morning room, Hargreaves," Lucinda said, a definite sternness underlying the tremor in her voice.

"We won't be having our elevenses at all," Prescott said, "if we don't get our talk finished."

"Don't be ridiculous, Prescott. We've nothing to talk about, and you know it."

Hargreaves noted the way in which the earl all but glared at his young cousin, his jaw developing a hard edge to it as a vein began to throb at his temple. If he didn't know better, he would swear that the close friendship between the cousins had become strained. So strained, in fact, that it looked to be on the verge of breaking in two.

"What I know is that I'm dealing with one of the hardheadedest women I've ever met in my life."

"Me, hardheaded? What about you? You refuse to face the truth."

"What truth?"

"You know very well what truth."

Uncomfortable with the situation developing in front of him, Hargreaves cleared his throat and backed toward the door. "We shall inform Mrs. Sweet that your lordship wishes to postpone his elevenses."

Prescott ignored his valet completely. "Darlin', if I knew what truth you were talking about, would I be asking you to explain it to me?"

"Oh, you can't be that blind, Prescott. Mule-headed, perhaps, but not blind."

"We shall postpone high tea as well," Hargreaves said, and closed the door behind him.

Hearing the latch click, Prescott turned loose of Lucinda long enough to stalk to the door and turn the key in the lock. He wanted no more interruptions from anyone. "I may be a little dense about some things, but I ain't mule-headed. And my eyesight's as good as it's ever been. It's you that's shortsighted."

"Me? At least I know a potential disaster in the making when I see it."

"What disaster are you talking about?"

"Us, of course. If we continue on in this vein, Prescott, we shall be courting certain disaster. No good can come of it. No good at all."

"But I love you."

Fresh tears sprang up in Lucinda's eyes. His words, so simply spoken, began chipping away at her stern resolve to distance herself from what he wanted and needed, and especially from what he desired. For she feared that his wants and needs and desires were exactly the same as hers. But now, hearing him say that he loved her, she knew it would be easier for her to stop living and breathing than to go on denying her true feelings for him.

"And I love you," she said. "But that still doesn't change the fact that I can't marry you. That I *won't* marry you."

"Why the hell not?"

"Oh, for God's sake, Prescott. Why do I have to keep repeating myself? You're an earl, and I'm a—"

"Don't say it. Dammit to hell, Lucinda, don't you dare say it."

"But it's the truth. We can't ignore it. You and I—we can never be as you wish us. We can never be man and wife. I'm a low-born bastard who doesn't know the name of her own father, and you have a centuries-old, honored lineage with a position in society to maintain. Think how it would look to your peers if you should marry someone like me."

"I don't give a damn how it would look to them, because I don't give a damn about them or what they think. And I'll let you in on a little-known fact—I never wanted this title. I want it even less now, 'cause it's the one thing that's standing in the way of you becoming my wife. Hell, I've got half a notion just to give the damn thing back."

"You can't do that."

"Watch me."

Frightened by the hardness in his tone, she knew he was serious and that he might well relinquish his title solely for the sake of obtaining her hand in marriage. But she couldn't let him do something so rash; the consequences would be too far-reaching.

"Don't you care what happens to Ravens Lair?"

"Not a whole lot, no. It's fixing to fall down around our ears now; let it go ahead and do it."

"What about the people?"

"What about them?"

"Simply put, Prescott, they depend on you as their liege lord, and they depend on this estate, *your* estate, for their livelihoods. They have done so for centuries. If you relinquish your title, you will harm them irreparably."

"Well, hell, I'll just deed all the land over to them then. They're the ones who work it, they're the ones who ought to have it, not me."

"You forget that Ravens Lair is entailed. You can't simply step aside with no heir to take your place. Every square inch of the earldom of St. Keverne will revert to the crown. I'm sure that, in time, Queen Victoria would name a new earl, but—"

"But nothing. Let the queen have it. That suits me just fine."

"But don't you see? It mightn't suit the farmers and villagers who have lived here all their lives. The new earl could quite easily take it upon himself to have everyone evicted from their homes and install his own people. They would have to roam the countryside looking for new places to live and raise their families."

"Oh, come on. You know as well as I do that that ain't gonna happen."

"I know no such thing. History has an unfortunate way of repeating itself. Mass evictions have happened before; they could happen again."

Feeling trapped by Lucinda's logic, as well as her unending sympathy toward the people of St. Keverne, Prescott emitted a frustrated groan and stalked toward the window. Blindly, he stared out at the green sweep of lawn below, catching a tiny glimpse of the white-capped ocean in the far distance. How could one woman have so much concern for others and so little for herself? For that matter, how could she have so little for him?

"I only know one thing, darlin'," he said, turning to face her. "I love you. I've done a lot of things in my life—some of them I'm not too proud of. But I'll tell you this, I've never told a woman that I loved her before."

"Oh, Prescott."

"I hate this life I'm having to live. It's not who I am. But, as much as I hate it, I love you even more. If you want me to stay on here and be a dadblamed earl, then, by God, I'll stay on. I'll do whatever I have to to make you happy, to make you love me."

"But don't you see? I already love you. I think I fell in love with you the first moment I saw you, when you came sweeping into my life and rescued that silly bonnet for me."

He took her in his arms and held her close, his eyes closed as he breathed in the clean scent of her hair. "Then have mercy, Lucinda, and marry me. Be my wife. Be the mother of my children. Grow old with me."

Well aware that her hour of reckoning had at last arrived, she knew that if she were to try and deny Prescott his needs and desires she would only be denying her own. She was his—heart, mind, soul, and, if he so desired it, body as well.

She pulled out of his embrace and took his face in her hands, looking deeply into his eyes as her fingers sifted through the long, thick hair that brushed his neck. "I'll bear your children—as many as you want. I'll be by your side whenever you need me, for as long as you need me." *For as long as you want me,* she added to herself.

"You mean that?"

"Yes."

"Thank God." His mouth swooped down and claimed hers, his arms crushing her body to his as his tongue plunged past her honeyed lips.

The few kisses they had shared had been heady and soul-stirring in their own right, but Lucinda knew that they didn't begin to compare to this one. Before there had been warm, pleasurable sensations, but now flames blazed within her. Hungry flames that she wished could go on forever. Being with Prescott this way was so right, because she belonged to him in the most basic way.

Though overwhelmed by an all-consuming joy that she eagerly welcomed, a small shred of regret remained in one tiny corner of her mind. If only things could be different. If only she were different. She loved Prescott with all her heart, and she knew by his own admission that he loved her, yet she wanted so much more than his simple, earnest declaration. She wanted them to be as one for all time, and she knew that would never happen.

What she had now had to be good enough, she decided, relegating that one regret to the back of her mind, where it could do no harm. Then, wrapping her arms around Prescott, she returned his passions with full fervor. They were together now, at this moment in time, and that was all that really mattered.

Feeling Lucinda's response was all the encouragement Prescott needed. Unable to wait a moment longer to give as well as to receive pleasure from the woman he loved so deeply, he scooped her up in his arms and carried her into his bedroom.

"Stop me now, Lucinda," he said, placing her gently on his bed. "If you don't want this as much as I do, if you don't want me as much as I need you, then for God's sake stop me while you've got the chance."

She stared up at him, studying his face and seeing the sincerity in his eyes. Until now, she had never seen honest hunger in a man before. Lust, yes. Desire, certainly. But never a hunger so strong that it seemed to pulsate throughout his entire body.

For a response, Lucinda simply lifted her hand, beckoning him to join her.

With an eagerness he hadn't felt in years, Prescott stretched out beside her on the bed and took her in his arms once again. Wanting to be gentle with her, for he knew she had never been with a man before, he began slowly, worshiping her body through her layers of clothing with his hands and partaking of her sweetness with his mouth. He explored her feminine curves, starting at her waist and working his way up to her breasts where he found and teased areas that elicited tiny gasps and moans of excited pleasure from her. And when touching and kissing her wasn't enough, when he wanted to feel her flesh against his, he began undoing the buttons on her blouse, carefully at first, but then ripping them open in a fit of frustration.

"Oh, hell, darlin', you gotta help me out here," he groaned. "I've never been real good with handling ladies' dainty things."

Her heart pounding, her full lips parted and, desire for him brimming in her deep gray eyes, she unfastened the few remaining buttons on her blouse and tossed it aside. Then, with nervous fingers, she removed her skirt and petticoats.

And as she undressed, Prescott began pulling at his clothes like a man possessed, totally unconcerned that his valet would have a few things to say about the now shabby condition of his shirt and trousers. He didn't care. The need to hold Lucinda, to be one with her, was all he could think about.

All too soon, the midday light that streamed through the windows cast a golden glow on their naked bodies. Prescott felt his breath constrict in his lungs at his first sight of Lucinda's glorious form. He had seen many women in his life, but never one so lovely. Raven-black hair cascaded in loose curls down the middle of her back, one lone tendril curling over her shoulder. Pale, firm breasts with hard, coral-pink tips, a small waist, full hips, and long, slender legs. He must have done something really wonderful in his life, he thought, to deserve someone this perfect.

Lucinda knew she should avert her gaze from his naked form, but she found herself too enraptured by his unquestionably masculine anatomy to even think about being modest. The hair on his chest was a shade darker than that on his head. It swirled around his flat male nipples only to meet in the center of his broad chest then dip down to his navel, where it grew thick and dark around his—

"Oh, my word!"

"Easy, darlin'." Sensing her alarm, he closed in on the bed where she knelt. "Don't let it frighten you."

"But, Prescott, it's—"

"Just me. That's all it is. It's what you do to me."

"I did not do that. Did I?"

"Don't you know by now that you just being you does this?"

"No, I don't."

"Well, don't worry. It'll be all right."

"The question is, will you? Doesn't it hurt?"

"Oh, more'n you know. But it's a good kind of hurt. The kind that'll go away in a while."

He knelt on the bed as she did and reached out to her, running his hands under her wealth of hair and letting them settle on her neck, where he felt the delicate bones beneath her satin-smooth skin. Looking at her, he couldn't help but notice the curiosity in her eyes, as well as the twinge of apprehension behind the inquisitiveness. He knew of only one way to rid her of both those feelings, and he did so by letting his hands glide down her arms until they fell on small hands that were clenched into tight fists. He opened them, slowly spreading the fingers apart and guiding his thumbs over her sensitive palms. Then he brought them up to his body and placed them over his heart.

"See? Just ordinary flesh and blood, darlin'. That's all I am."

He was hardly ordinary, Lucinda thought, finding herself suddenly unable to put that fact into mere words. The hardness of his muscles, the heat from his skin that penetrated the cold pads of her fingers, and the coarse, springy hair on his chest robbed her completely of speech. But the steady thud of his heart had the most profound effect. Hearing her own pulse drum loudly in her ears, she realized that his heart and hers were beating in perfect unison.

"I want you," she whispered. "But I've never done this before. I don't know what to do."

"I know, darlin', I know. That's why we're gonna take this nice and slow."

He leaned toward her and brushed his lips against hers, wanting so much more, but holding back for her benefit. Because he had never made love with a virgin before, he supposed they could sort of be virgins together in this one, very special act.

Deepening his kiss, he wrapped his arms around her and drew her closer. The feel of her breasts brushing against him, their tips growing as hard as he, sent the blood racing through his body. Heaven help him wait, he prayed. All would be ruined if he went too fast.

With bare flesh touching bare flesh, he gently laid her on her back, moving to hover over her as his hands began a slow exploration of her hidden secrets. And where his hand led, his mouth soon followed, finding and tasting the sweetest joys he had ever known.

Following Prescott's lead, Lucinda began to explore as well. She hadn't known that a man's body could hold so many mysteries while, at the same time, reveal so many secrets. The skin on his back was as supple as soft leather stretched across a base of hardwood, the muscles beneath growing tight then relaxing again as he moved above her. His ribs felt like a well-padded washboard; his hips were equally firm. And letting her curious hands glide lower, over the springy hair on the flat plane of his belly, she finally encountered that which truly made him a man.

Prescott's tenuous hold on his control almost escaped him. Knowing he wouldn't last much longer at the rate they were going, he stepped up the pace of their mutual seduction, his mouth leaving the slender column of her neck to search for and find one of her hard peaks. As his tongue paid homage to it, eliciting a tiny groan from deep inside her throat, his hand delved to the silky nest between her thighs. A rich moisture bathed his fingers, and he knew she was ready.

He slowly pulled away and, with the gentlest of urging from his hands, he parted her legs and poised himself above her.

When he touched her, tremors began to pulsate throughout Lucinda's entire frame, causing her heart to pound loudly and her breaths to come in ragged gasps. She felt something quite magical just within her reach, but though she strove determinedly to claim it, it continued to elude her. And then she felt the warm weight of Prescott on top of her and his hard length begin to penetrate her virginal barrier.

Feeling a moment of harsh discomfort, one part of her wanted to cry out and make him stop. But the other part of her knew that if she did, the delicious excitement he had given her would cease altogether and she might not be able to recapture it.

Yet, in the end, she did cry out when the discomfort grew so severe she thought she would faint. Feeling her pain as strongly as if it were his own, Prescott captured her cry in his mouth, his tongue plundering its honeyed recess as another part of him took possession of her. Then he erased the last of her pain and fears by wrapping her in the security of his arms, his hands tunneling under her to bring her hips up to his.

With their bodies completely united, Lucinda sensed the return of the magical sensations she'd had earlier and strove once again to claim them, her body telling her that she would succeed if she matched Prescott's movements. Though at first hesitant, she began to meet each of his thrusts with one of her own, her hips soon undulating with his in an age-old rhythm as her breathing grew more ragged and her hunger more profound. The magical feeling became much brighter, more close at hand, and then the moment of true deliverance arrived.

The most powerful pleasure Lucinda had ever felt began to surge through her, bathing her all over in the warm, soft light of completion. Feeling her body arch under him, and hearing the tiny cry come from deep in her throat, Prescott let go and poured himself into her, giving her not only his seed, but his heart and soul as well.

Moments passed as they held each other, both desperately wanting the pulsating sensations to go on forever, both wishing silently that they would never have to part.

But inevitably, they did, Prescott poising himself above her so that he could look down at her rapturous expression.

"I love you," he said simply.

"Oh, God, I love you, too."

He brushed the hair out of her face and kissed her forehead. "Then it's settled. We'll get married as soon as possible. I'll go see the preacher, or the vicar, or whatever y'all call them here, and I'll tell him that—" He broke off as the tears forming at the corners of her closed eyes filled him with a sense of certain dread. "Lucinda, darlin', don't do this. Please, don't do this."

"I have to. Don't you see? We can't marry. It would ruin your life and demean your position at court."

"To hell with court. Living without you will ruin my life."

"But you won't be without me. I'll be yours in every way that matters for as long as you want me."

"Just not as my wife, is that it?"

Lucinda averted her gaze, her heart wrenching in two at the thought of what she had done to them. "In England, a mistress is a valid position to hold. She's almost as good as a wife. In some cases, she's even better than a wife."

"Mistress, huh? That's how you see yourself, as my mistress?"

"That's what I am. That's all I can ever be to you."

Prescott studied her for a long moment, wishing things could be different between them, but knowing he could never change her stubborn, hardheaded mind if she didn't want to change it herself.

"Well then," he said at last. "If that's the way you

want it, darlin', then I suppose that's the way it'll have to be."

The hard ring to his words formed a vast hollowness in the pit of her stomach. What had she done? By denying him her hand in marriage and giving him her heart and body instead, she had tried to save him and the Trefarrow family name. Yet, in doing so, she had possibly broken her own heart. Heaven help her, what was she to do now?

17

"What's a barbecue, Uncle Prescott?"

Prescott turned away from the hole in the ground that two villagers were digging and frowned down into Alexandra's inquisitive face. "Well, let's see. It's kind of like a picnic. No, it's more'n that. See, it's where a whole bunch of people get together and— Oh, dang, sugar, it's just a plain old cookout."

"What's a cookout?"

Lucinda came up behind them carrying Elizabeth and holding Victoria's little hand. "It's where a lot of food is cooked outside of the house rather than inside the kitchen, where it's normally prepared. Isn't that right, Uncle Prescott?"

Prescott couldn't help but notice how the four women in his life had changed during the past weeks. Alexandra, Victoria, and Elizabeth, now well-fed and obviously well-cared for, thanks to Lucinda's attentions, had bloomed into beautiful little ladies.

Especially the baby, because she had stopped wetting the bed at night and no longer cried out in her sleep for her mother. But, to his way of thinking, Lucinda was the most changed of all. Though she still remained distantly polite to him when others were around, it was a whole different story when they were alone. And they seemed to be alone quite often these days. Every moment they could find they were in each other's arms, and beds, filling each other's needs and sating each other's passions, which only seemed to grow more intense instead of fading with time, as so many of his other relationships with women had.

"Yeah, that's a barbecue all right," Prescott said, knowing that if he didn't change the direction of his thoughts, he'd be tempted to ignore the children and the pit the men were digging in favor of whisking Lucinda off to some secluded place so he could make love with her for the rest of the afternoon. He'd done it before; it wouldn't take much for him to do it again, and, right now, he couldn't afford any distractions. Not even the most pleasant one he could think of. The Calderwoods were due to arrive within the next two days, and things still needed to be done around the estate.

"'Course now, I've known some folks who like to roast ears of corn and potatoes and even turnips over an open fire," he said. "But this time we're just gonna cook meat. Half a cow, a whole pig, and . . . lamb." He added the last with a visible grimace, well aware that if any Texan worth his salt ever found out what he was planning to do he'd round up a lynch party and have him strung up so quickly he wouldn't have the chance to know what hit him. Kind of like the way realizing he was in love with Lucinda had knocked him off his feet.

Tears formed in Alexandra's blue eyes and her bottom lip began to tremble. "You're going to cook Princess?"

"Oh, no, darlin', not Princess." Wanting to reassure the four-year-old, he knelt down so that he was at eye level with her. "She's— Well, she's one of the family now, living with us and all. You don't cook one of your own family. We'll let Tom or one of the men here pick out one of her little friends. How's that sound?"

"I won't eat any," Alexandra said, wiping the tears off her cheeks. "I don't like eating lamb."

"Me neither, sugar. Tell you what—you and me'll stick strictly to the beef and pork, and everybody else can eat all the lamb they want."

"All right."

"Good. Now how about you and me going to the stables and telling Tom to go pick us out a sheep that he thinks is just about right?"

"The lad ain't 'ere, milord," said Ethan, one of the villagers working on the pit.

Prescott rose to his full height. "Where'd he go?"

Ethan shrugged. "Wouldn't be knowing that, milord. Far away, I reckon. Ain't seen 'im since Wednesday night, when 'e 'ad that large bag with 'im."

"You saw him Wednesday night, carrying a large bag?" Prescott said. "But that was two days ago. I could have sworn I saw him in the stables just yesterday morning."

"Nay, thee couldn't 'ave seen the lad yesterday, milord. 'E took off Wednesday night. 'Ere, Josh, it were Wednesday night we seen 'im, weren't it?"

"Aye," Josh said, leaning on the handle of his shovel. "Coming out of the Proud Ram, we were, remember?"

"Oh, aye, aye, that's right. Which way would thee say 'e was 'eaded? Truro?"

"Nay, I reckon it'd be more like Bristol."

"Why the Sam Hill would he want to run away?" Prescott asked. "Tom Sweet was one of the best stable hands I've ever come across."

"Probably found 'imself a girl, is all," Ethan said. "Lads Tom's age need to sow their wild oats. Beggin' your pardon, Miss Lucinda, but it's a fact of life, can't be ignored. So if 'e is sowing 'is oats, milord, I wouldn't worry none about 'im. 'E'll come 'ome when 'e's good'n ready."

"His grandmother must be beside herself with worry," Lucinda said.

"You can say that again." Prescott scooped Victoria up into his arms and grabbed hold of Alexandra's hand.

"'Ere, don't go running off yet," Josh said. "'Ow deep does thee want us to dig this 'ole?"

"No more'n a foot," Prescott said. "And you'd better make it a foot longer while you're at it. Gotta have enough room for everything to cook at once."

As they started up the hill to the castle, Prescott wondered why Tom would decide to leave so suddenly without telling him. Though he'd had only a few conversations with the young man, Prescott had assumed that he liked his work. He'd always been cheerful and talkative, wanting Prescott to tell him stories about life in the American West. He'd never shown any outward signs of dissatisfaction that Prescott could recall.

Entering the kitchen a few minutes later, they found Mrs. Sweet standing at the long work table, furiously plucking feathers off a chicken. When she saw Prescott, her stout frame stiffened and her face, already rosy from the kitchen heat, grew as dark as a thundercloud.

"We just heard," he said, depositing Victoria on the floor.

"Heard what, milord?"

"About your grandson, Tom. He's run away?"

"Aye, and with your blessing, it seems."

"*My* blessing?"

Mrs. Sweet snorted derisively. "Thee told him to go to that heathenous Texas, and off my Tom went."

Prescott couldn't have been more shocked if the housekeeper had suddenly hit him on the head with a frying pan. "I didn't tell him any such thing, Mrs. Sweet. I swear I didn't. We talked about the Triple T a few times, and he asked me what it was like to live on the ranch. I didn't think there was any harm in it, so I told him."

"Well, that's where he's gone. To work for your brother, he said."

"My brother Payne?"

"Aye. My Tom said he wanted more than just a life as a stableboy here at Ravens Lair. Said he wanted to be his own man and see the world, America in particular."

"I didn't know," Prescott said. "If I had, I sure wouldn't have told him all those tales."

"Tales, bah! Nothing but lies, they were. Lies about red Indians and cattle thieves and bank robbers. Filled my Tom's head, thee did, worse than any of those novels he was always reading."

Miranda came hurrying into the kitchen, an anxious look on her face, but Prescott ignored her. "They weren't lies, Mrs. Sweet. There are Indians and cattle thieves and bank robbers in Texas."

"Thee's seen them, I suppose?" the housekeeper asked with a sneer of disbelief.

"Indians a couple of times, and cattle thieves almost every year. They're all over the place; you can't avoid them. I've never come across a bank robber, though. Just been lucky, I guess."

"Well, if my Tom gets himself hurt, or if he dies, it'll be on your head, milord. I'll see to it."

"He won't get hurt, Mrs. Sweet. If your grandson heads for the Triple T like he said he was gonna do, my brother'll make dang sure he doesn't get hurt." The moment the words were out of his mouth, Prescott wanted to take them back. He couldn't guarantee what would happen to Tom if, or when, the boy ever got to Texas. There were a thousand ways a young man Tom's age could get himself maimed for life, and all of them doing an honest day's work. Busting broncs and bulldogging calves, the staple chores on a working ranch, a man could take a bad fall off a horse and end up paralyzed. Even going into town on Saturday night with the other hands, he could get caught in the crossfire of a saloon shoot-out and end up dead. Nothing was really all that safe. No place was that, either, he decided. "Not unless he goes there looking for trouble."

"Trouble? My Tom? Not bloody likely. He's a good lad, he is."

"I know, ma'am."

Rubbing her hands together, Miranda stepped forward. "Milord. Your —"

"Please, not now. Look, Mrs. Sweet, your Tom is one of the finest young men I've come across in a long time, and I've met quite a few. I wouldn't worry if I were you. I know you've heard a lot of stories about Texas and all, but it ain't as heathenous a place as you seem to think. Couple more years, we might be as civilized as y'all are here." But Prescott prayed he was wrong. He never wanted to see Texas become like England, full of condescending stuffed shirts who upheld social rules that made no sense at all. In his opinion, Texas was fine just the way it was.

"Bah!"

"No, I'm serious. Oh, sure, it can get a shade wild at times, but no more than London gets."

"Satan's den, London is. My Tom wanted to go there once, but his father wouldn't let him. Maybe he should have gone, though." Her voice cracking, a big tear appeared in the corner of Mrs. Sweet's eye. "Maybe if he'd gone to London, he wouldn't have run away to America."

Realizing he was losing the battle with the housekeeper, because her aching heart was ruling her head, he decided to try and reassure her. "Listen, he should make out okay. Trust me, a young man like Tom has got a better chance of making something of himself over there than he does here."

"Milord," Miranda said.

"I said not now. It's happened before, Mrs. Sweet. He may start out as a ranchhand, but with a lot of hard work and determination, he could end up owning his own spread one day, being his own boss. That's what he wants; that's why he left."

The housekeeper dabbed her eyes with the hem of her apron. "Own his own land?"

"Sure, why not? Lord knows, we got plenty of it in Texas. In some places, that's about all we got. Land that's spread out as far as the eye can see, just waiting for somebody to come along and claim it. Now, you can't say that about England. All the land here is already owned by somebody else."

"Aye, that's true."

"Milord," Miranda said again, trying to get Prescott's attention.

But Prescott wouldn't be interrupted. He sensed the housekeeper was beginning to soften up and might even be willing to listen to reason for a change. One had to strike while the iron was hot when dealing with a woman who would listen to reason. And he did, walking over to Mrs. Sweet and wrapping an arm around her plump shoulders in a gesture of comfort. "Your Tom's a real hard worker. Why, in no time at all, he could round himself up some wild mustangs, buy a few head of cows, and have himself a nice little place. All before he's thirty, I'll bet."

"Before he's thirty?"

"Yep."

"Does thee truly think it's possible?"

"I wouldn't put it past him."

"And he wouldn't be scalped by red Indians?"

"Milord!" Miranda pleaded.

"Scalped? Lord, no, ma'am. I ain't heard of a scalping taking place in years, not since I was a toddler. You've been told all the bad tales about Texas and none of the good ones. Land sakes, there's cities back home even got their own orchestras and operas. And we've had street lights and indoor plumbing for some time now. There's even talk of putting in a trolley car system in Dallas."

"Is that where your ranch is, Dallas?"

"Well, no, ma'am, not exactly. The Triple T's closer to Waco. Lays just right outside of town. But we're only a short train ride away from Dallas."

Miranda stomped her foot and glared at him. "Milord, I must insist thee listen to me."

Prescott heaved an impatient sigh. "What is it, Miss Miranda?"

"Thee has guests, milord."

"Guests?"

"Aye."

"Well, it's about time," he said. "I've been expecting the sheriff to bring the judge by for over a week now. We can finally get Emerson out of the dungeon."

"'Tis not Sheriff Penhalligan and Judge Chenoweth, milord," Miranda said. "'Tis your family, the Calderwoods."

He looked at her and shook his head. "No, no, it can't be them. They're not due for a couple more days."

"They're here, milord. Their three coaches just pulled up. That's what I've been trying to tell thee."

Prescott's stomach clenched into a hard knot vaguely reminiscent of the one on a large noose, and he felt his knees go weak. "Oh, Lord have mercy. Somebody do something, please."

"*You* do something, Prescott," Lucinda said, scooping up the baby and grabbing Victoria's hand.

"Me?"

"Yes, you. They're your family."

All reason escaped Prescott. The only thing he could think of offhand was to find himself the deepest, darkest hole in the castle and hide in it until his family decided to leave.

"Wh—what do I do?"

"I would suggest you go welcome them," she said.

"Do I have to do it alone?"

"Yes, you must. I need to get the children settled in the nursery; it's time for their nap. Mrs. Sweet, put the kettle on and begin making sandwiches. Lots of them. It's quite possible that his lordship's family are quite famished after having traveled all the way from Truro. Rowena, dash down to the stables and get Will and some of the other men to carry in the Calderwoods' luggage. I imagine there's plenty of it. Miranda, find Hargreaves, and the two of you check all the guest rooms and make certain they're as we left them. And open the windows to air them while you're at it."

As Lucinda barked out an order, each of the women dashed about to obey it. Only Prescott continued to stare at her with a blank, somewhat dumbstruck expression. For the life of him, he couldn't find the strength or ability to even move.

"Go on, go greet your guests," she said. "They're waiting for you."

"I'd rather go shackle myself to the dungeon wall next to Emerson."

With a heavy sigh, Lucinda placed a hand in the middle of his back and shoved. "You can do that later. Right now, you've your family to welcome."

Prescott wasn't sure how he survived the next few hours. He only knew that as he headed for the front door it swung open on its creaky hinges, and a herd of chattering people swarmed into the castle, overtaking it and him like a conquering army.

Various aunts and female cousins he had met briefly in London, ones he couldn't name even under the threat of death, kissed his cheeks until he thought the skin would wear off. Their male counterparts, equally unidentifiable, shook his hand and slapped him heartily on the back, leaving him with bruises and, thanks to one burly young male cousin, the distinct possibility of a dislocated shoulder. And, as they greeted him, they all talked incessantly and at the same time, telling him about the thoroughly boring summer season in London, the hot, dirty train trip from Scotland with its absolutely deplorable food, the even dirtier coach ride from Truro, and how pleased they were to escape to his delightfully quaint house. Prescott tried to tell them that Ravens Lair was a castle, not a house, but he never quite managed to get out the first syllable.

"Your charwoman really should do something about those windows, my boy," said one bony middle-aged woman—his Aunt Charity, he thought, wanting to laugh at the absurdity of her name, because she didn't look or sound the least bit charitable to him. "They allow far too much light into the room. Such as it is. Far too much. Just look at how your Aubusson has faded."

"I kinda like—" he began, only to be cut off by one of his uncles.

"St. Andrews, now that's the place to golf," the man said. "Absolutely smashing course. Played nine holes every morning without fail. I tell you, it leaves you feeling like a new man. Golf does wonders for the soul. You really must try it, Preston."

"Prescott," he said. "And I would, if I knew what gol—"

"I say, Cousin," interrupted one of his younger male cousins, who behaved more like one of the girls, "is there a WC in this drafty old place?"

"A WC?" Prescott had lived in the castle now for three months, in England for almost five, and until now he had thought he had a grasp of their quirky language, but he had no idea what a WC was.

"Yes, the loo," the young man said. "Is there one, hmmm?"

Prescott merely frowned. "What's a loo?"

A giggling young woman came up and patted his cheek, fluttering her lashes at him. "Isn't he an absolute delight, Harold? Auntie Margaret told us what an entertaining goose you were, Cousin Prescott, but silly old me, I didn't believe her."

"Nor I," Harold said, giving Prescott a look that made him decidedly suspicious.

"Now do stop playing the fool, darling, and tell Cousin Harold where that loo is. He has the most embarrassing problem, you see, and —"

"I do not!" Harold said, blushing furiously to the roots of his curly blond hair. "You're always telling tales on me, Cressida—you have done so most of our lives—and I shan't have it any longer. Do you understand?"

"Oh, pah, Harold. Don't get your little knickers in such a twist."

"See there? You've done it again."

"Done what?" Cressida asked.

"Questioned my masculinity, that's what."

"I've done nothing of the kind. You question it quite well enough on your own, just by being flighty old you."

"Flighty! Now see here, Cressida, I . . ."

Caught between the feuding cousins, Prescott closed his ears to the remainder of their argument. Now more than ever, he wanted to find himself a good hiding place, to just slip under the faded Aubusson and crawl into one of the cracks on the floor—anything to get away from his unruly bunch of relatives. But he changed his mind in an instant and considered himself truly reprieved from a fate worse than death when Lucinda's calm voice suddenly sounded above the chaotic din.

"Mr. Calderwood, you'll find our facilities up these stairs. Just turn left at the landing, and it will be the third door on the right."

Heads turned and conversation slowly ceased as she came gliding down the stairs, the perfect picture of grace and elegance under fire. Pride, love, and eternal gratitude surged through Prescott. While one part of him wanted to run to her, take her in his arms, and show her just how much love he had for her, another part of him wanted to spirit her away from this seemingly endless madness. But he did neither. He knew if he did his behavior would be questioned, and this bunch already had enough fuel to stoke their verbal bonfire to last a lifetime.

Instead, he broke through the Harold-Cressida barrier and advanced to Lucinda's side. "Everybody, I'd like you to meet my cousin, Miss Lucinda Trefarrow."

"Your cousin?" Aunt Charity said, studying Lucinda through her lorgnette.

"Yes, ma'am," Prescott said, "on my father's side."

"What a fine-looking country filly," came a man's hushed voice somewhere in the crowd.

"Oh, do shut up, Walter."

"Well, she is, my dear."

"I said shut up."

"Yes, dear."

"If Lord Prescott hasn't already done so," Lucinda said, knowing by the way he acted that he hadn't, "we would both like to welcome you to Ravens Lair. Your rooms are ready whenever you wish to adjourn to them. We should be having tea in the drawing room quite soon, so if you wish to freshen up from your long journey beforehand, might I suggest that you do so now?"

"First sensible thing I've heard all day," Aunt Charity announced. "I could stand a good cup of tea."

A wave of mumbled agreement rolled through the throng.

"And," Lucinda added, "Cook has informed me that dinner shall be served promptly at eight."

Cook? Prescott cast her a questioning look that Lucinda answered with an apologetic lifting of one eyebrow.

"What does she mean by '*we* wish to welcome you'?" one female cousin asked another as the horde began filing up the stairs.

"She lives here, you ninny," said the second cousin. "It's her house, too, I suspect."

"But what's she to Cousin Prescott? That's what I'd like to know."

"Didn't you just hear him? She's his cousin, the same as we are."

"Oh, drats, not another one."

The second cousin merely grinned. "Adds more spice to the competition, wouldn't you say?"

Prescott overheard the conversation and wondered what competition they were talking about.

"It seems as though you're to be the target of more than one young lady's undivided attentions this upcoming fortnight," Lucinda said moments later, when the last of the Calderwoods had disappeared from sight at the top of the stairs.

"Huh?"

"Oh, really, Prescott. Don't tell me you didn't notice."

"Notice what?"

"Honestly! There are at least a half-dozen marriage-minded young women here, and each one of them has you in her sights."

"Well, having me in her sights is one thing, but snaring me is something else."

"Taking yourself out of the running even before the hunt has begun, have you?"

"I was never in no running, and there ain't no hunt. Not to my way of thinking, least ways. I thought I made that clear to them months ago in London."

"Obviously, not clear enough. Don't you know what a prize catch you are?"

"I ain't no prize."

"I beg to differ, Prescott. You're unmarried, and you've a title and an estate."

"This crumbling old pile of rocks?"

"It's much more than they've got."

"If there was some way I could give it to one of them, trust me, I would," he said. "But while we're on the subject, you got your fair share of looks as well."

"From your cousins, you mean?"

"Uncles, too."

"Oh, that's ridiculous."

He leaned close and whispered in her ear. "Better watch yourself, darlin'. I know that bunch, and they're sneaky. Real sneaky."

"One could give you the same warning, you know."

"Yeah, well, I can handle myself around women."

Lucinda's quick peal of laughter echoed off the rafters in the now-empty foyer and sent a warm surge of pleasure through Prescott. "Oh, you can, can you?"

"Yeah, I can."

"Is that why you're always running off whenever one comes in your presence without warning?"

"I don't run off."

"Yes, you do. Take yesterday, for instance."

"What about yesterday?"

"You started to leave your chambers—I saw you—but you ducked back in again when you saw Esmeralda coming down the hall."

"I can explain that. Every time that woman sees me, she screams rape."

"Once," Lucinda said. "She only screamed rape once—the first time she met you."

"Well, a man can take just so much, and once was enough for me. Besides, I worry that she might take a notion to kick the bucket."

"Kick the bucket?"

"Die. Be a helluva thing to try and explain why an old woman hollering rape would just up and die on a man without something causing it."

"All right. But that still doesn't excuse your behavior around Miranda and Rowena."

"Those two?"

"Yes."

"I've never run away from them."

"Yes, you have. One day last week they were having one of their incessant petty arguments. You walked in and heard them and, just as they were about to turn to you for your invaluable advice, you ran out."

"The hell I did."

"You did, Prescott. Don't bother to deny it."

"Well, there's a difference between knowing how to handle women and stepping smack dab into the middle of a cat fight. A man could wind up maimed for life doing a fool thing like that."

"They were arguing, not brawling."

"Sure looked to me like they were about to come to blows."

She studied him through narrowed eyes for a

moment. "I never suspected that you had a cowardly streak where women were concerned."

"Now wait just a dang minute. I ain't no coward. I'll take on any man my size, any time, anywhere."

"But not a woman, is that it?"

"Darlin', I'll take you on anytime you want."

Lucinda released a small yelp of surprise as Prescott backed her into the library and slammed the door shut with his foot. He pushed her against the wall with his body, his hands braced on either side of her as he bent his knees, his mouth claiming hers. Then he kissed her so hard that it made her head reel. But she welcomed the dizziness brought on by his kiss and the pressure of his body against hers.

His hand delved under her skirts and brought her leg up to wrap around his waist, all the while his tongue plundering the innermost recesses of her mouth. In an instant his fingers had slipped inside her knickers and were gliding up her inner thigh, blazing a course to a destination that Lucinda knew would bring her pleasure. Then he ripped off the fragile garment, gaining him freer access to that which he so fervently sought.

Infected by his fevered excitement, she fumbled with the buttons on his trousers and went on a short expedition of her own. In due course, she found him, her fingers curling around him and gently bringing him to life.

Prescott groaned and pulled her down to the floor, letting her roll on top of him while he took the more subservient position beneath. With his eyes closed, he couldn't see, but could only feel her wet, velvety softness surround him, and the tight constrictions she magically induced.

Just as he was about to come in a blinding, heartwrenching rush, he opened his eyes to watch her. Her head was thrown back and her mouth open, gulping in short gasps of air followed by the release of soft moans. Then she issued a long, quiet cry and fell forward, totally replete as he filled her.

"You're gonna be the death of me, darlin'," he whispered when he was once again able to think clearly. "All night last night, once this morning, and now this. You ever run out of steam?"

Still breathless, she laughed. "I thought you said you could handle women."

"This your way of testing me?"

"You started this, Prescott, I didn't." She pushed up on her elbows and stared down into his face.

The sun pouring in through the library windows turned her hair a brilliant blue-black, her eyes as bright as black bits of coal. He lifted a hand and rested it on the side of her neck, his thumb caressing her chin and lower lip. "God, you're beautiful. The most beautiful woman I've ever seen in my life. I love you, Lucinda."

Without hesitation, she smiled. "I love you, too."

Prescott knew she meant it. He wanted to ask her to marry him again, but he knew what her answer would be, so he didn't waste his breath. Instead, he took a different approach, one he felt certain would remind her of the precarious position in which she had put herself. "You think we made ourselves a baby this time?"

His dose of reality caused some of the light to fade from her eyes. "Do you want one?"

"With you? Hell, yes. I want a whole houseful of babies."

"Ravens Lair is an awfully large house, Prescott."

"Yeah, it is. Looks like you and me are gonna be busy, don't it?"

She carefully disengaged herself and rose to her feet, turning her back on Prescott as he straightened his clothes.

"Don't do this to me, Lucinda," he said, following her to the window. "Don't do this to us."

"Do what?"

"Walk away from me when I talk about our future and our children. There will be babies, you know. We can't keep making love and not make them."

"I know."

"Then what's bothering you?"

She shook her head. "How sad all this is, I suppose."

"Nothing sad that I can see about a man and a woman in love having a baby. That's the way God intended it."

When she turned around to face him, tears were glistening in her eyes. "They'll be bastards, Prescott, like me."

"Only if you let them be bastards. I could give them my name in a shot, and you know it, but you've got this bullheaded notion that— Hell, that don't matter. They *will* have my name."

"You'd adopt them?"

"Adopt? A natural father can't adopt his own kids. The minute they're born, I'll have them baptized as Trefarrows. Each and every damn one of them."

"They would be Trefarrows anyway."

"Yeah, well, you know what I mean. I'll see to it that my name is listed as the father in the county records, or the parish records, or whatever kind of records you people here in England keep."

"And you wouldn't be ashamed for everyone to know that you've fathered illegitimate children?"

"Ashamed? With you as their mama, I couldn't be ashamed of any child we ever had. I love you, goddammit, don't you know that by now?"

"I know, and I love you, too. But the fact remains—"

"Shit!" He grabbed her hands and held them tight. "I, Prescott, take thee, Lucinda, to be my wife. To have and to hold from this day forward, for richer, for poorer, in sickness and in health, 'til death do us part."

"What are you saying?"

"The same thing you're gonna say."

"Prescott!" She tried to pull her hands free, but he only tightened his grip.

"Say the words, Lucinda."

"But —"

"If you love me, you'll say them."

Handfast, she thought. Though their union wouldn't be legal in the eyes of the Crown or the Church, they would be a handfast man and wife. If she could have him no other way, then so be it. "I, Lucinda, take thee, Prescott, to be my husband."

"To have and to hold . . ."

"To have and to hold from this day forward, for richer, for poorer, in sickness and in health."

"'Til death do us part."

"Yes, Prescott. 'Til death do us part."

"I forsake all others who have come before you and who might come after."

"I do as well. You should know that without asking. There's only you. There will never be anyone but you."

"And wherever I go, you'll go with me."

She frowned. "I don't believe that's part of the traditional vows, is it?"

"This ain't a very traditional wedding, but I know it's in the Bible somewhere. Say it."

"Wherever you go, I'll go with you."

"Good girl. What comes next?"

"I'm not sure. It's been a while since I've attended a wedding. I believe that at some point rings should be exchanged."

"Rings, right. I don't have one on me."

"I don't need one."

"I don't care if you need one or not, I'm gonna get you a ring."

"Nothing gawdy, please."

"Darlin', I can't afford gawdy. You'll be lucky if I can come up with something plain. One that don't turn your finger green."

Lucinda laughed, pleased that he had once again found his sense of humor. And it comforted her to know that she had recaptured hers as well. With Prescott, she couldn't stay serious for long. "I don't wish to sound too forward, you understand, but I think now, at this point in the ceremony, the groom is supposed to kiss the bride."

"I can handle that." He wrapped his arms around her and lowered his head, sealing their unorthodox union with a kiss as powerful as any other he had ever given her.

19

Sheriff Penhalligan finally brought Judge Chenoweth to Ravens Lair five days later, on the morning of July third. Though Prescott had been expecting the two men for well over a week, he was no more prepared for their arrival than he'd been for the Calderwoods. Still, he welcomed them just the same.

"I don't know how you go about doing what you do, Your Honor, but I'd just as soon you make your decision quick so I can get that piece of hog scum out of my dungeon."

"All in due course, milord. All in due course." Judge Chenoweth settled his ample girth into one of Prescott's leather library chairs. "Sheriff Penhalligan has told me some of the events that led up to your incarceration of, er . . ."

"Emerson," Penhalligan said. "Garrick Emerson."

"Ah, yes, Emerson. You have alleged that he stole a

vast sum of money belonging to you, and that he beat his wife to death?"

"Yes, I did, Your Honor. But the money belonged to Ravens Lair, not me. And he beat Anne Emerson, his wife."

"To death, isn't that correct?"

"Well, she didn't die right off. She lived long enough to give birth to their stillborn baby, and then she died."

"You witnessed Emerson's attack on his wife?"

"No, sir, I didn't. I saw the bruises and the welts that his beating left on her body. If it helps, my cousin, Lucinda, saw them, too. She assisted Mrs. Emerson in delivering the baby. It was a little boy. Do you want me to send for her, have her come in and confirm it?"

"No, no," Chenoweth said. "Must protect the gentler sex from horrors such as this if we can. It's a pity, a sad pity indeed that some men cannot seem to control the more violent side of their natures."

"Yeah, well, Emerson's one who can't. That's why I've kept him locked up in the dungeon all this time. I'm afraid he might try to harm his daughters."

Chenoweth glared at Penhalligan. "The man has other children? Why didn't you inform me of this?"

The sheriff fumbled for the right words. "I—I didn't think that—"

"Your not thinking is quite obvious, my good man." To Prescott, "Where are the children now, and how many are there?"

"There are three of them, and right now they're upstairs in the nursery. My cousin is caring for them. I take a turn at caring for them, too, when I can find the time."

Chenoweth shook his head. "Nasty business, this. Poor tykes will probably end up in a foundling home. That is, of course, if they haven't grandparents or aunts and uncles who will consent to care for them."

"Don't worry about that, Your Honor. I intend to adopt all three little girls."

"You, milord?"

"Well, yeah, if it's all right. There ain't no law in England against somebody adopting orphaned children, is there?"

"No, but, milord, those children are not really orphans, are they? Their father is still alive and, by English law, he's responsible for their upbringing."

"No, *I'm* legally responsible for that. I made myself responsible the day I brought them home to the castle with me. I don't want them to have anything to do with Emerson, or him with them. They're better off not even knowing that piece of human outhouse slime."

"Milord, while I realize that your intentions may be of the purest design, need I remind you that you are an unmarried man?"

If the Queen's magistrate only knew, Prescott thought. In his mind, he was about as married as any man could be. But he doubted the judge would see it from his point of view. "No, you don't need to remind me of that."

"Well, for an unmarried man with no plans to acquire a wife in the near future, to adopt three little girls and try to raise them alone— It's—it's unheard of, milord."

"Okay, maybe it is unheard of. But is it illegal?"

Chenoweth thought a moment. "No, I should say that it's more of a moral issue than a legal one, milord."

"So I can't adopt them, is that what you're saying?"

"Your lordship would have a deuced hard time of getting the Crown to approve of such an adoption; that much I know."

"All right, all right." Lucinda had told him almost the same thing. Too bad he hadn't paid more attention to her. "Then how 'bout this—can I make them my wards?"

"I should think that would be a bit more acceptable, milord."

"And Emerson, their father—can I arrange it so that he can't see them, be around them . . . hurt them if he feels like hitting someone smaller than him?"

"Well, milord, he is their father. Fathers have rights with regards to the welfare of their offspring."

"I know, that's the problem. A man like him shouldn't have any rights at all."

"If your lordship could get the man to agree to such a condition . . ."

"Yeah, I'll talk to him," Prescott said with a decisive nod. Offhand, he could think of at least a dozen different ways in which he could sway Emerson into handing the girls over to him all legal-like. He would try offering him money first, even though he didn't have much of it to hand out. And if that didn't work, then he'd let his fists do some of the talking. Whatever it took, he'd try it. The sooner the girls were his, the better off they'd be. The *safer* they would be from Emerson. "And once they're my wards the way I want?"

"Mr. Emerson cannot go near them without your lordship's permission. He will virtually cease to exist as far as their guardianship is concerned."

"Good, that's what I wanted to hear." Assuming

that the meeting was over, Prescott rose to his feet and crossed to the judge to shake his hand. "I'm glad you stopped by." *Even though it took you dang near a whole month to get here,* he added to himself. "I've got a houseful of relatives visiting, but I'd appreciate it if you'd stay and have a bite to eat with us. It seems the least I can do, considering how far you had to come."

"Perhaps I will share a meal with you," Chenoweth said, "after we've dispensed with our most unsavory business here."

"I thought we had."

"No, milord. We've only just begun. There is still the small matter of your illegal incarceration of Mr. Emerson to discuss."

"Illegal?"

"Yes, milord, illegal. You haven't the right, nor the authority, to incarcerate anyone."

"But Penhalligan didn't have a jail to throw Emerson's sorry ass into."

"Yes, so I've been told." The sheriff got another of Chenoweth's disapproving looks, and Penhalligan had the good grace to hang his head in embarrassment. "But the fact remains, milord, you've taken the law into your own hands, and the Crown frowns upon such activity."

"Well, I wouldn't have taken it into my own hands if I could've been assured that Penhalligan here wouldn't let Emerson skip town. He was gonna put him under house arrest. You ought to see Emerson's house, Your Honor. It's the biggest, the nicest one down in the village. It even puts Ravens Lair to shame. But that's not surprising, considering everything he put in it was either bought with money from Ravens Lair or stolen outright from the castle."

"You can prove this allegation?"

"You bet I can. Just give me a few minutes to round up the books Emerson tried to doctor, and I'll show you."

"Sheriff, have you seen the records to which his lordship is referring?"

"Er . . ."

"Never mind," Chenoweth said on an impatient sigh. "If only the local constabulary were more helpful in situations such as these, my job would be considerably less taxing. As it is, it seems I shall have to review your claim and documents at length."

"Take all the time you need. I'm in no hurry to let that scalawag outa my dungeon."

"You're most gracious, milord. I appreciate your kind invitation, and I humbly accept."

Prescott looked at the judge a moment. "Invitation?"

"To reside here at your castle until I've made my ruling, of course."

Reside? Prescott couldn't recall offhand having asked Chenoweth to actually reside at Ravens Lair. But since the magistrate was the only one with the necessary authority to put Emerson away for a good long time, and he seemed to have taken a liking to the place anyway, how could Prescott refuse?

"Of course," Prescott said. "Just let me go tell my housekeeper to fix up a room for you. You will be wanting a room, I take it?"

"Naturally. If it isn't too much trouble."

"No. No trouble at all. Pardon me a minute, will you?"

Prescott made his way out of the library and down the hall to the kitchen, wondering with every step where the hell he was going to put the corpulent barrister. Every bedroom in the house was already occupied by the Calderwoods. He couldn't very well put him up in the nursery; the girls might take a notion that he was a new toy or something. The attics wouldn't do, either, even though there was enough room up there to house a good ten people. And the staff's quarters were out of the question. Esmeralda might come upon him during one of her nightly excursions, scream rape, and scare the living hell out of him. For the time being, Prescott needed a live judge, not a dead one.

"Down in the dungeon with Emerson?" he muttered.

"Beg pardon, milord?"

He whirled around and saw Hargreaves closing the cellar door behind him, his face oddly flushed. "Oh, I was just thinking out loud is all."

"About your lordship's guest in the dungeon?"

"Yeah. How's he doing?"

"The miscreant is as well as can be expected, under the circumstances."

"Mean-tempered bastard, ain't he?"

"Er, your lordship has a most proficiently direct way with words."

"Huh?"

"Yes, he's a mean-tempered bastard."

"Yeah, well, I knew that. Has he ripped the shackles out of the wall yet?"

"Still trying, milord, but not having much success, we're happy to report."

"Good. By the time me and the judge are through with him, Emerson's gonna wish he'd never stolen a nickel from Ravens Lair. *Or* laid a hand on his poor dead wife."

"Judge, milord?"

"Yeah, Judge Chenoweth."

Hargreaves coughed. "We've a magistrate of the Crown now staying at the castle?"

"Sure do. He sort of invited himself to visit with us a spell."

"We see."

"Wish to hell I did. You want to know something funny, Ed? I ain't got no place to put the man. We're all full up. I'm thinking maybe, as a last resort, we can put him on a Baptist pallet down here in the library."

"A Baptist pallet, milord?"

"That's what we call 'em back home. When kinfolks come in to visit a spell with you, and you run out of beds, you just spread a couple of quilts and a pillow or two down on the floor and let them sleep there."

"Milord, with all due respect, we feel that a Baptist pallet would not be an appropriate enough accommodation for a representative of the Crown."

"Too disrespectful of his position, huh?"

"Inarguably, milord."

"Well, where the hell else am I gonna put him?"

"Your lordship's dilemma is understandable, but might we make a suggestion?"

"By all means, fire away."

"Well, milord, it has come to our attention that, er . . . that your lordship has been spending more time in Miss Lucinda's chambers at night than his own."

"Dammit. We were trying to be so careful, too."

"We are blessed, or cursed, I suppose, with an acute sense of hearing."

"You heard me traipsing up and down the hall to her room?"

"Not quite, milord. It seems as though the head of Miss Lucinda's bed makes a distinct thumping sound against her chamber wall whenever any, er, mmm, physical activity, shall we say, takes place there. And as my room is directly above hers . . ."

"Yeah, I see what you're saying."

"Thank you, milord. We were hoping you would. But back to the matter of finding accommodations for Judge Chenoweth during the duration of his stay. Would it not be possible, not to mention more sensible, to let him have Miss Lucinda's room? She, of course, would sleep with—I mean, sleep in your lordship's chambers."

Prescott gave the suggestion some thought. "It's gonna raise a few eyebrows. You know that, don't you?"

"It has obviously escaped your lordship's attention that, as earl, your lordship has every right to conduct himself in any manner which he sees fit, without fear of contradiction or reprisal from those who are obviously of lesser rank than himself."

"I can do what I damn well please, within reason, is that what you're trying to say?"

"Precisely, milord."

"Thanks, Ed. We'll put the judge in Lucinda's room, and she can move her stuff into mine."

"Very good, milord. And the name is Hargreaves, not Ed."

"Yeah, I know. You'll tell Mrs. Sweet what we've decided to do?"

"With all due haste, milord."

Prescott started to turn and walk away, but something stopped him. "One thing, Ed."

"Yes, milord?"

"What were you doing down in the cellar?"

"Er, taking stock of your lordship's wine inventory, of course."

"Of course. Do you think we're gonna have enough?"

"If your lordship's relatives choose not to stay more than a fortnight, we should have. However, if their tenure is longer, we fear your lordship will have to restock. In vast quantities."

"Yeah, they do seem to drink a lot, don't they?"

"I believe the popular term is as though they have hollow legs."

"Right. You go talk to Mrs. Sweet. I'll go see Lucinda."

"Stay with you in your chambers?" Lucinda looked shocked. "Have you taken leave of your senses, Prescott?"

"Darlin', it's the only thing we could think of."

"We?"

"Yeah, I talked it over with Ed, and he agreed. Well, the truth is, he's the one who suggested it."

"Hargreaves? You spoke to your valet before you consulted me, and he suggested that we— My God, we're ruined. Absolutely ruined."

"Now, don't take on so. He already had it figured out that we were visiting each other at night."

"You've visited *me*, Prescott. I've never visited you."

"Well, now we don't have to visit at all." In the privacy of her bedroom, he wrapped his arms around her and pulled her close. "Think of it this way—it's gonna save us a whole lot of time at night. Time we can spend doing other things."

"Yes, I'm well aware of that."

Giving her a quick kiss on the cheek and a playful swat across the back of her skirts, he stepped away. "Now hurry up. We've got to get your things moved out of here before Mrs. Sweet brings up the judge."

"I'll never be able to face your family again; you realize that, don't you?"

"Lucky you."

"Don't be so cavalier about this, Prescott. What your family thinks may not matter a great deal to you, but it does to me."

"It shouldn't."

"But it does so, nonetheless. No, there's got to be another solution to this dilemma into which you've so rashly thrust the two of us."

"Darlin', I've thought of everything, believe me I did. This is the only thing I know of that'll work."

"No, not the only thing."

"Well, all right, if you've got a better idea, I'm all ears."

"The nursery," Lucinda said simply.

"What about it?"

"I'll sleep up in the nursery with the children until Judge Chenoweth leaves."

"No! Absolutely not. I won't hear of it."

"Why not?"

"Because, it—it just won't work, that's all. You'll be stuck up there with them, and I'll be down here all by myself."

"Only for a few days, Prescott. Surely you can . . . restrain yourself for a few days."

Restrain himself? Prescott saw the warmth in her deep gray eyes and felt a surge of pure unadulterated lust shoot through him. He could no more restrain himself from this woman than he could cut his own throat, and keeping his distance from her would be tantamount to doing that very thing. But he supposed he would have to abide by her wishes, if for no other reason than to assure her that her good name would be kept intact.

"All right," he conceded. "We'll do it your way."

She leaned toward him and kissed him on the cheek. "Thank you, Prescott."

"But the minute Judge Chenoweth packs his bags and leaves, we're moving your stuff back to your room. And the minute my family's gone, you're moving into mine. You got that?"

"We'll discuss that when the time comes," she said with a smile, and glided out the door.

The Fourth of July dawned cloudy and cool, a fine mist of rain covering the tiny Cornish peninsula of St. Keverne for the better part of the morning. Staring out of the library window at the seemingly incessant drizzle, Prescott was convinced that his carefully laid-out plan would end up in nothing but a soggy failure. Rain meant a wet ground. A wet ground meant no fire could be built in the outdoor pit he'd had dug especially for today. No fire in the pit meant no barbecue, and he'd had his heart set on eating some good barbecue.

"Probably didn't have the right kind of sauce for it anyway," he mumbled. "Can't have a good barbecue if the sauce ain't good."

"It's your Aunt Em's recipe, isn't it?" Lucinda asked.

"More or less. What I could remember of it. Mrs. Sweet had to make a few changes 'cause she didn't have all the right ingredients."

"I wouldn't worry if I were you. Your barbecue should be a smashing success. I'm quite looking forward to sampling some of it; you've told me so much about it."

He turned away from the window. "Really?"

"Yes, really."

"You're not just saying that to make me feel better?"

"No, I honestly want to taste a piece of real Texas barbecued meat. It sounds ever so spicy."

"Oh, it is. One bite of it with Aunt Em's sauce is guaranteed to put hair on your ch— Well, not yours. You know what I mean."

"Yes, I'm afraid I do. And I can do without the hair, thank you."

Prescott eyed the fullness behind her prim, white blouse and grinned. He liked Lucinda's chest just the way it was, without hair. Smooth, creamy, pale, firm yet supple to the touch, and with two of the tastiest nubs his mouth had ever—

He broke into his own reverie, knowing that now was not the time to start fantasizing about her bosom or the pleasure he gained from feasting on it. Fantasizing would lead him to want to do other things with her that he just didn't have time for at the moment.

"What are the girls up to?" he asked.

"They're in the nursery. Rowena is reading to them."

"Well, the minute this rain stops, we'll— It is gonna stop, isn't it? It's not gonna be miserable like this the whole dang day."

"Really, Prescott. Sometimes you worry so needlessly over the most inconsequential matters." She crossed to the window and stood beside him, looking out. "I should say it will all be over in less than an hour."

"You think so?"

"Yes, I do. Look there. See, the sky is already growing brighter along the coast."

"Yeah, it is, isn't it?"

"In an hour or two, after the sun's shone a while, the ground should begin drying out, and you can do whatever you need to do to construct your barbecue. I gather that is your main concern at the moment?"

"One of them, yeah."

As he turned his attention to the weather once again, Lucinda eyed his profile thoughtfully. He was such an enigma, she thought. On the surface, he looked and behaved like a Texas country bumpkin, yet behind his handsome boyish face lay the mind of a complex man, one with his own unique moral code. When he lowered his guard, she had seen signs of his intelligence, and she knew him to have the soul of a hopeless romantic. He might bluster and complain a lot about his family, but she knew that, deep down inside, a part of him secretly wanted their approval. And, if not their approval, then at least their respect.

He looked away from the window and saw her intense scrutiny. "What's the matter?"

"Nothing. I was just looking at you."

"See anything interesting?"

"Oh, lots of things."

"Like what?"

"For one thing, the fact that you've a conscience."

"Everybody's got one of those, darlin'. Well, almost everybody," Prescott added, thinking of Emerson.

"Not like yours. And if I'm not mistaken, it seems to be bothering you."

"Naw, it ain't."

"You're worried about something, Prescott, I can tell."

"What have I got to worry about?"

"The outcome of today's festivities, perhaps?"

"You just told me it was gonna stop raining, so it can't be that."

She studied him a bit longer, staring deeply into his green eyes. "You've planned something, haven't you? Something none of us expects."

He turned to move away from the window, but not before Lucinda saw the redness steal into his face. "Well, I guess the cat's out of the bag now."

"What have you done?"

Sitting down on the top of his desk, one leg bent while the other rested on the floor, he grinned. "I just planned a little surprise for the kinfolks is all."

"What kind of surprise?"

"Naw, I can't tell you. It'll spoil it."

She moved to stand directly between his legs. "Prescott."

"Just make sure everybody knows they're to wear a costume tonight."

"Costumes?"

He slipped his arms around her waist and pulled her close to him. Burying his face in her neck, he breathed in the delicate fragrance of her soap and toilet water.

Feeling his warm breath along the side of her neck did strange things to Lucinda's pulse. "Prescott, I seriously doubt your family thought to bring costumes with them. They appear to have brought everything else, but no costumes."

"Then they'll just have to make do with whatever we've got up in the attic, won't they?"

"I suppose."

"Make sure you choose something pretty for yourself."

Lucinda vaguely recalled seeing an old Regency gown in one of the attic trunks. A gauzy, cream-colored little thing with high waist and a low, but not scandalously low, neckline. However, if she felt modesty was in order, a lace kerchief would solve that problem. She would have to hurry and fetch the gown, though, before the others began picking through the array of centuries' old garments. And shoes. She would need the proper kind of—

Her thoughts scattered to the wind as Prescott began nibbling on her neck. "You mustn't do that," she said.

"Why not?"

"We've the issue of your masked ball to discuss."

He leaned back. "Masks? I hadn't thought about that. Now that you mention it, though, it sounds like a good idea. We'll even give prizes." Grinning, he went back to feasting on the column of Lucinda's throat and the sensitive area behind her ear, eliciting a tiny groan from her.

"And later?" she asked between gasps.

"Later?"

"Yes, later. After the ball."

"We'll go to bed. Together."

"But what about all those crates you received a few days ago?"

"What crates?"

"The unmarked ones. The ones you're keeping in the outbuilding behind the stable."

"Oh, those crates."

"Aren't they for tonight's festivities?"

"Naw, don't worry about them. Just think about bed, about you and me snuggling beneath a nice warm blanket."

"I'm sleeping in the nursery now, remember? How can I snuggle with you in your bed when I'm up there in mine?"

"Leave it to me," he said. "I'll figure out a way."

Lucinda gave up the battle with her self-control and let her needs take over. She grasped Prescott's head, her fingers weaving through his thick hair, and took possession of his lips. Assuming a more aggressive role than ever before, she began doing things to him that she had always wanted to do but until now had never had the courage. Her tongue plunged deeply into his mouth, grazing the rough edges of his teeth and stroking the surface of his tongue. Heavens, he tasted so good.

Though somewhat surprised by the energy behind her unexpected assault, Prescott didn't protest. He relaxed and let her have her way with him. When she pushed herself against him, he lay back on the desk surface, holding her tight in his arms so they wouldn't fall off. A sharp object pierced the middle of his back, and he arched it long enough to sweep the desk top clean with one arm.

Lucinda climbed on top of him, her legs straddling his thighs, her teeth tugging so deliciously at his earlobe that it sent his blood pressure soaring. Unable to restrain herself any longer, she was about to tackle the buttons on his trousers, and Prescott was about to help her, when the door to the library suddenly opened and someone coughed. Both froze, Prescott holding Lucinda's face close to his chest as he turned to see who had caught them.

"Beg pardon, milord."

"What the hell do you want, Ed, can't you see we're busy?"

"Er, yes, milord. We merely thought your lordship would like to know that the Italian has arrived."

"Italian?"

"Yes, milord. A Signore Luigi Mannetti, we believe he said his name was."

"Mannetti, Mannetti. Yes! Er, er, give me a minute."

"Very good, milord."

The door closed and Lucinda leaped to her feet, her face red with embarrassment. "I knew someone was going to catch us. Didn't I tell you that if we continued carrying on this way, someone would catch us?"

"Yeah, well, it was only Ed."

"Oh, God, Prescott."

"Well, it could've been worse."

"How much worse?"

"Esmeralda could've walked in, seen us just now, and had a stroke."

"Never again," Lucinda said, straightening her clothes. "Do you hear me? Until all the guests and visitors have left this house, you're not to do this sort of thing ever again."

"Me? You're the one who started it, darlin', I didn't."

Back rigid, chin held high, she walked primly to the door. "You're imagining things."

"The hell I am. Two more minutes, and you would've had me deflowered for sure."

She shot him a startled look then laughed. "Deflowered you?"

"Well, you know what I mean."

"Yes, I do, and I might have done just that. We'll never know, though, will we?"

"Wanna try again later?"

"Maybe."

"Maybe's not good enough."

"All right. Later."

"Promise?"

"You have my word on it."

And the parting look she gave him told him she was one lady who kept her word. Lucky him.

21

"A what?" Cousin Harold whispered to Cousin Cressida.

"A barbecue, I think he said."

"God, I hope it's not one of those red Indian ritual things. I've heard about them, you know. They tie people to stakes and roast them alive, and then they—"

"You're disgusting. Cousin Prescott isn't going to roast anyone. But if he were, I'd put your name at the top of his list."

"That will be quite enough, you two." Aunt Charity tilted her parasol to keep the sunlight off her face, wishing the frilly piece of stretched fabric could keep the smell of burning wood out of her nostrils. "As your cousin has been so generous in allowing us to visit him, you should accept his rather odd form of hospitality without slander."

With the exception of one or two, all of the Calderwoods were sitting on the grassy slope in front of the castle watching Prescott supervise the tending of the fire in the pit.

"But we've never heard of a barbecue, Auntie," Cressida said. "Not one like Cousin Prescott's, at any rate."

"Perhaps you'll learn something of his heritage then," the old woman said. "If you can keep your eyes open and your mouths shut long enough."

"He can't hear us," Harold said. "And even if he could, I doubt he would do anything about it. He doesn't look that intelligent to me."

"*Au contraire.*" Cressida eyed the play of muscles in Prescott's tanned forearms and the way his broad shoulders moved beneath his shirt. "Our esteemed cousin might appear like some half-civilized savage, but I shouldn't wonder that he would take great delight in teaching you a few of his Western manners." He looked as though he knew how to satisfy a woman in bed, too, but she wasn't about to apprise simpering old Harold of that fact. It might intimidate him.

"Well, you're right about him being a half-civilized savage, but Western manners? The man has none, that I can see."

Heading for Prescott with a large pitcher of lemonade, Lucinda overheard only a small portion of the hushed conversation, but it was enough to set her teeth on edge.

"He's got a lot more than you," she mumbled as she swept past the trio.

"What'd she say?" Aunt Charity asked.

"I don't know, I didn't quite catch it," Cressida said.

"I wonder if she thinks she's the lady of the manor," Harold said. "She certainly acts as if she is."

"She may well act like it, but she isn't," Cressida said. "She's merely one of Cousin Prescott's poor relations. A bastard, from what I understand."

"Quite a fetching one, though," Harold said.

"You aren't becoming smitten with her, are you, cousin?"

"I could be."

Cressida tossed her head back and laughed. "She's totally unfit for you, Harold."

"Here, here," Aunt Charity said.

"Unfit, how?"

"For one thing, she lacks breeding."

"Dear cousin, when one is born a Trefarrow, one has breeding."

"All right then, she's the wrong gender for you."

"There you go again, you sniveling cow, besmirching my manhood."

"What manhood?"

"Oh, I've heard enough," Aunt Charity said, rising to her feet. "The two of you have succeeded in giving me the most beastly headache. I shall need at least three hours rest before I can even think of being sociable again."

"Three hours?" Harold said when the old woman had walked out of earshot. "She couldn't be sociable in three years."

"You're one to talk."

Standing near the edge of the barbecue pit, waiting for the flames to render the split pieces of oak into uniform pieces of white, glowing coals, Prescott took a sip of the lemonade Lucinda had poured for him. He stared up the hill and saw his cousins trudging back toward the castle, bickering with every step they took.

"I didn't think they'd last long," he said. "Neither one of them look like they've seen a lick of sun in their whole life. Heat must've got to them."

"The heat or the boredom," Lucinda said.

"If I thought there was a chance in hell of you being right, darlin', I'd cancel tonight's little shindig and let them entertain each other. Get rid of them real quick that way."

"Or you'd have a double murder on your hands. Your cousin Cressida doesn't appear to like your cousin Harold very much."

"Neither do I, but I don't think I'd resort to murder to get rid of him."

"Then perhaps he will murder her."

"Now there's an idea." Prescott looked back at the fire and liked what he saw. "Won't be long now. A few more minutes and we can put the meat on to cook. How's everything going in the kitchen?"

"As well as can be expected, I suppose. Mrs. Sweet has prepared your sauce recipe down to the very letter, but she refuses to taste it."

"Why?"

"She says it looks poisonous."

Prescott laughed. "No, it won't kill you. It might give you a bad case of the belly-wobbles long about midnight, but it won't kill you."

Belly-wobbles, Lucinda thought, smiling. Prescott had such an interesting way with words.

"Did you find the costume you wanted before the others picked our attics clean?" he asked.

"Yes, I did, thank you."

"Bet it's pretty."

"I think so."

"Can't wait to see it."

"I think you'll be pleasantly surprised," she said. "Have you chosen what you're going to wear?"

"Yep. Had it in mind all along when I first thought of all of us wearing costumes."

"What period is it?"

"Recent."

"How recent? Georgian? Regency?"

"Naw, more recent than that."

Something in his tone alerted her, made her feel uneasy. "Prescott?"

"Yes?"

"What's going on in that mischief-riddled mind of yours?"

"Why, nothing, darlin'. Whatever gave you the idea something was?"

"That devilish look in your eye."

His gleam vanished into a face of feigned innocence. "You must be seeing things. There ain't a mischievous bone in my whole body."

"You're up to something no good, aren't you? I can feel it."

"Just trying to keep the kinfolks entertained, make them feel at home, is all."

"Yes, and I'm the Duchess of Windsor."

He leaned over and kissed her on the cheek. "Run on up to the house and tell Mrs. Sweet I'm ready for the meat and the sauce."

As she turned to leave, he swatted her playfully on the behind. The men helping him with the fire chuckled as she yelped and took off running.

"'At's showing 'er, milord."

Prescott simply grinned.

* * *

"'Make them feel right at home?'" Lucinda echoed when she finally saw Prescott's costume later that night. "I thought you meant their home, not yours."

Prescott leaned over to tie the leather straps of his holster around the lower part of his thigh. When he straightened, he adjusted the belt and heavy revolvers to a more comfortable position around his waist. He was wearing faded blue Levis, a faded blue shirt, scuffed boots with spurs that jangled, and a rather despicable-looking kerchief around his neck. All he had to do, Lucinda thought, was slip the kerchief up over his nose and he would be ready to hold up a stagecoach.

"Man's got to make the best of the hand he's been dealt, darlin'. If had my way, this place would be my home. I'd turn it into the Triple T."

"Graze cows on the front lawn?"

"Maybe. For starters, though, I'd get rid of them dang suits of armor downstairs and replace them with longhorns from a few of my steers back home. Dress this place up a bit."

"And would you be holding nightly gunfights in the drawing room?"

"If I had the hankering to, maybe I would."

She eyed the twin revolvers at his hips. "Those things aren't loaded, I hope."

"Man ought never wear one 'less he's got bullets in all six chambers and is prepared to use it. My daddy taught me that."

"Are you going to shoot anyone who crosses you tonight?"

"I might. Them Calderwoods get out of hand, these'll put them in line right quick-like."

"Honestly, Prescott, you are incorrigible."

"And you're beautiful, darlin'. That's the prettiest little dress I believe I've ever seen."

"You really like it?" She fanned out the full muslin skirt and did a quick pirouette in front of him.

"I love it. Problem is, every man tonight's gonna love it, too. You really think you ought to be showing that much of your bosom?"

Her hands flew up to her chest. When she had first tried on the dress and saw herself in the mirror, she had thought the neckline modest, with only a hint of provocativeness about it, but now she wasn't so sure. "Well, it was designed to show a woman's bosom, but if you think it reveals too much . . ."

"No, it ought to be all right, I guess." He moved to a much closer proximity, towering over her and peering down at her cleavage. "Just don't do much bending over."

"Perhaps I should wear a lace shawl."

"Might be a good idea to take one along. Just in case, you understand. It might get kind of cold out tonight."

"Out? We're dining outside?"

Prescott laughed. "Darlin', you don't eat barbecue inside. You eat it outside."

"Like a picnic?"

"Kinda. The stuff's messier'n hell to eat, but it sure is tasty."

"Oh, my. I don't think your family will be very delighted with the idea of dining out on the lawn."

"We won't be on the lawn. We'll be up on the porch. Er, I mean, terrace. Got the tables and chairs all set up and everything. Even had Mrs. Sweet find us plenty of napkins and washrags, too. We're gonna need all we can get before the night's over."

Lucinda merely shook her head and turned to leave.

"Where you going?"

"I'm just going up to the nursery to check on the children. I shouldn't be long."

"They ought to be in bed by now."

"That doesn't necessarily mean they are, though, as you well know. They've been somewhat rebellious all day."

"That's 'cause they're bored."

"Bored?"

"Yeah, they ain't got nothing to keep them busy. I know we've been out riding with them a couple of times, but mostly they just sit up in that nursery playing together, getting read to, or taking naps. You did that all day, you'd get bored too."

"I do try my best to —"

"Aw, it ain't your fault, darlin'. You're doing the best job you know how, and it's a good one. It's just that they're little kids. They got a lot of energy they need to use up 'fore they can sleep good at night. What they really need is some wide open spaces to run around in, a few trees to climb, and when the mood strikes 'em, a chance to go skinny-dipping. Or whatever it is little girls do when they're alone near a puddle of water. They'd get so plumb tuckered out doing that, they'd have a hard time holding their heads up at the supper table."

"Well, we have wide open spaces here, but not many trees. And if I've understood your terms 'skinny dipping' correctly, they would probably catch cold in the puddles of water 'round Ravens Lair. You wouldn't want them to get sick, would you?"

"Nope, sure wouldn't. But most kids are a lot stronger than they look."

"But they're little girls, too; remember that. You can't apply your childhood experiences to them, because you were a little boy. And little boys and little girls are made differently."

"That's what makes y'all so special." Prescott kissed the tip of her nose and turned her around to face the door. "Now run along and check up on our young'uns, and I'll meet you downstairs when you're through."

Lucinda did check on the girls and found that her concern for them had been groundless. All three were curled up fast asleep in their little beds, looking like three tiny blond angels. Ursula, who had volunteered to watch them rather than help serve at what she called "his lordship's barbaric feast," sat beside a flickering lamp, knitting.

"If they should awaken at any time," Lucinda said, "you will let me know, won't you?"

"Mmm," the woman said, her squinting eyes never leaving her flying fingers.

"Thank you, Ursula."

"Mmm."

"Those children are very dear to his lordship. Were he here now, I'm sure he would thank you, too."

The woman squinted up at her. "All babies be dear, Miss."

"Yes, well, I'm sure you're right. I shall come up and check on them again later."

"Mmm."

Leaving Ursula to her knitting, Lucinda descended the stairs to join Prescott. Music and laughter and the clinking of glasses greeted her as she rounded the landing. The Calderwoods, she strongly suspected, were either so well into their cups that they didn't care about the evening's dining arrangements, or Prescott had not yet informed them. Either way, his festivities for the night were off to a rollicking good start.

Reaching the bottom of the stairs, she started toward the drawing room, where large doors opened out onto the wide stone terrace. But a movement at the back of the stairs caught her eye. She glanced back and saw Hargreaves going down into the cellar. Surely he wasn't going to fetch more wine. He had brought up enough bottles earlier to last Prescott's guests more than a few hours.

She started to call out to him, but stopped when she saw how stealthily he moved and how furtively he looked over his shoulder in both directions as if to make certain that no one saw him. Then he slipped through the door and closed it behind him.

What on earth was he up to? she wondered, knowing instinctively that something was amiss. She knew, too, that Prescott needed to be made aware of his valet's actions.

She found him outside on the terrace, overseeing the carving of the huge haunch of beef.

"I must speak with you a moment, Prescott."

"Now?"

"It's important."

A huge burst of light suddenly filled the sky, followed by another and another, drawing the guests inside the drawing room out onto the terrace.

"So's this, darlin'. Ain't it pretty?"

"Fireworks? That's what was in all those huge crates? And that's why you brought the Italian here?"

Prescott beamed. "It's the Fourth of July, darlin'. Can't celebrate my nation's independence without a good old-fashioned barbecue and fireworks show."

"Fourth of July?" Aunt Charity, dressed to look like Queen Victoria in crisp black taffeta and a headdress of ostrich feathers, made her way over to Prescott, her usual scowl deepening into a look of pure malevolence. "You insult us with this display of what can only be described as—as Colonial insolence!"

"I ain't insulting nobody, Aunt Charity, least of all you. I'm just celebrating, like any normal, red-blooded American back home would do."

"But this is England, you surly boy, not America."

"And I'm an American, not English. 'Bout time y'all understood that."

"I think it's wonderful," said Cousin Harold, who was dressed as Lord Byron in satin knickers and lacy ascot. "Good show, old man. Jolly good show."

"Here, here," said Cousin Cressida. Like Lucinda, she had chosen a Regency-period gown, only her cleavage was more daring, leaving little to the imagination. "Shows you've not only Calderwood blood in your veins, you've our spunk as well, Cousin. Something some of us lack."

"If that jibe was intended for me," said Cousin Harold, "it fell short by a bloody mile."

"Oh, you think you have spunk, Cousin?"

"I know I do, you spiteful cow."

Realizing the cousins were about to begin another of their lengthy arguments, Lucinda tugged hard on Prescott's arm. "I need to speak to you *now.*"

The urgency in her voice finally caught his attention. "Okay. Y'all excuse me a minute. Enjoy the show. And the vittles. Supper's ready."

He followed her into the drawing room, and then on into the foyer, where the loud explosions didn't drown out her voice. "What's going on?"

"That's what I'd like to know," she said. "Why is Hargreaves in the cellar?"

"How the hell should I know? He's a grown man, able to take care of himself. I got a houseful of kinfolk to feed; I can't be worrying about him. Maybe he's just down there doing something."

She raised her eyebrows and stared at him, her look speaking volumes.

"Oh, come on," he said. "Only thing down there is a bunch of dusty old wine racks and—and the dungeon."

"Yes?"

"And Emerson is in the dungeon."

"Are you sure of that? When was the last time you checked on him?"

"Er, day before yesterday, I think."

"Well, your man Hargreaves has been spending an inordinate amount of time visiting the cellar recently, or hadn't you noticed?"

"I noticed. But he told me he was just checking on the wine we had."

"I hate to be the one to tell you this, but you've been deceived. We've enough wine in that cellar to last us well into the next century. He's there for some other reason."

"No. No, no, no. He wouldn't set Emerson loose. Would he?"

"I know very little about the man. He's your valet, not mine."

Prescott took off like a shot, running to the cellar door. "By God, if he's gone and let that son of a bitch out of his cell, I'll—I'll wring Ed's scrawny Limey neck."

Lucinda was a half step behind him, her slippers

sliding on the polished marble floor. "Temper, Prescott. Please, do mind your temper. And you'd best take along a lamp; it's frightfully dark down there."

"Where do you think you're going?"

"With you, of course."

"The hell you are. You're staying up here."

"The hell I am. Where you go, I follow. Remember our vows?"

"Goddammit, Lucinda, I ain't got time to argue those vows with you now. Keep your pretty little butt outa my way, you hear?" He bent down and gave her a quick kiss on the cheek. "I'll be back directly."

As he disappeared through the cellar door, she stood there a moment, debating whether to follow her own instincts and go after him, or to be the dutiful common-law wife that she had made of herself and obey him. It took her no time to decide on the former.

Grabbing up a nearby lamp and lighting it, she pushed the door open and began descending the steep stairs.

22

"When did you find it?" Hargreaves stared at the side of the wine rack, barely able to see the narrow slit all but hidden on the wall behind it.

"Just before you came down," Emerson said. "I've been searching this place top to bottom for weeks, like you told me, and I finally found that."

"You've not touched anything have you?"

"Nothing, sir. I would have, of course, but I couldn't move this rack. Not alone."

"Good man. *His lordship* is occupied with his guests, making a complete ass of himself, so we shouldn't be bothered by him or his doxy for a long while. We'll just move all the bottles out of the way, and then we'll both have a look, shall we?"

Doxy? Prescott stood in the shadows on the far side of the cavernous cellar, watching his valet and Emerson and listening to every word they said. He didn't mind being called an ass, even a complete ass, because there were times when he thought of himself that way, but he drew the line at the likes of Ed calling Lucinda a doxy.

He started to step out of the shadows to make his presence and his objections known, but a slender hand suddenly grabbed his arm and pulled him back.

"Let it go, Prescott," Lucinda whispered, grateful that the sound of clinking wine bottles covered her voice.

"But that son of a bitch just called you—"

"I know. I heard him. Let it go."

"What the hell are you doing down here anyway? I thought I told you to stay upstairs."

"I didn't listen, obviously. What in heaven's name are they doing?"

"Beats the hell out of me. They're not taking inventory of Ravens Lair's wine stock, that's for damn sure."

"For some time I've suspected that he's been searching the castle for something. Maybe now we shall find out what he's looked for."

"Who's been searching the castle? Emerson?"

"No, your valet, Hargreaves."

"You've seen him?"

"And heard him. So have the girls."

"Why didn't you say anything?"

"I thought he might have been carrying out your orders."

"My orders?"

"Yes, you have been rather secretive about your goings-on here of late."

"About the party and fireworks tonight, yeah, but nothing else."

They fell silent as Hargreaves removed the last

bottle and carefully placed it on the floor alongside the others. "Ready to shift this unwieldy beast?"

Emerson spat on his hands. "Let me get a solid hold first."

The two men clutched the same shelf, one at either end, and, on the count of three, they gave a mighty heave.

The wine rack didn't budge as much as the veins in their neck and the muscles in their backs.

"God bless sturdy English oak," Hargreaves said.

"Bless it or damn it, sir, it's not going to move."

In the shadows, Prescott turned to grin down at Lucinda. "They ain't got a brain between 'em."

"Shhh!"

"Perhaps we both should try to move the same end," Hargreaves said.

"Aye, maybe that'll work, sir."

"Now they're thinking," Prescott whispered.

Emerson moved to Hargreaves' end, and both men gave another mighty heave. The rack screeched across the floor a fraction of an inch, leaving a deep groove embedded in the dirt floor.

"Again," Hargreaves said.

"They're gonna be here all night at this rate," Prescott said.

"Will you shut up?" Lucinda hissed. "They'll hear you."

Another dozen attempts succeeded in moving the wine rack away from the stone and solidly packed dirt wall no more than two feet. But it was enough for Hargreaves and Emerson to squeeze through.

Prescott started after them, but again Lucinda stopped him. "You can't seriously be thinking of following them, can you?"

"Dead serious, darlin'."

"Prescott, have you forgotten that Garrick is a—a madman? I don't want you getting hurt."

"Aw, you're so sweet." He leaned over to kiss her but she stepped away.

"If you go after them, I'll— I'll —"

"What, go back upstairs where you belong?"

"No! I'll go with you."

He wrapped an arm around her neck and pulled her close. "Darlin', I've never hit a woman in my life. But right now, I'm tempted to knock you clean out just to keep you out of my way. Out of trouble, too."

"You wouldn't dare."

"No, 'course I wouldn't. But I don't want you following me, either. Why don't you go up and check on the girls. I'll bet all the racket from the fireworks has woke 'em up."

"When they fall asleep," Lucinda said, "nothing can wake them, so think of another excuse why I can't go with you."

"You won't get in the way?"

"I'll stay a good two feet behind you."

"Uh-huh, sure you will."

"I swear, Prescott, I will."

"Jesus save me from hardheaded women. All right, come on. But take one of these, just in case." He handed her one of his revolvers and almost laughed when the weight pulled her arm down.

"I might carry it, but I shan't use it."

"Do you even know how?"

"Of course I know how. You just aim it this way and pull the trigger."

Prescott ducked when she swung the barrel in his direction, then reached up and pushed her arm aside.

"You just hold the damn thing, will you? If any aiming and firing needs to be done, I'll do it."

Lucinda smiled angelically. "Whatever you say."

Prescott growled and started for the opening in the wall. As she had promised, Lucinda remained behind him all the way through the opening and into the dark, seemingly endless tunnel that lay beyond. And the farther they journeyed into the unknown, the distance between them lessened from two feet to one, then to hardly any space at all, her body all but hugging his with every step he took.

"You scared?" he asked in a voice just above a whisper.

"N—no, of course not."

He grinned at her obvious lie. "'At's my girl. Better give me the lamp."

"Why?"

"I'm taller, I can hold it higher and out in front. We'll see better."

"Oh." She handed him the lamp, then resumed her place right behind him. "Where do you suppose they are?"

"There's no telling. What is this place, anyway?"

"The smuggler barons' cavern, I suspect."

"Smuggler barons?"

"Yes, you remember, I told you about them."

"No, I don't think so."

"I must have done, Prescott."

"You told me about the first earls, but you never said anything about any smuggler barons."

"Oh, well, I should have done."

"Any of them wear dresses and wander the castle halls at night stealing women's jewelry?"

"No, you silly goose, the barons raped, and pillaged

unsuspecting ships they lured onto the rocky coast."

"Oh, pirates, huh?"

"Some were. Most were nothing more than lazy louts who eked out a living pillaging—"

"Unsuspecting ships they lured onto the rocky coast. Yeah, I think I understand. What happened to them?"

"The last one sailed with his family and henchmen for Jamaica, or some such island in the Caribbean, when Oliver Cromwell dethroned and beheaded Charles I."

"Didn't much care for Cromwell's politics, huh?"

"More likely the last baron feared for his life. Cromwell was a nasty bit of business, quite avid in his quest to purify the whole of England. His followers, from what I've read, were even worse. They closed down all the theaters and gaming houses in London, made religion and piety the only acceptable forms of entertainment, if you can call it that, and they hanged or burned at the stake any person they suspected of practicing witchcraft."

"Packing up and sailing to Jamaica would sound good to me, too, if I had to live like that."

"It's said that the last baron made his departure from Ravens Lair so quickly he left behind a vast treasure room full of stolen bounty."

"Treasure here, right under our very noses?"

"It's only a rumor, Prescott, a tale that's been handed down from generation to generation. Always told, I might add, when times were tough."

"I don't 'spect anybody's gone looking for it, have they?"

"At one time or another, every Trefarrow has looked for it. Unfortunately, they never found anything."

"Yeah, well, that's the direction the Trefarrow luck usually runs, ain't it? We're always in need of money, and we can never get our hands on it."

They left one tunnel and turned down another, the walls growing damper, the air mustier, and the dirt floor at a steeper angle.

"Money isn't everything, Prescott."

"It is when you don't have any, darl—" He broke off abruptly, seeing a faint light flicker up ahead, and hearing the sound of voices.

"That's gotta be them. From here on, no talking, understand?" Feeling Lucinda nod behind him, Prescott whispered, "Stick close to me and keep that gun handy."

Suddenly one of the men gave out a loud whoop. "This is it!"

Prescott recognized his valet's voice and wondered what "it" was. The last baron's buried treasure, he hoped.

"I knew it had to be here," Hargreaves said, "I knew all along."

"What is it?" Emerson asked. "A book? You've had me scouring the dungeon and this filthy cellar all this time for a bloody book?"

"This, my good man, is more than just a book. It's my grandmother's journal, her private accountings of what transpired here before my birth."

"But there's plenty of journals up in the library."

"Not like this one. This one will identify the true lord of Ravens Lair. I suspect that's why Grandmama had it hidden away down here. My grandfather refused to accept the truth. She knew it and, in her own way, tried to preserve this legacy for me. God love the dear woman."

Keeping close to the dirt wall, Prescott stopped at the entrance of the small alcove, where a faint light spilled out into the main corridor. He handed his lamp to Lucinda and chanced a quick look inside the chamber. Hargreaves and Emerson knelt on the floor, their backs to him. Between them sat a small wooden sewing box, its lid opened, its prized contents resting in his valet's hands.

Lucinda, too, had a peek, and the sight of Hargreaves' shadow on the wall startled her. Until that moment, she had never paid much attention to the valet, therefore she had never noticed the remarkable resemblance his profile bore to Prescott's. They had the same angular cheeks, the same strong, determined chin, the same wide forehead. Thinking back, she knew they were both tall and lanky in build, even though Prescott was more muscular from having labored hard through his years spent in Texas. Why, even their eyes were the same shade of green.

"Yes, yes, yes!" Hargreaves said. "Listen to this, Emerson.

> *. . . they returned from Gretna Green in such high spirits, not to meet with well wishes but the wrath of my good husband. I know not what drives him. He not only swore to disown Giles but promised to have Giles's bride, Helena, tried, convicted, and sent to the penal colony in Australia on the charge of theft and prostitution if my darling son did not agree to have his new marriage annulled. The devastation I saw in their young eyes filled my heart with such pity for them, I now take matters into my own hands with the hopes that my good husband,*

the earl, never learns of my perfidy. Though Giles' marriage to Helena is surely torn asunder, I shall keep their wedding document as proof of their innocent young love. Perhaps one day, if not in England, then surely in Heaven, they shall be united again.

"And this is it." Hargreaves unfolded the piece of old parchment he found tucked inside the journal. "The document that proves my father was indeed married to my mother at the time of my conception. It's legal, and so am I."

"You bastards!"

Emerson's angry growl had Hargreaves looking up, and the knife in Emerson's hands had him moving back. Seeing the direction of Emerson's gaze, he looked over his shoulder at Prescott and Lucinda, who stood in the entrance.

"Put that away," he told Emerson. "We've no need of violence now. No need for more secrets, either. I'm glad you found me out, Prescott. Or should I say, Cousin Prescott?"

"Cousin?" Prescott stepped into the alcove, making sure Lucinda stayed safely behind him.

"Don't pretend you didn't hear," Hargreaves said. "I'm sure you heard every word."

"Yeah, I did, but I don't think I understand."

"It's quite simple, really. I'm the tenth Earl of St. Keverne, and you are an impostor. This"—Hargreaves waved the marriage document—"is proof of my birthright."

"All I see is a piece of paper." Though Prescott tried to keep his tone light, hoping he sounded confused, his mind groped for a way in which he could get

Lucinda safely out of this situation. Emerson had a knife, and Prescott didn't want to find out if the man knew how to use it.

"Ah, but it's more than that, Cousin. This document ends nearly fifty years of well-intended deceit and treachery by my dear grandmother, your great-grandmother, the Eighth Countess of St. Keverne. It proves that I am the legitimate heir to Ravens Lair."

"Heir?" Prescott's attention on Emerson and the knife he wielded faded somewhat. "You're claiming to be the real heir to this place?"

"Yes, I am," Hargreaves said proudly.

Prescott tried, but he just couldn't stop himself from laughing. He'd left his home, his family, everything he'd known and loved, to come to a wretched, unfriendly country where, with the exception of Lucinda and the three little girls, hardly anyone liked him or trusted him, and it had all been for nothing? "Jesus Christ, I can't believe it."

Certain that his upstart American cousin was mocking him, Hargreaves rose to his feet, his expression indignant as he inadvertently put himself between Emerson and the two standing in the entranceway. "Well, you had better begin to believe it, Cousin. As soon as I can present this document and my grandmother's journal to one of Her Majesty's magistrates, and he verifies their authenticity, it shall only be a matter of time before you are out on your ear."

"You want a magistrate, Ed? I just happen to have one upstairs right now."

"Yes, Judge Chenoweth," Hargreaves said.

"That's right. What do you say you and me go see him, see what he has to say about those papers of yours?"

Emerson flashed his blade. "No! Nobody leaves here until his lordship and I have settled the matters between us."

"You've no matters to settle, Emerson," Hargreaves said.

"No matters? He took my life, all that I worked for, from me."

"You didn't work," Prescott said. "You stole everything."

"I worked," Emerson said. "From sunup to sundown for a mere pittance of what that miserable, dying old bugger could afford."

Lucinda stepped out from behind Prescott. "Uncle Herbert was not a miserable old bugger. He was a kind, decent man, Garrick, and you took advantage of him when he hadn't the mental or physical ability to defend himself."

"Oh, aye. So kind and decent he preferred his bastard niece over his own son."

"Uncle Herbert had no son. He—"

"Had only daughters? No, not quite."

A brief silence ensued, giving Emerson's unspoken words time to register.

Prescott groaned. "Oh, God, not another relative."

"*You?*" Lucinda asked, shock widening her eyes. "You're Uncle Herbert's son?"

"His bastard son," Emerson said. "And your cousin."

"I don't believe it," Lucinda said.

"You had better, because it's true. My mother apprised me of their liaison as she lay dying. I'm the one who should have the title and the estate, not this barbarian you've bedded down with."

"A liaison is not a legal marriage," Hargreaves said.

"Neither is that claim of yours."

"But it is, old man."

"Not for much longer."

Emerson reached for the journal, but Hargreaves turned sharply, stretching his arm full-length to keep it out of his reach. Taking action, Prescott jerked the revolver out of Lucinda's hand, pointed it at Emerson, and fired just as Emerson shoved Hargreaves aside, putting the valet directly into the line of fire. As the deafening shot rang out, Hargreaves sank to the floor, blood slowly beginning to stain the sleeve of his coat.

"Son of a bitch!" Prescott took aim again, but Emerson was too quick for him. He fled the chamber and disappeared down the tunnel.

Prescott started to take off after him, but realized that Hargreaves needed his attention more. After all, his whole future depended on the life of the valet.

Lucinda sank to her knees beside Hargreaves and began to examine his wound.

"How bad is it?" Prescott asked.

"I can't be certain, of course," she said, "but I think it's only a flesh wound."

Hargreaves stared up at him. "You shot me."

"I'm sorry," Prescott said. "It's not my fault. I was aiming at Emerson, and he—"

"Well, you bloody well missed him by a bleeding mile, didn't you?"

"Such language, Mr. Hargreaves," Lucinda said. "Or should I call you Cousin?"

"Call me any bleeding thing you like. Goddamn, this hurts!"

"He'll be all right," Lucinda said.

"You sure?" Prescott frowned.

"As sure as I can be of anything at this point."

"Good, then you take care of Ed."

"Me?" she said. "What about you? You can't just leave him here like this."

"Then take him back upstairs, and don't let him lose too much blood. I can't afford to have him bleed to death."

"Such sincere concern for a man who's about to claim your inheritance," Hargreaves said with a sneer.

"Yeah, some inheritance," Prescott said. "But we'll talk about that later. Right now, I've got to go after Emerson."

"Don't be daft, Prescott," Lucinda said. "He'll kill you."

"Not likely, darlin'." Prescott waved his revolver in front of her face. "I got this; he's only got a knife."

"Americans," Hargreaves said as Prescott ran out of the chamber.

In the dim lamplight, Lucinda examined the valet's injury and found it to be just as she had suspected; only a minor flesh wound that looked more unsightly than life threatening. "You're very fortunate, Mr. Hargreaves."

"I'm bleeding, Miss Trefarrow, and in quite a lot of pain. What's so fortunate about that?"

"Had Prescott wanted to kill Garrick instead of merely incapacitate him, as I suspect was his original intent, you would most probably be dead by now."

"Yes, but he missed him and got me instead, didn't he?"

"He's a crack shot, Mr. Hargreaves. Fate sometimes has an odd way of putting even crack shooters off their targets. Can you stand?"

"I'd rather lie here for a while longer, if you don't mind."

"But we need to move you to a more sanitary location. If this dirt should get into your wound, you could develop an infection. Blood poisoning. Gangrene, more to the point."

Hargreaves stared at her incredulously. "You're honestly concerned about my welfare, aren't you?"

"Of course. Why shouldn't I be?"

"Quite simply put, my dear, if I should die, your lover will maintain the title of Tenth Earl of St. Keverne. And eventually, as soon as that barbarian from Texas decides to make an honest woman of you, you will become Countess."

She averted her gaze, but not before color slowly crept into her cheeks. "That isn't likely."

"What, that he will marry you?"

"No, that I will marry him. I'm sure you know of my . . . my circumstances, Mr. Hargreaves."

Hearing the quiet note of shame and pain in Lucinda's voice, the valet realized that he had done her a great wrong by misjudging her. She was no power-seeking adventuress out to get what she could from the current earl, as he had thought, but merely a young woman thrust into the most untenable position that life as a bastard could offer.

"In that case," he said, "I believe I owe you an apology, Miss Trefarrow. Or should I say, Cousin Lucinda?"

"Apologize to me? For what?"

He groaned and tried to stand. "Help me up first. This is the sort of thing a gentleman should explain while on his feet, not flat on his back."

With a lot of pulling and tugging on Lucinda's part, and moaning and groaning from Hargreaves, Lucinda helped him to stand. Once upright, he swayed a bit, forcing her to wrap an arm around his waist to support him.

"You'll have to forgive this weakness of mine," he said. "It's quite unlike me, I assure you. But then so is my being shot. You see, I've never been wounded before."

"No, I didn't think you had. Let us pray that you never get shot again."

"Yes, let us."

Hargreaves leaning on Lucinda, they headed back toward the entrance to the wine cellar.

"Umm, now then, about your cottage . . ." he said.

"My cottage?"

"Yes. I'm frightfully sorry, Cousin."

"Thank you. I think."

"I didn't intend to set fire to it."

"You?"

"Yes. It just sort of happened, all on its own, you see."

Lucinda abruptly removed her support, allowing Hargreaves to fall with a loud groan against the tunnel wall. "You burnt down my house?"

"Not intentionally. I was looking for Grandmama's journals."

"In my cottage?"

"Yes."

"But your grandmother never lived there."

"Ah, but her elderly paid companion did, many years ago. I knew her living arrangements, of course, and I thought that she might have hidden Grandmama's journals there, to keep them away from Grandpapa. While searching for them, I accidentally upset one of your lamps, which I had lighted, and the oil and fire spread faster than I could stop it. Before I knew what was happening, flames had engulfed the whole place, and I was running for my life. I didn't mean for you to lose your home, Cousin. I only wanted to find proof of my birth. My *legitimate* birth. Surely you, of all people, should know how important that sort of thing is."

"Yes," she said, "I know."

"Then you forgive me?"

"For wanting to find proof of your birth, yes. For burning down my cottage, never." She turned around and stalked back in the direction from which they had just come.

"Oh, Cousin, really," Hargreaves called out. "You've made out all right, haven't you? I mean, I know you lost everything, but what are a few trifling possessions when compared to what you have now?"

She changed directions again and came back to him. "And what, pray tell, would that be?"

"Well, that bloody Texan, of course."

"You mean, thanks to you, we're lovers?"

"Well, yes."

"You arrogant ass. Don't you realize that, thanks to you, whatever he and I may have had, may have been, is no longer possible?"

"What are you saying?"

"I'm saying that thanks to your untimely intervention, you've probably ruined both our lives."

"Ruined them? How?"

"Don't you see? Prescott and I no longer have a future together. As it stands now, if you are indeed the legal heir, and I suspect you are, he will be returning to Texas, and I'll be left here, with nothing." No home, no future, and especially no man to fill the long, empty days and nights that remained of her bleak life.

"Don't be ridiculous, Cousin. Even I can see that the two of you love each other."

"Love doesn't last forever, Cousin," Lucinda said. "In time it will fade to nothing more than a pleasant memory. Maybe not even that."

"I think not. A man in love will move heaven and earth to be with the woman of his choice, and you are clearly Prescott's choice."

"A fat lot you know." She turned and headed back into the tunnel, away from the wine cellar entrance.

"Where are you going?"

"Someone must help Prescott find Garrick before Garrick finds and kills him."

"But what about me?" Hargreaves called out.

"For all I care, you can stand there and bleed to death."

Ten minutes later, with minimal light from her lamp to guide her way down one long dark passage after another, Lucinda heard the sound of fighting just up ahead. She stepped up her pace and turned a corner just in time to find Emerson ramming his fist into Prescott's face.

"Stop it!" she cried. "Stop it right now!"

Neither man listened. Both were too intent on trying to best the other.

Prescott dodged one of Emerson's blows and landed a punch of his own in the man's midsection, knocking the breath out of him for a brief moment. When Emerson snapped back, he did so rapidly, lunging for Prescott, and shoving him hard into and through the wall of stone nearby. As rocks tumbled to the dirt floor, Lucinda stepped back, fearing the whole tunnel would collapse around them.

His breathing labored, one eye nearly swollen shut,

blood trickling from his split lip, Emerson lingered for half a heartbeat before he turned and snarled at Lucinda. He shoved past her, nearly knocking her to the ground, and darted away down the tunnel.

She regained her balance quickly enough, hurrying to Prescott's side and throwing off the rocks that had fallen onto him. "Are you all right?"

"Yeah," he groaned. "Where is that son of a bitch?"

"Gone, I'm happy to say. Perhaps this time he'll stay away permanently."

"Not if I can get to him first." Now free of the heaviest stones, Prescott pushed aside the smaller ones and eased himself to his feet.

"You're not going after him again, are you?"

"If I don't, who will?"

"Sheriff Penhalligan, that's who. Oh, do listen to reason, Prescott. You cannot confront Garrick single-handedly."

"I did it before, I'll do it again," he said, holding a hand to his aching ribs.

"And perhaps next time you'll die in the process. I won't hear of it."

"Darlin', I know you're worried and scared, and I know you mean well, but just stay out of this, will you? This is between me and Emerson."

Without another word, he turned around and staggered out into the corridor, not giving Lucinda a backward glance as he headed off in the direction Emerson had gone.

"You fool!" she cried out. "You bloody, stupid fool! Oh, God, save me from bullheaded men. Bullheaded Texans in particular."

No matter what Prescott believed, she knew she couldn't let him face another uncertain confrontation with Emerson alone. She could either go back up to the castle and send for Sheriff Penhalligan and wait heaven only knew how long for the man to arrive, or she could once again follow Prescott and pray that she reached him before he did something to Emerson he would later regret, or before Emerson did something unthinkably ghastly to him.

Of course, the latter notion won out.

However, as Lucinda started to turn, the light from her lamp caused an object inside the collapsed wall to glimmer. She paused a moment, wondering if her eyes were playing tricks on her, then her curiosity got the better of her, and she looked inside.

"My God!"

Tired and winded, his ribs aching, Prescott raced out of the long, dark tunnel. He found himself on a rocky beach, the full moon and bright stars overhead enabling him to see the silhouettes of moored boats bobbing at the wharf just below St. Keverne. And in the distance, running on the beach, heading toward that wharf, was Emerson.

"Stop!" he called out.

If Emerson heard him, he gave no sign, for his feet continued to rapidly churn up the damp sand.

"I said stop!" Prescott withdrew the second revolver from his holster and cocked the hammer. "Don't make me do this, Emerson."

Intending only to fire a warning shot over the man's head, he took careful aim and squeezed the trigger.

At the same moment, Emerson veered to the left, where a slight rise on the beach caused him to ascend. Prescott's bullet caught Emerson squarely in the back, sending him headlong into a powerful wave which crashed against the shore and the craggy, sharp-edged rocks.

"No!" Fearing the worst, and praying to heaven that he was wrong, Prescott raced toward Emerson.

But when he reached the spot where he had seen Emerson fall, the rolling surf had already carried the man's body off the beach and out to sea.

"Oh, God, not this way." He fell weakly to his knees. "Not this way. Not again." He had already killed one man in his life, in self-defense when that man had tried to steal his horse; he had hoped never to have to do it again. But it appeared as though fate, or God, or whoever was directing the events in his life, had had other ideas. Emerson was gone. For good this time.

Without warning, an image of Alexandra, Victoria, and Elizabeth flashed through Prescott's mind. How could he face those three sweet little girls knowing that he had killed their father? But if he didn't face them, tell them what he had done, how could he live with himself and the guilt?

Minutes later, when Lucinda exited the partially-hidden tunnel entrance, she saw Prescott in the distance. He was so still, kneeling there, she feared that Emerson had hurt him badly and was now lurking somewhere in the rocks, just waiting to finish the job or for Prescott to be washed away by the tide. But as she started toward Prescott, she noted the slump of his shoulders, the angle at which he hung his head, and her fears began to dwindle. He was hurt, all right, she decided, but not a physical kind of hurt. His despair reached out to her, engulfed her, and made her realize that he had dispensed with Emerson in the most primitive way known to man.

Without a word, she knelt down beside him, uncaring that the cold, wet sand seeped through her thin gown as she wrapped her arms around his broad shoulders. Prescott turned and embraced her, holding her so close to him, so tightly, he almost squeezed the breath out of her.

"I didn't want it to happen this way," he said in a voice cracked with emotion. "You've gotta believe that."

"I do."

"The last thing I wanted was to kill him."

"I know. It's all right, my love."

Prescott buried his face into the curve of her neck, letting her feel even more profoundly his guilt and sadness.

"Are you sure he's dead?"

"Yeah, I'm sure. I shot him."

"You could have missed him again."

He pulled back and looked down into her upturned face. "Again?"

"Well, you did miss him back in the tunnel, you know, and shot Hargreaves instead. I mean, Cousin Edward."

Prescott considered her suggestion for a moment, but then shook his head. "No, I'm sure I hit him this time. Everything happened so fast, though . . . I thought I was shooting over his head, but somehow the bullet hit him instead, and then a wave got him and washed him out to sea. If he'd still been alive, I'm sure he—"

"Shhh. Don't talk about it. It's over and now best forgotten."

"But I never even saw his face."

"Is that so important?"

"Yeah. No, I guess not. It's just that— Well, I don't know what I'm gonna tell the girls. His girls."

"*Your* girls, Prescott. Alexandra, Victoria, and Elizabeth have been your children, not Garrick's, since the moment you took them out of that hovel he'd left them in and moved them into the castle."

"My girls or his, it doesn't change the fact that sooner or later I'm gonna have to tell them something."

"Well, of course you will, if they ask."

"They will."

"They haven't so far. I've spent a great deal of time with them."

"Yeah, I know."

"And not once since they've been at Ravens Lair can I recall them ever so much as having spoken his name. Their mother's name, yes, many times, but not Garrick's. He was never a part of their lives. Not like you, at least. You're their father."

"Not yet," he said, rising to his feet and then helping Lucinda to stand, "but, God willing, I soon will be. Those three little girls will never know another day of hunger or lack of love or attention." He issued a mirthless snort. "I wish I could say they'd never know another day of being poor, but as soon as I change their name to Trefarrow, that's probably all they'll ever know."

"Perhaps not." Lucinda dipped a hand into the wet folds of her gown and produced a round object that glittered in the moonlight.

"What's that?"

"A pretty bauble I found. Here, have a look."

He took it from her outstretched palm and found it to be a ring. A man's ring, he realized, feeling its considerable weight, with one large stone in a wide band. Despite the moonlight, he couldn't determine what kind of stone it was, but something told him it was real and probably quite old.

"Where'd you find this?"

"In the hole in the stone wall that Garrick pushed you through. There was more in there along with this."

"More?"

Lucinda nodded. "Much more."

A knot the size of a turkey's egg began to grow in the pit of Prescott's stomach, but he ignored it. "Show me."

With a smile, she led him back inside the tunnel, and a few minutes later, both crawled through the small opening in the now-collapsed stone wall, the light from her lamp guiding their way.

"Good Lord Almighty, is this the last baron's hidden treasure?" He stared in wonder at the three small wooden casks resting on the floor.

"That would be my guess."

"So it was more than just an old family fable after all, huh?"

"So it would seem," she said. "I didn't have time to look into all of them, just the one there that's open, but what I found was enough to excite me."

Lucinda could only guess what the sight of the opened cask laden with gold and silver coins and jewels did to Prescott. He suddenly seemed to have lost the ability to speak coherently, muttering slurred, disjointed words and phrases as he fell to his knees to sift through the contents of the first cask. When that one had been inspected, he went on to the second, and then the third, sifting his hands through their contents and bringing them out into the open after centuries of being hidden away.

"Do you know what this means?" he asked at last,

pulling her down beside him. "Do you have any idea at all what this means?"

"Er, we Trefarrows are no longer destitute?"

"More'n that, darlin'. Much more. We're rich. Filthy, stinking rich."

"I suppose we are, if all of this is worth anything."

"Worth anything? It's worth a fortune; I'd stake my life on it."

"But if it's so valuable, why did the last baron leave it behind?"

"You said he left Ravens Lair in a hurry, didn't you?"

"Yes."

"Well, maybe he just plumb forgot it. Who knows, who cares, darlin'? It's ours now—yours, mine, and the girls—and I'm gonna—"

"Share it with Cousin Edward, I hope."

An image of his valet—his *former* valet—suddenly flashed into Prescott's mind. "Oh, yeah, him."

"It's his as well as yours, you know. Or it will be his when his claim is proven valid and he assumes your position as the rightful Earl of St. Keverne."

"But isn't there some law here about—"

"I wouldn't know about legalities, Prescott. I only know that, morally speaking, you are not the earl."

"The hell I'm not. Until someone tells me different—until someone tell's *him* different—I'm the one in charge here."

"But not for much longer. Cousin Edward will soon have legal right to everything. Even this."

During his quick inspection of the casks, Prescott had found a lady's ring with a pretty little blue stone—a sapphire, he hoped—that looked to be just about Lucinda's size. He took her left hand in his and slid it on her ring finger. "It's a perfect fit. Almost like it was made 'specially for you."

Lucinda looked at the ring in the lamplight, admiring the deep color of the unfaceted stone. It did fit her very well, and it was quite lovely, but she knew that to wear it any longer than necessary would be courting certain heartache.

"But it wasn't made for me," she said, pulling at the ring, wanting to take it off and give it back to Prescott. "And because it's not mine, I can't—I can't wear it. Damn, I think it's stuck."

"Then just leave it alone."

"I can't. Didn't you hear me? It's not mine."

"I found it, I say it's yours, so leave it alone."

"Do be serious, Prescott. I can't wear this ring. What will everyone think?"

He took her face gently in his hands and turned her gaze up to his. "That we're engaged. It's about time we made it official, don't you think?"

She froze, unable to breathe properly as a thousand conflicting emotions warred within her. More than anything, she wanted to say yes, she loved him, and yes, she wanted to marry him, wanted to spend the rest of her life with him. But nothing had changed. They had found some long-dead smuggler baron's hidden treasure and the Trefarrow family's financial status was now on a sounder footing, but even that couldn't change the fact that she was illegitimate, and always would be.

Excitement forced Prescott to his feet, and he pulled her up after him. "Come on. We gotta go see Ed, tell him our good news. Gotta see how he's doing, too."

"Cousin Edward is fine." Much finer than she was at the moment.

"I hope you're right. Sure would hate to see him die on us when we're so close to going home. Hey, while we're at it, we'll even make our big announcement."

"Big announcement?"

"Yeah, that we're engaged. Maybe even get Judge Chenoweth to marry us before he leaves. Unless you're wanting a big church wedding with all the trimmings."

"No!"

"Yeah, you're right. We're better off keeping it small. Just family, right?"

"No, I mean, we—we can't get married."

Prescott merely laughed as he pulled her out into the tunnel. "That's what you think, darlin'."

Prescott Trefarrow had to be the most bull-headed man Lucinda had ever known. He understood why she couldn't marry him, because she had explained it to him a thousand times over, yet he simply would not take no for an answer.

She had remained calm, standing by him silently as he had announced to his mother's family that, due to certain facts that had just recently come to light, he was no longer the Tenth Earl of St. Keverne and that his former valet, Edward Giles Hargreaves Trefarrow was, and that he intended to renounce his title and hand the estate over to his newly-found cousin at the first opportunity. But when he took her hand in his and told everyone that they would soon be marrying, she had the immediate and most uncomfortable feeling that all eyes in the room focused directly on her. A small coterie of his unmarried female cousins, standing in a close huddle, actually shot visual daggers at her.

She could well imagine what they all thought of her, they with their smug, condescending, disapproving expressions and she with her muddy gown, her wind-blown hair hanging in wet tendrils about her face and shoulders, and an embarrassed blush creeping into her cheeks. Prescott's poor relation could only have set her snare for him and caught him in the oldest manner known to womankind.

But they were wrong. She hadn't set out to trap Prescott, or any man for that matter. Nor had she set out to fall in love with him, or have him fall in love with her, which he obviously had. God in heaven, when would this nightmare end? When would they all leave—Prescott included—and let her get back to her boring, uneventful, yet safe life? Never, from the looks of it.

"This is most unbelievable, your lordship," Judge Chenoweth said, stepping forward. "You're not the true earl after all?"

"Nope," Prescott said with a satisfied grin, "not if Ed's document is the real thing, I ain't."

Hargreaves, holding his bandaged arm close to his side, shifted to a more comfortable position in his chair and held up his grandmother's journal. "It is the real thing, I assure you."

"Well, we must have it authenticated, you understand," the judge said.

"Of course," Hargreaves said.

"The sooner the better," Prescott said.

The judge nodded. "Then I shall make a point of looking into it first thing in the morning."

"Good, you do that," Prescott said. "In the meantime, I want y'all to eat, drink, and have yourselves a high old time, 'cause it looks like this'll be the last time y'all'll be coming here to Ravens Lair. I don't 'spect Ed here's gonna want my kinfolks dropping in for a visit. And you," he said, turning to Hargreaves, "better get yourself up to bed and take care of that wounded arm of yours. I can't afford to have you getting sick and dying on me. Not now. Not when I'm this close to getting to go home."

Hargreaves shook his head. "I must confess, I'm most thoroughly confused."

"About what?"

"About your attitude, of course. Ordinarily, one would expect you to protest—at the very least proclaim me a lying impostor and have me thrown out of here on my ear. Yet you seem almost pleased with the notion."

"I am. The fact is, Ed, I couldn't be happier if I was a speckled pup. Besides, I wouldn't throw you out. Hell, you're a wounded man."

"Yes, I know." His gaze never leaving Prescott's, Hargreaves touched his arm, clearly reminding Prescott of just how he'd come by that wound. "But as I'm laying claim to your title and estate, what better reason could a man have than to want his usurper out of his home?"

"This ain't my home. It never has been. As for the title, well, I never wanted the dang thing in the first place."

"Never wanted it?"

"Hell no! I ain't no earl. I'm a cattle rancher from—"

"Texas, yes, I know," Hargreaves said.

"Born and bred and proud of it. And the first chance I get, I'm going back." Prescott tightened his hold on Lucinda's hand and pulled it up to his chest. "Taking all my girls back with me, too, as soon as his honor here can get them adoption papers and marriage license drawn up and signed for us."

"That will be my second duty of business tomorrow morning," Judge Chenoweth said.

"And about the matter of me shooting Emerson tonight?" Prescott said.

"What about it?"

"Am I gonna have to stand trial or something?"

"Are you sure you shot him?"

"About as sure as I can be of anything."

"It is rather dark out, despite the full moon," Lucinda said.

"Yes," the judge said, "and one's nocturnal vision can easily be deceived by darkness, you know."

"I shot the man," Prescott insisted. "I took point-blank aim and shot him in the back."

"Still," the judge said, "if the tide washed his body out to sea, as you claim, we have no absolute proof that your bullet actually hit him."

"No proof?"

"Yes, no proof. We must have a body in order to determine that a crime has been committed."

"But I give you my word I shot him."

"I'm sorry, milord, but in this case I'm afraid your word just isn't good enough. However, to salve your conscience, I shall have Sheriff Penhalligan look into the matter at first light."

"Good. And if you don't find Emerson's body?"

"It's quite simple really," the judge said. "With no body, there can be no trial. With no trial, or even the slimmest of hopes of one, no charges can be made."

"And I can leave for home as soon as Ed proves his claim is real?"

"I would say so, yes."

Relieved to know that he wouldn't have to stay in England any longer than necessary, Prescott released a long breath and turned to Hargreaves. "I need to have a little talk with you."

"Certainly, Cousin."

"In private, if you don't mind."

"Of course." Hargreaves tried to stand, but quickly sank back in the chair. "I fear I'm going to have to ask you for a bit of assistance. It appears as though this wound of mine has made me rather weak."

Prescott helped his former valet to his feet and led him out of the drawing room, his mother's family watching every step they took.

"Nosy bunch, ain't they?"

"Who, your family?"

"Yeah. After me shooting you and all, I don't imagine you think much of being related to me, but just be grateful you're not related to any of them. There are times when I wish to hell I wasn't, but I didn't have much say in the matter. But then, none of us ever do when it comes to picking our families. And with that bunch— Well, with the way my luck's been running, they'll probably try to follow me home."

"Oh, I rather doubt that, Cousin. They don't seem to be the kind who are interested in visiting locales that are more exotic than rural England."

"I hope you're right."

Once they were well away from the drawing room and anyone who might attempt to eavesdrop, Prescott said, "I've got something to tell you."

"Oh?"

"Yeah. Seeing as how you're gonna be the new earl around here pretty soon, and even though we're the ones who found it, it rightly belongs to you. So I—"

"What belongs to me, your debts?"

Prescott grinned. "No, not debts."

"Are you sure? I shouldn't wonder that your little family gathering tonight cost the estate close to a small fortune. All those pyrotechnics, especially."

"Trust me, all of that's covered. After tonight, I've got a feeling money will be the least of your worries." Prescott shook his head, still finding it hard to believe that good luck—not to mention good fortune—had finally come his way. "Mine, too, if you see things my way."

"What are you talking about?"

"See we—me and Lucinda, that is—we sort of found ourselves a buried treasure while we were chasing after Emerson."

Hargreaves stopped dead in his tracks. "Buried treasure?"

"Yeah."

"Have you been sampling the single malt whiskey again?"

"No, I'm sober as a judge. It's buried treasure, Ed. Well, it ain't buried now, but it was. Lots of gold coins and jewels and silver stuff in little boxes."

"And you found it here, at Ravens Lair?"

Prescott nodded.

"Where?"

"In a kind of cave off one of the tunnels."

"My word."

"Lucinda thinks it might have belonged to the last baron who lived here."

"I know nothing about any baron. We Trefarrows have always been earls."

"Not in the beginning. According to Lucinda, we were barons long before the first Trefarrow became an earl. And some of those barons were about as crooked as you can get. Mean, ruthless bastards, who did a lot of raping and pillaging. Lucinda can tell you more about them, of course, if you're interested, but it all boils down to the fact that the last one left behind some pricey little trinkets, and tonight she and I found them. Which is why I'm telling you all this now. You're gonna be taking over here pretty soon, and I was kinda hoping you'd show a little Christian charity and share it with the ones who found it. Don't rightly know how much any of it's worth, if anything at all, but it's bound to be worth something."

Speechless, Hargreaves stared at Prescott. He couldn't believe that his cousin could be so forthcoming with such a tale, however farfetched it might seem, when he could have just as easily kept the story, not to mention the treasure, to himself.

"I've only been here a few months," Prescott said, "but I can tell you, running this place is a mighty expensive proposition. The roof needs fixing, there's dry rot in the walls, rats in the cellar, there's more than a dozen windows gonna need replacing 'fore winter sets in—and that's just scratching the surface here in the castle. It don't even begin to cover what the tenant farmers need done to their cottages. I figure half of what we found tonight might cover some of the cost, but not all of it. You'd need to find ten more buried treasures twice the size of this one to get this place back to the way it once was."

"I don't know what to say, Prescott."

"Only one thing to say, Ed. Say you'll share it with me and Lucinda. We need money back in Texas as bad as you need it here. Oh, one more thing."

"What would that be?"

Prescott eyed him directly. "Promise me you'll go find yourself a woman, marry her, and start having kids. Namely sons."

"I beg your pardon?"

"You heard me. Get married and have a family. I don't want to have to come back over here in twenty or thirty years, or however long you might decide to live, and claim this infernal title again. Having it the one time was enough for me, thank you."

Hargreaves dipped his head to hide a smile. "I don't think you have to worry about inheriting it a second time."

"You planning on living forever?"

"That's not what I meant. I meant that I don't need to get myself a wife. You see, I already have one."

"You're married?"

"Very much so."

Prescott grabbed hold of the man's hand and pumped it heartily. "Well, that's just great. Damned great, Ed. Congratulations."

"Thank you. Though, I must say, your felicitations are rather late in coming."

"Late?"

"Yes. Almost eighteen years too late, as a matter of fact. That's how long I've been married to Marguerite."

"Eighteen years, huh? Well, ain't that something."

"By some standards, I suppose it could be considered a milestone of sorts."

Prescott heard the underlying note of wistfullness in Hargreaves' voice and knew his marriage was a good one. "How come you didn't bring her here to Ravens Lair with you?"

"Er, there was only the one position for a valet that

needed filling. Ordinarily, we work as a team, Marguerite and I, but with no Countess of Ravens Lair in residence, her services as a lady's maid weren't needed. Besides, it would have been too dicey, were she and I to come here together. I needed to be on my own to search for my grandmother's journals. Now that I've found them, of course, I shall be wiring her at the first opportunity."

"Of course. Can't wait to meet the little woman."

"She'll most certainly be surprised to meet you."

They started to return to the drawing room, but Prescott had another thought. "Just one more thing."

"What would that be?"

"Not that it's any of my business, you understand—I'm just being curious is all—but how are you and Marguerite fixed for kids?"

"Fixed?"

"Yeah, do you have any children?"

Hargreaves chuckled. "Rest easy, Cousin, the Trefarrow line will be protected for many, many more years to come. I've three sons to inherit the title after I pass on."

"Three?"

"Yes."

"All healthy and happy and, er, normal, I hope."

"Without question, they are all red-blooded Englishmen with eyes only for the fairer sex. Of that much, I am certain. At the moment, they're all at boarding school. The oldest is scheduled to enter Cambridge next term."

"Cambridge, huh? Must be a pretty smart boy."

"He is. He's very intelligent. As are his younger brothers. They shall elevate this title of ours, not to mention our family name, to new heights. Politics, law . . . perhaps even medicine, if my youngest son has his way."

"Well, I can't tell you how happy hearing all this makes me, Ed."

"Yes, Cousin, I can see you're ecstatic. Under other circumstances, I might feel saddened by the abrupt end I've put to your short dynastic reign, but I don't. I don't feel the least bit sad at all."

"Neither do I. This is one reign that never should have begun in the first place."

"Then you'll soon be leaving England?"

"As soon as you get hold of this title, and I can make all the arrangements. Course, that may take some time. I've got to adopt those little girls first, make it all legal, and then marry Lucinda, if I can talk her into it, and—"

"That shouldn't be too difficult for a man of your strong determination. Our cousin loves you, you know."

"Yeah, well, I love her, too. More'n I ever thought I could ever love a woman. But she's got this damned silly notion that just because she was born without her father's name, she's not good enough for me. Ain't that the craziest thing you ever heard? I mean, it ain't her fault she was born a bastard. She can't help what her mama and daddy did."

"She's a proud young woman who knows her place, Cousin."

"That's a bunch of bullshit, Ed. Her place is with me."

"Not in this society."

"We ain't gonna be in this society much longer if I can help it."

"I understand, but I'm not the one you have to

convince. You must try and see it from her perspective. She knows of no other way of life except our British one. She feels that to marry you would be to bring you shame and disgrace. Give her some credit for thinking of your welfare, your position within the community, and not her own comfort."

"To hell with my welfare and position. It's her stubborn pride that's got me over a barrel. I don't know how to get around it, how to talk sense to her."

Hargreaves clapped a hand on Prescott's shoulder. "I suspect that if you put your mind to it you can make her see things your way in time."

"You think so?"

"I have all the faith in the world in you, Cousin."

"I hope you're right, Ed. I sure hope you're right."

But deep down, Prescott had his doubts.

25

"What's a Texas?" Alexandra turned her wide, blue-eyed gaze on Lucinda, who stood behind her, brushing the tangles out of her hair.

Lucinda had to look away for fear that she would begin weeping and frighten the child. They were leaving soon—Alexandra, Victoria, Elizabeth, and Prescott. They were all leaving for Texas, while she would be remaining at Ravens Lair, her life far less complicated to be sure, but empty as well.

"The way your Uncle Prescott tells it," she said, "Texas is quite close to paradise."

"Paradise," the four-year-old said, smiling at the sound of the word. "That's a pretty name. Will I like it there?"

"Oh, I'm sure you will, darling. You and your sisters should love it. You'll each have horses to ride and all kinds of little animals to play with."

"Of course we will. We're taking Princess with us."

"Princess, your lamb?"

"Mmm-hmm."

"Oh, I shouldn't think that Uncle Prescott will want to take Princess all the way to Texas. It's ever such a long ocean voyage from here to America. She might get sick."

"We can't leave Princess behind," Alexandra said. "I won't go if she can't go, too."

"Then we'll just have to take her along with us, won't we? I'm not leaving without all my girls."

The unexpected sound of the masculine voice behind her made Lucinda turn sharply. Prescott was leaning against the doorjamb, his thumbs tucked into the front pockets of his Levis, his familiar, easy grin on his face. She looked away, unable to stop the ache that began to throb in her heart.

"How long have you been standing there?" she asked.

"Long enough. Lexie sugar, would you run on up to the nursery and tell Miss Rowena that Mrs. Sweet needs her down in the kitchen? Me and your Aunt Lucinda will be up in a while to have supper with you and your sisters."

The little girl broke out of Lucinda's arms and skipped over to Prescott, where she stood on tiptoe to hug his waist. "I love you, Uncle Prescott."

"I love you, too, darlin'." He dropped a kiss on the top of her head and, as she scampered off down the hall, he called out to her, "Y'all wash your hands now, y'hear? Kids," he said with a chuckle. "Little girls are as bad as little boys 'bout getting dirty. They've been playing with that lamb all day."

"Are you serious about taking Princess with you?"

"Yeah, I guess I am. Don't really have much

choice. Leaving the little critter behind would break their hearts, and I ain't about to do that after all they've been through."

"You could get them a puppy instead, couldn't you? Or a kitten?"

"I could try, but I don't think they'd like one as much as they love that little lamb. It's their pet, their baby. They've bottle-fed it from the day I found it and brought it home." He started toward Lucinda slowly. "Never liked sheep very much."

"Yes, I know."

"But I've gotten used to living with that one. Wonder if I'll ever get used to living without you?"

"One does what one must, Prescott."

"That's just it. I wouldn't have to get used to living without you if you'd come with me."

"Don't." She moved away before he could touch her, hold her, bring to life the feelings within her that she had to keep buried. She had to let him go, though she wanted desperately for him to stay and never leave. "We've been through this more times than I care to recall, Prescott. You know I can't go with you."

"I know that's what you've told me, but I still can't make any sense of it. We belong together, Lucinda." Before she could move out of his reach again, he took hold of her left hand and held it tightly in his, looking down at the ring he had put on her finger. "We even exchanged vows, remember?"

"Those vows were just words. They didn't mean anything, not really."

"They meant something to me. Otherwise I wouldn't have said them. I think they meant something to you, too. You're my wife, dammit."

"Your handfast wife, perhaps, but not your legal wife."

"We can change all that. I'll get Judge Chenoweth to—"

"No! You'll do no such thing. I will not be the cause of ruining your good name or—"

"Bullshit! My good name is mine to ruin, not yours—don't you know that by now? And you wouldn't be ruining it. For once you'd be giving it some meaning."

Lucinda pulled her hand free and moved away. "That's not what your family thought."

"To hell with them. They're gone. They've been gone for nearly a week now, and I still haven't changed my mind."

"I'm afraid you'll have to."

Realizing that he wasn't making any headway using the direct approach with her, Prescott decided to back off for a while. But he wasn't through with her yet, not by a long shot. He still had one ace in the hole, and, if he had to, he wouldn't think twice about playing it. "So, that's it, huh? I'm gonna leave, and you're gonna stay?"

"That would be best for everyone."

"Best for you, maybe, but not for me, darlin'."

When Lucinda looked over her shoulder a moment later, she saw that he was gone, and her feelings of desolation increased tenfold. Why couldn't he understand? She loved him with all her heart and being, but she couldn't marry him. She had to keep denying him her hand in marriage to save him from disgrace and humiliation, two things she was sure he would come to despise her for in the years ahead.

* * *

"So, this makes it official, does it?" Prescott studied the documents before him and nodded.

"Yes, it's official," Hargreaves said. "Judge Chenoweth had a messenger deliver them just moments ago. I thought you should be the first to see them."

"'Bout time, that's all I gotta say."

The past three weeks had been the longest of Prescott's life. He'd done nothing but wait and worry, all the while planning and making arrangements to leave England. Two of those three weeks he'd waited for the judge to announce that Alexandra, Victoria, and Elizabeth were his adopted daughters—officially, whether he was married or not. Where the children were concerned, he half expected Emerson to come back from his watery grave, if he was indeed dead, or to walk in with Sheriff Penhalligan and charge him with attempted murder. But Emerson hadn't appeared, and the girls were now his.

His cousin, Edward Giles Hargreaves Trefarrow, however, was a different matter. Something in the back of Prescott's mind told him to expect word from the good judge that Ed's documents were invalid, that the Queen's record keepers hadn't been able to verify their authenticity, and that he, God help him, was still earl. But this now proved that he'd done all that worrying for nothing. He was a free man again.

"Congratulations, Ed," he said. "You're gonna make a dandy earl around here."

"A better one than you were, if you don't mind my saying so, Cousin."

"Don't mind at all."

"I must confess, though, your short-lived stint as earl wasn't the complete and utter failure I thought it would be. You made one or two changes here at the estate that I intend to keep as they are."

"Such as?"

"Well, such as giving the tenant farmers more credit than they've been given in the past. And giving them a larger share of the annual harvest profits as well. It's only fair, considering they do all the work."

"If you're as much of a Trefarrow as I think you are," Prescott said, "you can count on doing your share of the work. You can't just sit up here in the castle and wait for the profits to come to you. You've got to go where the money's being made, down there with the farmers in the shearing shed. Just hope you don't mind getting your hands a little dirty and coming home smelling like a flock of sheep, because, believe me, you will."

At this, Hargreaves looked a bit disgusted. Prescott went on.

"You've got to get out in the fields and help them with haying, too. Round up some of those dang sheep y'all put such great pride in. Putting in a hard day like that makes you feel good inside. Useful, you know? Besides that, the farmers will respect you more, knowing you're willing to act like one of them, even though they know you're not."

Hargreaves nodded. "Yes, useful. I suspect it's been quite a while since Ravens Lair has had an earl as active, or even as interested, in the day-to-day operation of the estate as you've been. Mostly, our illustrious—or should I say infamous—ancestors were inactive to the point of being lethargic and quite uninterested in anything but the profits the estate could make for them."

"Yeah, that's the impression I got from what little

Lucinda's told me about the castle's history. Learning what a bunch of scalawags our kinfolks were, it's a wonder we Trefarrows were able to last here this long. I'm amazed one of those earls didn't up and lose this place in a poker game."

"Or to their creditors."

"Them, too." Prescott winced at the memory of the long line of money lenders he'd been beholden to in his lifetime, and his father's and grandfather's lifetimes, too. But he supposed that was just part and parcel of being born a Trefarrow—owing almost as much as you owned, and always worrying that you'd lose even the shirt on your back when you couldn't pay the next note that came due. "Things ought to be different now, though, don't you think?"

"You mean now that you've found the last baron's hidden treasure?"

"It sure can't hurt none."

"Not to disillusion you, Cousin, but I have a feeling that most of that so-called treasure is fairly worthless."

"Worthless? Aw, it can't be, Ed. Some of it's gotta be worth something."

"I wouldn't count on it."

"But there's gold and silver and gems of all kinds."

"The gold and silver look real enough, but for all we know, those gems could be nothing more than colored glass. Of course, I could be speaking out of turn. We won't know what they are until we've had them appraised by an expert. I can contact a reputable one that I know in London and have him here within the month."

"A month? Hell, Ed, I can't wait around that long. Me and the girls are leaving for London tomorrow morning, and two days after that we're heading home to Texas."

"Then I suppose you've little choice but to trust me to send you your share after everything has been appraised and sold."

"No, I can't do that, either. It's not that I don't trust you—I do! It's just that I need the money right now."

Hargreaves stroked his chin, mulling over the possibilities. "Would you consider dividing it?"

"Have I got much choice?"

"Not if you're to let me have my share of it, as you promised."

"Then I guess we'll do it your way. Divide it, and both take our chances. Just hope I don't choose the bad stuff."

Later that morning, as he and Hargreaves crouched over the desk in the library, picking and choosing the pieces they liked best, Prescott couldn't help but be disheartened by the notion that an expert's examination of his treasure could prove it all to be little better than fool's gold. Though it sure didn't look like fool's gold to him. It didn't feel like it, either. The weight of the gold jewelry and the clarity of the gems seemed real enough to him. Even the silver pieces, though badly tarnished, looked authentic. But then, he was no expert. He was just a poor, debt-ridden rancher in bad need of money.

With his share of the treasure tucked into a pillowcase and flung over his shoulder, he trudged upstairs to his room, finding it empty and quite lonely without Lucinda there. The last time he'd seen her, she'd been about to take the girls out for a walk. She'd wanted some time alone with them, she'd said, to say good-bye.

He tossed the pillowcase onto the bed and stalked toward the window, shoving aside the drape and looking down at the lush green pasture below. Damn it, why couldn't she set aside her silly pride and love him the way he loved her? Why did she have to be so concerned about him maintaining his good name and position in society? He didn't care about any of that. He never had and never would care about it, either.

Then a thought struck him, one that had been in the back of his mind for some time but only now seemed like a feasible solution. He'd give her one more chance. He'd ask her to marry him and go home with him as his wife, and if she said no one more time . . .

Well, it had worked for Payne. Hell, it might just work for him. If nothing else, it would sure get her attention.

Lucinda stood in the upstairs corridor, peering through a crack in the heavy drapes at the scene taking place in the drive, just below the front terrace. Prescott was waving his hands in the air, overseeing the placement of the children's meager pieces of luggage alongside his own. In a matter of minutes, they would be climbing into the carriage and driving away, leaving Ravens Lair, St. Keverne, Cornwall, and, in time, the whole of England. And, God save her aching soul, they would be leaving her.

Tears trickled down her pale cheeks and a sob rose in her throat. She had been such fool, falling in love with a man with whom she'd known she hadn't stood a chance. She had given herself to him time and time again, dreaming that they might have a future together, yet knowing all the while that they had no hopes of a future at all.

"Fool," she muttered in a voice hoarse with emotion. "You stupid, stupid fool."

Flinging the drape shut, she turned and raced down the hall to her room. Well, it would be her room for a while longer, she thought, leaning weakly against the door. As soon as Prescott departed, she would have to find other lodgings. Where those lodgings would be, she had no idea. Once Cousin Edward's wife arrived from London, Lucinda doubted the new countess would allow her to stay on at Ravens Lair.

Desperation and hopelessness welling up in her soul, Lucinda threw herself onto her bed and wept openly, loudly, until she had no more tears to shed.

Assured that the luggage was bound securely to the back of the carriage and wouldn't fall off on the trip between Ravens Lair and the train station in Truro, Prescott turned with a satisfied nod. He started to call out to Mrs. Sweet, who had been observing him somberly from the terrace, but a movement higher up caught his eye. He saw the drapes flutter and then close at a window on the second floor, and he knew Lucinda had been watching him; he could feel it in his soul. She had been standing there, watching him, thinking . . .

No, not just thinking. She had been remembering. How could she not remember? They had shared so much in the few short months they'd had together—the heartless cruelty of a thief; the death of a kind woman; the unconditional affection of three orphaned little girls; and the discovery, the acknowledgment, and the heartbreak of love.

Or perhaps Lucinda had been watching him and wondering what might have been, what they might have had together had she not been so stubborn and single-minded.

Well, she wouldn't have to think, or remember, or wonder much longer.

Prescott lowered his gaze from the upstairs window to the housekeeper on the terrace. "The girls about ready to go, Mrs. Sweet?"

"Yes, mil—" She broke off abruptly, drawing herself up to her full five-feet-two-inches as she remembered, almost too late, not to address him by his former title. "Yes, Mr. Prescott, they are. Ursula and Rowena are up in the nursery, helping them finish dressing."

Prescott started up the wide steps. "Then I 'spect we'll be on our way when they're done."

"Yes, I expect thee shall be."

He crossed to where the housekeeper stood and looked down at her. "Want me to tell Tom anything once I reach the ranch?"

"Tom?"

"Yeah, your grandson. Got a letter from my brother the other day. He said Tom had settled in right quick."

"Hmmph!"

"He likes ranch life. Likes the work. Likes the men. More'n that, they've taken a shine to him." Prescott thought it wiser not to mention the other news that Payne had imparted in his letter—that soon after Tom's arrival at the ranch, the hands had taken him to Carrigan's Saloon in Waco, where he had met Carrigan's girls. That they had not only made him a man in every sense of the word, but had given him a feeling of what it was like to be a true cowboy. If Tom's grandmother was anything like his Aunt Em, she wouldn't want to know that her grandson had tasted and thoroughly enjoyed some of the more delightful sins of the flesh. Enjoyed them so much, in fact, that Payne now had a hard time keeping the boy on the ranch.

"As long as he's happy," Mrs. Sweet said.

"Oh, he's that, all right."

"Well . . . good."

"You don't want me to tell him anything?"

"Nothing to tell, mil—Mr. Prescott. Nothing at all. He's chosen his path."

"Yes, ma'am, it appears that he has."

"Then that's the end of it." She turned to go back into the castle, but stopped after a few feet and looked back at Prescott. The stern look in her eyes had been replaced with one of sadness. "But if thee wouldn't mind . . ."

"Wouldn't mind at all, Mrs. Sweet."

"Well, thee could tell him to write his grandma'am more often. One letter in two months ain't enough. We likes to hear from him more often."

"I'll be sure to tell him that very thing, ma'am. You can count on it."

"Thank thee, Mr. Prescott." Out of habit, she bobbed a curtsy. "I'll be hurrying up the babes for thee."

"We're in no big rush. I got one more thing to do before we leave."

Lucinda pushed herself up on the bed and wiped her hands across her damp cheeks. She couldn't, and wouldn't, let Prescott's departure affect her this way. She still had a life of sorts. Though it wouldn't be as full or as exciting as it had been with—

No! Mustn't think about that, she told herself.

Mustn't think about Prescott, either. Not any longer. He was part of her past. Or, rather, he would be very soon. And as soon as he was gone, she would get on with her life. Yes, she would make a new beginning, a fresh start. But not at Ravens Lair. Not at St. Keverne, either.

Perhaps, if he could spare it, Cousin Edward might see it in his heart to loan her a small amount of money. Just enough to get to Penzance, or Bath, or maybe even London. Though what she would do when she got there—

No, she wouldn't think of that, either. She was healthy and strong and hardworking. Surely she wouldn't have much trouble in acquiring a job. She liked children well enough, but she doubted that a family of breeding would hire her as a nanny or a governess. One needed credentials for that sort of post.

A shop. Yes, working in a shop would be splendid. She could sew and knit, and she wasn't at all averse to soiling her hands. More than that, she had been taught from birth to speak with a cultured accent, not a Cornish one. Perhaps she could deal with the public as a clerk instead of being merely a dressmaker's assistant.

Sitting on the side of her bed with her back to the door, Lucinda failed to hear the door open quietly, or the footsteps on the thick rug. She did, however, hear something rustle behind her, but by the time she turned it was too late to investigate.

A massive piece of cloth dropped over her head and was soon followed by a heavy cord being wrapped around her waist. With her arms pinned close to her sides, and feeling that something dangerous was happening to her, she issued a loud shriek from deep within her throat. But the shriek was cut short when she felt herself being picked up off her bed and flung carelessly over a broad shoulder.

"You can't do this!" she cried.

"Oh, yes, I can."

Instantly recognizing the voice, her struggles ceased. "Prescott?"

"No, darlin', I'm a kidnaper."

"Kidnaper? Prescott, have you taken leave of your senses?"

"Don't think so." He headed out of her bedroom and made his way down the hall to the stairs. "No, as a matter of fact, I know I haven't. Guess you could say I've finally come to my senses. Might be a bit late, but if I waited for you to come to yours, we'd probably be stuck here the rest of our lives, and I can't wait that long."

"You're mad."

"Probably. You do strange things to a man. Driving me mad's just one of them."

"Put me down this instant."

"Can't. Morning, Miss Miranda."

"Mil— Er, Mr. Prescott."

Hearing the hesitant feminine response, Lucinda realized that at least one of the household staff had encountered them and was witnessing Prescott's insanely disgraceful behavior and her humiliation. She supposed it was a good thing that a sheet hid her face and the blush which now covered it. Though whether that blush was due to her own sense of shame, Prescott's outrageous deportment, or the blood rushing to her head, she wasn't sure. Most likely it was a combination of all three.

But she didn't have time to think about that. She needed help quickly. "Miranda!"

The young maid had turned to leave, but the sound

of the familiar voice stopped her. "Miss Lucinda? What's thee doing in that bundle?"

"Mr. Prescott is—"

"I'm kidnapping her." Prescott grinned at Miranda over his shoulder, and received a flirtatious smile in return. "Don't tell nobody."

"No, you must tell," Lucinda said. "Run fetch his lordship."

"His lordship, Miss?"

"Yes, the new earl."

"But he—"

"Please, Miranda. Find him and bring him to me quickly before this madman succeeds in ruining his life and what's left of my reputation."

"But, Miss, his lordship ain't here," Miranda said, her voice fading as Prescott walked farther and farther away from her.

"Not here? Where is he?"

"He left the castle early this morning to fetch her ladyship in Truro. She be arriving on the noon train."

"Damn!"

Prescott shifted her weight on his shoulder, eliciting a grunt from Lucinda and making her wriggle indignantly. "Watch your language, darlin'. We're coming up on some ladies who might take offense."

"Who? Who's there?"

"Miss Lucinda?" said a voice.

"Mrs. Sweet? Thank God. Please, help me!"

"Pay her no mind," Prescott said. "She's just being a bit testy is all."

"Is she going to Texas with you, mil— er, Mr. Prescott?"

"You bet. Gonna have ourselves a high old time on our honeymoon."

"Honeymoon?" Lucinda repeated. "Ha!"

"Congratulations, Mr. Prescott," Mrs. Sweet said.

"Yes, congratulations," Ursula echoed faintheartedly.

"Thank you, ladies."

As he rounded the corner, leaving the housekeeper and her assistant gaping at them, Prescott encountered the one woman he had managed to avoid since his arrival. He thought about turning around and heading the other way as quickly as his feet would carry him, but he suddenly decided to face the old woman head on instead of retreating.

"Morning, Miss Esmeralda."

Her arms laden with neatly folded linens bound for a location known only to her, the elderly woman ceased her humming, straightened her bent body as far as it would straighten, and craned her neck. Through squinted eyes, she stared up at Prescott. Instead of flinging aside her linens, falling into a faint, and screaming rape, as she had done on their first encounter, she did a most remarkable thing. She actually smiled at Prescott.

"Morning, milord."

"Just Prescott. I ain't a lord no more, Miss Esmeralda."

"Esmeralda?" Lucinda said. "Oh, please, Esmeralda, you're my last hope. You must help me."

The old lady squinted at the large bundle Prescott carried. "Who be that?"

"This?" Prescott said, shifting Lucinda higher up on his shoulder. "Oh, it's nobody, Miss Esmeralda. Pay it no mind."

"It?" Lucinda said. "How dare you call me 'it'!"

Esmeralda's laughter rang out through the vast,

high-ceilinged corridor. "Thee treat her well, milord. She's a good girl, she is."

"Yes, ma'am."

"And no raping her."

"Esmeralda!"

"No, ma'am, I won't be raping her."

"Good, good. Will thee be having elevenses in the morning room as usual?"

Prescott grinned and shook his head. "No, not this morning. Y'see, I'm leaving."

"Oh, aye. Then have yourself a safe journey."

"I intend to. 'Bye, ma'am. Nice meeting you."

Esmeralda smiled one last time, then her body resumed its bent stance, and she shuffled off down the hall humming a mindless little tune under her breath.

"Nice old lady," he said as he turned and advanced toward the front door. "When she's in her right mind, that is."

"Which is more than I can say for you," Lucinda said. "You'll never get away with this, you know. Someone will stop you."

"Care to bet on it, darlin'?"

"With what? You know I haven't a farthing to my name."

"Hell, if it's money you're worried about, I'll be happy to loan you some."

"I wouldn't take a tuppence from you, Prescott Trefarrow."

"Now that's what I like to hear. A woman who ain't interested in bleeding her husband dry. Being frugal's a good thing, I say."

"I'm not that frugal, and I'm certainly not your wife."

"Not yet."

"Not ever!"

Prescott laughed. "Care to bet on it, darlin'?"

Lucinda could only growl in frustration.

Were it not for Prescott's arm around her waist steadying her, Lucinda felt certain her knees would give way, that she would topple over and disgrace not only herself but Prescott, the girls, and the minister standing before them. Heaven above, help her. After days of teasing her—when he wasn't making love to her—and generally doing a thorough job of breaking down her willpower and resolve all the way across the English Channel from Dover to Calais and down into France to Paris, she had agreed, finally, to marry him.

"By the powers vested in me," the American embassy chaplain said, "I now pronounce you man and wife. You, sir, may now kiss your bride."

Grinning broadly, with the three little girls looking on, giggling, Prescott turned Lucinda to face him and kissed her soundly.

"This is utterly ridiculous, you know," she said breathlessly when he pulled back a moment later. Looking around, she saw that the chaplain had slipped out of the small sanctuary attached to the embassy, leaving her and Prescott alone with the girls.

"What, us getting married?"

"Yes."

"Don't seem all that ridiculous to me, darlin'. You're doing the right thing."

"I only hope you don't live to regret it."

"The only thing I'd ever regret is leaving you behind in England, not taking you with me. With us," he added, a sidelong glance encompassing the trio of little girls. "We belong together. All of us. Don't you know that by now?"

As she searched his green eyes for some trace of mockery or disappointment, she felt intensely relieved to find only sincerity in their depths. If she had ever doubted that he loved her, his look erased it forever. She had no doubts, no fears, and, thankfully enough, not too many regrets. Still, one matter continued to haunt her.

"Now that we're man and wife," she said, "I think I should tell you something."

"Don't tell me you don't like cows."

"What?"

"Cows. Big critters that go 'moo' and give milk."

"No! I don't dislike them in the least."

"Good, 'cause liking cows is the one thing I expect out of the woman I marry. They're my business, my livelihood. Without cows, we Texas Trefarrows—"

"I swear, Prescott, this has absolutely nothing to do with livestock," she interrupted impatiently. "Cows or sheep or whatever else you might raise on that ranch of yours are not the issue."

"Horses. We raise horses, too."

"All right, horses."

"Some pigs every now and then, but no sheep."

"What about Princess?" Alexandra said. "She's a sheep."

"Well, Princess, of course," Prescott said. "But she's special."

Satisfied with his answer, Alexandra crawled up onto the chaplain's settee to watch and listen to the interplay between her new parents.

"May I continue?" Lucinda asked.

"I'm all ears," he said with a grin.

"Now this may sound rather strange, I know, but I—oh, heavens—I think I've known you before."

His grin faded. "What?"

"In another life, perhaps."

"Another life?"

"Yes, I believe it's called reincarnation. I've only heard about it, you understand, but it's the only explanation I can think of that makes any sense."

"Uh-huh."

"Well, if I didn't know you from another life, how can I explain why you came to me so often in my dreams?"

Prescott swallowed audibly. "Your dreams?"

"Yes. I used to see you all the time in them."

"All the time, huh?"

"At first, you frightened me. I don't know why; you're not the least bit frightening. A bit intimidating at times, not to mention damnably infuriating when you've got your mind set on something, but never frightening. But then, of course, I didn't know who you were or what you were like, as I do now."

"In these dreams of yours, what did I do? Or did I do anything at all?"

"You would look at me. Smile. Hold out your arms."

"And that frightened you?"

"Very much."

"What would you do?"

"Nothing," she said. "I told you I was afraid of you."

"You didn't try to get away, run for help?"

Lucinda thought for a moment, then shook her head. "I don't know why, but the idea of running for help must never have occurred to me. I only know that I used to wake up feeling frightened."

"I see."

"Oh, I knew you wouldn't understand. I did warn you that it would sound strange. Now you must think I've taken leave of my senses."

"Well, if you've taken leave of your senses, darlin', then I 'spect we're two of a kind."

"What?"

"I never told you, but I used to dream about you all the time."

"What?"

He nodded. "Hell, I've been dreaming about you ever since I was old enough to know there was a difference between girls and boys. And that's a pretty long time, let me tell you."

"Prescott?"

"It's true. That first time I saw you, that day I chased down your bonnet?"

"Yes."

"Well, I thought my eyes were playing tricks on me. I mean, you were the spitting image of my dream mate. That's what I called you, 'cause I didn't know what your name was. Then, as I got to know you, found out what kind of woman you were, that you were sweet, caring, and funny, when you weren't being stubborn—it's the damnedest thing—I couldn't help myself. I fell in love, darlin'. Head over heels and knee deep."

"Oh, Prescott." She moved closer into his embrace, winding her arms around his broad shoulders and placing her head on his chest. The last of her regrets, her doubts, vanished into oblivion.

"It's kinda like we were meant to be. You know?"

"Yes, I know. I tried to fight it—"

"Don't I know it."

"—but it did no good. No good at all."

"Well, no need to fight it any longer, darlin'. We're together, right where we belong."

27

Payne marched into the kitchen and tossed the mail onto the table before going out the back door onto the porch. Aunt Em sat in her rocking chair snapping green beans for supper while Chloe knelt beside a big tub nearby giving their daughter one of her many daily baths. Though only a year old and quite dainty looking, with her thick golden hair and huge blue-gray eyes, she had the most unnatural penchant for getting dirty. Only yesterday, when Payne had pulled her into his lap to read her a bedtime story, his fingers had casually brushed her little knees and he'd realized they were as rough as the siding on the barn. And, like her mother before her, she had already developed a fondness for horses rather than dolls. He had to face it—he had another tomboy on his hands.

"Did we get anything interesting in the mail?" Chloe asked.

"Prescott wrote us another letter, but I wouldn't call it interesting." Payne stepped back a bit and laughed as the baby splashed the bath water with a merry giggle, soaking Chloe and half the back porch.

"Has he gone back to England, or is he still gallivanting around Europe?" Aunt Em asked.

"His letter was from Venice," Payne said.

"Venice? What the devil is he doing there?"

"I suspect much the same thing that he did in Paris, Berlin, and Rome," Payne said. "Playing the tourist and seeing the sights."

Emmaline grunted. "That boy ought to be back here, helping you out with all the chores that need doing instead of running around over there, spending money he doesn't have."

"Oh, let Prescott have some fun, Aunt Em," Chloe said. "You have to admit, he had very little of it, working the Triple T all those years."

"I never once heard him complain," Emmaline said. "Besides, work can be fun if you let it."

"But it's nothing compared to taking the grand tour of Europe," Payne said, recalling the months he'd spent on the continent, traveling from one great city to another—usually at the behest and expense of one of his well-heeled lady friends—dining, drinking, and dancing the night away, and coming home at dawn, only to wake up in the afternoon with a blistering headache and, usually, a strange woman in bed beside him. Heaven help Prescott if he were following in his footsteps. Then again, maybe that sort of lifestyle was more suitable to Prescott than it had been to him. "It could be the one highlight of his life that he'll always remember." *Or, in my case, wish he could forget.*

"Did you ever take the grand tour?" Chloe asked.

"Of course. But I was much younger and more foolish back in my callow youth."

"Real footloose and fancy-free, huh?"

"You could say that." Payne had an idea where his wife's thoughts were going and he wished she would change the subject. He didn't mind discussing his past with her in the privacy of their room, but he hated the thought of shocking dear Aunt Em.

"Sowed your share of wild oats, too, I imagine," Emmaline said, snapping her last bean.

"Er . . ."

His aunt chuckled and rose to her feet. "Never mind. You don't have to answer that. So, where's Prescott going to next, or did he say?"

"No, he didn't," Payne said. "He only said that the Grand Canal didn't look a thing like the Brazos. And it didn't smell like it, either."

"What does the Grand Canal smell like?" Chloe asked.

Payne thought a moment. "Bad, as I recall."

"Sounds to me like Prescott's beginning to get a little homesick," Emmaline said.

"Homesick for England or here?" Payne asked.

"Here, of course," Emmaline said. "I'm going in and putting these beans on to cook. Supper ought to be ready as soon as the sun goes down. Chloe, don't you keep that baby in the water too long now, y'hear? It's starting to get cold out here."

"I won't, Aunt Em. We're fixing to get out right now. Aren't we, Miss Prissy?"

Payne reached out and grabbed the towel off the

porch railing, handing it to Chloe. "Prissy is hardly a suitable name for our daughter, my love. How we ever agreed on it, I'll never know. She's anything but prissy. Perhaps we should have named her Junior."

"For a girl? Hardly. Just give her a little time, Payne. Priscilla's gonna grow up to be one the finest ladies in Waco. Maybe in all of Texas—who knows?"

"I hope you're right, but I doubt it. She all but had a tantrum the other day when I took her to the stables. I know she wished to ride my horse."

"You didn't let her, did you?"

"Good heavens, no! Well, not alone, at any rate."

"Uh-huh. You may pretend you're worried about her growing up to be a tomboy, but every time I see the two of you out together you've always got her up in the saddle with you."

"I was merely teaching her the finer points of handling a horse early in life, my dear. Teaching her to be a lady is your job, not mine." Payne extracted his towel-wrapped daughter from Chloe and cuddled her close, loving her fresh baby smell almost as much as he cherished the unconditional love that she always gave him.

"Oh? Just what is your job?"

"To spoil her rotten, of course. You're papa's little girl, aren't you, my sweetness?"

Priscilla wrapped her pudgy arms around Payne's neck and gave him a big, wet kiss on the cheek, afterwards making a face and giggling as his day's growth of beard scratched her mouth.

"She'll be yours until she grows up and some handsome young man comes along and steals her heart," Chloe said.

"Your mama must be daft, darling. Papa will never let that happen."

"You won't?"

"No, I won't. I have every intention of spiriting her away to a convent at the first sign of budding womanhood."

"You say that now, but—"

"I'll say it then, too; just watch me. No man is good enough for my precious daughter. You'll remember that, won't you, sweetness? All men, except your papa, are swine. Horrible, lecherous swine who have only one thought in mind."

Chloe sidled up close to Payne and gave him a long, provocative look. "Speaking from experience, are you?"

"Yes, I—" He caught her eye and felt a familiar heat rush through him, one that only she could create. One that only she could extinguish. "I think it might be time for our little Miss Prissy to take a nap, don't you?"

"A nap. Now?" Chloe traced a finger around the open collar of his shirt. "But supper's almost ready."

"We can dine later. I don't mind eating a cold meal."

"You might not mind, but Aunt Em will be awfully upset."

"Not as upset as I'm going to be if—" He broke off abruptly, hearing a strange sound in the distance. "What the devil?"

"What?"

"I could have sworn I just heard sheep bleating."

"Sheep? Here? You are hearing things, Payne. There are no sheep in this part of Texas."

He heard the sound again, closer and much

louder this time. "Then what would you call that?"

Emmaline stuck her gray head out the back door as Payne started around the porch to the front of the house. "What is that noise?"

"Payne said it was sheep," Chloe said, starting after her husband.

"Sheep? Here?" Emmaline followed in her wake, wiping her hands on her apron.

"That's what he said."

"Lord Almighty, if it is sheep, we're all in for trouble."

As they reached the front porch, Chloe's curiosity and Emmaline's worries vanished in the face of surprise. Still holding Priscilla, Payne stood in the yard next to a very large wagon that seemed to overflow with bags and trunks and bouncing, giggling little girls and one sheep with a pink satin ribbon tied around its wooly neck. Getting down from the seat with some degree of difficulty was a dark-haired young woman, obviously in the latter stages of pregnancy. And helping her down was—

"Prescott?" Both Chloe and Emmaline called his name at the same time as they hurried down from the porch and raced toward the wagon.

"Thank the Lord, my boy's finally come home," Emmaline said, wrapping her nephew in a warm, teary embrace.

"Yeah, I'm home, Aunt Em. For good."

"What do you mean, 'for good'?" Chloe asked as Emmaline stepped aside.

"I mean I'm here for good," he said. "I ain't ever leaving Texas again."

"You can do that?" Chloe asked.

"Well, yeah, why not?"

"You're the Earl of St. Keverne. You can't be an earl and live here, too. Can you?"

"I wouldn't know." Prescott grinned at the comforting sight of his sister-in-law's happy but bewildered expression. "It don't matter much no how, 'cause I ain't the earl no more. Seems that Sir Henry Wilberforce fella made a big mistake in naming me the earl."

"Mistake?" Payne had a horrible sinking feeling in the pit of his stomach that Sir Henry's mistake might somehow involve him. "You're not the real earl?"

"Relax, little brother. You ain't neither. Seems we got us a long lost Cousin Edward for that job."

Payne breathed a sigh of relief. "Thank God."

"Lord, Prissy's grown," Prescott said. "When I left here, she was just a little bitty ol' thing."

"Yes, well, babies do have a nasty habit of growing," Payne said, eyeing the pregnant woman and the three little girls, who were keeping their distance. "And speaking of babies . . ."

"Oh, yeah. Where are my manners?" Prescott crossed to the woman and wrapped his arm around her shoulder. "Everybody, I want y'all to meet my wife, Lucinda."

"Wife?" all three said in unison.

Prescott grinned and nodded. "That's what I said. She's my wife. It's all legal, too, Aunt Em, so don't go getting all starchy on us now. Me and Lucinda were married a year ago come July in a little chapel right close to the American embassy in Paris, France."

"Paris, France?" Chloe whispered in awe.

Taking into account that next July was still over three months away and Prescott's new wife looked as though she might deliver her baby any day now, Emmaline realized that Lucinda must have already been in the family way when her nephew married her. Why that should surprise her, she wasn't sure. After all, the boy was a Trefarrow, and most Trefarrow men had a nasty habit of putting the cart before the horse. Prescott, it appeared, was no different from his brother Payne where matters of the flesh were concerned.

But she put aside her thoughts and crossed to Lucinda to envelop her in a welcoming hug. "Nice to have you in the family, Lucinda. I'm Emmaline, Prescott's aunt, but you can call me Aunt Em. Everybody does."

"Thank you . . . Aunt Em," Lucinda said hesitantly.

"All I've got to say is, I'm pleased as punch that somebody as nice and pretty as you finally got this young scalawag nephew of mine to settle down." Then, to Prescott. "Was he Baptist?"

"Who?"

"The preacher who married you in Paris, France?"

"No, but he was a man of the cloth. Methodist, wasn't he, darlin'?"

"Episcopalian, I think, Prescott." Where before she had seen only cool curiosity on the faces of her husband's aunt and sister-in-law, Lucinda now felt an outpouring of warmth. These women didn't know her or her unfortunate status of birth, yet she had the feeling that their welcome was sincere.

God, could Prescott have been right all along? Lucinda wondered. Could she possibly find a home of her own, a family who truly cared for her, and a life free from gossip and speculation in this new, wild land called Texas? She certainly prayed so.

"Yeah, you're right, he was Episcopalian, wasn't he?" Prescott said. "Not that it really matters. We're married, and that's all that counts."

"And these sweet little children?" Emmaline couldn't help but smile as she walked toward the little girls. "Are they yours, Lucinda?"

"No, ma'am, they're mine," Prescott said.

A stunned expression replaced Emmaline's smile. "Yours?"

"Yep, mine."

"I always knew you had odd proclivities, Prescott," Chloe said, "but how in the name of heaven did you fath— I mean, you've only been gone from here for a year, and they're obviously— Well, that is, the little one there looks to be at least two."

"She is," Prescott said, going down the line of little blond, blue-eyed girls. "Elizabeth's two, Victoria's four, and Alexandra's five, going on six. She's gonna be ready to start school come fall. Victoria wants to go with her, but me and Lucinda think she ought to wait a while. At least another year."

"But that still doesn't tell us how you of all people became their father," Payne said.

"Oh, that's simple," Prescott said. "I adopted 'em."

"Adopted them?" Emmaline shook her gray head in wonder. "My word. Oh, my word!"

"What's the matter?" Payne asked.

"My cornbread," she said. "I just remembered I've got a pan of it still cooking in the oven. Lordy mercy, I hope it's not burned."

As Emmaline turned and ran toward the house, Chloe crossed to her new sister-in-law and embraced her. "We're so happy to have you here. All of you."

"Thank you," Lucinda said.

"I'm sorry if we seemed a little distant at first. It's just that we were all so surprised to see Prescott."

"Not to mention his sheep," Payne said.

"I can explain about that," Prescott said.

"I certainly hope so, brother."

"It's just that we didn't expect him to show up here at the ranch," Chloe said. "Well, not so soon anyway. We just got the letter he wrote us from Venice."

"You just got it?" Prescott asked.

Payne nodded. "This morning, as a matter of fact. If I hadn't gone into town for supplies and stopped at the post office, we never would have known you were even in Venice."

"But I wrote the dang thing over three weeks ago, just as we were getting ready to leave Italy. We would probably have beaten it here if we hadn't made that stop in Barcelona."

"That's my fault, I'm afraid," Lucinda said.

"Your fault?" Chloe asked.

"Aw, now darlin', don't go blaming yourself for that," Prescott said. "It was my fault, if it was anybody's."

"But I'm the one who began feeling odd aboard ship. You and the girls positively delighted in the voyage."

"Just a touch of seasickness is all it was," Prescott said, wrapping an assuring arm around his wife's shoulders. "Course, at the time, I thought the baby might be coming early, and I wasn't about to take any chances. You and the little one mean too much to me." He turned to Chloe. "As it was, though, the doctor who saw her said everything was all right, and that Lucinda should just take it easy and enjoy the voyage. Which she did—once she got over being seasick."

"When are you due?" Chloe asked.

Prescott all but beamed. "Within the month. That's why we left Europe and came home. I couldn't have my firstborn coming into the world as a foreigner. I wanted her to be born a Texan. Only way to do that was to get Lucinda home. Just hope little Miss Prissy there don't mind sharing a room with her new cousins."

"Don't listen to him, Lucinda," Chloe said. "Your baby won't have to share a room or anything else with my daughter. She, or he, will have a room of her own. Or his own. Payne and I don't live here at the Triple T."

"Y'all don't?" Prescott asked.

"No, we don't," Payne said. "We haven't lived here since shortly after you left for England. We moved over to Chloe's cottage. Just the three of us."

"Is that a fact?" Prescott said. "I know it must be nice for y'all, but I can't see Aunt Em cottoning to that arrangement. Must be pretty lonely here for her with y'all gone."

"We're not gone," Chloe said. "We're just a short distance away. And Aunt Em's not all that lonely. How can she be with all the ranch hands down in the bunkhouse? The baby and I just came over today to spend some time with her while Payne went into town."

"Supper's ready!" Emmaline called from the front door. "Y'all come eat it while it's hot."

A look of sheer delight crossed Prescott's face. "Mmm-mmm-mmm! Ladies, y'all are fixing to experience one of life's greatest wonders: my Aunt Em's cooking."

* * *

Shortly after supper, when Prescott had helped himself to seconds, and then thirds, of Emmaline's fried chicken, green beans, mashed potatoes, cornbread, and peach cobbler, Chloe and Payne bade everyone goodnight and left with their sleeping daughter for the cottage. Emmaline helped Prescott and Lucinda tuck the three little girls into bed, promising they would awaken to a day full of excitement and adventure in their new home. Lucinda offered to help Emmaline with the dishes, but was politely refused.

"After all the hard traveling you've been doing?" Emmaline said. "You'd best just take yourself and that baby off to bed and get some rest."

Lucinda eyed the stacks of dishes beside the sink. "But I surely can't leave you to do all this work by yourself."

"Why not? I've been doing it by myself for the past forty years or more. It won't take me but a minute. Now you run along and keep that husband of yours company."

"Well, if you insist . . ."

"I do. Now skedaddle. I'll see y'all in the morning. And if you feel like sleeping in, go right ahead, I'll understand."

"She's . . . wonderful," Lucinda said much later as she lay beside Prescott in their bed.

"Who? Aunt Em or Chloe?"

"Both really, but I was speaking of your aunt."

"Yeah, she's all right. You couldn't find a better, more kindhearted woman if you searched the world over."

"As wonderful as she is, though, I don't think she much approves of the fact that we're cousins."

"Distant cousins, darlin'," Prescott said. "And she understands. Didn't you see the look on her face when we explained just how distant we were?"

"Well, yes, but I just hope that—" Lucinda broke off as a strong pain suddenly shot through the lower part of her back.

"What's the matter?"

"Oh, my goodness!"

"What?"

"It's my back."

"Your back? You didn't do any heavy lifting, did you?"

"No, nothing more than usual. Just let me turn over onto my side." Maneuvering in the small space that Prescott's large frame allowed her on the mattress, she turned and almost immediately began to feel some of the discomfort subside. "Yes, that's better. Much better. I must have exerted myself much more than I thought, climbing into and out of that wagon. It wasn't the least bit comfortable, you know."

"Yeah, the ride from town was kind of bumpy," Prescott said. "Gotta do something about those dang roads. You sure you're all right now?"

"As all right as I can be while still in this condition."

"Well, you've only got a few more weeks to go then it'll all be over."

"Will it?"

"For a while, sure," Prescott said, smiling as he placed his hand on Lucinda's round belly. A strong kick from the baby made him laugh. "Lord, did you feel that?"

"Of course I felt it, silly. How could I not? I've

been feeling it for the past five months. Day and night. It's a wonder I can get any sleep at all."

"Hey, there's another one."

"Just wait, there'll be more. Your daughter or son is just getting started. It kicks like a mule."

"Yeah, but it makes you look so beautiful."

"What, the kicking?"

"No, being in the family way," he said. "I'm gonna hate to see it all come to an end."

"I'm not," Lucinda said. "I'm looking forward to it ending. I'm looking forward to seeing my feet again, too. I don't think I've seen them in weeks."

"Don't you like being this way?"

"Not particularly. You wouldn't either, if you were a woman."

"Then you don't want any more kids?"

"Of course I do. I love children; you know that. It's just that I don't like having to be in this condition to have them. Now if *you* could somehow have the next one . . ."

"I'll try, darlin'. I'll try my dangdest, but I don't think we'll—" He broke off as Lucinda's stomach suddenly grew hard under his hand and she inhaled a sharp gasp. "What's happening?"

"Oh, God!"

"Lucinda?"

The pain in her back, coupled with the warm wetness that gushed between her legs made her incapable of an immediate response.

"Are you losing the baby?"

"Mmm!"

"Jesus, I knew it." He threw aside the sheet and leaped out of bed. "I'll run get Aunt Em."

"No, not yet."

"But she'll know what to do."

"So do I."

"You've never lost a baby before."

"I'm not losing it, Prescott. I'm having it."

"Now?"

"Yes, now."

"But it's too early."

"Tell that to the baby. Ew, heavens!"

"What now?"

"I've drenched the bed. My water's broken."

Prescott could only stand there in his underwear and stare at her. "Yeah, you're having it, all right."

"Help me up so we can change the sheets."

"No, you stay right where you are. Don't move. I'll get the sheets. And Aunt Em."

"Not yet. It's too soon. Stay and talk to me."

"Talk to you?"

"Yes. I need some distraction."

Prescott scratched his head. The woman was in pain, having his baby, for God's sake, and all she wanted to do was talk. He'd never understand women if he lived to be a hundred.

"Okay," he said, "what do you want to talk about?"

"Your brother."

"Payne?"

"Yes. He seems like a very nice man."

"He is. At times."

"He's very like you in many ways. In others, you're total opposites."

"Well, we're different people, that's why."

"Why didn't you tell him about the money?"

"What money?"

"The baron's treasure that we found. Don't you think he should know that he's not as poverty stricken and as debt ridden as he believes?"

"No, I don't," Prescott said. "A little suspense never hurt anybody. He kept me in suspense when he kidnaped Chloe; I'm just doing the same to him now about the money."

"He kidnaped Chloe?"

"Yeah, but I'm not gonna go into that now."

"Yes, you are. Is that why you kidnaped me, because your brother kidnaped his wife?"

"Well, it worked, didn't it? If I hadn't, you'd still be back in Cornwall, pining your little heart out, and I'd be— Well, I don't know where I'd be, but I sure as hell wouldn't be here with you where I belong."

"Then I'm glad you did."

"You mean that?"

"I never say anything I don't mean, Prescott. Don't you know that by now?"

"Yeah, I do." Lucinda, his wife, his very reason for living, was the one woman he could always trust, always rely on to tell him the truth, no matter what the situation.

"I love you," she said.

He sat back down on the bed and held her hand. "I love you, too, Lucinda. And considering you're about to have my baby, I'd say that's a damn good thing." Leaning over, he kissed her forehead. He wanted to do more, but he dared not. They would have time to share their love, their passions, their bodies. They had all the time in the world. The rest of their lives, in fact.

"Prescott?"

"Yes?"

"I think you'd better go get Aunt Em."

* * *

Payne, Chloe, and Priscilla returned to the Triple T bright and early the next morning, having received word from one of the ranchhands that they were needed at the homestead.

"What's the matter, Aunt Em?" Chloe asked as she rushed through the front door. "Is one of the little girls sick?"

"No," Emmaline said, looking quite haggard from a sleepless night, but nonetheless happy. "Nobody's sick. Everybody's about as healthy as you can get."

Prescott loomed up behind his aunt, looking even worse. "Y'all should've stayed around last night. You missed all the excitement."

"What excitement?" Payne asked, thoroughly confused.

Chloe, much quicker to read between the lines, gasped in surprise. "Lucinda had her baby?"

"Yep, she sure did," Prescott said.

"Oh, I want to see it."

"Then come on."

The proud new father led the way down the hall and quietly opened the door to his room. Lucinda lay sound asleep in the middle of his bed, two tiny little bundles sleeping on either side of her.

"Twins?" Chloe and Payne chorused on a whisper of disbelief.

"More'n that," Prescott said, beaming. "Twin *boys.*"

"Sons?" Payne asked. "You have twin sons?"

"That's right, little brother. Looks like the Trefarrow legacy's gonna live on forever."

AVAILABLE NOW

FOREVERMORE by Maura Seger

As the only surviving member of a family that had lived in the English village of Avebury for generations, Sarah Huxley was fated to protect the magical sanctuary of the tumbled stone circles and earthen mounds. But when a series of bizarre deaths at Avebury began to occur, Sarah met her match in William Devereux Faulkner, a level-headed Londoner, who had come to investigate. "Ms. Seger has a special magic touch with her lovers that makes her an enduring favorite with readers everywhere."—*Romantic Times*

PROMISES by Jeane Renick

From the award-winning author of *Trust Me* and *Always* comes a sizzling novel set in a small Ohio town, featuring a beautiful blind heroine, her greedy fiancé, two sisters in love with the same man, a mysterious undercover police officer, and a holographic will.

KISSING COUSINS by Carol Jerina

Texas rancher meets English beauty in this witty follow-up to *The Bridegroom*. When Prescott Trefarrow learned that it was he who was the true Earl of St. Keverne, and not his twin brother, he went to Cornwall to claim his title, his castle, and a multitude of responsibilities. Reluctantly, he became immersed in life at Ravens Lair Castle—and the lovely Lucinda Trefarrow.

HUNTER'S HEART by Christina Hamlett

A romantic suspense novel featuring a mysterious millionaire and a woman determined to figure him out. Many things about wealthy industrialist Hunter O'Hare intrigue Victoria Cameron. First of all, why did O'Hare have his ancestral castle moved to Virginia from Ireland, stone by stone? Secondly, why does everyone else in the castle act as if they have something to hide? And last, but not least, what does Hunter want from Victoria?

THE LAW AND MISS PENNY by Sharon Ihle

When U.S. Marshal Morgan Slater suffered a head injury and woke up with no memory, Mariah Penny conveniently supplied him with a fabricated story so that he wouldn't run her family's medicine show out of town. As he traveled through Colorado Territory with the Pennys, he and Mariah fell in love. Everything seemed idyllic until the day the lawman's memory returned.

PRIMROSE by Clara Wimberly

A passionate historical tale of forbidden romance between a wealthy city girl and a fiercely independent local man in the wilds of the Tennessee mountains. Rosalyn Hunte's heart was torn between loyalty to her family and the love of a man who wanted to claim her for himself.